The Traitor's Tale

MARGARET FRAZER

BERKLEY PRIME CRIME, NEW YORK

THE BERKLEY PUBLISHING GROUP
Published by the Penguin Group
Penguin Group (USA) Inc.
375 Hudson Street, New York, New York 10014, USA
Penguin Group (Canada), 90 Eglinton Avenue East, Suite 700, Toronto, Ontario M4P 2Y3, Canada
(a division of Pearson Penguin Canada Inc.)
Penguin Books Ltd., 80 Strand, London WC2R 0RL, England
Penguin Group Ireland, 25 St. Stephen's Green, Dublin 2, Ireland (a division of Penguin Books Ltd.)
Penguin Group (Australia), 250 Camberwell Road, Camberwell, Victoria 3124, Australia
(a division of Pearson Australia Group Pty. Ltd.)
Penguin Books India Pvt. Ltd., 11 Community Centre, Panchsheel Park, New Delhi—110 017, India
Penguin Group (NZ), 67 Apollo Drive, Rosedale, North Shore 0632, New Zealand
(a division of Pearson New Zealand Ltd.)
Penguin Books (South Africa) (Pty.) Ltd., 24 Sturdee Avenue, Rosebank, Johannesburg 2196,
South Africa

Penguin Books Ltd., Registered Offices: 80 Strand, London WC2R 0RL, England

This is a work of fiction. Names, characters, places, and incidents either are the product of the author's imagination or are used fictitiously, and any resemblance to actual persons, living or dead, business establishments, events, or locales is entirely coincidental. The publisher does not have any control over and does not assume any responsibility for author or third-party websites or their content.

THE TRAITOR'S TALE

A Berkley Prime Crime Book / published by arrangement with the author

PRINTING HISTORY
Berkley Prime Crime hardcover edition / January 2007
Berkley Prime Crime mass-market edition / January 2008

Copyright © 2007 by Gail Frazer.
The Edgar® name is a registered service mark of the Mystery Writers of America, Inc.
Cover art by Teresa Fasolino.
Cover design by George Long.

ISBN: 978-0-425-21902-7

BERKLEY® PRIME CRIME
Berkley Prime Crime Books are published by The Berkley Publishing Group,
a division of Penguin Group (USA) Inc.,
375 Hudson Street, New York, New York 10014.
The name BERKLEY PRIME CRIME and the BERKLEY PRIME CRIME design
are trademarks of Penguin Group (USA) Inc.

PRINTED IN THE UNITED STATES OF AMERICA

10 9 8 7 6 5 4 3 2 1

The Middle Ages Come to Life . . . to Bring Us Murder.

The Dame Frevisse Medieval Mystery Novels
By Two-time Edgar® Award Nominee Margaret Frazer

THE TRAITOR'S TALE

"Painted on a much broader canvas than usual . . . Plenty of real history presented to the reader in the most enjoyable way . . . Ms. Frazer portrays the curse of living in 'interesting times,' making it all seem as fresh and vibrant as a news bulletin. Possibly the best in the series to date, and that is saying a lot. Miss it at your peril."
—*MyShelf.com*

"Illuminating . . . An interesting history lesson."
—*Publishers Weekly*

"Frazer makes her characters live . . . [She] once again shows her remarkable ability to lead her readers through the thickets of medieval history. She knows the period and provides settings that take us back to a time that makes ours look placid . . . For readers who have any interest in historical mysteries, this book is a winner."
—*Gumshoe Reviews*

"When you pick up a Margaret Frazer novel, you know you're in for a treat. She has a marvelous way of weaving historical details, facts, politics, and the ins and outs of everyday medieval life into the fabric of her novels. If history texts were written in such a fascinating way, I'm convinced that every schoolchild would become a scholar."
—*CA Reviews*

Also in the series

THE SEMPSTER'S TALE

A couple is bound by forbidden love, as a country teeters on the edge of revolution . . .

"What Frazer . . . gets absolutely right . . . are the attitudes of the characters."
—*Detroit Free Press*

continued . . .

THE WIDOW'S TALE

*A threat to king and country forces Dame Frevisse
to choose where her loyalties lie . . .*

"Action-packed . . . a terrific protagonist."
—*Midwest Book Reviews*

THE HUNTER'S TALE

*Dame Frevisse finds that the evil that men do
sometimes lives after them . . .*

"The book's charm lies in the author's meticulous research . . .
The plot moves at a stately pace appropriate to its time and
setting." —*Publishers Weekly*

THE BASTARD'S TALE

*Even in the charmed circle of medieval England's lavish
royal court, no one is immune from murder . . .*

"Frazer executes her . . . dramatic episode in fifteenth-century
history with audacity and ingenuity." —*Kirkus Reviews*

THE CLERK'S TALE

*Dame Frevisse must find justice for the murder
of an unjust man . . .*

"As usual, Frazer vividly recreates the medieval world through
meticulous historical detail [and] remarkable scholarship . . . A
dramatic and surprising conclusion." —*Publishers Weekly*

THE SQUIRE'S TALE

*Dame Frevisse learns that even love can spawn anger,
greed, and murder . . .*

"Meticulous detail that speaks of trustworthy scholarship and a
sympathetic imagination." —*The New York Times*

THE REEVE'S TALE

Acting as village steward, Frevisse must tend to the sick—
and track down a killer . . .

"A brilliantly realized vision of a typical medieval English village . . . Suspenseful from start to surprising conclusion . . . Another gem." —*Publishers Weekly* (starred review)

THE MAIDEN'S TALE

In London for a visit, Frevisse finds that her wealthy cousin
may have a deadly secret . . .

"Great fun for all lovers of history with their mystery."
—*Minneapolis Star Tribune*

THE PRIORESS' TALE

When the prioress lets her family stay at St. Frideswide's,
the consequences are deadly . . .

"Will delight history buffs and mystery fans alike."
—*Murder Ink*

THE MURDERER'S TALE

Dame Frevisse's respite at Minster Lovell turns deadly
when murder drops in . . .

"The period detail is lavish, and the characters are full-blooded." —*Minneapolis Star Tribune*

THE BOY'S TALE

Two young boys seek refuge at St. Frideswide's—
but there is no sanctuary from murder . . .

"Fast-paced . . . A surprise ending." —*Affaire de Coeur*

continued . . .

THE BISHOP'S TALE

*The murder of a mourner means another funeral,
and possibly more . . .*

"Some truly shocking scenes and psychological twists."
—*Mystery Loves Company*

THE OUTLAW'S TALE

*Dame Frevisse meets a long-lost blood relative—
but the blood may be on his hands . . .*

"A tale well told, filled with intrigue and spiced with romance
and rogues." —*School Library Journal*

THE SERVANT'S TALE

*A troupe of actors at a nunnery is a harbinger of merriment—
or murder . . .*

"Excellently drawn . . . Very authentic . . . The essence of a truly
historical story is that the people should feel and believe according to their times. Margaret Frazer has accomplished this
extraordinarily well." —Anne Perry

THE NOVICE'S TALE

*Among the nuns at St. Frideswide's were piety, peace,
and a little vial of poison . . .*

"Frazer uses her extensive knowledge of the period to create an
unusual plot . . . Appealing characters and crisp writing."
—*Los Angeles Times*

Don't miss Margaret Frazer's mysteries featuring Joliffe:

A PLAY OF ISAAC
A PLAY OF DUX MORAUD
A PLAY OF KNAVES
A PLAY OF LORDS

To my sons.
Well-loved, may they live well.

"It nere," quod he, "to thee no greet honour
For to be fals, ne for to be traitour . . ."

GEOFFREY CHAUCER
The Knight's Tale

Chapter 1

Revolts and riots lesser and greater had been flaring and fading across the south and east of England all through the spring into this fine-weathered summer of 1450, but Jack Cade's rebellion had proved to be something more than all of them. Given a leader better than most and driven by years of rough injustices and this past year's failure of the war in France, men had gathered to him in the thousands and marched on London, demanding justice from the king and his lords; and the king and his lords had fled, had disappeared northward.

Their thought had maybe been that London would be safe enough with the wide river Thames and the towered gates and drawbridge of London Bridge to keep the rebels at bay; but four days ago London, angry enough at its own wrongs and angrier still at the king's betrayal, had opened the bridge's gates and let the rebels in.

And riding toward London, Joliffe had watched the sky, thinking to see smoke from burning buildings, expecting to meet with droves of escaping citizens. He had counted on learning from them how bad matters were in the city, but the few he met with were more interested in keeping going than talking, had seemed more grumbling than terror-struck. With that and the lack of any black towers of smoke, he chose to stop at an inn outside London's Newgate in hopes of learning more about what was happening in the city before going in himself.

The innkeeper, his business slack—"You're the first traveler in here these three days past. Such folk as pass are going away from London, not to it."—was more than happy to sit drinking the good wine Joliffe paid for and talk of what he knew. "Not that there's even been many of those, from what I've seen. Cade's kept his men under his hand, I'll say that for him. No rioting, robbing, and raping through the streets, if you know what I mean. That's small comfort, mind you, to those as Cade set his men on purpose to pillage. Them as were rich enough and disliked enough for it. Malpas and that lot. Nor any comfort at all to the half-dozen or so men he's had killed." The innkeeper chuckled with deep satisfaction. "Not that anyone's minded Lord Saye's and that bloody thief Crowmer's heads hitting the pavement in Cheapside. There were more than rebels cheered that. Nor it hasn't hurt that Cade's seen to it his men have been paying for what they take otherwise—food and drink and the like."

"You haven't been into London yourself to see how it's going?" Joliffe asked.

"Go into London now?" The innkeeper sounded disbelieving Joliffe could think him so short of wits. "Not likely! This isn't going to last, this love-match between London and Cade. Those he hasn't robbed are going to be wondering when it'll be their turn, and his men will be wanting more than drink and taking orders and chopping off a head now and again. No, hereabouts we're laying bets on when it's all going to turn uglier than it is. I want to be around to collect my winnings and I'm keeping out of London the while, thank you. If you've good sense, you'll do the same, man."

"Now there's a problem," Joliffe said cheerfully. "I gave up claim to good sense years ago." Instead of it, he paid for two nights' keep for his horse and set off on foot by way of Holborn bridge and to Newgate. The guards set there by Cade asked him his business, and his tale of needing to see how his aged aunt did—"Or more to the point, how my hoped-for inheritance does."—got him in without trouble.

"It's Cade's curfew soon, though," one of the guards said. "See you're out of the street by then or you'll be hustled over to Southwark with the rest of us."

"She only lives in Forster's Lane," Joliffe said with a wave of one hand and kept on going.

As the innkeeper had said, Cade seemed to be keeping his hold over his men, but the quiet in the streets was wrong. Where there should have been the city's late afternoon busy to-and-fro flow of people, bright-arrayed shop fronts, and crowding market stalls, there were barred house doors, shops blank-faced behind shutters, no crowding market stalls. The only places he saw open were taverns and a few cookshops, and almost the only people seemed to be rebels, and they were either drinking or else wandering as if at a loss of what to do, those that weren't already drifting toward the London Bridge now that late afternoon shadows were beginning to fill the streets.

That was something the innkeeper as well as the gate-guard had warned him of—Cade's order that every day by sunset his men were to withdraw across London Bridge, out of the city into Southwark. The order was maybe the more readily obeyed because all London's brothels were there, but for such as needed help remembering where they were supposed to be, Cade had his officers going through the streets to turn and herd them the right way.

Since Joliffe's way lay bridgeward—but had nothing to do with any aged aunt—no one troubled him. The worst he met with were four drunken men lurching along broad Cheapside arm in arm and singing together happily, even if not all the same song. They looked far enough gone to want any passer-by's company and be offended if it wasn't given, so Joliffe put a slight stagger into his own step and raised a hand in fellow-feeling as he passed them, in the hope that they would know a fellow drunk must have business as important as their own and leave him to it. They did, with a cheerfully shouted something at him as they passed. He cheerfully shouted something back, doubting they would get much farther before they were gathered up and sent toward Southwark. For himself, when he was far enough away to suppose they had by now forgotten him, he returned to his own long stride, out of Cheapside into Poultry and from there into the Stocks Market. Five streets met there, but the one Joliffe wanted still went enough toward the bridge that he'd hoped to have no trouble, nor did he, save that men plainly Cade's officers were there before him, herding a score of men—probably collected from the surrounding streets—toward the street Joliffe wanted for himself. If he got herded with them, he might well find himself going over the bridge before he knew it; but he'd not for nothing spent years pretending to be a great many people besides himself. He set back his shoulders, lifted his head, changed to a bold stride, and crossed the marketplace like a man firmly about his business. As he passed the nearest of the officers, he raised a hand in easy greeting. The man lifted a hand in return and no one made him any challenge as he strode on, safely into Lombard Street.

The George Inn, with its sign of an armored knight on a white horse spearing a writhing dragon, was near the farther end. Like everywhere along the street, its door was shut, its windows shuttered. For good measure, the gate into its yard was unwelcomingly closed, and when Joliffe knocked at it, a man on the other side demanded to know who he was and what he wanted.

"I've come to see Matthew Gough," Joliffe answered, half what the man had demanded but enough. There was a scrape and thud of a bar being pulled aside, and the gate opened just enough to let a very lean man slip through. Fortunately, Joliffe was and did, with the man shutting it on his heels while saying, "His rooms are the first along the gallery up there," and already reaching to put the bar in place again.

The George was one of London's best inns. It stretched long along its cobbled yard, with stables and lesser guest rooms on the left, its public rooms on the right, sheltered from ill weather by an open gallery that ran the building's length, reached by stairs at both ends and lined with doors to the inn's best guest chambers that were sheltered in their turn by the eaves of the steep-pitched roof. Even in these strained days all was cleanly swept and cleanly kept, but where there should be people on the come-and-go, and talk and laughter from the tavern-room, and servants on the move, the empty yard, the crushed, taut silence, the servant on guard at the gate, a wary face at a lower window, were unsettling, and Joliffe went quickly up the stairs and along the gallery to the first door there.

It stood open to a well-sized room, low-ceilinged under golden oak beams but with a wide window overlooking the street. There were clean rushes underfoot, a curtained bed, a table and chair and several stools, and space along the walls for travelers' chests and baggage to be set, though presently table and chair were shoved aside, leaving the room's middle to a large chest from which a man was just lifting an elegantly curved breastplate undoubtedly meant for the man standing, already in a thickly padded arming doublet while a third man knelt behind him, buckling the straps of a leg harness around his thigh.

Joliffe rapped at the doorframe. They all turned toward him. The man holding the breastplate was the youngest and not very young—somewhere around Joliffe's own age. The other two were nearer sixty years than not, with faces roughworn by weather and hard living that looked to have agreed with them.

"Master Gough?" he asked.

The man standing to be put into his armor answered, "I am, yes. You want what?" The Welsh of his younger years was still in his voice despite the decades he had spent in France as one of England's great captains in the war now being so headlong lost there, and the other two men must be his squires.

Joliffe went into the room, away from the door, before he answered, "I'm from the duke of York."

"Are you?" said Gough, committing to nothing.

Joliffe answered the question behind that question with, "Sir William said I should remind you about the *damoiselle* in Caen."

Gough laughed and a taut wariness went out of him. "I remember. Though I did have hope Sir William had forgotten." The kneeling squire went back to buckling the leg harness' straps behind Gough's thigh and the other squire came to fit the breastplate over Gough's chest. "So you're York's man," Gough said past him. "Any good with a sword?"

"I've been taught."

"By anyone who knew what they were doing? Or catch as catch can?"

Finished with the leg harness, the older squire stood up and went to the chest for another piece of armor.

Joliffe named a name.

Gough looked up in surprise from helping his squire shift the breastplate to lie most comfortably against his waist. "He had you in hand? How did that come about?"

"Someone I once worked for thought I should have that skill to add to my others."

"Did he?" Gough had likely survived years of battles, raids, and changes of lords over him by not only how well he fought, but by how well he could assess the worth and skills of men around him when their lives and likely his own might depend on how right he was. Just now he was assessing Joliffe. "Does my lord of York know this?"

Evenly, Joliffe answered, "I'd not tell you something about myself that my lord of York didn't know."

The older squire brought the backplate that went with the breastplate. He and the other squire began to buckle the pieces together at Gough's shoulder while Gough's look held on Joliffe and Joliffe's held on him, until finally Gough said, "So he knows, and here you are." He raised his arms for his squires to come at the straps and buckles at his side. "I'd trust York's judgment before I'd trust most other men's. So. You'll have your chance to use that sword-skill tonight."

Among things Joliffe preferred to avoid was chance to use his sword-skills, and blandly, deliberately misunderstanding, he asked, "You mean I'm to fight you for whatever it is you wanted Sir William to know? My lord of York will have to find himself another messenger, then. I don't favor being too dead to take it to him."

Gough chuckled. "Not me. No. Cade's had his chance in London and tonight he's losing it. We're taking the bridge back from the rebels."

"I can't say I see the four of us having much likelihood of that," Joliffe said. "Begging your pardon for doubting your skill as a fighter, of course."

"What are you? York's jester?" No longer prickly with

doubt, Gough was in sudden good humour. One to a side, his men were now fastening armor around his upper arms. "No, I've gone back and forth much of today between Lord Scales in the Tower and the mayor and his men at the Guildhall to set this up."

"Him being about the only man who could go freely back and forth from one to the other," the older squire said. "Some cur among the rebels would challenge him, 'Who are you and where are you bound?' and he'd come back at 'em, 'Matthew Gough, new-come back from France. Who are you?'"

The other squire laughed. "There wasn't one of them didn't know who he was and gave him way."

"There's many of them been in France themselves," Gough said. "They know who's at fault for there and here, and the shame is we're against them when we ought all to be against the curs around the king who've brought us to it. But Cade shouldn't have taken to robbing one rich man after another through the city. Your London merchants will lie down for a lot but make them afraid for their wealth and they'll fight. Even Lord Scales, whatever else he's been ordered, isn't minded to let London go to ruin in front of him."

"What's planned for tonight?" Joliffe asked. "Wait until Cade's men are into Southwark, then seize the bridge and shut them out of London again?"

"You have it," Gough approved. "Straight and simple." He looked out the window where the shadows in the street were deepening toward twilight. "So we're heading for the bridge when dark comes down—Londoners and some men-at-arms from the Tower for stiffening."

"And us," the younger squire said happily.

Joliffe silently wished them all joy of it and said, "That should make it the easier for me to go out of London some other way with whatever it is you want my lord of York to have."

"Well thought and likely," Gough agreed. He laid a hand over the left side of his waist. "Your trouble is, the letter's here. Under my doublet."

Joliffe stared at Gough's lean-boned, strong-sinewed hand, browned and weathered and spotted with the beginnings of old age, laid over the smooth steel of the breastplate buckled and tied over the thick-padded doublet. Gough had sent word to Sir William Oldhall that he had something it would be worth the duke of York's while to have but someone must come for it. Now Joliffe was come but very plainly he could not yet have whatever it was. Not yet. Because whatever it was, Gough had not wanted it out of his keeping, even when going into a fight on London Bridge.

"Um . . ." said Joliffe.

Gough patted his side. "This letter. If it were a cat, there'd be blooding among the pigeons when it's let loose. Beginning with that bastard-bred duke of Somerset, our king's thrice-damned governor of Normandy."

"He won't be for much longer," Joliffe said with feigned lightness. "Not at the speed he's losing the war there."

Gough's grim laugh agreed with that. "This letter has something to say about that, too, and it's yours when we've done this business with Cade. Rhys, get out Jankin's gear. This fellow can wear it."

Leaving the younger squire waiting with Gough's padded cap that would make his helmet sit more comfortably, the older squire had begun to shrug into his own padded doublet, but now he went to another chest while Gough said to Joliffe, "Killed at Formigny battle, was Jankin. Damn Somerset to Hell."

"I only came for the letter," Joliffe said carefully. "Not for fighting."

Gough gave him a dog-toothed grin. "Should have come sooner, then."

Joliffe eyed the dark red, padded doublet Rhys was bringing toward him, particularly misliking the black stain of old blood down its front.

"Took an arrow in the throat," Gough said, frowning at that same darkness. "If there's any justice this side of Hell, worse will happen to Somerset."

But in the meanwhile the letter Joliffe wanted was inside Gough's armor, with no way to come at it short of Gough unarming, and that was not going to happen; and with a grim vision of Gough going over London Bridge's edge into the black-running tidal water of the Thames, taking the letter with him, Joliffe began to unfasten his own doublet.

When setting him to this task, Sir William had told him not much beyond the bare fact that Matthew Gough had sent word that he had something that would tell York why the war in France was gone so fast and so far to the wrong. "Whatever it is," Sir William had said, "he isn't trusting it out of his hands, nor does he think it would be to his good or mine for him to be seen to have anything to do with my lord of York. That's why I need you to fetch it." Sir William had drummed impatient fingers on his desktop and said what he had said often enough before. "I would to all the saints that York wasn't gone to Ireland." Sent there as the king's lieutenant and effectively into exile, most probably because his even-handed rule while governor of Normandy—making a notable best of an incurably bad business—stood out too sharply against England's ill-governing by the lords around the king.

Or maybe it was simply enough that King Henry VI, after five years of marriage, had fathered no child, and that made those same lords uneasy, because until King Henry sired a son, Richard, duke of York, was his heir to the crown.

But there was a matter more than that. As corruption and ill-government took deeper hold around the king, men were beginning to remember that if King Henry's grandfather had not seized the throne for himself by force fifty years ago—if he had not wrenched the crown out of the right line of succession and taken the throne by right of arms, not by right of blood—Richard, duke of York and not even born then, would not now be heir to King Henry's crown.

He would be king.

It was a claim he had never pressed, but to the lords whose hold on power depended on King Henry's weakness, York was a threat to them simply by being alive.

Until three years ago another threat had been King Henry's uncle, the duke of Gloucester, likewise his heir but, unlike York, constantly challenging the lords around the king—until he was suddenly accused of treason, arrested, and then, before any trial, suddenly dead.

Which, Joliffe thought, showed that for a king's heir there were worse things than being sent to govern Ireland. Still, just now and speaking for himself, "worse" very easily included going into a night-battle on London Bridge behind a battle-eager Matthew Gough. Though he supposed it could have been worse: he could have been going into battle *ahead* of Gough.

Or against him.

Fully armed now except for helmet and gauntlets, Gough said, "Owen, you help with him," and Joliffe submitted not only to the dead Jankin's arming doublet but his half-leg armor and then a sleeveless brigantine of small, overlapping metal plates riveted to a canvas tunic covered by red cloth that matched the doublet—even to the shape and color of the stain, unfortunately—while Gough told how the night's plan had been put together in snatched meetings during the day as the Londoner's fears against Jack Cade grew.

"So it had to be simple and it is. When the curfew bell

rings from St. Martin-le-Grand, that's when we all make a run for the bridge. By then all of Cade's men that are going back to Southwark will be gone over. We rush Cade's guards on the bridge-gate, retake it, hold it, and the city is ours."

Joliffe shifted his shoulders to settle the brigantine's weight better and asked, "What about Cade's guards on the other city gates?"

"The aldermen for the wards there are supposed to see to them."

"And those of Cade's men still in London? The ones who've avoided obeying the curfew order?"

Rhys answered that with a curt laugh and, "Gough wrung promise from Lord Scales that there'll be men from the Tower to hold this end of the bridge against attack on our backs."

Warily, Joliffe asked, "Why would a promise to help against Cade have to be wrung from him?"

"Because he's gone soft," Gough snapped. "In France he was good enough. Maybe talked a better game than he gave sometimes but was good enough. Now he's cuddled in with that lot around the king and doesn't want to unfeather the soft nest he's made for himself. God knows he's let things happen in London these few days as make no sense if he wasn't taking someone's orders for them, that's sure."

"What about a sword?" Rhys asked. "Is he to have one, or just his dagger?" That most men wore hanging from their belts, and especially in these days.

"Give him Jankin's," Gough said curtly. "No reason not to."

Joliffe had left his own sword with his horse, not wanting to walk too openly armed in London, as if looking for trouble. He had already shifted his belt and dagger to wear over the short-skirted brigantine and took the sword Rhys now handed him, still in its leather scabbard wrapped around with its long belt. While Joliffe buckled on the belt and settled the scabbarded sword on his left hip, Gough crossed to the window. By the deepening shadows in the street, Joliffe guessed the sun was gone or nearly so; darkness would come fast now, and Gough, abruptly cheerful, came away from the window, saying, "Come on. Let's be on our way before the bell starts."

He took up his helmet—a full, visored bascinet—from the table, was slipping it down over his close-fitted arming cap and fastening the buckle along his jaw as he moved for the door. Rhys and Owen had lighter, wide-brimmed, open-faced kettle-helmets, and Owen tossed a like one to Joliffe as they followed Gough toward the door. With nothing like their open pleasure, Joliffe strapped it on and followed them. Over his years, he had been, at one time and another and among other things, a scholar of sorts, in a company of traveling players, what could only be called a spy, and now was in uncertain service to a man who might someday be as suddenly dead as the late duke of Gloucester if the men around King Henry decided on it. On the whole, Joliffe was not sure it had been a sensible life, but he had mostly enjoyed it and as much for what he had *not* done as for what he had. And among the things he had not done was ever take liking to throwing himself into fights. Whatever was in Gough's letter, it had better be worth this.

The same man let them out the innyard gate and as quickly shut it behind them. There were already clots of men in the street and steadily more after they turned the corner into Gracechurch Street, coming from side streets and all of them headed toward the bridge. Londoners, not rebels, armed with cudgels and sometimes swords, with an occasional breastplate and helmet among them. Most of the rebels Joliffe had seen had been no better armed and armored, so that was well enough. It was in their plain great numbers the rebels were most dangerous, and the narrow space of London Bridge would be to the Londoners' advantage in a fight.

Horatio at the bridge, holding back Lars Porsena's army and living to tell the tale, Joliffe thought encouragingly.

Or, less encouragingly, Roland at Roncesvalles and very dead.

From across the city St. Martin's bell began to ring, mounting with sharp, hard strokes past the simple declaration of curfew into a brazen clamor. Gough broke into a dog-trot. Rhys and Owen matched him. So did Joliffe. Four fully armed men moving with clear purpose drew the scattering of other men to them, after them, with purpose, too. Nearly at the bridge, with the bell still clamoring over the London rooftops, they met with a score of Lord Scales' men from the Tower coming out of Thames Street on their left. Gough paused to share words with their captain, then turned to the gathering Londoners, more still joining from surrounding streets. With his visor up so they could see his grinning face, he called in a battlefield voice, "What we want is a hard rush, some sharp pushing, and then, if they fight us, some head-bashing! Who's with me?"

He was answered with the formless yell of men with their blood up—if not their wits, thought Joliffe—and when Gough drew his sword, swung away from them, and charged onto the bridge, the Londoners charged after him, still yelling.

To Joliffe's surprise Rhys and Owen pulled aside and hung back, but only so they could close on the crowd's rear flanks to urge it and any stragglers forward with shouts of their own. Not bothering with the shouting, Joliffe went with them.

From the London end of the bridge to almost the other, narrow-fronted shops and houses lined and overhung both sides of the street, closing off all sight of the river. From other times of crossing the bridge, Joliffe knew that near to the far end the houses ended, leaving a gap before the double-towered stone gateway set to guard the drawbridge there. The rebels had been caught unready, with warning enough that some had started to shove the gates closed, but Gough and the Londoners smashed into the few rallying to meet their on-rush, jamming them backward into the gateway past any chance of the gates being closed, and after that it was melee work, the narrow gateway and bridge working in the Londoners' favor against the rebels' greater numbers in the push-and-shove the fighting rapidly became.

Joliffe had never favored hazarding his life—had done so somewhat too many times but did not *favor* doing so—and he held to the back edge of the struggle. Not that coming to the fore of it would have been easy. Packed into the gateway, men lacked room for clear sword-work. Shoving, yelling, fists, pommels, and sometimes a dagger-stroke were the main business as the struggling mass lurched one way, then the other, neither side able to force the other back enough to gain the gates for themselves, but in it Joliffe's own blood roused, and even knowing it was the other men's heat kindling his own, he shoved into the gateway with them, his dagger in one hand, dead Jankin's sword in his other.

The struggle went on far longer than he would have thought it could. Full dark came while they were at it, leaving them to fight by the flaring yellow light of torches and in the thick shadows under the gateway's tower. As the men at the front tired and faded back, those at the rear pushed forward to batter and push and be battered and pushed. Sometimes a man on one side or the other would go down and fighting would turn fierce again, but the first hot edge of fighting was long since gone, and more and more often there were brief drawings off on both sides, the fighting replaced with shouts back and forth.

Joliffe, resting in one of those lulls, sitting on his heels with his back against the low stone wall of the bridge-edge in the long open space between the last of the houses and the gateway, thought the shouting seemed to do about as much good as the fighting was. He had seen at least two men dead and a good many bloodied and bashed, but except for that and that the fire of fighting was mostly turned to bloody-minded stubbornness on both sides, nothing was much changed. Still, the street here was still full of men milling about, waiting to start again, with Gough standing a few yards away from him, close to the last housewall, in talk with some of the Tower men, probably about how best to press forward and take the gateway once and for all. Rhys and Owen were a little further away, in the better light of a torch there, Owen wrapping a cloth around a cut across Rhys' arm above his gauntlet, taken in the latest squall of fighting. They were a little laughing together, while Gough, with his helmet off and wiping sweat from his forehead, was frowning and shaking his head at whatever one of the Tower men was saying.

Joliffe was listening not to them or the general shift and talk of men but to the river in the darkness behind and below him, the muted thundering of the water foaming and fighting its way between the bridge's wide stone pillars, so many and so thick they held the river back from where, with all its force, it wanted to go. He couldn't tell if the tide was at ebb or flow or on the turn, but knew for certain he'd rather be up here than down there—and now that his blood was cooled again, would rather be some place else altogether. The brigantine was more weight than he cared to carry; the helmet was awkward on his head; he didn't like trying to hurt people or have them trying to hurt him; he hadn't had supper; he wanted to be in his own bed sound asleep; he . . .

Gough strode out into the midst of the Londoners. His reputation and authority from the years when England had been winning the French war still served him well. More than once this night Joliffe had seen him rally the Londoners into believing they were the bold warriors they had never been, going not into an untidy scuffle on a bridge but into a battle with a leader of legend. Now Gough was doing it again. By voice and gesture he was gathering up the Londoners and Tower men out of their weariness into readiness to fight again. He pointed toward the gateway and said something that brought laughter from the nearest men. Other men jostled to be closer. They were crowded around him now, and the laughter changed to a cheer. He was urging them on to a final great rush and push, and Joliffe shoved himself to his feet as the men around Gough swung from him and surged yet again toward the gate, Gough urging them on from behind. Joliffe guessed he meant to drive them rather than lead them this time, probably in the hope of bringing the weight of men in the rear to bear on the forward fighters, finally driving them through the gateway by plain weight of bodies. Good. Then there would be an end to this and he could get that letter and be away.

Just as there had been all night, more men were coming along the bridge in scattered fews and handfuls, belated to the fight. Gough turned from the fight to call out welcome to them, gesturing them past him, into the gateway scrummage, then turning toward it himself. Rhys and Owen, done with their bandaging, were moving to join him. They none of them saw four more, club-bearing men come out of the shadows along the street, pause, point, and then two of them spring into a run straight for Gough's back, the other two at Rhys and Owen.

Joliffe shouted warning as he broke forward into a run, too, and although Owen went down from a club alongside his helmet, Rhys dropped into a crouch below the blow meant for him and without straightening spun around, his dagger out, and went for his attacker as Joliffe barreled into the man who had felled Owen. Both his fight and Rhys' were sharp and short, with Joliffe's man making to swing the club two-handed at him but Joliffe, already too close, using his free hand to grab and shove the man's arms higher and the man backward, his head lifting, clearing his throat for Joliffe to drive his dagger under the man's chin and up.

He did not stay to see the man fall, just shoved him away while jerking his dagger out, saw from the corner of his eye that Rhys' man was down, too, and spun with Rhys toward Gough.

Gough was down, but his attackers had dropped their clubs. One of them had a dagger out but they had caught Gough under the arms, one on either side, and were making to drag him toward the bridge's edge. Their confidence in their fellows was too great: they did not look around until just the instant before Rhys and Joliffe took them from behind. Joliffe's man was wearing no back-armor, only a breastplate, its leather straps crossed across his back. Joliffe stabbed into his left side, thrusting up toward the heart. By the time he had his dagger out again and the man was falling, Rhys had shoved the other fellow staggering forward to thump against the bridge railing and slump to the ground. Dead, Joliffe supposed, but was already shoving his own man roughly aside from Gough, lying face-down where they had dropped him.

Together, he and Rhys turned him to his back just as Owen came staggering over, too late for everything. But it had been too late from the beginning. Gough's dead eyes staring past them into nothing told them that. And the blood on Rhys' hand from where he had held Gough to turn him over told the rest.

"Under his arm," Rhys said. "They clubbed him down and one of the cozening shits stabbed in under his arm. He never had chance at all."

Nor had it been a chance attack. There were answers Joliffe would like to have, but, "Are they dead?" he asked, looking around at the four sprawled bodies.

"Right they are," said Rhys. He was closing Gough's

eyes. A few men were falling back from the rear of the fight, gathering around, beginning to ask questions that the squires and Joliffe ignored, Rhys instead ordering, "Owen, see what's on them." And at Joliffe, "Watch him," leaving him with Gough's body while going himself to rifle through the clothing of the two dead men who had done for Gough, moving with the expert quickness of someone who had done this uncounted times on a battlefield, looking for what might be worth his while to have.

This time, though, he was looking for the same thing Joliffe wanted—evidence of who these men had been and why they had wanted Gough dead—and said angrily when he had finished, having found nothing but small pouches that clinked with coins inside each man's doublet and tucked them inside his own, "Nothing." He looked up at the surround of faces. "Anybody know any of these curs?" he demanded. "They look like Londoners."

Heads shook in general denial echoed by voices saying no one knew them. In truth none of the dead men looked anything in particular. Their clothing was ordinary, serviceable. They could have been anybody from anywhere. Rhys picked up the dagger that had fallen with the second man Joliffe had killed and gave it a hard looking over, but except it had Gough's blood on it, it had nothing to tell; and suddenly, fiercely, Rhys stood up and with a wide swing of his arm flung the thing out into the darkness above the Thames.

Owen came back from the other dead men, carrying their belts with their daggers in one hand, two more pouches with probably coin in the other, but, "Nothing else on them," he said.

From the gateway the yells and clashing and scuffle had gone on, most men not knowing what had happened behind them, but now someone shouted, "They've fired the bridge!" and the night burst past yellow torchlight into the vicious, leaping red and orange of unleashed flames. The men who had gathered around Gough's body disappeared in a rush toward the gateway, shouting. Rhys, with the calm of a man who's seen worse, said, "The gatehouse is stone. There's no wind, no houses close to take fire. It shouldn't spread."

"It's the drawbridge that's burning," Owen said.

"That's good, then," Rhys said, level-voiced. "They've given up hope of retaking the gate and want to see we can't go after them when they retreat." Then with the heaviness of a man not able to hold the worst at bay any longer, "Let's shift him back to the George. Where's his helmet?"

Joliffe found it and slung it from his arm by its chin-strap while Rhys unbuckled and slid Gough's sword belt off him and laid it, the scabbard, and Gough's sword on his body. Owen carefully folded Gough's hands over the sword, and Rhys said gruffly, "Come on then," and with Joliffe at Gough's feet and Rhys and Owen at his head they lifted him and set off along the bridge, keeping well aside, out of the way of men and women running toward the gateway with buckets and long ropes to haul up river water against the flames.

Looking back as they came off the bridge, Joliffe saw the rising black roils of smoke lighted by flames from below and wished the bridge-folk good luck. Then he had to give all his will to setting one foot in front of the other up the slope from the bridge to the turning into Lombard Street, leaving it to Rhys and Owen to answer, when they wanted to, whatever questions were thrown at them by Londoners come out of their houses to ask what was happening. Mostly Rhys simply snapped, "Go and see, if you want to know." Only as they came into the yard at the George did they pause for the innkeeper's questions, and to his credit he was more distressed by Gough's death than by the bridge, saying with wonder and regret, "Matthew Gough. All those years fighting the French, only to die against some rebel scum here in London. There's fate for you."

"There's fate," Rhys agreed bitterly. "Send someone for a priest. We're taking him to his room."

The climb up the stairs with Gough's body fairly well finished the last of Joliffe's strength, he thought. Until he crossed the threshold into Gough's room. At sight of the strewn chaos—chair and table and joint stools overset, bedding and mattress stripped from the bed and dumped into a heap against the wall, everything that had been in the chests dumped and scattered across the floor, the chests themselves up-ended—he jerked to a halt. Behind him Owen started, "What . . ." and Joliffe forced himself forward.

Like him both Rhys and Owen stopped on the threshold. Then Rhys snapped, "Let's get him in," and they carried Gough's body to the bed, laid it on the floor long enough for the three of them to put the mattress and a sheet back in place, then lifted Gough's body onto them.

Only then did Rhys take a long look around and swear, "Bastards and curs!" while Owen started shaking his head in silent protest and went on shaking it. Joliffe settled for righting a joint stool and sinking onto it, his legs done for a while. Slowly, he set to ridding himself of helmet, arming cap, and brigantine, dropping them onto the floor beside him.

Of nobody in particular, Owen demanded, "What happened?"

"Robbery," Rhys answered dully. He began to take off his own gear. "Only they didn't find anything, because we've put it all somewhere safer than here."

"Then when they didn't find anything, they came and killed him," Owen said. "Bastards."

"That makes no sense," Rhys said.

Nor did it; but neither of them were any more ready for thinking than Joliffe was. Owen joined Rhys in stripping down to their arming doublets and hosen. With hair sweat-plastered to their heads and shirts to their bodies, they looked very much the way Joliffe supposed he looked, and certainly for a moment they stood as slackly as he felt, until Rhys said with a nod at Gough's body, "Let's have him out of his armor anyway."

Taking Gough's armor off him after a fight was something they had surely done many times before now, but this time, the last time, their fingers were slowed by weariness and the weight of their grief and Rhys' sometimes-falling tears as he bent to the work.

Joliffe saw them but made no move to help. He had no place here. Gough and Rhys had likely started young together in the war; had maybe been surprised to find themselves both alive at the end of it; had probably talked of what they'd do with themselves now it was over; and now, when least looked for, all that could be planned was where to bury Gough and how many Masses for his soul could be afforded.

Joliffe had known Gough too briefly for grief anything like Rhys' and Owen's must be. What he had instead was a slowly growing anger at the way Gough had died and he kept that to himself, leaving the two squires to their grief and duty until Rhys lifted off Gough's breastplate and set it aside. Then Joliffe forced himself to his feet and said, "You can come at that letter now. I still want it."

Both squires turned to stare at him. Owen started angrily to say something, but Rhys said first, "Best you have it. Yes."

He made quick work of unfastening the front of Gough's arming doublet to come at a thin, many-folded square of parchment tucked tightly into the waist of Gough's braies. He pulled it out, faced Joliffe, and thrust it at him with, "This is what they killed him for, isn't it? They didn't find it here, came to kill him at the bridge, and meant to throw him into the Thames to be rid of him and it together. That was the way of it, wasn't it?"

His gaze locked to Rhys', Joliffe took the thing from him with slowly nodded, silent agreement.

"Then if I were you," Rhys said grimly, "I'd watch my back from here to wherever you're going with it." And turned back to Gough's body and what still needed to be done.

Chapter 2

The church was plain and not over-large, its windows small and set high to give no outward view to the world, only let the blessing of sunlight into the unpillared nave and the nuns' choir where the two double lines of tall-backed seats faced each other, ready beside the altar for those six or seven times a day St. Frideswide's nuns gathered there to their Offices of prayer.

Just now, though, with the dawn Office of Prime and morning Mass past and time for Tierce not yet come, the church was empty save for a single nun kneeling in her choir stall, head bowed forward on her hands clasped on the slanted board meant to hold psalter and breviary through the saying of the Offices. Veiled and gowned in Benedictine black, her bowed head hiding the white wimple that encircled her face

24

and hid her throat, she would have been a shadow among shadows save the morning sunlight through the church's east window had banished shadows to the rafters and corners for the while. Only the shadows in her mind held her, and against those the church's deep quiet at this hour was a balm laid over the raw, hurt edges of her thoughts.

To her very heart, Dame Frevisse knew here was where she belonged, here inside these cloister walls, in this nunnery, in this church in this far corner of Oxfordshire. In all the world, this was her place, and most especially here in this choir stall that had been her own—as much as anything in the world was a nun's own—since the day she had taken her vows. Day after day, through all the years into years she had been in St. Frideswide's, she came here to pray and chant the daily Offices with St. Frideswide's other nuns. There were only ten of them now, because St. Frideswide's had never grown as its founder had hoped, but it survived and here were Frevisse's comfort and certainty, here was where she wanted to live, reaching toward God. That reaching was the struggle and the joy to which she had given her life, and although sometimes, for other people's needs, she was drawn out into the world, whether she would or no, here was where she wanted to be, with no wish at all, for any reason whatsoever, to leave her place and peace here.

But she was going to.

Her knees were complaining at her about too-long kneeling, and for pity of them and because their ache was growing into pain, she eased up and back onto the seat behind her, hands now clasped on her lap but her head still bowed, her eyes still closed.

By constant edicts of the Church, nuns were supposed to be cloistered—enclosed inside their nunnery's walls from when they took their vows of poverty, chastity, and obedience until their death. About that, bishops were very firm, but in practice the enclosure was not so narrow and there was sometimes unseemly laughter in the nuns' daily chapter meetings when a new reminder from their bishop was read aloud, listing all the reasons for which a nun should not leave her cloister. There were always reasons for a nun to go out into the world—to visit relations in their need, or to go on pilgrimage, or to tend to nunnery business best done by no one else, or simply to enjoy some nearby pastime like fishing or watching the harvest in nearby fields. As Dame Amicia once said, the bishop's list seemed to be longer each time it came; and although St. Frideswide's prioress, Domina Elisabeth, kept her priory more strictly than some were kept, there were nonetheless times . . .

Frevisse bowed her head lower and lifted her hands from her lap to press them, still clasped, to her forehead. Try though she would, the one prayer that kept coming to her was, "Lord, give me strength," which was a sort of answer to her need but not enough of one. For her cousin Alice of Suffolk's sake she had been out of St. Frideswide's all too lately, and almost everything—admittedly through no fault of Alice's—had gone so far to the bad that at the end there had seemed no good to any of it, only varied layers of wrong. And now her cousin needed her again and Frevisse had been given leave to go to her.

Or not so much been given leave as been ordered to it. Alice had written, as was proper, to Domina Elisabeth, asking that Frevisse be sent to her in her need; and less for Alice's need than because Alice was duchess of Suffolk and wealthy and not without power despite lately widowed by her husband's murder, Domina Elisabeth had told Frevisse she had leave to go. Leave that Frevisse did not want.

But because obedience was one of a nun's vows, Frevisse was here, trying to pray not only for strength to do what she did not wish to, but that she be not angry at Alice for demanding her help and even angrier at Domina Elisabeth for sending her away so readily.

Or at least not *so* angry.

Alice had chosen a life in the world. She had married and been widowed from her first husband very young, then had married the earl of Salisbury, and when he was killed in the French war, had married William de la Pole, earl of Suffolk. Through the years after that, Suffolk had risen to a dukedom and become the most powerful of the lords around the king, and Alice had risen with him. But he had used his power badly, had finally raised such a storm of hatred and protest around himself that King Henry had, early this year, exiled him to save his life.

Instead, sailing to that exile, Suffolk had been seized at sea by unnamed English enemies—pirates, it was said—been crudely beheaded, his body thrown onto the beach at Dover and his head set on a stake beside it.

The pity was that his death had done nothing to right the wrongs he had helped to make in England. From spring until now at almost harvest time, rebellions had been breaking out all over England. Jack Cade's had been the worst. That one was ended now, but there were steady reports of lesser ones still happening, with men's angers still fierce not only at dead Suffolk but at the men who had misgoverned with him and were still close around the king. Among loud demands for justice and good government, hatred of Suffolk seemed hardly dimmed. And now Alice, his widow, wanted Frevisse's companionship and comfort.

Fiercely and not quite as the words were in the psalm, Frevisse sharply whispered, *"Eripe me, Domine, ab homine malo, a viro violento custodi me."* Rescue me, Lord, from the evil man, from the violent man defend me. *"Salve me, Domine, e manibus iniqui, superbi qui cogitant evertere gressus meos, qui abscondunt laqueum mihi."* Save me, Lord, from the hands of the wicked, the arrogant who plan to overthrow my course, who conceal a trap for me.

She dropped her hands into her lap and opened her eyes.

That was not the prayer she should be making. Or at the least not be praying it with anger. She did not believe Alice was evil or setting a trap for her, and if she could not pray better than that, she were best not to pray at all.

But she needed prayer, and if not with words, then otherwise; and she closed her eyes again and with the deliberant skill she had learned through her nunnery years, steadied her breathing, slowed it, deepened it, let her mind rest on her breathing, rest in her breathing, let her breathing ease her out of her taut anger into quietness, breathing slowly, deeply, finding quiet in herself, drawing quiet into her . . .

"Dame Frevisse?" someone whispered to her.

Frevisse opened her eyes and looked at Sister Margrett hovering in front of the choir stalls. No nun should go out of the cloister unaccompanied by another nun. Sister Margrett, the youngest of St. Frideswide's few nuns, was Domina Elisabeth's choice to accompany Frevisse, and although Sister Margrett's Benedictine clothing concealed, as it should, all of her except her face and hands, nothing could hide her glowing eagerness to be out and away as she said, "They're ready." The half-dozen men and two women whom Alice had sent with her message, so certain she'd been that Frevisse would be sent to her and their company be needed. She had slipped into the church while they were readying to ride this morning but they must be waiting now on their horses in the courtyard outside the cloister door, with nothing needed save Frevisse and Sister Margrett themselves. "Domina Elisabeth says you should come," Sister Margrett urged, and with a nod that was already weary of the journey she had yet to make, Frevisse obediently rose to her feet.

Chapter 3

The manor of Hunsdon lay along a green swell of Hertfordshire countryside, quiet among its fields. The manor house was old, with parts added to and taken from it over the years, with newest to it a square, brick-built tower at one end. Sir William Oldhall had his study there, high enough that, with a squire left at the stair-foot, he could be certain nothing said in the wide room would be overheard by anyone.

Not that either he or Joliffe was saying anything. With Sir William's clerk sent out when Joliffe was shown in, the silence had settled while Sir William read the letter. Finishing it, he had laid it on the slanted top of his clerk's desk and paced away to the window and had been standing there several long minutes now, looking out over the manor's outer wall and the gentle roll of countryside all green and golden in the warm light of the quiet summer evening.

Joliffe, leaning a hip against a corner of the heavy desk, watched him and waited. Sir William was much about Matthew Gough's age, and Joliffe knew that, like Gough, Sir William had spent more years of his life than not in the French war. Unlike Gough, he had risen beyond the plain leading of men-at-arms to a place on the king's council in Normandy and had served the duke of York when York was governor there for the king.

York had depended heavily on men like Sir William, experienced in the ever-shifting warfare along the borders between English- and French-held territories, to advise him as he had steadied and strengthened matters into an uneasy peace but peace nonetheless.

The trouble had been that governing and the garrisons that went with it in Normandy cost money; and while the war had been one thing when it was a matter of lands to seize and pillage to be had, it was another now it had ceased to be profitable, when there was neither glory nor fortune to be had, only trouble and costs. The war had poured wealth from France into England, and the lords around the king had not been minded to pour it back, too busy running the king's household into wallowing-deep debt and the royal government to hell, their greed and corrupted justice grinding down the law and lesser men.

King Henry—reputedly busy with his prayers—gave no sign of knowing or caring; and Richard of York had been recalled from Normandy, and with Edmund Beaufort, duke of Somerset made governor in his stead, the war was now being disastrously lost.

Sir William had left France when York did; had become one of York's household councilors and, quietly, the man who kept York informed, now he sent away to Ireland, of how matters went in England. And Joliffe was among the men used by Sir William to learn the things York needed to know.

Sir William turned from the window and pointed at the letter. "It hadn't been sealed. Did you read it?"

"Yes." If men were being killed because of the thing, and he was carrying it, he assuredly had read it.

"It's proof of nothing," Sir William said. "It's one man's word of what he saw."

It was that, but, "Very detailed word," Joliffe said evenly. "Who and where and when, and what happened afterward that made this Robert James remember about that who and where and when." And a more damning set of statements he had never read, if they were true. They looked true, with anger there in every blot of ink and pen-gouge into the paper, with Robert James' name scrawled furiously at the bottom, followed by an equally scrawled assurance that all the above was true, so help him Christ and Mary and all the saints.

Joliffe's own grim thought was that if what he claimed was true, there were men who were going to be in need of help from all the hosts of heaven far more than Robert James was.

Sir William turned back to the window, his hands behind his back, the back of the right one slapping up and down in the palm of the left as he muttered, "But it's still not proof. We could name names until blue in our faces and be no further along, because Suffolk's people and Somerset would deny everything just as fast as we said it."

Which was true, but Joliffe offered, "It ties together pieces that otherwise hang oddly, left on their own, and it gives us somewhere to ask questions we didn't have before."

"Where?" Sir William demanded, turning around again. "Did Gough say where this Robert James is now?"

"No."

"Probably dead. Somewhere in the rout the war's become. Like Gough."

Joliffe held back from pointing out that Gough had not died in the war, had not even been killed by one of the rebels he'd been fighting. Sir William was right that this Robert James' angrily written accusations were proof of nothing. A great deal more would be needed to bring an indictment that would hold against men so powerful as the duke of Suffolk had been and the duke of Somerset now was. But James' accusations were a place to start, and Joliffe had thought Sir William would take them up more readily than this.

"Damn it about Gough," Sir William said. "He deserved better than that."

Joliffe kept to himself his thought that a great many men deserved better than what they got. Instead he said, "There's use can be made of these accusations, even so."

Sir William moved away from the window, began to pace the chamber, still restlessly slapping his hands into each other behind his back. "There is. Yes. We have names, anyway."

"Men who might be ready to talk," Joliffe prompted. "If asked."

"It's just that this Robert James is nobody. Who's going to believe him?" Sir William said. "He was with Surienne, too. That makes anything he says suspect. He could just be setting up to defend himself."

"He's too nobody to need to defend himself," Joliffe said, putting more patience than he felt into the words. "He's a plain man-at-arms, briefly stuck with being lieutenant of Bayeux. He's not anyone who's likely to be sought out and blamed for anything."

Sir William pointed at the paper. "He saw things. He heard things. Surienne *told* him things."

"He saw what a lot of men must have seen. He *overheard* what Surienne said because Surienne said it in the great hall where surely any number of other men heard it, too." And how dearly Joliffe wished they had those men's testimonies to go with James', because it was Sir François de Surienne who had kicked out the keystone that had held together the whole structure of peace in France. A mercenary captain under English command, he had, despite the truce, swept a force into the Breton border town of Fougères early last year. His men had pillaged the town and then held it in the teeth of angry Breton and French protests to the duke of Somerset that he rein in Surienne and make restitution for the wrong.

Thereafter came the part that had made no sense. That a mercenary captain might run mad was one thing, but Somerset had done nothing—either against Surienne or to save the truce; and when finally, after months of unanswered demands, the French king, allied with the duke of Brittany, attacked Normandy's border in return, Somerset had done nothing to stop him. Town after town, castle after castle had fallen or been surrendered to the French, until—in a few short months—Somerset himself was besieged in Normandy's chief city, Rouen, with his family and most of the English army's best captains. Then, with a haste that bordered on what some might call cowardice, he had surrendered Rouen and its castle and left a good many of those captains as hostages to the French while he retreated with his goods and family toward the coast, to Caen. There, after another few months and more towns and castles lost, the French army had again closed in on him, and word was lately come that Somerset had now agreed to surrender Caen, too, giving up England's last great stronghold in Normandy.

In hardly a year almost everything the English had gained in France through the thirty-five years of war since King Henry V's great victory at Agincourt had been lost, and there was no hope of saving the rest.

From the beginning, the great, blazing question had

been: What had possessed Surienne to seize Fougères and break the truce?

Then: Why had Somerset done nothing either to punish him or to save the hard-won peace?

And finally: When all the French attempts to mend the truce were ignored and they finally attacked, why had Somerset done nothing, had simply let Normandy fall to them, like a poorly made house of sticks?

Robert James' scrawled words gave something close to answers to all that. Joliffe leaned over and picked up the paper. "This Robert James was there in Rouen. He saw Suffolk's steward, Sir John Hampden, there two months before the attack on Fougères. He says Hampden was in close talk with the duke of Somerset and Surienne together."

"There could be reasons for that besides . . . treason."

The word "treason" seemed to come hard to Sir William. It came less hard to Joliffe. There were men—essentially sound but not wanting to know how bad their fellows could be—who preferred not to see the great many layers of treachery and ugliness there were in the world, or at least to look no closer than could be helped. Joliffe preferred to know. Instead of shying clear, he watched, he saw, he thought about it, and he was willing to believe in the ugly picture this probably-dead Robert James had put together from what he had seen and then had thought about.

But Sir William was trying, "Suffolk still has . . . had lands in Normandy. Hampden as his steward was there to see about them, that's all."

"Surely Suffolk would have had a separate steward for his Norman lands," Joliffe said.

"Some other reason of business then. He would see Somerset simply in the usual way of things. Bringing a message or simply greetings. Suffolk and Somerset were friends, after all."

If two carrion crows looking to pick over the same carcase

could ever be thought to be friends, thought Joliffe. He was also willing to warrant that if anyone cared to look, they would find Suffolk had sold those Norman lands of his a safe while ago. But he only said, "And that kept Hampden in close talk with Somerset *and* the mercenary captain a full turn of the hourglass?"

"What was this James doing, keeping such close note of them, anyway?" Sir William said almost fretfully. "It was no business of his."

Joliffe held back from saying Robert James had noted it because it was odd; instead persisted, "And Suffolk's chaplain? Why would he be in Normandy? His place is in the household, or else in his own parish, supposing he has one."

"Pilgrimage," Sir William promptly answered. "Like Hampden, there for one reason but bringing greetings and some message from Suffolk since he was going that way anyway."

"He was there twice. And in talk with Surienne at least one of those times. And Suffolk's secretary? What was he doing traipsing off to Normandy? A secretary overseas isn't very useful for writing the daily letters."

"If it was Suffolk's secretary. James said the man 'was said' to be." Sir William pointed almost angrily at the paper still in Joliffe's hand. "Even if he has the right of it, *that* is proof of nothing! No one can be accused of anything on simply that—one bitter man's assertion scrawled when he was angry and in pain with defeat and wounds."

Only with effort could Joliffe grant all of that was fair enough counterargument. But, "He was at Fougères, too. On *Somerset's* order he took a supply train there from Bayeux." Given the distance between the towns, that made as little sense as everything else Somerset had done, but the point he added was, "Somerset was supporting Surienne in holding Fougères, and that's proof of it."

"It's Surienne I'd give a hand to talk to!" Sir William said with raw frustration.

"Does anyone know where he is?"

"Gone," Sir William said disgustedly. "Vanished out of Normandy. As I would be, if I were him."

So would Joliffe. A mercenary captain as successful over the years as Surienne had been would have seen clearly enough who would be handily blamed for the utter rout the French war had become after his attack on Fougères. He would have known that away was the best thing for him to be, and away he was gone.

Sir William crossed back toward the desk. Joliffe straightened from it. There was sufficient difference between his place in the world and Sir William's for him to show that much respect. At the same time, Joliffe knew his usefulness lay in being bold beyond what otherwise he should be, and he said, "The point is that this report gives more weight to all the suspicions and accusations already abroad that Suffolk set about deliberately to lose the war. This makes plain it was he and Somerset together, and even if it isn't proof in itself, it gives us somewhere more to ask questions. Of Hampden and the priest and even Suffolk's secretary on the chance he really was there."

Sir William sat down in the chair behind the desk and said heavily, "It does." He rubbed at his temples with his fingertips. "The trouble is that I don't want it to be true. But I agree it may well be. So there are three things to be done. Learn where Hampden and the priest—what was his name, John Squyers?—and our late duke of Suffolk's secretary presently are. My spy in the Lady Alice's household can find that out. Once we know it, you will find out what you can from them. Suffolk's death may have them frighted enough they'll be willing to buy safety by telling what they know. In the meanwhile of all that, I'll send word to my lord of York in Ireland of what's toward. My messenger taking my report about this Jack Cade's rebellion to him can take that word, too."

Sir William paused, looking in two minds about saying more. Joliffe waited, and Sir William finally said, "You've not been long in my lord of York's service."

"I've not," Joliffe agreed; and he had come to it by cross-ways rather than by purpose.

"Nor do you go by a name that's your own."

"I don't, no."

"But my lord of York trusts you. Without saying why, he's said his reasons are sufficient."

"Yes," Joliffe agreed again.

Sir William paused again, then said sharply, "There's something I've heard. From court. From inside the king's own household." He leaned forward, toward Joliffe, bracing both hands on the desk. "It's coming from that high. What I want is for you to keep your ear out for it. We have to know how wide they've spread the word and if they're going to follow through on it. Because if they do, the danger is doubled and more than doubled. You understand?"

"Not yet. For what am I listening?"

With mingled anger and unwillingness, somewhat strangling on the words, as if it were a struggle to get them out, Sir William said, "That my lord of York is guilty of treason."

Joliffe's first stab of disbelief was replaced by feeling he was a fool not to have foreseen that. The duke of Suffolk was dead but the lords and other men who had held power with him around the king were still there, were too deeply set in the royal household and the government to be shifted easily, even with all this summer's rebellions against them. What was more likely than that they would try to turn England's anger away from themselves and toward York? To find him guilty of treason would serve two purposes— provide a scapegoat for the rebellions and rid the lords of him. And never mind that he had never made anything of his blood-claim to the throne, had so far lived and served only as King Henry's cousin. All that had got him so far was nearly no place on the king's council, recall from Normandy when he was too successful, and now all but exile out of the way to Ireland.

The trouble was that he was not out of men's thoughts.

With England's government given over these past ten years to men more interested in gain than the country's good, York's right to the throne, so easily forgotten under the strong rule of King Henry's father and grandfather, was being remembered and not only by those who wished him well.

With one thing and another and memory of the duke of Gloucester's fate—dead of uncertain causes, the men around King Henry said; murdered, said most others—Richard of York had to feel less than easy about his place in the plans of the men around the king.

"It's this Cade," Sir William said tersely. "He's made it the easier for them by claiming his name is John Mortimer. You know that."

"Yes," Joliffe said, as tersely as Sir William. He knew that, and that "Mortimer" was the family name of York's mother and that it was through her that York's royal blood most dangerously came.

"Why Cade claimed to be a Mortimer, I don't know," Sir William said irritably. "It likely makes no difference in the long run of things, because some sharp-wit around the king would have come up with this treason thought anyway."

"You mean they're going to claim my lord of York was behind Cade's rebellion."

"Behind his uprising and all the other ones, too, very likely. That's why I want to know if you hear anything that way. Anything. From anyone."

Because after all, if an untried and unproved charge of

treason had brought the king's own uncle, the duke of Gloucester, to his death, why couldn't a treason charge do the same for Richard of York?

And for any men too loyal to him, such as Sir William. And Joliffe.

Chapter 4

Only with St. Frideswide's behind them had the man in charge of seeing Frevisse to her cousin told her they were not bound for one manor or another but would meet with Lady Alice and her company somewhere on the road.

"To where?" Frevisse had demanded.

"I believe my lady is going to her manor of Wingfield," the man had said. Wingfield, in the heart of the late duke of Suffolk's lands in East Anglia, at least three days' ride from St. Frideswide's.

Frevisse had wanted to know more but that was the last she had from him or anyone else; and they did meet Alice at some lesser crossroads near nowhere in particular so far as Frevisse could tell; but while Frevisse had thought to find her carried in a horse-litter with drawn curtains, making slow progress as a bereaved widow through the summer countryside, Alice was sitting on a black palfrey among some twenty other horses and riders and two lightly burdened packhorses, while her small son, John, played some running game with himself around the base of the tall wayside cross there, its shadow thrown long across the road by the late afternoon sun.

It was a lonely place, no village in sight, and yet there was a wary alertness to the men around Alice, one of them saying tersely to the leader of Frevisse's own company, "Any trouble?"

"None. You?"

"Only some, and that was yesterday."

Frevisse rode past them then to Alice, dressed all in widow's black save for the elegantly tucked and pleated white widow's wimple around her face and over her chin as well as her throat, and even that subdued by the black veil over her head, hanging below her shoulders on either side. Only her face showed, making her as swathed from the world as a nun; and both her face and voice were likewise swathed from showing anything as she said formally, "Dame Frevisse. Thank you for coming."

Frevisse returned in kind, "Your need was enough to bring me, my lady," while trying quickly to assess how much was wrong here. A year ago, she and Alice had parted in anger and disappointment at each other. Since then, once, Alice had asked her secret help and Frevisse had given it despite deep doubts. She and Alice had briefly met afterward, had found last year's wounds still there but their kinship—their mothers had been sisters—still strong and their friendship maybe ready to stir to life again.

By Alice's stiff greeting it looked dead again, and in the same formal way, Alice looked past her to Sister Margrett and said, "You're welcome, also," but was gathering up her reins as she said it. Welcome was over. One of her men had taken John up in front of him in his saddle. The rest of her escort were forming a double column, half the men riding ahead, half behind, except for John's man who rode with Alice's six women, Frevisse, and Sister Margrett in the middle of them all.

Frevisse noted that the women, like herself and Sister Margrett, all rode astride rather than fashionably side-saddled, the better to match the men's pace, she supposed. She also noted that the duke of Suffolk's badge was nowhere to be seen, nor the ducal banner of three gold leopard heads on azure, a golden fesse between them, despite small John was now duke and had right to it. It was rare for a great lord— or even a great lord's widow—to ride in obscurity, unless there was grievous necessity for it. Was the hatred against dead Suffolk still so widespread that Alice had to hide who she and John were?

She could expect no answers from Alice any time soon, she supposed; could only meet Sister Margrett's questioning look with a shake of her head as the column rode on. At a trot as often as at a walk, and sometimes at a canter along straight stretches of the road, they kept on through the long end of the summer's afternoon. Their shadows stretched far aside from them, across the road's grassy verge into the thickening shadows of hedges, coppices, walls, and villages by and through which they rode. The sun touched the horizon and began to slide from sight. Time was come to stop at an inn or a monastery's guesthouse but still they rode with no word passed among them.

Even Sister Margrett, who might well have been querelous, asked nothing; but on her own part, Frevisse wanted very much to take hold on Alice and demand explanation for why their going had the seeming of a flight, of someone afraid or with something to hide. Even the two packhorses were so lightly burdened they kept up easily with the others; and now the sun was fully gone and still they rode. Twilight faded into full dark but the night was clear; even without moonrise there was starlight enough by which to ride, if only at a walk now. The hour was long past when Frevisse and Sister Margrett would have gone to their beds. Frevisse drowsed and jerked awake, drowsed and jerked awake again more times than she counted. Beside her, Sister Margrett did the same; and once one of the other women reached out to push the woman beside her straight in her saddle when she began to slump sideways.

By the stars Frevisse thought the hour was close to midnight when finally there was a general drawing of reins to a halt. Beside her, Sister Margrett whispered, "Where are we?" but Frevisse could only answer, "I don't know." As best she could make out, it was empty countryside around them. She could hear a stream but that was all. Around them everyone was dismounting. She and Sister Margrett did, too. A man led their horses away, toward the stream, Frevisse thought, and then she made out that a bustling away to one side was the setting up of small tents nothing like the fine pavilion she had known otherwise for Alice; but when she and Sister Margrett had eaten the bread and cheese someone gave them, had washed it down with warm ale from leather bottles shared around, and used the privacy given by a canvas screen stretched between poles for other necessities, they both willingly ducked into the tent pointed out to them. That they were to share it with four other women cramped together on scant bedding mattered less to Frevisse at that moment than that she was lying down; sleep came without trouble.

Morning was another matter.

First, it came too soon. Called awake by one of the men, the women rose with soft groans of stiffness and little exclaims of pain and came out into dew-wet half-darkness, the sun not yet risen. The men had likely slept even less, taking turns at guard, and unsheltered, but neither they nor the women made any complaint or said much of anything at all. Frevisse, Sister Margrett, and the other women did what they could to straighten wimples and veils and shake wrinkles from rumpled gowns, all with very little talk. More bread and cheese and ale were handed around while the horses were being saddled, and Frevisse realized past her yawns and aches that they were going to ride on with no more explanation than there had yet been.

Enough was enough, and she went purposefully toward Alice, at that moment standing alone, a little apart from everyone, looking eastward as if to hurry the sunrise. To her back and with no friendliness, Frevisse said, "My lady."

Alice turned around. In the half-light of the almost-dawn her face was drawn with more than lack of sleep, with more than the weariness of hard riding; and instead of the demand Frevisse had meant to make, she surprised herself and maybe Alice by asking almost gently, "Alice, by all mercy, what is this about?"

Alice made as if to answer, stopped as if words would not come, then finally forced out, "This is me being afraid for my life and the life of my son. When we're at Wingfield I'll tell you more. Until then . . . please."

Alice was not someone given to pleading but that was a plea, and Frevisse said, "Yes."

Low and unevenly, Alice said, "Thank you," with tears sounding very near; but it was with dry eyes and lifted chin she moved past Frevisse and toward the man leading her horse toward her. In the saddle, she even smiled around at her people before nodding for her lead men to ride on.

They rode that day much as they had ridden the day before. When they paused at noontide to eat—more bread and cheese and ale, none of it very fresh now; they seemed to be avoiding market towns where new could have been bought— Frevisse judged they were all—men, women, young John, and the horses—nearing the end of their strength; and indeed sometime in the afternoon the packhorses and the men leading them fell behind and were left. Frevisse hoped that was sign they were near Wingfield, but more in early evening than late afternoon they rode under gathering clouds around a last twist of road, passed a church and straight toward a towered gatehouse set in a long wall the far side of a moat. "Wingfield," one of the women riding behind Frevisse sighed in aching relief.

They seemed not to be expected. At the shut gates the two men on watch took a while to grasp that Lady Alice was indeed there. Then one went shouting the news while the other unbarred and swung open the gates, letting them into the manor yard. As they rode across the yard to the fore-porch of the great hall, a man came out in flustered haste, catching Alice's reins and holding her stirrup while she dismounted, all the while apologizing that all was not fully ready for her yet, that he had thought she meant to arrive tomorrow, that he . . .

"The apology is mine to make," Alice assured him. "We're before our time. Whatever is ready will serve very well for now. We're very tired. Anything will be welcome, Master Thorpe. No, Sir Edmund, let the servants take the horses. All of you come into the hall. There'll be wine for everyone. You've deserved that of me, and more. I'm in your debt." Save that she was very pale, Alice gave no sign of being anything but the lady caring for her people. Smiling, she added, clear enough for all to hear, "Nor do I doubt that Master Thorpe will have a goodly meal on the table for us almost before we've had time to unstiffen from our ride."

"Be assured, my lady," Master Thorpe said with a low bow, sounding far more sure of that than he probably felt.

But Alice leaned near to him and said in a false whisper, meant to carry to everyone around them, "Mind you, we've lived on bread and cheese for two days, so any meal that's more than that is going to look most excellent to us."

On the lift of the general laughter that answered that, Alice held out her hand for John to come to her from among the women. His eyes were large and shadowed. With that and the mourning-black of his doublet and over-gown, he looked even younger than his seven years; looked very young to be burdened with a dukedom and a murdered father and a very frightened mother. But straight-backed and head up, he went to take his mother's hand, and with Master Thorpe they led the way inside, through the foreporch into the screens passage low-ceilinged under the minstrels gallery and then into the great hall.

It was perhaps as large as St. Frideswide's whole church but far more elegantly proportioned with stone-mantled fireplaces and tall windows of clear glass set with heraldic beasts in bold color, and its high-beamed roof decorated with painted shields. For all that, it was presently less than it would usually be, with the walls naked of tapestries over the white plastering, the fireplaces empty, the floor swept clear and no fresh rushes yet laid down. But that did not lessen Sister Margrett's, "Oh. My," as she stared around her. Even as the daughter of a well-off merchant of Northampton town, she was unused to such display and withdrew, somewhat subdued, to one side of the hall with Frevisse, who was as uncertain as Sister Margrett was of what their place was here.

The others were breaking into small clumps and beginning to talk among themselves in a mingling of weariness and relief. A haste of servants were setting up a trestle table down the hall's length and bringing out the household's cups from wherever the tablewares were locked away in the lord's and lady's absence. For her own part, Frevisse looked forward to the promised wine and then food and then rest, and beside her Sister Margrett groaned quietly, "I'm not going to be able to walk tomorrow."

"I only pray I don't need to ride again for a month," Frevisse said from the heart.

Sister Margrett groaned again, maybe at the very thought of riding; then said with startled dismay, "A month? Will we be here that long?"

"I don't know. Lady Alice has told me nothing about why we're here at all." And Frevisse was beginning, coward-wise, to think she did not want to know why Alice needed her.

She had not even seen Alice and John leave the hall, but looking around, she saw they were not here. But as she thought that, Master Thorpe, who must be the household's steward here, approached her and Sister Margrett, bowed to them both, but said to only Frevisse, "My lady asks that you come to her," adding to Sister Margrett, "She asks your pardon, but she would like to see her cousin alone."

"Of course," Sister Margrett said as courteously.

Feeling far from courteous, Frevisse followed Master Thorpe up the hall and through a doorway there. Other rooms lay beyond it, and stairs, and it was up the stairs Master Thorpe led Frevisse and to more rooms. They opened one into another, one after another, making a wing of the house away from the courtyard, with walls wainscoted with panels of golden oak below, plastered and patterned above, or else painted. Because a lord's and lady's comforts traveled with them in a lumbering train of wagons when they moved from manor to manor, these rooms were barren of most furnishings, except it seemed the de la Pole wealth was sufficient that not everything had to be moved when they moved. In one chamber through which Master Thorpe led her a tall, posted bed was centered against the far wall, lacking the curtains that would usually have hung around it but with several servants unrolling a mattress onto the bedframe while others waited with folded sheets and blankets piled in their arms. Alice at least would have a bed tonight, Frevisse thought.

But Alice was not there, and Master Thorpe led on to the room beyond it. A much smaller room than the others, it was as bare, with only a flat-lidded chest against one wall and a narrow window set in a thickness of wall that made Frevisse guess this was the older part of the house. Rather than a bench set under the window, two stone seats ran with the several feet of the wall from the room to the window, facing each other, and Alice was there, standing between the stone benches, looking out at the day's end.

Master Thorpe said, bowing, "Dame Frevisse, my lady."

Without turning even her head, Alice answered, "Thank you. Leave us until I call."

Master Thorpe bowed again and went out, closing the door, and at the soft snick of the falling latch Alice swung sharply around and started toward Frevisse, a hand thrust out so desperately that Frevisse went toward her in return, reaching out, too. Alice grabbed her hand as if grabbing for life, saying nothing, simply holding to her with eyes shut, taking the shallow, shuddering breaths of someone wanting to cry but unable to give way.

With no thought of what to say, Frevisse clasped her hand in both her own and simply held it as tightly as Alice was holding to hers, until Alice pulled sharply away and with seeming anger began to fumble at the pins holding her black widow's veil of heavy linen over her wimple, so clumsily that Frevisse said, "Here. Let me. Sit down."

With a trembling gasp, Alice obeyed, dropping onto the chest. Frevisse deftly removed pins and veil, would have loosed Alice from the confining circle of the wimple around her face and throat, too, except Alice with that same anger stripped it off herself and threw it across the room.

"There!" she said fiercely. "So much for grieving!" She bowed her head, clutched it from both sides, her fingers digging into her fair hair as if her head might fly apart without she kept hard hold on it, but said no less fiercely, "If he wasn't dead already, I think I'd kill him."

Assuming that Alice meant her late husband, Frevisse did not pretend to a dismay she did not feel. Regrettable though Alice's urge might be toward any man, Suffolk had done more than most to earn it, and she contented herself with folding Alice's veil, carefully putting the pins in it for safe keeping, then laying it on a rear corner of the chest. By then Alice had dropped her hands into her lap and was sitting with her head leaned back against the wall, staring dry-eyed up at the ceiling with such despair and weariness that Frevisse would have given comfort if she had known what comfort might serve. Not knowing, she instead asked, "How much danger are you truly in?"

Alice jerked her head forward from the wall. "Danger?" she demanded, sounding almost ready to turn her anger on Frevisse.

Keeping her own anger to herself, Frevisse returned evenly, "You all but said it in so many words to me on the way here. Besides that, you deliberately sent word to Master Thorpe that you would arrive here a day later than you meant to. I assume that was to forestall any ambush that might be planned against you."

"You might be assuming wrongly," Alice snapped.

"I might be," Frevisse granted. And waited. Whatever Alice's anger, it was not really at her, and whatever her own anger at Alice, there was no useful purpose in showing it.

And Alice suddenly gave a choked laugh, tried to say something, failed, and put her hands over her face, bowed her head again, and gave way to crying, her body shaking with terrible sobs that somehow she kept almost soundless, as if even now she had to hold as hidden as she could. Frevisse, having no better comfort to offer, offered none. That probably served best. Alice had begun to quiet by the time there came a soft scratching at the door and a woman called, "Wine, my lady."

Alice hurriedly arose and went to the window, putting her back to the room and herself as far from the door as might be, leaving Frevisse to let in a servant carrying a tray finely balanced between a tall pitcher of Venetian glass painted with swirling gold vines, two matching goblets, and a clear glass plate with narrow slices of toasted, buttered bread. Frevisse took the tray from the woman with thanks and nodded for her to withdraw.

Even at sound of the door closing, Alice, now wiping her eyes, did not turn from the window. Frevisse set the tray on the chest and poured the dark red wine into the slender goblets, took one to Alice, who murmured thanks without fully looking around. Frevisse went for the other goblet and the plate. The bread looked to be plain kitchen-bread, not the fine, white kind that would be the duchess of Suffolk's usual fare. That this was the best to hand told again how sudden her arrival was, but it was certainly better than drinking wine on empty stomachs, and joining her cousin at the window, she held the plate out in front of Alice.

Alice, with her goblet already half-emptied, made no move to take any.

"Eat," Frevisse ordered. "You don't make a practice of letting your household see you drunk, do you? Which you'll be if you don't eat something."

Alice, about to drink again, gave a choked, unwilling laugh, lowered the goblet, and took a piece. Frevisse set the plate down on an end of one of the window seats where they could both reach it and for a few moments they ate and drank in silence, standing because they had been sitting on horseback for a great many hours and the bare stone of the seats promised little compensation of comfort. But with the edge taken from her hunger and thirst, Frevisse returned to her curiosity. She had no doubt at all that Alice wanted her here for something more than her companionship. Only Alice's unwillingness to come to it surprised her, and carefully schooling any particular feeling from her voice, she tried, "Since you wrote my prioress for my company at your husband's funeral, may I ask where is his body?"

Calmly, still looking out the window, Alice said, "It's here. In the church. He's been here almost from the beginning." She hiccuped on a small, bitter laugh. "Or from his ending. Depending on which way it's looked at." She sat suddenly down on one of the window benches and looked up at Frevisse. "Sit, please. You're too tall."

Frevisse sat on the other bench, facing her, and waited. Alice ate more of the toast, gathered herself, and went on, "I was afraid of what would be done to his body if anyone had chance at it. The hatred is still so high against him. Even with him dead. I didn't want worse than was already done. Not more than . . ."

Her throat seemed to close against saying what had already been done to Suffolk's body—butchered by a crude beheading and thrown like rubbish onto the stones at Dover's beach with his head rammed onto a stake beside it.

"I know," Frevisse said, to save her saying more.

Alice nodded sharp acceptance and went on, "The king's men who found him . . . it . . . his body . . . they took it into the castle there at Dover but it couldn't stay there." She turned her head away to look out the window and into her memories. "I sent orders for it to be lead-coffined and taken from Dover by ship and part way up the Thames, as if it were going to Ewelme, but before it reached London, it was shifted to a coast-hugging balinger and taken the other way, north around the coast to Aldeburgh and wagoned from there under a load of cloth to here and buried secretly in the church at night with enough of the rites to satisfy but no ceremony to draw anyone's unwanted heed. The other ship went on up the Thames to London with no sign there'd ever been a coffin aboard."

So that if anyone was looking for revenge beyond Suffolk's death, the trail had gone cold and confused, Frevisse thought.

"And now you're here to give him proper funeral," she said.

"Yes," Alice agreed, stood abruptly up and moved away, saying bitterly as she went, "I didn't want him buried at Ewelme where I mean to be buried. I don't want him near me through eternity."

To her back, Frevisse said quietly, "You're that angry at him."

Alice spun around. "I am *that* angry at him, yes. You know as well as I do the part he played in bringing on this disaster in France. What else he's done . . ." She started to pace the room. "You've no thought of what else he's done. I don't know everything, have only a guess at how much I don't know. But I know enough . . ." She had begun pacing again. "Have you heard about the letter he wrote to our son before he sailed from England?"

Frevisse had not, nor would it have mattered if she had, because Alice did not wait for answer but went scathingly on, "He ever had a way with words, did Suffolk. He wrote this letter that urges John to honor God and the king, and to obey his mother, shun the company of bad men, and never follow his own mind but only the advice of others. Told him that if he did all that, he'd come to a good end." Anger etched Alice's words with scorn. "All that and none of it meant for John at all. All of it no more than shallow wisdom-by-rote, meant to show the world what a fine and noble man the duke of Suffolk was." Alice did not actually spit as she said his name but came near enough as made no difference. "How *dare* he write things like 'Never follow your own wits but ask the advice and counsel of good men. Draw to your company good and virtuous men'? This from the man who protected and kept company with men like Fiennes. And Tuddenham. And Danyell. Cheating, thieving, grasping, vicious . . ." She strangled on her anger, recovered, and burst out, "I doubt he spoke a straight thing in all the last ten years of his life!"

With a mildness wholly feigned, Frevisse suggested, "So when he wrote all that to John, he knew whereof he spoke?"

Alice stared at her, then gave a sudden fragment of laughter and said, "I suppose so, yes." She returned to sit facing Frevisse again. Hands clasped tightly around the glass goblet now resting on her lap, she asked bitterly, "But do you know what he did with that letter? He had his secretary write out I don't know how many copies of it. John got his, yes, but so did the world at large. It wasn't meant for John at all, only for Suffolk. Just like everything else he did in his life. All for himself and nothing for anyone else."

And so Alice was tangled in bitterness as well as grief; but what Frevisse so far failed to understand was her fear—or rather, why she was so much more afraid now than she had been when Frevisse last saw her, far sooner after Suffolk's death. She did not ask, though. Not yet. Just now Alice's need was to pour out her anger and her pain, like lancing a sore to let out the festering pus, that healing might begin. And indeed it was with far less anger, as if she were gone away on some side thought, that Alice said, "I just wish I knew what had become of Burgate. He'd still be of use to me."

"Burgate?"

"Suffolk's secretary. Edward Burgate. He's taken himself off without a word to me. All our people that sailed with Suffolk were put ashore along with his body. Burgate, too. Most of them came back to me. Some stayed with the body and came later. Everyone but Burgate, but no one has been able to tell me where he's gone or even when he went. He was there and then he wasn't."

"Did anyone else go missing? Then or later?"

Alice made a dismissing shrug, more irked than worried. "The expected fleeing rats from a sinking ship. Not more than expected. Our chaplain, though," she added with faint surprise. "He came back with the rest but asked my leave to go to his parish." She gave a curt laugh. "That's something he never wanted before. It will be a wonder if anyone there even recognizes him." It being all too usual for a priest to be given a parish, take the income from it but hire a lesser priest to serve there in his place for a very small portion of the tithes. "Just another rat from my sinking ship," Alice said bitterly.

Carefully, Frevisse asked, "Are you sinking?"

The question seemed to give Alice pause. She sat silently awhile before saying slowly, "I don't know that I am. I'd say that presently I'm bailing fast enough to keep afloat."

"But you're afraid," Frevisse said quietly, "of some sudden sea-surge that, if it comes, could overthrow you."

"Yes." Alice drew a deep and trembling breath and let it go. "Yes. Some sea-surge of circumstance. That's what I'm afraid for. That something will come that will unbalance and overthrow everything."

"Is it likely?"

"I don't know!" Alice spoke with both despair and anger. "That's the trouble. I don't *know*. I only *fear* there's something but don't know what, so there's nothing I can do about it." She flung to her feet again. "I just want to be done with Suffolk! I want to give him his funeral so that's off my conscience, and then get on with John's life."

"And your own," Frevisse said gently.

"My own? I don't know that I have one anymore. Or not one worth the living, now Suffolk has so thoroughly destroyed it."

Frevisse let go by that declaration of despair. Whatever else came, Alice was wealthy in her own right, not merely her husband's, and well-witted and strong-minded. Given time enough for her raw wounds of heart and mind to heal, she would survive and almost surely even prosper again. Probably Alice, under her grieving and anger, knew that, too, because she turned from that particular course of misery and said with sudden, quiet gratitude, "Thank you for coming, Frevisse. I haven't seemed grateful, but . . ." She broke off as if her throat had closed. Tears swam into her eyes and she looked away, out the window again. "Just 'thank you'," she whispered.

Chapter 5

To Joliffe's mind, the only fault with Wales was that, more often than not, it was so far from where he was when he had to go there. Added to that Sir William had been unable to give good reason why Suffolk's steward Sir John Hampden was there, only that he was and therefore Joliffe should be and as soon as might be, never mind that Wales was the other side of England from where he started, so that even with mostly fair weather and the best will in the world—and Joliffe was never certain how best, or even good, his will truly was—he had had five days of steady riding from Hertfordshire to Chester and something like another half-day's ride to come, finally, into Flint, where Hampden was reported to be.

His somewhat concern was that he would find Hampden

had moved on. That of course would be solved by following him. Of greater concern was how to have from him what Sir William wanted to know without the world and its cousin coming to know of it.

Sir William had been sanguine about it. "He's a man who's lost his lord. As Suffolk's man, he was laying hold on properties and getting royal offices. With Suffolk dead, he can't be sure of anything, including keeping what he has. Offer him money and let him understand, without you saying it in so many words, that you're from a lord very near the king who's hoping to be nearer. Someone who could do him good in time to come."

But no names, Joliffe noted. Since York was nothing like "near the king", and the lords around King Henry looked to keep him that way.

"You'll have to feel your way once you're in talk with him, that's all," Sir William had said. "Maybe let him think you're from the duke of Buckingham."

Riding into Flint's marketplace, however, Joliffe's interest was more in finding somewhere to stay than in finding Hampden. A bank of dark clouds had been rising up the eastern sky behind him since midday, promising the fair weather was going to turn to rain, and before he did anything else, Joliffe meant for him and Rowan, his roan mare, to have somewhere dry to stay the night.

As it happened, that proved easy enough. Flint was built outward from one of the great castles used to hold Wales to English obedience; was set on the wide coast road across northern Wales and, besides that, was a seaport as well, and so there was more than one inn in the town and several facing onto the marketplace. He chose the Green Cockerel for its sign of a green, crowing cock hung out over the street and asked a half-grown boy in the stableyard about bed and stable-room there for the night.

"Two days ago you'd have been without," the boy said

with a gap-toothed grin. "Today's good enough, though."

Joliffe gave him a farthing to hold Rowan and went into the tavern-room where there was only an aproned man setting pottery cups along a shelf above a wooden cask that was bunged and spigoted and ready for when business came. The long tables around the walls were well-scrubbed, the rushes on the floor clean, and the man cheerful as he admitted Joliffe could have a bed there tonight. He tipped his chin toward the raftered ceiling and said, "A good, clean bed in a good, clean room. You'll maybe have it to yourself, too. The bed, not the room. The only one-man room I've got is taken. It's his men have the other room, though, and they seem a quiet lot. No trouble out of them. They . . ."

A grumble of thunder turned both his head and Joliffe's toward the streetward door, standing open to the afternoon light that was gone gray and darkening in just the little while since Joliffe had come inside.

"Best get your horse into stable and yourself in here," the man said, still cheerful. "It's two pence the night for you, another two pence for the horse, but that covers his feed and drink. Your food and drink cost more."

"Fair enough," said Joliffe. Knowing that paying ahead without being asked was ever the way into an innkeeper's good graces, he brought out eight pence from his belt pouch and handed it over. "For tonight and tomorrow night," he said. "Do you lay on a supper here or . . ." Thunder rolled closer overhead. ". . . or will I have to go out?"

"We do meals, master. There's a lamb on the spit in the kitchen right now, and I'm minded my wife made berry pies this morning. Very good pies she makes, does my wife."

"Then I'm like to be a happy man," Joliffe said and went out to the stableyard again.

He found the boy still holding his reins but eyeing the over-clouded, grumbling sky like someone willing to be elsewhere. At the other end of the reins, Rowan was standing hipshot and disinterested, unbothered by thunder over her head. In truth, few things bothered her. She and Joliffe had kept company together long enough to be accustomed to each other, and he had decided that if a horse could have a philosophy, then hers was that life happened, there it was, and she wasn't going to make a bother about it unless she had to. Her answer to Joliffe's light slap on her rump as he said to the boy, "To the stable, then. I'd see where she's to be," was to stir and straighten with the sigh of someone much put upon, and start toward the stable at the yard's far end, taking the boy with her.

The stable looked to be as well and cleanly kept as the tavern-room itself. Joliffe was well content to leave her to the stableman's care, with a penny given to win her the man's favor. He gave the boy another farthing to carry his saddlebag for him back to the inn, playing the gentleman to have chance to ask him as they recrossed the yard among the first spatters of rain, "So why would I've been out of luck for a bed here two days ago?"

"Because of the murder, look you," the boy said happily. "We had the crowner here and all his folk. The sheriff's man and his men and a brace of Sir Thomas Stanley's, they had to stay at The Lion across the way. Right to the rafters with guests we all were."

"The Cockerel and The Lion are the only inns in Flint, then, that they were all here?"

"Well, the murder happened at The Rolling Man," the boy said cheerily. "Or just outside it, anyway. So they couldn't stay there, like. It would have been . . ." He paused to find the word, then offered triumphantly, ". . . prejudicial, see."

They had to break then into a sharp, short run to the inn's door as the rain began to come down in earnest. They ducked together into shelter just as the clouds dumped their buckets, as the saying went. The boy laughed at their escape and Joliffe was glad both to be done with riding for the day and to see the innkeeper holding up a wide drinking-bowl in one hand and a pitcher in the other, asking, "Ready for refreshment now, maybe?"

Joliffe agreed he was.

"See the gentleman's bag to his bed, Jack," the innkeeper said. "Then your mother wants you in the kitchen."

Joliffe, for whom being called "gentleman" was still a source of hidden mirth, sat down on a bench at one of the long tables, saying with a nod toward the open-backed stairs at the far corner of the room where Jack had disappeared with all the clattering eagerness of youth, "He's a ready-witted boy."

"He is that." The innkeeper set the bowl in front of him and began to pour a clear, golden ale from the pitcher. "I'm thinking to keep him at school a while longer, to see if there's the makings of a lawyer in him. He has a way with words, does our Jack."

"He was telling me I'm in luck to have a bed here tonight."

"True enough. Today there's just five, come in yesterday. Two days ago we were full up. The boy likely told you why."

"He did," Joliffe agreed, and asked, with a gut-set feeling he wasn't going to like the answer, "So who was murdered?"

"Some fellow named Hampden," the innkeeper answered easily.

Joliffe had deliberately raised the bowl for a deep drink as he had asked his question. That served to mask his face and saved him having to make quick answer while he drank, and when he finished and held the bowl out for more, he only said, "Grand ale. Your wife brews it, Master . . .?"

"Cockerel," the man obliged with both answer and more ale. "Like the sign. Only I'm not green." He chuckled at his own jest. "Nay. It's her sister in the next street that brews for us."

Joliffe made a friendly gesture at the bench across the table from him. "Join me?"

Master Cockerel took the offer by reaching for a cup from the nearby shelf, saying while pouring for himself, "I'll not mind getting off my feet awhile, nay."

Jack came clattering back down the stairs and disappeared through a rear doorway.

"This Hampden that got himself murdered, he was English?" Joliffe asked.

"English, aye. More than that." Master Cockerel leaned forward. "He was the duke of Suffolk's man."

Joliffe took that with becoming surprise. "Was he? There's ill fortune around that name these days."

"If I were one of Suffolk's men, I'd be watching my back these days, that's sure," Master Cockerel said. "Things come in threes, and there's two deaths."

"I'd have thought Suffolk's death was part of the three made with those two dead bishops this year. Chichester and Salisbury." Men who had been as high as Suffolk in the king's favor and both murdered—Adam Moleyns of Chichester in January by a rout of soldiers angry at being denied their pay once too often; William Ayscough of Salisbury dragged from Mass in a parish church and beaten to death by more angry men in June.

"Ah." Master Cockerel paused in thought. "There's that, isn't there?" He chuckled. "Well, we'd best hope then that this fellow isn't the start of another three."

Except he might be the second, rather than the start, if his murder were part of whatever Gough's death had been, Joliffe thought darkly while sharing the innkeeper's laugh. Then, since it never did to keep questions too long one way, he turned the talk to weather and how long the rain was likely to last and whether there would be more. That saw him through to the end of his ale, and then Master Cockerel showed him up the stairs to the long dormer room he would share—judging by the saddlebags much like his own lying on beds—with four other men.

"There's pots under the beds and the washbasin and towel here by the door," Master Cockerel said. "If there's anything you need, just shout down the stairs. You'll be going out?"

"Not for a while. I stopped riding to miss the rain." Which was still battering on the thatched roof close above their heads and in the street beyond the open-shuttered window at the room's far end. "I'm not minded to go wandering in the wet for no good reason."

"A man after my own heart," Master Cockerel said and left him.

Joliffe lay down on the one vacant bed. The mattress and pillow rustled with new-straw stuffing, the rough-woven wool blanket was thick and clean. He had slept worse in his day. Far worse. Besides that, there were small bundles of herbs hanging here and there around the room in a business-like way that made him guess they were for keeping many-legged vermin away. Given all of that, and if Mistress Cockerel baked as well as her sister brewed ale, he was going to regret how short his stay was going to be. Hands behind his head, he looked at the rafters and considered things. He had come to find Sir John Hampden, had meant to follow him if he had moved on. Well, Hampden *had* moved on, but Joliffe was not inclined to follow where he'd gone. What else to do, then? Ask questions, he supposed, but they would have to be *about* Hampden rather than *of* him, and The Rolling Man was probably the place to start.

The rain was a steady downpour likely to last an hour or more. Joliffe shifted his arms, folded them across his chest and settled himself to sleep. Having so narrowly avoided getting soaked, he saw no reason to go deliberately into the rain. People would be as ready to talk about murder in a few hours as now, and looking forward to roasted lamb and Mistress Cockerel's berry pie, he slept.

Not so deeply, though, that he did not awaken the moment there were voices in the tavern-room below him—a sudden quantity of voices that made him think his fellow guests were come in, and he rose from the bed. The rain had slacked to nearly nothing, and though the overcast made judging the time difficult, he thought supper must be near. He was hungry enough for it, anyway, and headed down the stairs, meeting a man coming up. They both turned sidewise, Joliffe's back to the wall, the other man's to the open side of the stairs, to clear way as they passed each other, Joliffe taking chance for a good look at him—a younger man, maybe no more than thirty; a long, smooth face with dark, sharp eyes; hair in the longer cut lately made fashionable by the king's abandoning the above-the-ears crop of his father's time.

Stranger-friendly, he said as they passed, "Wet out."

"It is that," Joliffe agreed. "I rode in just before it broke."

"Your good fortune." The other good-humouredly lifted the arm over which he was carrying a wet cloak. "I wasn't so favored."

Then they were past each other, with nothing to think about it, except that Joliffe did not like his clear certainty that the other man had taken a deep, close look at him in passing, as if to be very sure of knowing him if they met again.

The same kind of look that Joliffe had taken of him.

In the tavern-room four more men, as openly just come in from the rain, were gathered to a table around a pitcher and pottery cups, dice already rattling out on the boards between them. Nearly Joliffe joined them, to learn what he could about and from them; but if they were only lately come to Flint, they had nothing to do with Hampden's death, were not his problem. Besides, he was surely going to share the dorter with them and have chance enough then to learn as much as he likely needed. Best for now that he eat, then go out and about in Flint to learn what he could about Hampden—at best, why he had been in Flint and how he had died.

He failed to set about that so soon as he could have, because both the roast lamb and the berry pie were so savory and served in such fulsome shares it would have been a crime to cram them down. Willing to be law-abiding when he could, Joliffe took his time over the meal, and the men across the room did likewise, even leaving off their dicing while they ate. The man on the stairs did not come down again, but Jack took a laden tray up to him, and before Joliffe was done, the room had filled with assorted, ordinary townsfolk— several men alone, a young couple with a small child, an older man and woman together. None of them looked likely for the kind of talk Joliffe wanted, even if he had not already asked enough questions of Master Cockerel that it would be better if he were not heard asking more, so when he had regretfully finished eating and had had a final tall cup of the excellent ale, he strolled out of the Green Cockerel.

The rain had fully ended but the air was still thick with damp and late twilight was well-come, the first lanterns already being lighted beside doorways. The Rolling Man was easily found in a side street not a far walk away from the marketplace. It was more tavern than inn, with no yard that Joliffe saw but a tavern-room facing the street under the sign of a man rolling a wine cask. With the heavy damp and evening coming on, Joliffe had supposed he would find it busy and it was, but differently from the Green Cockerel to judge by the mixed roar of laughter and angry shouts inside the tavern-room, and the man who lurched out a side door to relieve himself against the wall. That done, he turned his back to the wall and sank down in apparent stupor. It was early hours to be so publicly drunk or even a tavern to be so loud. It looked to be just what Joliffe had hoped for, and putting on a swagger, he went inside.

Noise and smell hit him together. The first he was braced for. The second did not surprise him. The room was cluttered with battered, unscrubbed tables and benches already crowded with drinking men and some women, many of whom looked equally battered and unscrubbed and most of whom had plainly started their heavy drinking some hours ago. No one had troubled to sweep out the floor's old rushes with their stinking spills and thrown-down food. Fresh rushes had simply been thrown on top of foul and not very lately, either. Slut-run, such places were called, though from what Joliffe had seen of them they seemed as often—or more often—run by men as women. Only when even the owner could no longer stand the stink and squelch underfoot—or maybe when he began to fear patrons would sink and be lost in it before they paid—would the floor be cleared, to start again.

For his part, Joliffe had never understood either that degree of laziness or some people's seeming delight in filth for filth's sake, as if life were more real if it were dirty. But then neither had he ever understood people for whom cleanliness was all in all, as if a polished tabletop were enough to earn them a crown in Heaven.

And if a polished tabletop *were* the way to Heaven, he had no hope of salvation.

Having bought a tall leather jack of what proved to be poor ale, he sat himself on the end of a bench along a table where two men were slapping greasy playing cards down at each other and half a dozen other men were sitting somewhat watching them but mostly drinking and talking among themselves. Joliffe, as he had intended, was soon drawn into their talk. Asked where he came from and what brought him to Flint, he answered with ready ease that he was from Warwick way, heading to Caernarfon, to a cousin doing business there for the while, with papers for him to sign and word that his wife had safely birthed him another son.

"Not that he's going to be so pleased about that," Joliffe said with the ease of a man who thought himself well out of it. "That's their fifth, and three girls besides."

He had used this imagined cousin before, moving him about the countryside as need be, with the number of children increasing every time. Now one of the men here, more sorrowful over his ale than the rest, sighed into his almost-empty bowl and mourned, "Not one do I have. Not one to carry my name on after me."

His fellow on the right poked an elbow into his ribs. "You've not a wife either, Dai. Try getting yourself one of those before you start in about having no childer."

Dai straightened. "A wife?" he said indignantly. "Do I look mad, man, that I'd be saddling and bridling myself with a wife?"

"Drink up," said someone across the table and poured more ale into Dai's bowl from the pitcher they were all sharing. Dai buried his face in that as solace for his griefs, and Joliffe said at large to the rest of them, "I hear I've missed a murder. Some fellow was killed in here lately, was he?"

In some times and some places there was need to take the long way round to find out things, but he'd guessed rightly that here a straight question would be enough.

"Didn't happen in here," one of the men said with good cheer. "It was in the street right outside."

"Started in here, though," someone else said.

"The fight started here. The dead fellow wasn't part of it then, though, was he?" a third offered.

"Wasn't part of it at all," Dai said, still brooding into his ale bowl. He seemed the sort given to brooding about all and everything. "The fellows didn't even know him. Hell's blowsy bottom, nobody here even knew *them*, let alone them knowing anybody."

Letting himself look as confused as he was by then, Joliffe asked, "It was all strangers? The dead man and the men who killed him?"

"Nay," the first man said. "We knew the dead man, well enough."

"He wasn't dead then, though," said Dai.

His fellows ignored him, one of them saying, "Didn't know

him all that well. Had seen him hereabout now and again of late. Knew he was the duke of Suffolk's man . . ." Two of the men spat aside into the rushes. ". . . and that he came sometimes to see Sir Thomas."

"Sir Thomas Stanley, that is?" Joliffe asked.

"Aye. Him," the man said, with no great liking.

Another man spat into the rushes, maybe simply because he needed to, but by a swift glance around the table, Joliffe saw several other men who looked as if they wanted to. "King's chamberlain here in North Wales, isn't Sir Thomas?" Joliffe asked, raising a hand for another pitcher of ale to be brought, the present one running low.

"That's him, and a quicker man to the bribe you'll not find this side of the border."

"Thank St. David he's a royal officer. If he were not, he'd be the kind of thief as would have every sheep off the hills and into his bag."

"Not that he might not anyway, the way he goes on," Dai said into his bowl.

"Wasn't for Sir Thomas that Hampden was this end of town that night, though," one of the men said, grinning.

Others chuckled or grunted appreciatively. Taking a guess, Joliffe said, "Some woman?"

"One of Sweet Mabli's, yes. Has her place in Trudge Alley. If you've a mind," the man beside him on the bench said with a wink and a nudge.

"Not tonight," Joliffe said with a regretting shake of his head. "I've done enough riding for the day."

That brought laughter and let him lead the talk on about Hampden. The way the men told it—and they had all been here the night it happened and given testimony at the crowner's inquest since then—there had been three men in here that night that no one had seen before. They had kept themselves to themselves, drinking, throwing some dice, not talking much among themselves but making no trouble.

"Sitting right there," Dai said, pointing at a table near the streetward door. "At that very table there."

Then suddenly two of them had sprung to their feet and started shouting and shoving at each other. The other one had joined in and without anyone had time to tell them to take it outside they had gone out the door, quarreling and shoving at each other.

"None of us saw them with any daggers drawn," the man next to Dai said now. "Those must have come out as soon as they were out the door."

"Hampden's bad fortune was he was out there, too," another put in. "On his way back to the castle from Sweet Mabli's. Just passing by."

"In time to take a dagger-thrust under the ribs." Dai shook a brooding head. "It goes to show. It does indeed."

No one asked him what it showed.

"More than one thrust," someone else said. "Three. One to the heart from the front. Another in the back. A third in the gut."

"Couldn't have done it better if they'd been trying," said Dai to his ale bowl.

"So what's happened to them?" Joliffe asked.

"Nothing. Killing the wrong man must have sobered them out of their own quarrel on the instant. By the time any of us were into the street to see if they'd come to fist-punching each other yet, Hampden was lying there . . ."

"Took us a moment to realize it was him and not one of them, but he was dead already anyway."

". . . and they were run off into the dark. They had horses somewhere . . ."

". . . and sense enough to clear off while the clearing off was good. Never hide nor hair of them did we see again, no more than did Sir Thomas' men out hunting them next day."

"Left us the trouble and cost of the crowner and not a single good hanging in return," said one of the card-players.

He threw down a final pair of cards and added, "Damn them." Whether at the cards or the fled men was unclear.

The game was over, anyway. His fellows threw down their cards, too. One of them scooped the little pile of far-things toward him from the center of the table, asking of Jo-liffe while he did, "Want to play?"

That being as good a way out of talk about the murder as he was likely to get, Joliffe took it, meaning to keep at the game long enough for, hopefully, his questions about the murder to be lost in the general fog of drinking and good fellowship and no one likely to remember him particularly. For that to work, he had to be sure not to win too much, but given his usual luck at games of chance, that was no prob-lem. By the time he drained a last draught of ale and stood up from the bench, saying he had to leave now if he was go-ing to sleep in the bed he'd paid for, he had won some money and lost more, enough that the other players were sorry to see him go but were unlikely ever to think about him again.

He had not drunk nearly so much as he had seemed to but put something of a drunken stagger into his steps back to the Green Cockerel, to see if anyone followed or wanted to overtake or waylay him along the street. Happily, no one did, but that did not lessen Joliffe's certainty that Hampden had not been chance-killed. Men drunk enough to stab a man three times before they realized he wasn't one of them weren't likely to have their wits about them well enough to make the clean escape these men had made. The thing was, they were long gone, and if whoever had hired them to do it was still here, he was probably clever enough to stay quiet, letting idle tavern-talk wear itself out rather than make trouble over it.

Had the man who set them on been the man keeping watch in the street? Because there had to have been one more. From where the three in the tavern had sat, they couldn't have seen Hampden coming from the direction Joliffe's late drinking companions had shown he'd come. Someone outside had signaled his approach in time for his murderers to start their sudden quarrel, lurch out the door, and kill him in a seemingly careless brawl. But murder it had most certainly been.

Gough murdered. Now Hampden.

It might be only his base, suspicious mind at work, Joliffe thought, but he did not much like that pairing, linked by Normandy and the duke of Suffolk as both men were.

Nor did he like, as he came into the Green Cockerel's now-crowded tavern-room, that the man he had earlier passed on the stairs was sitting now with his men and turned his head to watch him cross toward the stairs. Joliffe saw him only from the corner of an eye and briefly, but the sense of the man's gaze on his back made him uneasy all the way up the stairs, so that, although he went to bed, he did not let himself settle into sleep but kept awake until finally all five of the men had come upstairs to their own beds; and even then, with the man from the stairs gone into his own room and the door there shut, Joliffe waited until the four sharing the dorter with him sounded full asleep before he finally let sleep come to himself. And even then his hand was on his dagger under his pillow.

Chapter 6

The duke of Suffolk's funeral was more memorial than funeral, there being no coffin under the black damask pall laid over the carved, gilt-painted trestles that would have held it if it was not already interred with Suffolk's body somewhere beneath the church's paving stones, with no sign of where it lay. But that was the only lack. The church's altar and nave were draped in the heavy black of full mourning. There were carried torches in plenty and the dead man's heraldic arms hung on painted shields from the pillars. The Mass was done at full length, with the priest in black vestments embroidered with silver and gold that shimmered in the golden light of scores of candles gathered around the altar with its jeweled and golden chalice and paten, and the gorgeously gilded and painted Mass book. Alice herself was draped from head to floor in her widow's black, with John equally in black standing beside her, straight-backed and stiff-faced with a seven-year-old's determined dignity. But where the church should have been crowded to the walls with noble guests and other mourners come to give last respects, there was a thin gathering of household folk and no one else, not even villagers. It was a scant mourning for a man who, bare months ago, had held power greater than the king's.

The funeral feast afterward was likewise scant of guests and the removes sparse compared to how all would have been if circumstances had been otherwise.

How it would have been if William de la Pole, duke of Suffolk, had been otherwise, Frevisse thought.

Like most of the thoughts she had had these past few days, she kept that one to herself. Alice did not want her thoughts, only the comfort of her presence and the relief of talking to someone to whom none of it mattered.

That it did matter was something Frevisse likewise kept to herself. Beyond the harm Suffolk had done to England, she cared for what he had done to Alice and small John, left in worry and danger because of his deeds. From all she had heard and what little she knew for certain, he had grabbed hold on power and then used it with neither goodness nor conscience, had wielded it for no one's gain or good but his own and that of his close followers, nor been careful about the followers he drew to him—men who, like himself, had wanted power for no one else's good but their own and had not cared whom their ambitions ruined. Even given how easily any man in power could become hated simply because he had what others did not, the hatred turned against Suffolk had been—still was—great beyond the usual measure, not even his brutal death sufficient to curb it. That was the legacy his deeds had passed on to his widow and son. For John there was the burden of the dukedom laid on him years before it should have been. For Alice there was both her anger at Suffolk and her fear of what might come, knowing that hatreds not yet satisfied by Suffolk's death could still be turned on her and her child and followers.

In the face of all that, Frevisse accepted Alice's need of her as someone to hold to when the weight of it all became too much and she had to let go the tight control she kept for everyone else to see; but it meant that mostly Frevisse had no more to do than sit aside and watch as Alice dealt with all her duties, both of the household and the dukedom, John being far too young to take on any of it.

Unfortunately, for Frevisse sitting aside and doing little did not come easily. Days at St. Frideswide's were full of duties as well as prayers. The Benedictine Rule of life was founded on *ora et labora*—prayer and work—in balanced measure, seeking the good of soul and body together. Here at Wingfield, Frevisse had no work and it wore on her to be so idle. There were books and she read for hours at a time. There were the summer-flourishing gardens and she walked in them, sometimes with Sister Margrett to keep her company; but Sister Margrett was often happily busy keeping company with John and his nurse. His tutor had been left behind at Ewelme; Sister Margrett not only helped the nurse with her endless sewing but John with his reading, and played with him and told him stories.

When Frevisse asked her about it, she said simply, "I like children."

Frevisse did not—or not to any great degree. An hour spent in John's room, watching him and Sister Margrett sit on the floor playing with a foot-high builder's wheel and crane, lifting small stone building blocks and swinging them into place to build a wall that John then knocked down with a small battering ram and much laughter, was enough for Frevisse. So she was left mostly to her own company, save when she and Sister Margrett withdrew at the appointed hours to say the Offices together in the chapel off the solar beyond the great hall.

In St. Frideswide's the Offices' prayers and psalms wound through the days in a wreath of praise and hope, but here they seemed heavy with the weight of duty, and when they were done, Frevisse was still left with too many hours in which to work at calmness and not worrying, that she be ready to give calmness and comfort when Alice needed to make use of her company. So, a few days after the funeral, when the afternoon was softening among the long shadows of the westering sun, Alice found her where she had withdrawn into the gardens.

Gardens, with their square-cornered beds, graveled paths, arbored walks, and flowered bowers were an expected part of a great lord's home. Frevisse had never known one of Alice's houses to be without one, and she was sitting on the turf-topped bench at the far end of the farthest garden with a thin, softly-bound parchment book open on her lap when Alice sat down beside her, looked at the book, and said, "Father's book, where he collected verses and such as took his favor. I'd forgotten I'd left it here at Wingfield."

"One of your ladies brought it to me when I asked for something to read." And because Thomas Chaucer had been not only Frevisse's uncle-by-marriage but also her very good friend, it had been warming to see his handwriting again all these years after his death.

Leaning over her arm, Alice read aloud,

> " 'Now well and now woe,
> Now friend and now foe,
> Thus goes the world, I know.
> But since it is so,
> Let it pass and go,
> And take it as it is.'

Yes, I remember him saying that sometimes."

"And this." Frevisse turned back a few pages to read, "'Two lives there are for Christian men to live. One is called the active life for in it is more bodily work. The other is called the contemplative life, for in it is more spiritual sweetness. The active life is much outward and in more travail and more peril, because of the temptations that are in the world. The contemplative life is more inward and therefore more lasting, and more certain, restful, delightful, lovely, and rewarding. For it has joy in God's love, and savor in the life that lasts forever'."

Alice was silent for a moment when she finished, then said, "Richard Rolle. And so very apt at the difference between your life and mine." She stood up, moved across the path to pluck a spray of golden St. John's Wort flowers from among the herbs in the bed there, and returned to sit again. "I don't think Father liked my marrying Suffolk."

Frevisse suspected that was possible. Although the marriage had come long before Suffolk became what he became, Thomas Chaucer—like his father, Geoffrey—had seen more clearly into people than most people did, had been able to set what they said and seemed to be against what they truly were and did.

Alice began to strip the green leaves from the flower stem, dropping them to the path. "Did he ever say anything of it to you? Of my marriage? Or about Suffolk?"

"He never did. I was long gone into the nunnery by then, remember."

"Father came to see you there. He sent on a letter from you to me, too. After Salisbury died." Alice's second husband, killed by a chance-shot cannonball at the siege of Orleans the winter before the French witch called The Maid had made her trouble there.

Alice had never answered that letter, Frevisse remembered.

Alice had finished with the leaves, was now twirling the flowered stem between her fingers, staring at it while she said,

"If I had come back to England then, everything would have been different. But I was friends with Anne of Burgundy." Wife of the duke of Bedford, then-governor of France for then-infant King Henry VI. "So I stayed in France, and Suffolk was there and courted me and we married. Anne died, and then Bedford did, and Suffolk hoped to be made governor of France in his stead. When he wasn't, that's when he settled to winning young Henry to him and rising into power here in England. And here we are." She lifted her head, staring into some dark distance that had nothing to do with the herb-scented garden around them. "Father never said anything at all about him?" she asked. "Not then or later?"

"Nothing at all that I remember."

Alice gave a small, tear-denying laugh. "In its way, that's worst of all. That he wouldn't even talk about him." She dropped her hand with St. John's flowers into her lap and said wearily, as if even the words were almost too heavy to bear, "He became so small a man. My husband. It's as if the greater he became in the world, the less of him there was. That's been very hard to live with. To watch the man I loved change and dwindle until he was gone and I was left married to someone I would never have chosen to wed my life to."

Frevisse held silent. She did not think Alice wanted her words, anyway, simply her presence to lean on in the otherwise vast loneliness of loss almost beyond measure. To have given life and love to someone, only to find that neither was enough to save him from himself and then be left at the end of it all in danger and fear as well as bitterness—what could be said to that?

Alice abruptly tossed the flowers away, folded her hands firmly together in her lap, and said briskly, as if ashamed of having wandered into memory and now snatching at the first business that came to mind, "I sent an order a few days ago to my household priest that I want him back with me. I want Mass in my own chapel instead of needing to go out to the church every day. But do you know, this afternoon I had message back from him that he's presently needed where he is and begs leave to be excused a time longer. I'm minded to excuse him permanently."

"Maybe he *is* presently needed there," Frevisse said, less because she believed it than because Alice angry at a defaulting priest seemed better than Alice sinking further into the lethargy of her dark thoughts.

And Alice obligingly snapped, "It wouldn't matter to Squyers if he was 'needed where he is'. He's one of those well-fleshed, red-faced men who think God made the world for no better reason than to give them somewhere to live comfortably. 'Needed where he is'. They're probably praying to see the back of him there at Alderton." She suddenly laughed. "Poor man. He saw himself on his way to a bishopric by way of serving Suffolk. He was disappointed almost past bearing when Reynold Pecock was made bishop of Chichester instead of him this year, after Bishop Moleyns' death." Her momentary laughter dropped away. "After Moleyns' murder," she murmured.

That had been in January, three and a half months before Suffolk's own murder, five months before the bishop of Salisbury's, and five months and a little more before Jack Cade's rebels murdered some other equally-hated men of the king's government. It had been a brutal year.

Alice sighed, rubbed the heel of her hand hard against what little of her forehead showed in the tight surround of her widow's wimple, and said wearily, "Let's just say that Squyers has served better as a messenger than he's ever served as a priest." She stood up. "Let's go inside again. The sun is making my head hurt."

They were on a sunny path between low, square-cut borders of lavender, walking side by side in silence toward the house, Frevisse with her gaze to the graveled path a few yards ahead of her, when a sudden check in Alice's step made her raise her eyes to see one of Alice's ladies coming toward them, followed by a man whose plain, dusty clothing and tall riding boots made it likely he had just ridden in from somewhere. That he was brought so directly to Alice argued there was a pressing necessity to whatever word he brought, and Frevisse slowed, falling back just as the other woman did, to let Alice meet him alone.

Not alone enough, apparently. They met at a crossing of paths. The man went down on one knee, saying, "My lady," and Alice gestured for him to stand up and turned aside, leading him away along one of the paths, far enough that when she stopped and faced him again, what he said to her was well beyond Frevisse's hearing.

Whatever word he brought was brief, however; nor were Alice's questioning of him and his answers much longer before she said, somewhat more loudly, "Thank you, Nicholas. Master Thorpe will see to bath and food and bed for you. We'll talk more later, when you've rested and I've had time to think on it."

The man bowed. As Alice turned and started away, toward an arbored walk on the garden's other side, her lady came to Frevisse and said low-voiced and hastily, "Will you go to her, my lady?" Her words were respectful with suggestion but her tone demanded, and yet more earnestly and quickly she added, "She shouldn't be much alone as things are now and there's none seem able to help her so well as you do, my lady."

Before Frevisse could answer that, the man had joined them. With duty done, his face had sunk into dull weariness, making him look older than his young years, and when the woman said, "I'll take you to Master Thorpe now, if you please," his bare nod in answer looked more from his failing strength than from failure of courtesy; but despite that, he made a small bow to Frevisse as he passed her.

Whatever word he had brought must have been urgent,

Frevisse thought, and, yes, maybe Alice had best not be left alone with it; so with her hands tucked into her opposite sleeves and her steps more firm than her thoughts, she followed Alice, gone now into the arbored walk and out of sight. Coming in her turn out of the sun into the arbor's deep, vine-made shade, Frevisse momentarily failed to see her, Alice in her black widow's gown and veil being too nearly part of the small flickering leaf-shadows; and when she did see her, Alice was just turning back from the arbor's far end, having already paced its length. Not sure of being welcomed, Frevisse went slowly to meet her, but when they met at the arbor's middle, Alice only said, in a flat voice, "That was young Nicholas Vaughn. My father took him into the household when he was an orphaned boy and he's been in our service ever since. Father's, and then mine. Mine. Not Suffolk's," she said curtly, each word like another stone in the wall she had made between her and her dead husband.

"He brought ill news?"

"Ill enough. One of our stewards had been killed. In Wales. In a street brawl according to the inquest, Nicholas says. Not even his own brawl. He was simply passing and happened in the way of someone's dagger." She made an impatient sound, side-stepped Frevisse, and paced on.

Frevisse turned and kept step beside her. "When was this?"

"A little over two weeks ago. Nicholas found it out because I'd sent him with word I wanted Hampden back to his duties. He's among those who've started to distance themselves since Suffolk's death. I wanted his refusal to return so I could dismiss him entirely." Alice clapped her hands together angrily. "Why didn't someone send me word? Why did I have to find out by chance? Sir Thomas Stanley is the king's chamberlain in North Wales. He knew Hampden. Why didn't he send me word when it happened?"

That was a reasonable question, and Frevisse had another. To reach the almost-staggering edge of weariness Nicholas Vaughn had looked to be in, he must have hardly slept since leaving Wales nor bothered much with eating, and she asked, "Why did your man think he had to bring word of it in such haste?"

They had reached an end of the arbor walk. Alice stopped, still in its shade, staring out at her sunlit garden for a long moment before answering, "It was three daggers Hampden happened into the way of. Nicholas thought that was over-much for one man in a brawl not even his own."

Frevisse joined Alice in staring at the garden. Its summer quiet and ordered beds and clean-swept walks did not match her thoughts and in a while she said, "So Vaughn doesn't think it was a chance-killing?"

"No."

"Why not?"

"Frevisse . . ." Alice started with a stir of anger, broke off, swung around, and started back through the arbor. Frevisse followed her, letting her keep a little ahead, knowing she could not force an answer; and again, near the arbor's middle, Alice stopped, abruptly faced her, and said, "It's not that Hampden was a good man. Maybe he was. I don't know. Are there any good men anymore? I've begun to think not," she said with naked bitterness and added with anger, "Or if there are, none of them seems to have been drawn into my husband's service. The thing with Hampden is that he lately went twice to France for Suffolk. Or not so lately. Over a year ago. Just before and again soon after the attack on Fougères." The Breton border town whose seizure and sacking by an English-hired mercenary captain had broken the truce with France last year and led on to these months of English defeats and losses across Normandy.

Frevisse knew more about how that truce had come to be

broken than she wanted to know. It was a knowledge that she and Alice shared and it had estranged them until Alice's need of her had been greater than their mutual angers; but the shadow of their past angers and of what they knew still lay dark between them, and it was at the hazard of opening a wound only a little healed that Frevisse said carefully, "You're afraid this Hampden's death has to do with his having gone to France."

A taut moment passed before Alice snapped, "Yes."

"That his going to France had to do with Suffolk's . . ." She hesitated over the word, then said it. ". . . treason."

Alice drew a short, sharp breath. "You're bold to say that to my face."

"Did you want my companionship so I could lie to you?"

Alice put out a sudden hand and took hard hold on Frevisse's arm. "No." She spoke with something of the gasp of someone drowning. "No. I need your truth. It's only that sometimes the pain . . ."

She freed Frevisse and started to pace the arbor again. Again Frevisse went with her but now beside her as Alice went on, low-voiced. "No, it's not the pain so much as the fear. I know Suffolk set up with Somerset to lose France because the war was becoming nothing but a drain down which England was endlessly pouring its wealth, but people were unwilling to let it go."

Frevisse forbore to point out that much of that English wealth had come from the pillaging of France through the years of the war. Nor did she say that Suffolk's ill and greedy governing of England had been as costly to England's good as the war had been. No purpose would be served by saying it, and she settled for only, "We had the truce with the French. There could have been treaty made. That would have settled much."

But then that slight truce, when there should have been

a full treaty, was another of Suffolk's failures. When he had made the king's marriage to the French princess Margaret of Anjou, he had settled for a few years' truce when a treaty for full peace should have been part of the marriage agreement, the more especially since he had also settled for no dowry to come with the girl. All of that was among the reasons for all the angers at him, but Alice said defensively, "There still would have been the on-going cost of keeping our garrisons and maintaining the government there in Normandy."

"With a treaty that ended the fighting there, Normandy could have settled back to what it was—rich and prospering," Frevisse returned. "It would have come to support and defend itself."

"Not for years. The costs until then . . ."

"Were honestly England's to pay, considering we robbed and stripped everything we could from there when we claimed and seized the country," Frevisse said; but she heard the sharpening edge of anger in her voice and said quickly, "Alice, I'm sorry. That's not something worth debating between us. It's all beyond our help and always was. Nor is it what has you frightened here and now."

Alice had been drawing breath for probably an angry reply, but stopped, was silent a moment, and at last said, very low, as if her brief flare of anger was burned out, "No. It isn't. But the other thing . . . It's maybe nothing."

"Or it's maybe not," Frevisse said.

"Or it's maybe not. I only wish I knew where Edward Burgate is!" There was no anger, only despair in that cry, and wearily she went on, "I didn't tell you all the reason I sent Nicholas to fetch Hampden to me. It was more than to see if he would stay in my service. I wanted to warn him to say nothing about whatever reason he went to Normandy last year." She heaved a trembling sigh. "Well, he won't. I can only hope he never did."

Somewhere away across the garden John gave a happy

shout. Alice lifted her head toward it. "That's better, anyway," she said, a sob of half-laughter in her voice. "It's him I have to save from all of this. I want him happy, not robbed of everything that should be his." Her words sank into bitterness again. "Because of what his father was."

Chapter 7

Again the tower room at Hunsdon and again Sir William Oldhall standing at the window, gazing out, his hands behind his back. He might have been no more than considering his fields where the grain was standing golden ripe and the harvest was begun.

More likely he was not.

Joliffe, standing behind him and across the room, able to see only sky beyond the window, was holding in his impatience for Sir William's response to his word of Hampden's death. When told of it, all that Sir William had done was turn away to the window, and there he had stayed these several minutes.

The better years of Joliffe's life had been spent as a

traveling player, wandering England's roads, sometimes footsore, occasionally hungry, always homeless save for the cart that carried the band of players' few belongings. That he saw those as better years than this standing silent attendance on someone who paid him better than he'd ever been paid as a player told him nothing about himself he did not already know. But he also knew quite clearly the choices that had brought him to this and that he would likely make them again if he had to, given one thing and another.

But then, if ever he went back to being a traveling player, he'd now be able to afford a horse to ride and daily meals and forego the footsore and hungry part, which did add appeal to the possibility.

He was considering that and the small drift of a thin cloud across the window's view of sky when Sir William turned around and said, "I'm going to Ireland. My lord of York has to be warned."

That was so far aside from anything that Joliffe had expected that he said somewhat blankly, "About Hampden's death?" It had not seemed that great a matter. Except to Hampden, of course.

"No. Fastolf."

"Fastolf?" Joliffe echoed. "Sir John Fastolf?" Famed, like Matthew Gough, as a captain in the French war. Except Fastolf had seen what was coming far enough ahead that he had left the war, sold all his interests in France, and was now living comfortably and very rich in England.

"Him. Yes. You know there are to be commissions of oyer and terminer all over England to deal with all the troubles there've been these past months." Commissions of royal officers and other men appointed to hear reports of crimes and determine indictments. "Fastolf is named to the one for Norfolk and Suffolk, and he's sent me warning there's word been given—not official, not in writing, but with no doubt about what's meant—that the commissioners are to find out evidence against my lord of York."

Knowing the question was stupid even as it came out of his mouth, Joliffe blurted, "Evidence of what?"

"Of treason," Sir William said grimly. "That York stirred up all these uprisings and rebellions against the king this spring and summer past."

Joliffe held back startled exclaim against that; instead said with a steadiness he did not feel, "Treason. Allege it against him while he's in Ireland, beyond readily defending himself."

"Yes," Sir William said bitterly. He paced away from the window and across the room, tapping his fingertips on the desktop as he passed. "The charges would be laid and his property seized before he could do anything about it. Then he would be told to come back and face trial."

"And if he refused to walk into that trap, if he stayed safe in Ireland declaring his innocence, he would be charged with open rebellion and condemned anyway," Joliffe said. He turned to watch Sir William at his pacing. "Very smoothly done."

"Nor will Fastolf's commission be the only one that's been told." Sir William reached the far wall and turned back. "They've likely all been given to understand the same. Let even one of them 'find out' evidence against him . . ." He tapped at the desk again as he passed. ". . . and he'll be charged with being traitor to the king. And that . . ." At the window again, Sir William turned and said sharply at Joliffe, ". . . *that* will make all of us traitors, too, for serving him."

Which meant it would be best, for several reasons, not to let the business come to that, thought Joliffe; and aloud he said, "Who's ordered this?"

"Fastolf named no names."

"Because he couldn't or because he wouldn't?"

Sir William began to pace again. "I don't know." Again the tapping of fingers along the desk in passing.

"But it came from someone," Joliffe said. "Suffolk is dead. Who looks to be taking his place in running the king?"

"Who knows?" Sir William said bitterly.

You should, for one, Joliffe thought. Like every lord, York had spies in other lords' households as well as men like Joliffe not tied to one place who could be set to things best not done openly, and all their webs of information all came back to Sir William. If he did not know . . .

"The duke of Somerset?" Joliffe asked.

"Not from what I've heard." Back at the desk, Sir William stopped, rapped his knuckles on it impatiently. "He's had France to keep him occupied. He's surrendered Caen. By now Falaise is gone, too. That leaves us Cherbourg and nothing else in Normandy."

"Is he in Cherbourg then?"

"He's back in England. Landed at Dover with household, bag and baggage, a few days ago."

"If anyone's guilty of treason, he is. He's all but handed Normandy back to the French."

Sir William was frowning down at papers on the desk. "It will be interesting to see how King Henry receives him."

"With shackles and a prison cell would be best," Joliffe said darkly. "Followed soon after by a trial and a beheading."

"The last word I had is that he's riding openly toward London with no let or hindrance offered him." He looked up from the papers. "My lord of York has to be warned about this matter of treason. Of it and other things best not put into a letter or said by messenger. So I'm away to Ireland. You can report to Therry if there's need before I return."

Sir William was probably right that York should hear from him what was afoot, and Therry would keep a steady hand on things here, but, "What about Hampden's death?"

"Hampden. Too bad he was killed before you talked with him. But what's done is done. Best you try the Suffolk household priest. Sire John Squyers. I've found out where he is. Not with the Lady Alice as it happens. He's gone to his parish. At Alderton on the Suffolk coast. It's somewhere not much beyond Ipswich."

"When did he go there?"

"Two months ago." Sir William began to push papers around on his desk. "Or maybe it was a month and a half. A while anyway. He's not with Lady Alice. That's the point."

"You'd think now is when he'd be most needed in the household."

"Maybe he was more Suffolk's chaplain rather than hers. Maybe he and the Lady Alice don't get on."

"Or maybe he lately discovered a need to serve his flock instead of merely fleece them," Joliffe offered.

Sir William stopped moving the papers and looked up at Joliffe across the desk. "You find him out and ask him, that's all."

"There was another name on Gough's list."

"Edward Burgate. The duke's secretary. Yes. The nearest I've come to learning about him is that he may have been arrested at Dover."

"Arrested? For what? By whom?"

"Maybe by a royal officer. Maybe not. My man wasn't certain, but he's not been seen since, anyway. Not by anyone who's admitted to it."

"He's not at Dover, though."

"No, not at Dover, it seems. But nowhere else either. Best get as much from this priest as you can. With Hampden dead and unless we find Burgate, the trail we want back to Suffolk and Somerset is going cold and narrow."

Cold as dead men's bodies, Joliffe thought. Narrow as graves.

At least Ipswich was an easy enough ride from Hunsdon. Not much north from the manor was one of the roads the

Romans had made, Stane Street, running straight eastward toward the coast. With good will and fine weather, Alderton should be hardly two days' ride away, but he and Rowan had made a hard push of the ride to Wales and back, and he had no mind to push her again, nor trade off for a less-certain horse from Sir William's stable for the sake of faster going.

"Better the devil I know, yes?" he said at the back of her head as they ambled away from Hunsdon. She flicked her ears at him in what he chose to imagine was displeasure, and he granted, "You're not a devil then. You're an angel of patience and virtue. Is that better?"

She did not say whether it was or not, but she likely approved of their easy pace and later that morning made no objection to the hour they spent only standing in a copse of young trees on a hill above Stane Street for Joliffe to see who passed by. That way, if he saw anyone of them along his way again, he would have to worry they had been following him, realized they'd lost him, and been waiting to see if he came behind them.

Since no one but Sir William should know what he was about, that he would be followed from Hunsdon was unlikely, but Joliffe strongly believed, "Better safe than sorrowful."

But of course, if someone knew not only his business but where he was going, they'd have no need to follow him; could go happily ahead and wait for him to come, but about that Joliffe could do nothing, could only watch his back.

Making no haste, he rode into Colchester early in the second day. Ipswich lay some eighteen miles farther on and northward again. If he put effort into it, he could be past there today, but he spent an hour at an alehouse two hours' ride beyond Colchester, waiting to see if anyone familiar from his first day's travel happened by. None did and he rode on, somewhat easier in his mind but not much. Besides the possibility that he might be followed by someone as wary at this game as he was, he was bothered beyond the ordinary by both Gough's and Hampden's deaths.

Gough's surely had to do with the letter. Did whoever had wanted him dead know what had become of it, or were they still looking for it? And Hampden. There was the chance his death was maybe only by mischance and nothing more, but that "maybe" kept Joliffe wary. The only thing he knew Hampden and Gough had in common was that Hampden's name was in a letter that Gough had wanted the duke of York to have. That might mean nothing. It might mean much. What was certain was that Joliffe now had that letter in common with them, and since he was not minded to be dead before he had to be, he was taking care while care could be taken. One of his earliest-learned lessons in this life of twisted corners he now led was that suspicious was a better way to be than blindly trusting.

He spent the night in Ipswich at a comfortable inn where the ale was good and the wine better, and in the morning found someone able to tell him his way to Alderton lay through Woodbridge some eight miles farther along; and in Woodbridge a man leading a horse and cart across the marketplace readily pointed him toward the coastward road for Alderton. "Not much of a place to have business," the man said. He gave a squint-eyed stare at the sky with its milky overcast and added, "It's a good ten miles and I shouldn't be surprised if there's fog coming. But there's only the one road, so if you keep straight on and don't go wandering, you should do well enough. Shouldn't linger about it, though."

"I've no mind to." Joliffe assured him, thanked him, and rode on. He had half-promised himself a midday meal in Woodbridge but decided to forego it. Beyond the town, he even pressed Rowan into a canter now and again. The cool smell of the sea had been with him ever since Ipswich and was stronger here, carried on a small wind over the flat fields. He knew there was a wide-estuaried river to his right and the sea somewhere ahead, and as the man in Wood-bridge had said, if he kept straight on, he should not lose his way, but he would rather not ride in fog if he could help it. If he was fortune-favored, maybe he could find out what he wanted from this Squyers and be away ahead of the weather's change. But before he was as many miles along as he would have liked to be, the fog came sliding in over the low coast-wise sandhills and across the flat fields. In moments the world disappeared and Joliffe resigned himself to a longer ride at a slower pace.

He tried the comfort of telling himself he had been in thicker fogs than this and that he might ride out of it, but he did not. A street of houses formed out of the gray murk, and he asked a woman just going in at a door if this was Alderton, only to be told it was not.

"It's next along," the woman said. "Keep to the road and you'll come to it."

He did keep on, and after a tedious, blind ride that was probably not so long as it seemed, house-shapes along a village street again formed out of the fog. Since this must be Alderton, he now only needed to find this Sire John Squyers. He had long since decided against the roundabout-to-get-there he had meant to use with Hampden. Knowing for certain now how far this place was from the comforts of being a duke's household chaplain, and already doubtful that Sire John Squyers had suddenly come down with an attack of pi-ous desire to serve his parish, a straight appeal to the man's self-interest would likely serve best. Threat—much is known and more will be found out—leavened with some of the gold coins Sir William had given him to the purpose would very likely be all that was needed.

If it was not, he'd find another way.

So . . . the church first. That would be easily found, even in fog; and if Squyers wasn't there, his house was surely close by and someone could be found to point the way. Or if by ill luck Squyers was not here anymore, someone could say where he had gone. Joliffe just hoped if he wasn't here it was not because he had gone back to the duchess of Suffolk's household, because that would make talking to him the more difficult.

Besides those thoughts as he rode along Alderton's street—and whether it was Alderton's only street or one of several he could not tell—he was looking for an inn, not wanting to ride back to Woodbridge through this murk. He did not see one, but then he was not seeing much of anything besides house-fronts, closed doors, and no people, until the church thickened out of the fog into a solid shape beyond a low wall, and there on a backless wooden bench beside the wall, where they would have been enjoying the sun if there had been any, were two old men, one of them humped and shriveled inside his clothing, the other straight-backed with his knob-knuckled hands resting on top of a stout cane set firmly upright in front of him. Plainly not minded to be put off it by a mere fog, they had the look of having been on that bench for a fair while; and Joliffe drew rein in front of them and nodded friendliwise, sitting deliberately easy in his saddle to show he was here on no urgent matter.

Before he could ask anything, though, the bow-backed man said, "You're here about the priest?"

Just able to keep surprise from his voice, Joliffe answered, "I am, yes."

"Time someone got here," the other man said. "He's starting to stink."

While Joliffe hesitated, stumbled by that, the first man demanded, "You're from the crowner?"

With a sinking fear of where this was going, Joliffe said, "The crowner? No."

"What do you want with stinking Squyers, then?"

"I came to talk with him."

The bow-backed man gave a rattling laugh. "You can talk to him, but you won't be getting much answer from him."

Sounding ready to be unfriendly, the man with the cane asked, "Was he a friend of yours?"

"Never met him," Joliffe admitted with outward lightness.

The bent-backed man chuckled. "Won't meet him now, either."

"He's dead, see," his fellow said. "And not afore time."

"Mind yourself, Tom. The man's dead," his fellow warned.

"And good riddance to him." Old Tom had clearly not taken to heart the proverb of never speak ill of the dead. "Dead and lying there with his head propped in the crook of his arm and his soul burning in hell, the grasp-handed bastard."

"If you want to see him," his fellow said helpfully, "he's along there, in the lane alongside the priest-house."

Joliffe had no wish at all to see a body with its head in the crook of its arm, more especially one that had been dead long enough to start stinking.

"We've not moved it, like," old Tom said. "Just canvas-covered it over and left it for the crowner to come. We know the law."

The law was that a body found murdered was to be left where it was until the crowner could see it and begin inquisition into how it came to be dead. Mostly, though—because it could take days for a county's crowner to be found and then come—people chose to move a body safe away from dogs and vermin and pay the fine for having done so.

It seemed Squyers, in the villagers' opinion, did not warrant that trouble or cost.

Still with an outward lightness he was far from feeling, Joliffe asked, "So how does this Squyers come to be dead with his head in the crook of his arm?"

"Ha!" the bent-backed man said, more than ready to talk about it, but his fellow cut him off, saying at Joliffe, "If you didn't know him and you're not the crowner's man, then there's no need we tell you anything. He's dead and you'd best be on your way."

Joliffe would by far rather have been on his way than stay, but he needed to know more than he did and said with a shrug, "Ah well, if he's dead, he's dead, and I don't know anyone who's likely to care. It was sudden, was it?"

That brought a snort from old Tom and an outright bark of laughter from his fellow, but before either could answer, muffled hoof-fall and the chink of harness away along the street made them look and Joliffe turn Rowan toward the way he had come as five horsemen formed out of the soft gray wall of fog.

Joliffe curbed urge to lay hand to sword hilt. They were most likely the crowner and his men finally come. If so, then maybe he could learn by way of them something more about Squyers' death.

The next moment he re-thought all that. Crowners, as the king's officers, usually looked the part, went well-garbed in gown and authority and accompanied by clerks and guards. These five men were all rough-dressed much like himself, in plain doublets and boots meant for hard, long riding.

And then they were near enough for him to know he knew them.

Their leader was the sharp-eyed man he had met on the stairs of the Green Cockerel in Flint.

And the man knew him, too.

Choices being few, Joliffe decided to play it out. He stayed where he was while the riders drew rein and stopped, the lead man only a few yards from him and eyeing him coldly. Rather than leave it at that and because someone had to start, Joliffe said cheerfully, "We meet again. What brings you here?"

Response to his boldness glinted briefly in the other's eyes before the man said tersely enough there could be no mistaking his unfriendliness, "Report of Squyers' death came to her grace the duchess of Suffolk. She sent me to find out more about it. What I find is you. Again."

"And likewise I find you. Again," Joliffe said back.

"The difference being you're here before us this time."

"By no longer than a few switches of a horse's tail. These men will tell you as much."

"That's not to say you weren't here before."

"And came back for what reason? To be sure the priest was still dead? Because I wasn't sure the chopped-off head had sufficed?"

The man ignored that, said coldly, "Nor does it answer why you're here at all."

"No, it does not," Joliffe agreed. "But then why I'm here is no business of yours anyway."

Over his shoulder to his men, the man said, "Take him."

Chapter 8

That Sister Margrett was settled with reasonable content into the household was one less matter for Frevisse to worry on, and that they went to Mass and kept the Offices together as best they could, in Wingfield's chapel during the day, in their room for Compline and the night Offices, was more help to Frevisse's unease. The prayers gave some familiar shape to their days, but Frevisse still found herself, on the whole, much under-occupied. Alice wanted her companionship but perforce spent much of every day dealing with all the necessities of the household and such business as came in from the dukedom's far-spread manors, because however secret she might hope to keep her presence at Wingfield from the world beyond its boundaries, her officials had to be able to find her no matter where she was.

"Much of the trouble is that everything has been in change all of this year," Alice said, rubbing at her tired eyes in one of the brief times they were alone.

To Frevisse's mind, "change" hardly touched what Alice's life had been this year. From January into February there had been the fear and strain of Parliament's demand that Suffolk be impeached for treason, ending with the king first sending Suffolk into the Tower of London, then exiling him to save him. After that must have come the weeks of frantic readying for that exile, with much shifting of matters to provide for his family and properties in England and for himself abroad. Then had come his murder and everything had changed again, made the worse because through the three months since his death England had been constantly torn by outbreaks of rebellion that had thrown life even further from ordinary.

"I'm just so tired of change," Alice sighed. "I want things just to settle into one way and stay there. I get so tired of all the things I must not say aloud. Thank you for being someone I can freely say things to."

Frevisse tried to content herself with that, but between the whiles when Alice wanted her close company and needed her to listen, the days stretched long. She read much, but she thought, too, and the longer she was at Wingfield the more there was to think on and little of it was pleasant, knowing that even if Alice said nothing more about her fears, they must still be in her, with nothing Frevisse could do to help her, save listen while she talked of lesser things.

And then word came that the priest John Squyers was dead.

Frevisse was in the solar with Alice and some of her women when the crowner's man brought the message. To Alice's taut questions he was able to say no more than that the priest had been killed by some of his own people, that word of it had been brought to the crowner who was sending word on to her while he readied to go to Alderton. Alice thanked him, sent him away with one of her women to see that he was fed and rested, and sent another of her women to, "Find Nicholas Vaughn and say I want to see him."

Her order to him when he came was equally short. She told him what the crowner's messenger had said, then, "Go there and find out what happened. Take men with you."

He answered her with a bow and left. Frevisse watched Alice watching him leave, and said, "You put a great deal of trust in him."

"I do," Alice granted. "I can't decide if he's more the younger brother I never had, or the son there might have been if I'd had a child by Salisbury." She laughed at herself. "But if he had been either of those things, he'd not be free to serve me so well, and that would be a loss. He's a man without family or any ties except to this household. That, and that he's sharp-witted make him valuable. I've deeded him a steady income from various properties, but no lands of his own, to keep him free to go on serving me."

Free to serve her? Or bound to it, having small other choice? Frevisse wondered.

Three days later, in the warm evening after supper, Alice sent most of her women to walk in the gardens but chose to stay inside herself, in the solar off the great hall, playing at chess with John while Sister Margrett prompted him in ways to win. Alice laughingly protested but allowed it. Across the room, one of her women played in a small, pleasant way on a psaltery, plucking notes lightly into the quiet beyond John's laughter and Alice's feigned protests; and Frevisse, watching the game for a time, made a small prayer that this while of ease would draw out through the whole evening, for all their sakes.

She was restless herself, though, and wandered the room. The solar was a large room, meant for the gathering of family apart from the more general life of the great hall. It was also newly made, from the glazed green and russet floor tiles to the plastered patterns of the pargetted ceiling. One tall, stone-mullioned window looked onto a wall-enclosed corner of the gardens; two others faced the foreyard and its gateway. A wide fireplace on the inner wall was carved around with the leopard heads of the de la Pole arms, and if the several chairs and various tables had been made in England the work had been by French craftsmen, Frevisse thought. There should have been tapestries on the cream-yellow walls but they would have been moved when the household last left and had not come back with Alice.

All in all, it was a rich and gracious room, presently so at peace with quiet music and laughter that almost there might have been nothing amiss in all the wide world—nothing to weigh on the mind but the day's simple wending toward bed and a night's sound sleep. As she wandered the room, unable to settle, Frevisse deeply wished that were true.

She paused to run her hand along the curved and polished arm of a cross-legged chair sitting between the windows overlooking the foreyard, wondering, as she had wondered before, how much of this room's pleasant wealth had been stolen out of France. An ungracious thought but not an un-reasonable one. A great deal of French wealth and goods had flowed into England on the tide of victories that followed King Henry V's new-beginning of the war thirty-five years ago. Only when the profits of war had given way to the costs of peace and the hard business of governing a ruined coun-try back to prosperity—only then had the lords begun to turn against that war. The lords who had made the most profit from it and now no longer did. Not that the war would be a problem for them much longer, given the speed at which Normandy was being lost, Frevisse thought.

A call from the gateway, then the sudden sound of horses clattering into the yard drew her the two paces needed for her to see out the window. From across the room, Alice asked, "What is it?" but Frevisse hesitated over her answer. The evening gloaming was deep enough in the walled yard that she could make out men and horses—too many of them to be merely bringing a message—and that there were servants coming out to meet them but not who . . .

"The man you sent to find out about the priest. I think he's returned," she said.

"Nicholas Vaughn," Alice said. "John, I fear we must pause the game while I talk with him. It shouldn't take long." She was rising from her chair as she said that but paused to lean over the game board and add, mock-sternly, "And no moving of any pieces while I'm not looking."

"The way she used to do when she played her father," Frevisse said.

Alice laid a hand on her breast, humbly bowed her head, and said, with a preacher's sententiousness, the old proverb, " 'Things past may be repented but not undone.' " Then she fixed John with a stern stare and added, "So if you don't do it, you won't have to repent it."

He laughed, and she laughed with him and turned toward the door to answer the knock there with the order to come in. Her steward did, bowed, and said, "My lady, Nicholas Vaughn is returned with someone he says he would have you . . . talk with."

The pause was small but there. So was Alice's, before she ordered, "Let them come in."

Master Thorpe paused again, as if wanting to say more but uncertain if he should.

"What?" Alice asked.

Master Thorpe flickered his gaze toward John and the other women. "You might want to do this . . ."

He hesitated, not sure how far beyond bounds he ought to go but Alice said, "Without others here?"

"It might be best, my lady."

With every trace of ease and pleasure gone, Alice said, her words quick and clipped, "Sister Margrett, would you take John to his chamber, please. Agnes, you may go, too. The other women should come in from the garden now. See to it."

They all stood up, Sister Margrett and Agnes curtsying, John making a small bow, his disappointment all over his face though he said nothing as Sister Margrett took his hand. Master Thorpe stood aside to let them leave, gave a glance at Frevisse still standing beside the window because she had been given no leave to go with the others, then withdrew himself.

"Alice," Frevisse began.

But curtly, crisply Alice said, "Just be here with me."

There was a momentary silence then that ended with the scuffle of men outside the door, not in struggle but as if too many were there and trying to sort themselves out, until Nicholas Vaughn came in, followed by two other men shoving a fourth one roughly between them, his arms tied behind his back and his wrists together. When he stumbled from their last hard shove, they made no attempt to catch him, and he went to his knees as Vaughn bowed to Alice, saying, "This fellow was at Flint after Hampden was killed, my lady. Now he was at Alderton, asking questions. I thought you might want to ask him some in return."

By then the bound man, still on his knees, had straightened himself and raised his head, and Frevisse only barely caught herself back from an exclaim. He was dirty and disheveled, with several days' worth of beard and altogether more ill-kept than she had ever seen him, but she knew him.

So did Alice, because after an instant that Frevisse suspected was as startled as her own, she ordered, "Nicholas, you stay. You others may go. Leave him and go. My thanks."

The men, clearly confused by her sudden order, bowed and withdrew, and when the door was closed behind them, Vaughn said, sounding uncertain, "My lady?"

Rather than answering him, Alice said, "Master Noreys."

"My lady," Joliffe returned in dry-throated echo of Vaughn. He looked past her to Frevisse. "Dame Frevisse."

"What were you doing in Alderton?" Alice demanded.

Joliffe tilted his head toward Vaughn. "As he said. Asking questions."

"Why?"

Joliffe shrugged one shoulder and gave a smile made somewhat uneven by a scab-stiffened cut on one side of his mouth. "To learn things?" he offered. "Why was your man there?"

"My priest had been killed. I wanted to know more about it."

"There you are. The first thing I heard when I rode into this Alderton was that a priest had been killed. How could I not be curious and ask questions?"

"Why were you in Alderton at all?" Vaughn demanded. And added to Alice, "He won't say, despite I've asked him."

"Which is hardly reason," Joliffe said, mockingly aggrieved, "to handle me as if I were guilty of something. If I'd killed the priest, I'd not have been there asking questions about it, would I? Could I have these ropes off now?"

Vaughn looked at Alice. He openly wanted her refusal, but she nodded for him to do it, and he moved behind Joliffe to obey. Apparently not minded to waste good rope by cutting it, he took his time undoing the knots. Alice did not tell him to hurry, and Joliffe kept quiet until he had done. That was notable, Frevisse thought, knowing his fondness for words.

Vaughn pulled the rope away and Joliffe's arms fell free. He stiffly made to rise, but Vaughn put a heavy hand on his shoulder, keeping him to his knees. Cradling one arm in the other, tenderly rubbing a rope-grazed wrist, Joliffe shrugged from under his hand and said at Alice, "May I get off my aching knees? Your men have already used me somewhat roughly."

"When I told my men to take him, he decided to make a fight of it," Vaughn said.

"That wasn't well-bethought, Joliffe," Frevisse said dryly.

"My lady, he didn't say please."

Vaughn drew sharp breath to make reply, caught himself, and instead said at Alice, "Gyllam and Bowen have bruises that match his. Symond has a cut cheek. He handled us no worse than we handled him."

And far less worse than Vaughn *wanted* to handle him, Frevisse guessed.

"Besides," said Joliffe, "he didn't order me killed, so I shouldn't complain too much. Of course if he *had* ordered me killed, I'd not be able to complain at all." He took on a cheerful tone. "So maybe I've no grounds to complain at all."

"Get up," Alice snapped.

While he did, slowly, as if he did truly ache, Frevisse said, "Joliffe, this is gone past playing games. You aren't going to talk your way out of this. Why not simply answer straightly?"

"I don't remember the question?"

Vaughn still held the ropes in one hand. His other hand closed into a fist that he looked as if he'd very much like to use. Alice, her impatience growing, snapped, "Master Noreys!" Frevisse, impatient at all of them, took up her own half-drunk goblet of wine from a nearby table and crossed the room to hand it to Joliffe, deliberately putting herself between him and Vaughn while she did.

"Drink," she ordered.

He took the goblet, needing both hands to hold it, swollen and clumsy as they were from being bound, and drank with a readiness that told his need. Finished, he gave the emptied goblet back to her and said, unmocking, "My thanks, my lady."

Frevisse turned to Alice. Carefully, quietly, hoping to keep angers down, she said, "We've trusted Master Noreys before this. Let him sit. Let's all sit and talk this through as if we still trusted him, until we know we can't."

Before Alice could answer that, Vaughn said, insisting, "The thing is, my lady, he was at Flint, too."

"After Hampden's death," Joliffe returned. "As were you. Or were you there *before* his death? And why would I be hanging about if I'd had anything to do with his death? Or this priest's?"

"Because you hadn't found out whatever you wanted."

"And I was more likely to find it out after they were dead than before and therefore I killed them?" Joliffe said back.

For all his tongue was quick as ever, he looked ready to drop where he stood, but Alice did not offer to let him sit and without her leave he could not. Frevisse asked, "How were these men killed?"

Vaughn looked to Alice. She nodded for him to answer and he said, "Hampden is said to have been killed by accident by brawlers outside a tavern. The priest was killed by a rout of his own people. They pulled him out of his house, beat him, and cut off his head. I'm sorry, my lady," he added to Alice as she and Frevisse crossed themselves. "I learned little else. I wanted to have him . . ." He jerked his head at Joliffe. ". . . away before the crowner came. Please you, my lady, may I know when have you had cause to trust him?"

Alice hesitated, then said, "Three years ago. At the time of the duke of Gloucester's death. He helped me in a matter then. Helped us," she amended, including Frevisse with a nod.

"It would help," Joliffe said quietly, "if you trusted me now. And let me go."

"It would likewise help," Alice returned, "if you trusted me and told me why you're interested in these men's deaths."

"I wasn't. I was interested in the men alive."

"Why?"

Joliffe gave her a crooked smile but no answer.

Alice's face tightened with anger. She glanced toward

Vaughn standing tautly ready for whatever she might order. It said something to the good about him that he had held back from doing worse to Joliffe than he had, but he looked more than willing to change that if Alice gave him leave, and Alice looked near enough to doing that. Frevisse, unsure how much her presence would hold Alice back if Joliffe irked her further, said with a calm she did not feel, "May we all at least agree that none of us are pleased to have these men dead?"

They all three looked at her. "What?" said Alice.

"It would be a common ground we could begin on," Frevisse said. "That none of us wanted these men dead."

"Of course I didn't want them dead," Alice snapped.

"Nor I," Joliffe said.

"And neither of you are satisfied their deaths are only from mischance?"

"If there was only the one death or the other," Alice said. "I could accept mischance was all it was. But both? I have to doubt."

"And you, Master Noreys?"

"I have my doubts, yes."

"So if we are willing to consider they may have been murdered—"

Vaughn interrupted, "It was the priest's own people who killed him."

Saying it almost before she thought it, Frevisse asked, "But was it all by their own doing? Or did someone goad them on to do it?" That was almost-past-belief unlikely, but if it served to keep Alice, Joliffe, and Vaughn talking, then she was willing to sound a fool, and she went on to Alice and Joliffe both, "But if neither of you wanted them dead, then who did? If you didn't send to have them killed, my lady, and if it wasn't by your doing, either, Master Noreys, then who would have interest enough in them being dead to have them killed?"

Alice and Joliffe exchanged questioning looks. Each

seemed to hope the other had answer to that. Having drawn
them a step off from being open adversaries, Frevisse went
on, grasping at possibilities, "Or if you've no thought of
who, then *why* would someone want them dead? Joliffe,
you're unwilling to tell us why you were both places. If it
wasn't because of the men's deaths—or to cause their deaths—
it was because you hoped to learn something, yes? From
them?"

Slowly, probably considering how much his answer might
give away, he granted, "Yes."

"Will you tell me what?" she asked.

"No."

But she had known that before she asked it, and she
turned to Alice with, "You have two men from your household lately dead and a third man missing . . ."

"Missing?" Joliffe said. "You don't know where Burgate
is either?"

"No," Alice answered tersely. "What do you know
about him?

"That he was Suffolk's secretary and he's missing. That's
all."

Before Alice could ask more that way, Frevisse asked,
"Besides they were all of your household, these men, did
they have anything else in common among them?"

"Nothing. Nothing I know of," Alice amended. "They
held greatly different places in the household. I never saw
them keep particular company with one another when they
were here."

"You said Burgate was going with Suffolk into exile. The
priest stayed with you until after Suffolk's death. What of
Hampden?" Frevisse asked.

"It was never intended he'd go with Suffolk into exile.
He was needed for his duties here and besides had lands of
his own to see to."

"Why was he in Wales?"

"I don't know."

"Joliffe, do you know?"

He had been studying the floor while rubbing at probably a cramp in one arm. Now he lifted his gaze to her and smiled with a mild innocence that she no more believed in now than she had any other of the few times they had met over the years. Joliffe might be many things—and she had known him as a player, a minstrel, a spy, and a friend—but she had never thought him innocent. "No," he said.

"If none of us know any more than this, we're going to learn nothing," Frevisse said, impatient at him and Alice together. She did not trust Alice to tell everything and was certain Joliffe was holding back and she snapped at him, "Why did you say 'either' just now, when Alice said she doesn't know where Burgate is?"

"I said 'either'?"

"You were surprised that she didn't know 'either'."

"Was I? More likely, I'm tired and just saying words that don't mean anything."

"It means," Frevisse said, "that besides you sought out Hampden and Squyers, you have interest in Burgate, except you don't know where he is. How did you know where the other two were?"

Alice, coldly, not waiting for his answer, said, "Some spy here in the household could have told him. Which lord does your spy work for?" she said at Joliffe. "For whom do *you* work?"

"He won't say," Vaughn said. "I've asked him."

Joliffe touched one side of his face as if it hurt. "That you did," he agreed. Under the shadow of his coming beard a bruise showed.

Threat open in her voice, Alice said, "I can give him leave to ask again."

"More near the point, Joliffe," Frevisse said quickly, "do you know anything else about any of the three?"

He held silent.

More impatient with every unanswered and uselessly answered question, she snapped at him and Alice both, "Someone has to tell more than they already have or we'll never be anywhere with this. There has to be some reason you wanted to see these three particular men, Joliffe. No, I don't expect you to tell me what it is. There likewise is almost surely some shared reason two of them are dead and the other missing."

"Maybe there's no particular reason," Joliffe said. "Maybe someone is just setting to kill as many of Suffolk's people as he can."

"At least for the moment, let's doubt that," Frevisse said dryly. "Are there any others of Suffolk's household you were going to see?"

"Others we might be in time to warn," Vaughn said.

"There were only those three," Joliffe said. "That I'll swear to."

"Then that's something," Frevisse said. "If it's not a general killing going on, then whatever it is must have to do with those three." She faced Alice. "Is there *anything* you can think of they had in common?"

Now it was Alice who was staring at the floor in thought but slowly shaking her head as she said with matching slowness, "Not a single thing. Perhaps Master Thorpe would know of something. I don't."

Quietly Joliffe said, "Normandy?"

Alice jerked her head up, stared at him, then said, "No. They had nothing to do with Normandy. They . . ."

She stopped, some other thought coming to her. For a long moment she stared past Joliffe at nothing. Then slowly she said, "Normandy. Yes. In the last year and a half or so, at different times, they each of them went over to Normandy. Hampden went twice that I know of. He could have gone more without I knew it. Squyers and Burgate went, too.

Once for each of them. Or Burgate could have gone more and I'd not know, if it was while Suffolk and I were apart. But I know for a certainty they all went."

"Do you know why?" Frevisse asked.

"To take Suffolk's messages, I suppose. Why else?" Alice said with sudden impatience. "Probably to Somerset. And, no, I never troubled to ask why they went instead of one of the usual messengers. We have enough of those, both of our own and the king's. A whole array. Enough for two a week to cross to Normandy at usual times and oftener if need be." Her voice darkened with self-reproach. "But I never asked why he used our own household men those few times, and I should have."

"And now those three men are dead or missing," Frevisse said carefully. "Can anything be made of that?" Alice looked at her, and Frevisse knew to almost a certainty that they were thinking the same thing. A year ago, by chance, they had come to share a secret so dire that while Frevisse had pushed it aside from her mind as a thing about which she could do nothing, the weight of it had maybe been what kept Alice from asking why their own household men were being sent to Normandy.

"Yes," said Alice. "I can make something of that." She looked at Joliffe. "But I won't say it in front of him."

Frevisse offered, "He must already partly know it if he knows enough to say Normandy."

They both looked at him. Vaughn looked back and forth among all of them, seemingly understanding none of it.

"Will it make difference," Joliffe asked carefully, "if I say I have a dead man on my side, too?"

"Who?" Alice demanded.

"Did you know Matthew Gough, my lady?"

"From when I lived in France, yes," she said. "I was sorry to hear he'd been killed and so pointlessly."

"More than pointlessly," Joliffe said. "He was murdered."

Vaughn scoffed. "He was killed in that fight on London Bridge. How does someone go about to get murdered in a battle?"

"By being struck down from behind by men set on killing him and no one else," Joliffe said back at him. And to Alice, "Gough wasn't killed by the rebels. He was killed by men who had already ransacked his room and then came looking for him."

"How do you know that?" she demanded.

"I was there."

Frevisse was surprised into saying, "In the fight? I've never judged you were given to putting yourself into a fight if you could help it."

"My lady, you've judged rightly," Joliffe agreed. "Much though I shall joy to come into God's presence, I'm in no hurry for it. Nor," he added thoughtfully, "am I in haste to go the other way either, supposing I've miscalculated.

"Which is not," Frevisse said dryly, "beyond possibility."

Chapter 9

Joliffe was hungry and thirsty and ached from the uncareful handling of the past two days and a night's uncomfortable sleep tied to a post in a stable. When he had understood where Vaughn was hauling him, he had had hope the trouble and slight acquaintance he and Lady Alice had shared three years ago would keep things from coming to the worst before he found a way either to escape or else talk himself out of trouble. Not that he had thought either would be easy, because Lady Alice was no fool and did not employ fools. Whomever she set to keep him prisoner would likely do it thoroughly.

His closer worry, though, had been how to put off her questioning—or at least keep her questions away from where he did not want to go—until he had been fed and had chance to rest long enough to gather his strength and wits to him again. He knew both were fairly well worn away by the time he was dragged off Rowan in Wingfield's foreyard, and he had not been altogether pleased to find Dame Frevisse with her cousin. To his good, her presence would likely keep Lady Alice from much she might otherwise have done to him. To the bad, Dame Frevisse was sharp-witted beyond the ordinary. The few times they had met before this, they had been on what passed for the same side. If they proved to be against each other in this matter, he had doubts how far he could mislead her. And so far he had not been able to mislead her at all. He wanted food. He wanted rest. And here she was back to where he did not want her to be, asking at him, "Was it because of Matthew Gough you were on London Bridge and in that fight?"

He wanted away from her too-quick wits. Any answer he gave was going to bring more questions at him, and if he was caught in any lie, they'd be less likely to believe any truth he told them. "Yes," he said.

Sharply at him, Vaughn demanded, "Were you one of the men who killed him?"

"No," Joliffe snapped back. Vaughn had been wearing on his patience for two days now. "I was the man who killed two of the four men set on to kill him."

That was more than he should have said. Dame Frevisse's already grave face became harsher; but she kept to the point, damn her, asking, "Why were you there?"

Joliffe decided it was time to give enough that maybe they would be satisfied for a while and let him alone a time. What he needed was to be fed, then locked somewhere away from everyone and all their questions, somewhere he could lie down and sleep; and with sudden, seeming openness, he said, "Right, then. It was this way. Gough had information from someone in Normandy. He wanted to pass it on to someone who might make good use of it. I was sent to get it. By bad chance, that meant I had to follow him into that fight on the bridge. After he was killed, his squires gave a paper to me off his dead body." He swallowed thickly and said, looking at the goblet still in Dame Frevisse's hand, "Might I have something more to drink?"

"No," said Vaughn.

But Dame Frevisse was already turning toward a table where a pitcher and other goblets stood, and Lady Alice did not forbid her, instead asked tersely, "What was on this paper?"

Making show of watching Dame Frevisse pour wine into the goblet, Joliffe said, "I didn't read it."

"What *did* you do with it?" Lady Alice demanded.

"Gave it to the man who sent me to Gough."

"And this man is?"

"You don't truly expect me to——" He broke off to say, "Thank you, my lady," to Dame Frevisse as he took the goblet she handed to him. He still had to use both his hands, resenting his clumsiness not for the ungrace of it but because it told him how little he dared trust his body yet; and although he drank, he drank less deeply than he seemed to, wary of adding enough wine to his weariness to fuddle his wits more than they already were. He saw Dame Frevisse was looking at his hands, and as he lowered the goblet he told her, "They're better."

She reached out and pushed one of his sleeves a little up his arm, uncovering the red grooves left around his wrist from the rope that had held him. Then she looked him in the face. He hoped she could read his look no better than he could read hers before she turned to Lady Alice and said, "He should probably be fed, too."

"When he's told us what we need to know, he can have food and drink and rest. Noreys, you've only to tell us——"

"You'll pardon me," Joliffe interrupted, "if I worry about what sort of 'rest' I'm to be given once you've no more need of me."

"There's been enough killing!" Lady Alice said, sharp with believable anger. "I don't want you dead. I only want to know what you know. You didn't read this paper from Matthew Gough. You gave it to someone. You won't say whom. You then sought out two men who are now dead. I'm willing to believe you had nothing to do with their deaths, but did they have something to do with the paper you had from Matthew Gough?"

Joliffe considered his possible choices and his answer, then granted, "Their names were on it, I'm told. So was Burgate's."

"And that," said Dame Frevisse, "makes four men, counting Matthew Gough, with Normandy and that paper in common and all of them dead. Or missing."

She was too quick by half; but Lady Alice said at him angrily, "What was it you wanted to know from my men? Why did you seek them out?"

Joliffe could suddenly see no point in not telling her. Either she knew the thing and it would come as no surprise to her, or she did not know it and now she would. But he looked sidewise at Vaughn and asked, "Do you want him here to hear it?"

"Just say it out!" Lady Alice said.

Dame Frevisse began, "Should he . . ." perhaps in warning to her, but Joliffe was already saying, sharp-worded back at Lady Alice, "I was to find out what any of these men knew about whatever messages they took between Suffolk and the duke of Somerset. To find out how much they knew about the plan to deliberately lose Normandy to the French."

He looked swiftly among their faces as he said it. On Vaughn's he saw surprise shading toward denying anger, but the quick look that passed between Lady Alice and Dame Frevisse had no surprise in it on either side.

So there had been such a plan.

It wasn't only in anyone's imagination.

Normandy had been lost by deliberate treachery.

And Lady Alice and Dame Frevisse both knew it.

How?

Lady Alice because she was married to Suffolk, yes, though Joliffe would have doubted her acceptance of it. But Dame Frevisse? How did she come to share that knowledge? By way of Lady Alice, surely, because Suffolk almost certainly would have told her nothing, given what had passed between him and the nun the last time they had met. The last time so far as he knew of, Joliffe amended.

The only way it made sense, he thought suddenly, was that the two women had known by some way other than Suffolk himself.

He would give something to know how *that* had come about.

But Lady Alice was saying forcefully to Vaughn, "You will never tell anyone what you just heard. You'll never say it. Never write it. Ever. Understand? Never even think about it if you can help it."

Vaughn bowed. "Yes, my lady."

But he *was* thinking, and his quick looks back and forth at the women suggested he was guessing much the same as Joliffe had. But Lady Alice was saying sharply at Joliffe now, "Noreys, no more gaming with words. You know far too much that you shouldn't. I have to know who sent you to Gough. Who has this paper of his? Who else knows all this?"

Joliffe shook his head, refusing an answer.

"Joliffe," Dame Frevisse said coldly and with an edge of anger, "at this point I would not mind shaking you or maybe worse myself. You're hungry, you're tired, you're probably aching, and those cuts on your wrists are surely hurting you and would be the better for cleaning, ointment, and bandages on them. You very likely don't have your wits as sharp about you as you might have . . ."

Joliffe grimaced in acknowledgment of all those truths.

". . . so let me make this plain to you. We have three murders very much alike and all of them with this paper and Normandy in common. I think, you think, Lady Alice thinks these murders have something to do with one another. Now, if they're not being done on Lady Alice's orders and they're not being done by whomever you are serving in this, then we have to ask—all of us have to ask, including the man you're serving—who *are* they being done for? We can at least guess at the why of these murders. They have to be meant to hide whatever passed between Suffolk and Somerset concerning Normandy."

"Their *loss* of Normandy," Lady Alice said bitterly.

Joliffe noted the bitterness. Whatever she knew about Normandy's loss and however she knew it, she was angry about it. That was something he might be able to use to his good. He needed something to his good just now.

Still at him and giving her cousin no heed, Dame Frevisse said, "Will you grant me all of that? That the murders have to do with Normandy's loss?"

Deciding he would rather follow her than hinder her, Joliffe said, "Yes."

She waited, as if expecting him to say more. So he did not.

She made a small disgusted sound at him and went on, "Can we agree, too, that those most interested in keeping their part in it secret would be Suffolk and Somerset? If there are other lords involved, we don't know their names . . ."

She paused, looked questioningly at Lady Alice who shook her head that she did not.

"But of those two, at least, we're certain," Dame Frevisse said. "Likewise, although Suffolk and Somerset are not the only lords with power sufficient to effect the deaths of men, they both possessed such power."

Her sharp reasoning was wearing on already worn wits, and he could not hold back from saying, "Except Suffolk doesn't anymore."

"To a certainty, he does not," Dame Frevisse granted, dry enough to parch a desert. "Which leaves us—"

"Somerset," Lady Alice interrupted angrily.

Quietly, Dame Frevisse agreed. "Somerset."

Three years ago Somerset had been the earl of Dorset. Since then he had risen by the king's grant to be earl of Somerset and then, again by royal grant, to duke. When he had gone to be governor of Normandy two years ago, he was said to be second only to Suffolk in power near the king, helped to that place by Suffolk himself. His rise in estate and power had been swift. His fall would be even swifter if he were proved guilty of deliberately losing England's hold on Normandy. And to Joliffe's pleasure Vaughn burst out, "He's surely traitor enough to do it. The nothing he did to stop the French—that was treason. Sending no aid to any town or place the French besieged. Or else sending too little to matter. He stayed in Rouen and did *nothing* while town after town, castle after castle were taken. Then, when the French came to Rouen itself, he surrendered it, and did the same again at Caen. If even half of any of that is true . . ."

"It is," said Lady Alice grimly. "And, yes, it's treason to surrender a town without resistance. Although I believe he waited until the French had fired upon him once or twice before he surrendered." Lady Alice said that as dryly as Dame Frevisse might have done.

"That still leaves all the rest," Vaughn protested. "The king will surely arrest him, and that will be an end of anything he can do against you."

"I wish so. I hope so," Lady Alice said. "But our lord the king would rather be led than lead, be governed than govern. Suffolk and Somerset were both more than willing to oblige him. I strongly suppose Somerset means to take up where he left off, and I'm doubtful there's anyone who'll stop him."

"King Henry has a plenitude of other lords around him," Joliffe said. "Surely someone among them will oppose him, persuade the king to his arrest."

"They've had the months since Suffolk's fall to sort it out among them who would take Suffolk's place that way," Lady Alice answered, cold and precise on the words. "I've had no report that any of them have. They've pushed and pulled King Henry hither and thither but none has come to the fore and taken the high hand over the others or him. Their failing may be that despite everything King Henry has failed at, they still have it in their minds that kings are to rule, not to be ruled. I promise you Somerset won't be held back by any such thought. If once he's received into King Henry's presence—mark me on this—it will be as if Normandy never happened."

Dame Frevisse protested, "But it did, and if nothing else, people's outrage will force the king to bring Somerset to some kind of trial."

"Will it?" Lady Alice said with scorning disbelief. "I doubt it."

"The Commons in Parliament forced Suffolk from power," Dame Frevisse persisted. "They'll do the same with Somerset."

"They may," Lady Alice granted. "But not while the country is caught up in these uprisings still happening everywhere. There's a new one in Kent, and small outbreaks all over Essex that could turn into something more, and Wiltshire is still seething from Bishop Ayscough's murder hardly a month ago. Besides all that, there is no Parliament just now, and by the time another one is called, Somerset will be so deeply set in power it will be a long haul of work to get him out. Believe me."

Slowly Dame Frevisse said, "All of that would explain why Somerset might order these men murdered, if alive they could be a threat to his hold on power through the king. None of it is proof that he *did* order any murders, though."

Joliffe had leaned one hip sidewise against the back of a chair beside him and been watching the two of them over the goblet's rim as he sipped more wine, learning much and more than willing to have them taken up with something other than questioning him.

It couldn't last, though. Vaughn said suddenly at him, "You said whoever killed Gough never saw the paper with their names on it. Yes?"

"Yes," Joliffe answered, more inwardly wary than he outwardly showed and carefully keeping his pose of ease against the chair.

"Then it wasn't from the paper that someone knew these men knew too much," Vaughn said.

Dame Frevisse quickly picked that up. "And if it wasn't from the paper, then the only way that someone would know these were men they wanted dead would be if that someone already knew . . ."

Vaughn and Joliffe said it with her.

". . . that these men knew too much."

In the immediate quiet among them all, Joliffe heard the mumble and movement being made by those of the household who slept in the great hall bringing out and laying down their bedding there. Beyond the open window some bird—a nightjar likely—was welcoming the darkness now fully come; and into their own quiet it was Dame Frevisse who finally said slowly, "That brings us again to Somerset. Because he's the only one besides Suffolk we can be certain knew what these men knew about Normandy's loss."

Lady Alice had been standing rigidly silent this while. Now she said sharply at Vaughn, "Nicholas, pour yourself some wine and sit down. Let's all of us sit down. And you," she said at Joliffe, "once and for all, tell us for whom you're working, since it may well be his purpose and ours is the same."

Joliffe shifted into the chair but sat staring into his goblet, slowly swirling the wine there, not answering, still not sure he should.

Quietly Dame Frevisse said, "Joliffe."

He looked up at her. She had sat down, too—on a long, low-backed settle mostly facing his own chair. Vaughn was a little ways away, in the room's other chair. Only Lady Alice was still standing, for all she had said they should sit. But for the moment only Dame Frevisse and Joliffe might have been there as she said to him, "On my word, you can trust her grace of Suffolk. She isn't trying to play you or anyone else false."

Holding her gaze, Joliffe considered that and everything else that had been said, added it to what had passed unsaid among them, then looked at Lady Alice. "I serve Richard, duke of York."

That was probably not the best of the very many answers he might have made her. It meant he was a far greater matter than he might have been, and after a moment's silence Lady Alice said, "Ah." A flat sound that told him nothing of what she was thinking.

It was Dame Frevisse who said, very quietly, "The duke of York. Is that wise?"

No, it probably was not. Joliffe knew too well that if Sir William was right and someone close to the king was trying to find a way to charge York with treason, that was a charge that could all too easily be stretched to include those who served him, and traitors came to ugly deaths. But to Dame Frevisse's question he merely lifted one shoulder and said wryly, "Isn't the saying 'Experience is the mother of wisdom'? How will I know if it's wise until it's too late to change my choice?" But having gone so far, he saw use in going further, and looking at Lady Alice, he said, "There's this. Two of your household men have been murdered and a third is missing. There looks to be some manner of danger stalking your household and maybe you. In that you have some common cause with my lord of York, because he's under threat, too. With those commissions of oyer and terminer being issued all over England for the finding out who's had part in this summer's rebellions and troubles, secret word has gone to at least some of the commissioners that they're to find York guilty in it."

"Is he guilty in it?" Lady Alice asked.

Sharp at the foolishness of that, Joliffe said, "Of course. From Ireland. To be sure he's too far away to take any advantage of anything that happens or to protect himself when the accusations surely come."

As sharply Dame Frevisse said at him, "Her question is reasonable."

"It is," Joliffe granted just as sharply. "But whichever way I answered it, she won't believe me, so why ask me at all?"

"You're fighting so hard against being alive, I swear you want to be dead!" Dame Frevisse snapped.

"And I swear I don't!" Joliffe said angrily back at her. "I also swear I'm tired and hungry and in pain and I only want to lie down and sleep until my mind is fit for these games you all want to play!"

That was an unmannered over-boldness at his betters and it came more from his tiredness than from good sense, but it was also true. He needed away from their questioning and his answering until he could better judge what was safe to say and bargain better than he had so far. He needed sleep and he did not flinch when Vaughn started to rise in angry response to his ill manners, because if Vaughn hit him, he meant to collapse as utterly as if he had been beaten.

But Lady Alice slightly raised a hand, Vaughn settled back into his chair, and she said to Joliffe, "That's fair enough, maybe. You've been hard used and we're all tired and will maybe deal together better after a night's rest. All I lack is for Dame Frevisse to vouch that you're as good as your word."

She looked toward her cousin as she finished. So did Joliffe and found Dame Frevisse looking at him, considering rather than answering. Or else deliberately holding back her answer long enough for him to begin to feel a shadow of doubt before she finally said, "I've never known him to do a dishonorable thing. Things that were suspect, maybe. Things doubtful. But never dishonorable." She turned her gaze to Lady Alice. "And you know yourself what chance he ran three years ago with no likelihood of gain for himself. I think he's likely to deal fairly with you."

Lady Alice returned her gaze to Joliffe. "You'll not object, though, Master Noreys, when you've been fed and your hurts seen to, to being locked into a room for the night?"

Joliffe rose and bowed to her. "So long as there's somewhere to lie down and maybe a pillow for my head, I'll be content and wish blessings upon you, my lady."

"I think we can allow you a mattress as well," she said, and added to Dame Frevisse, "Will you see to his hurts if I send ointment and herbs for them?"

"I will."

She stood up and respectfully so did Dame Frevisse and Vaughn as she said, moving toward the door, "Then I'll go give orders for it all now. Nicholas, if you'll stay here?"

He bowed. "I will, my lady."

Joliffe bowed, too, and Dame Frevisse slightly curtsied. All our manners fine and right, Joliffe thought, and stayed on his feet until Dame Frevisse had sat again before he slumped down into his chair with a suddenness that he knew—and did not care—betrayed how hard he had been holding himself together. For good measure he shut his eyes, hoping no one would want anything of him, but Dame Frevisse demanded at him, "Why are you still doing this? With . . ." She paused over what she had been going to say. ". . . that man you served dead and that other matter done, why didn't you go back to being simply a player and out of all this?"

Joliffe neither opened his eyes nor bothered to keep the bitterness from his voice as he said, "I haven't been simply a player for a long time, my lady."

"How long? Since before we first met?"

"No. No, then I was everything I seemed to be. A travel-ing player hoping for better days." He smiled without open-ing his eyes. "Surprisingly enough, the better days came. Then other things came. Now, being a player is no longer something I can simply 'go back to'."

"But wish you could?"

"There are days, my lady. Believe me, there are days." Days when he would rather have been other than he was, days when he searched back to find a time when he could have chosen differently. But mostly there were days when he knew himself well enough not to waste time in thinking too long on what was not and never could have been.

Of course there were likewise times when he did not even want to think about the here-and-now. This was one of them, and given this respite, he took it, slacking his body and sink-ing into a silence in which the three of them waited until a servant came with warmed water, a jar of ointment, and some narrow-folded bands of clean cloth bandages, and said to Vaughn, "My lady said to tell you the rear storeroom would do, that you'd know the one she meant. She's having bed-ding taken there."

Bedding. A divine thought. Bedding and no need to struggle to keep his mind clear.

In a mercy of silence, Dame Frevisse tended to his wrists. She had kinder hands than, for some reason, he had thought she would, but she was thorough at the work and did not apologize when the cleaning of a deeper rope-cut made him wince. Thorough in her mind and in her ways, and practical beyond the point of pointless apologies. The several times they had met she had been a good ally. He did not want her for an enemy now.

She finished bandaging his wrists, wrung out the wash-ing cloth in the cooling water, gave it to him, and still with-out looking at him, said, "You'll want to clean the cut at the corner of your mouth, too," before she turned away, bade both him and Vaughn good night without quite looking at either one of them, and left the room.

She would not be his enemy in this, Joliffe thought as he began to clean the cut Vaughn's fist had given him yesterday. But she might choose not to be his ally either. If he read her aright, she was very angry and not just at him. At her cousin, too? It had to be at Lady Alice's doing that she was here at all, and it was little likely Dame Frevisse liked that, given to her nunnery life as she was. She might even choose to hold neutral in this whole business after tonight, helping neither him nor her cousin, and that could well be a bad thing for him. But worse would be if she set herself against him.

Chapter 10

Frevisse had not looked at Joliffe while she tended to his hurt wrists, and certainly had asked him nothing. Besides that Alice's man was there to hear anything else he said, too much had been said already for her mind's peace; she had kept the darkness of her thoughts to herself and took them with her when she left, going upstairs with slow feet and heavy mind. Alice was being settled into her bed by her women when Frevisse passed through her bedchamber on way to her own. She gave Alice, lying against the pillows, a light curtsy but Alice did not acknowledge her and she went on, to find Sister Margrett readied for their own bed but still up and a candle still burning.

"I waited to say Compline with you," Sister Margrett said.

"And to hear what passed after you left?" Frevisse asked.

That came out more tartly than she had meant it to. Sister Margrett looked startled, then said tartly back, "Only if you want to tell it and it's something I should hear. Which I doubt it is. So, no, I wasn't waiting to hear what passed after you left."

Immediately contrite, both for her own sharpness and for having unjustly goaded Sister Margrett to anger, Frevisse said, "I'm sorry. That wasn't fair. I'm tired." She raised her hands to begin unpinning her veil. "I am very . . . very tired. And no, what passed is not something you would want to hear."

As quickly out of her anger as into it and Frevisse's apology apparently accepted, Sister Margrett said quietly, "There's blood on your right hand."

Frevisse turned her hand over to find a red smear of Joliffe's blood along the outer side of her palm.

"There was a man a little hurt. I saw to bandaging him," she said in the same weary way she had admitted she was tired, and went to the waiting basin of water on a table beside one wall to wash it off, then took off her veil and wimple, leaving on only her cap for the night, and washed her face, both soothed and revived enough by that to be glad that Sister Margrett had waited Compline for her.

There was peace in that final Office of every day—*Visita, quaesumus, Domine, habitationem istam, et omnes insidias inimici ab ea longe repelle. Angeli tui . . . nos in pace custodiant; et benedictio tua sit super nos semper.* Visit, we beg you, Lord, this house, and all the snares of the enemy from here drive back. Let your holy angels . . . keep us in peace, and your blessing be over us always.

Frevisse gave herself up to it, sinking her mind into the comfort of the words, and afterward went to bed with quieted mind, able to leave until tomorrow what could not be helped tonight.

* * *

FOR all of that, though, morning came sooner than she wanted to face it, and despite she was ready for Alice's summons after Prime and Mass and breaking the night's fast were done, she did not go eagerly. Against good sense, she had liked Joliffe from the time they had first met. Against good sense, she still liked him. And beyond all her present angers, she still cared for Alice as kin and sometime friend. What hurt and frightened her was the doubt that either her liking or her care would be of any use at all against the dark tangles into which they were come, and she silently prayed from among last night's prayers—*Custodi nos, Domine. Sub umbra alarum tuarum protégé nos.* Guard us, Lord. Under the shadow of your wings protect us—before going into the small room beyond Alice's bedchamber where she and Alice had talked together on their first coming to Wingfield.

Cushions had been found and put upon the window seats but otherwise it was the same. Alice, though, had nothing sad or pleading about her this time. Straight-backed in her black mourning gown, her face encircled by the stiffly pleated folds of her white widow's wimple and framed by the long blackness of heavy veil spread over her shoulders, she was the great lady in whose hands power lay with the familiarity of years, and neither she nor Frevisse spoke, only slightly bent their heads to each other, then stood waiting in silence the little while until Joliffe and Vaughn came in by the room's other door.

Both men looked better than they had last night. Rested, shaved, washed, combed, and presumably fed, Joliffe even had on a clean shirt under his doublet, to judge by the clean cuffs showing at his bandaged wrists; and when he had bowed to her and Lady Alice, he stood quietly facing Alice, leaving it to her to begin whatever their business would be this morning and giving no sign of his own thoughts.

Vaughn, like Joliffe, had cleaned and straightened himself from last night, but he looked no happier about matters than he had then, and after his own bow to Lady Alice, he stood between the room's two doors with one hand resting on the hilt of his belt-hung dagger as if on guard. Whether against Joliffe or against someone coming in was unclear.

Against Joliffe was Frevisse's guess.

As the men had entered, she had faded aside, almost to a wall, and now slightly bowed her head and folded her hands out of sight into her opposite sleeves, making seeming of withdrawing from everything. Though Vaughn might believe that of her, she was certain neither Alice nor Joliffe would, but they were likely intent enough on each other to discount her for the while; and certainly Alice's first words to him were no mannerly inquiry about how he was this morning or a nonsense hope that he had slept well but the blunt question, "Why should I believe you when you say you serve the duke of York?"

As bluntly, Joliffe answered, "Because I'd be a great deal safer saying I served someone else."

"Why didn't you claim another lord then?"

"Because that would get us no further toward finding out who wants dead everyone who might betray what Suffolk and Somerset did in Normandy."

"You truly think that's the root of these deaths?"

"I do. Do you have a different thought about it, my lady? Or, come to it, how much about Normandy's loss could you betray if you chose?"

Maybe offended that someone as slight in the world as Joliffe dared question her in return but accepting that offense was an unuseful thing just now, she answered coldly, stiffly, "My lord husband never told me a single thing about it."

Frevisse doubted Joliffe missed the evasion in that answer of how she *had* known about it, then; but Alice took the talk back her own way with, "You claim order has been given to link York to these rebellions so he can be charged with treason. I gather you likewise think that is linked to the murders of my household men."

With a lightness that was surely feigned, Joliffe said, "I hope it is, because if there are several such plots going all at once . . ." He made gesture as if casting something away.

"Nonetheless," Alice said, "there may be."

"There may be," Joliffe agreed. "But one or all, they're surely by men close around the king. They're the men with the power to order such things. Power they must be in fear of losing."

"Who gave the order against York?"

"It seems it was slipped sidewise and around the corner to at least the man who warned us of it. He gave no name with it."

"But you're willing to consider it could be the same person or persons who ordered these murders and maybe Burgate's disappearance."

"We have to consider something, and the simplest beginning is likely the best. But plot or plots, you'll have better thought than I can about who around the king it could be."

"My lord the duke of Somerset for one," Alice said without hesitance. "Except he might have found it hard to know enough and give the necessary orders. At least for Burgate being seized. For the others, who can say?"

"And now he's back from Normandy," Joliffe said. "He landed at Dover with his household over a week ago."

Surprise—and alarm?—widened Alice's eyes. Joliffe saw it as well as Frevisse, and he asked quickly, "You hadn't heard that, my lady?"

"No," Alice said sharply. "I've heard nothing that way." And plainly thought she should have. At Vaughn she demanded, "Have we heard anything from . . ." She seemed to think better of saying any names and said instead, ". . . anything from either of them?"

"The last word we had was just before St. Mary Magdalene day. When I came back from Wales and found out there had been nothing since then, I sent someone to find out why. There's not been time for his return."

So that was Vaughn's place in things, Frevisse thought—master of at least some of Alice's spies set to watch in other men's households. That distrust and the ambition that fed it were among the things she found hardest to accept about Alice's life. But Alice was saying, "Nor was there reason to worry we hadn't heard because we didn't know there was news we should have had." She looked to Joliffe again. "Since you know so much, do you know if the king has received Somerset or, better, ordered his arrest?"

"No," Joliffe said. "As I last heard it, Somerset was riding openly toward London, no let or hindrance offered him."

"Blessed St. Michael," Alice said. "What is King Henry thinking of? Every person dispossessed out of France, every man, woman, and child who's lost their home and everything they had in Normandy are going to want Somerset's head. He has to be at least brought to trial. King Henry has to at least arrest him."

Dryly bitter, Joliffe said, "Our King Henry is a merciful man."

"This isn't mercy," Alice snapped. "It's foolishness. I swear, he . . ." She broke off, again thinking better of her words, and sharply reverted to where they had been. "You say that someone is plotting to have York accused of treason. You say he's guilty of none. I'm the more ready to believe that because it begins to seem to me that someone may be plotting much the same against my son. Not to find him treasonous but to betray into the open the full extent of his father's treason and thereby have the dukedom from him."

Frevisse jerked up her head to stare openly at Alice. Vaughn made a sound that might have been a smothered oath. Joliffe, with a calmness that did not quite mask satisfaction, said, "Indeed, my lady?"

By the twist of Alice's mouth, she heard the satisfaction as clearly as Frevisse did; and she said, somewhat mockingly, "Indeed, Noreys. And, yes, to spare you pointing it out, we may therefore have more reason to work together than against each other. If my lord of York and I do truly have a common enemy, then we had *better* work together."

Joliffe bowed to her, respectfully agreeing, "My lady."

Vaughn stirred as if very badly wanting to say something.

Alice, keeping her gaze on Joliffe, said, "I know, Nicholas. This may not be wise, but I somewhat think I'd be a full fool not to attempt it. So, Master Noreys, where to begin? We agree it's possible that someone has ordered these murders to conceal Suffolk's and Somerset's treason. We presume this someone to be Somerset. Yes?"

"Yes."

"My suspicion follows that, seeking to protect himself, he wants to break any link between him and Suffolk in the matter, because to satisfy all the angers at Normandy's loss, *someone* is going to have to pay the price of it. My lord husband is already well-hated and well-dead. Let a charge of treason be brought against him now and what defense is likely to be any good? And if he is found guilty of treason, then his title, properties, and all will be forfeited to the crown. My son will be left with nothing. Neither title nor inheritance nor future."

Frevisse forebore to point out that the considerable inheritance that Alice had had from her father would not be forfeit for Suffolk's treason. Young John would be left with far more than "nothing." He would have wealth and his life and not the burden of the dukedom. But for Alice the loss of the latter seemed to be the heavy weight in the balance. Or maybe it was from the taint to his blood and name she wanted to save her son, and with no answer to make to that, Frevisse protested instead, "How can Somerset hope to separate himself that far from it? People have to see they were hand-in-glove together in everything."

Joliffe drew himself very straight, threw out his chest, changed something in how he stood, and suddenly seemed a much larger man, full of lordly authority as he declaimed, hands spread in entreaty for other men to see reason, "I sent to my lord of Suffolk for aid. I begged him to send men, to send anything but paper answers. My pleas, my lords, went unanswered. What little came, came too late. I swear I did what I could with what nothing Suffolk saw fit to give me . . ."

"Yes, yes," Frevisse broke in. "I can see Somerset would play it that way. But would men be fool enough to believe it?"

"The better question," Alice said, "is would anyone be fool enough *not* to at least *pretend* to believe it, if Somerset comes back into the king's favor? Once Somerset has the king's favor, who's to move against him? Not his fellow lords. They've all failed to take full hold over King Henry while Somerset is gone. They won't take it once Somerset is fully back. Nor is there much likelihood of a Parliament being called any time soon, for the Commons to set on Somerset the way they did on Suffolk, not while there's this ongoing seethe of rebellions to distract them. Once Somerset is firmly back into the royal household, there's no one going to have power enough to challenge him."

"There's my lord of York," Joliffe said.

"Who is in Ireland and not likely allowed to return any time soon," Alice said. "Especially if Somerset takes Suffolk's place with the king."

Joliffe started to answer that, but Vaughn said first, "My lady, are you seriously thinking to ally with York? If he brings down Somerset for this treason, whatever he uses to do it could be used against young John as well, as Suffolk's heir. Unless we know for certain he's our enemy, we may do better to hope Somerset stays untouched."

"We could hope that," Alice granted. "But unless we find some other reason than Normandy why someone has killed Hampden and Squyers and, yes, Matthew Gough—and find out that someone is other than Somerset, then it's against Somerset I want to be protected. Besides that," she said and sounded suddenly very like her father the times Frevisse had seen him set himself against something that could mean deep trouble, "Somerset should be stopped for more reasons than my own. He's as corrupt and ill-able to govern as my lord husband was. They should neither of them have ever been let near power. So, Master Noreys, if we work together in this matter of murders and all, destroying Somerset and maybe even setting York into the place he should have near the king, will my help suffice to earn York's help in keeping my son's inheritance safe from any attainder for treason against his father?"

Joliffe hesitated before saying carefully, "I cannot give my lord of York's word for anything. You know that. But I *will* swear that I believe whole-heartedly he'll play you fair in this as far as lies within his power."

"More than that would be unfair to ask of you," Alice said. "Especially when, from all I know, I would trust York to do right long before I'd ever trust Somerset."

"Towards that trust, my lady, have you considered the use of an alliance of marriage between your son and one of York's daughters?"

"You're a marriage broker as well as a spy, Master Noreys?" Alice snapped.

"Rather than either, my lady, a purveyor of facts and pointer-out of possibilities. Among the nobility, York is isolated save for a few relatives-by-marriage. An alliance with you would lessen that isolation. He's of royal blood. Your grandchildren by one of his daughters would have that same royal blood, and who knows what might come of that. There would be benefits on both sides."

"You're right," Alice said, "that such a marriage would indeed sweeten our—alliance, if it comes to that. And after all, with God all things are possible."

That had been her father's way of ending talk when he wanted to be done with something, and Joliffe took it as such, saying with a slight bow, "My lady."

"The more immediate question," she went on, "is What is to be done with you while I consider all of this? Because my mind is not yet made up."

Joliffe bowed low with a courtier's excessive flourish. "All that I ask is that you let me live, that I may serve you, most gracious lady."

"We had already determined on leaving you your life, Master Noreys," she said so haughtily that both Frevisse and Joliffe had to look at her to see by her slight smile that she was deliberately matching his courtier's flowered words with her own. "I mean what's to be done with you for the present. We need to determine what to do next and I can't talk with you more just now, nor do I think it wise to have you become widely known in my household. Neither do I want to lock you away again. It would seem . . ." The slight smile returned. ". . . discourteous."

Joliffe silently bowed his appreciation of that.

She looked at Vaughn. "Nicholas, could you keep him company through the day in the upper parlor? No one should come that way if I don't."

Vaughn bowed. "My lady."

"Share what you both know about this business. See what happens when you think together on it."

Joliffe and Vaughn both bowed to that, but Frevisse saw them afterward trade mutually wary glances that made her want to say, "And play nice together." But she did not, and Alice dismissed them with a small gesture, and with another slight bow they both withdrew by the small chamber's rear door, the way they had come.

With them gone, Alice ceased to stand so straightly, went toward the window as if suddenly needing to sit but saying as she went, "The upper parlor is where I would withdraw when the house was too full of Suffolk's business and too many people. There's a back way to the kitchen yard from there, for Nicholas to fetch them food and drink. They'll do well enough."

"If they don't let their dislike of each other take over," Frevisse said, following her.

"Nicholas won't. He knows his duty."

And Frevisse would have to trust Joliffe knew and would hold to his own. It was what his duty was that worried her, because it surely had not started out to be making alliance between Alice and York, and she asked, "Will you truly consider a marriage between John and one of York's daughters?"

Lowering herself to one of the cushioned seats as if far older than she was, Alice said, "It would be good sense." She folded her hands into her lap. "Save that John is already married to Margaret Beaufort. The duke of Somerset's niece."

Frevisse felt her mouth fall open and only with difficulty closed it again, too taken aback for words. Beyond doubt reading her startled face aright, Alice went on, "The girl came into Suffolk's ward after her father's death. Somerset grabbed the title that should have come with her, but she has properties enough to make her worthwhile."

"Properties and royal blood," Frevisse said, sitting down across from her.

"And most especially her royal blood. Suffolk never lost sight of that for a moment." Because just as York was, the duke of Somerset was cousin to the king. The difference was Somerset's royal blood came from the adulterous coupling of the duke of Lancaster—a younger son of King Edward III—and his mistress several generations back. Lancaster had eventually married the woman and had their offspring legitimated, and through the years they and their children had risen to dukedoms and a bishopric and places very near the king—and none nearer than Somerset.

"Suffolk had the marriage done very quietly last winter," Alice said, as if glad to say it aloud. "Secretly. On the chance things might go to the bad. Which they did."

"John is too young to have made the marriage completely sure," Frevisse said. Far too young to have consummated it.

"So is she. Nor are they ever likely to. I suspect that Somerset will do what he can to have the marriage annulled and get her into his own hands, to his own use. After all, the king has two half-brothers available for marriage."

Frevisse startled. She knew those two children. Edmund and Jasper. Or had known them when they were small boys. But, yes, they were young men by now and, yes, she could see how Somerset would like to place himself more closely to the king by marrying his niece to one of them.

"Not that I much mind the thought of having her off my hands," Alice said. "I like young Meg Beaufort very little."

"Alice!"

"Well, I don't. It's why I left her at Ewelme. She's lovely to the eye, is little Meg—she hates being called Meg, so I'm afraid I do it. She's all large eyes and sweet-shaped face, but even at seven years old she's pie-faced with piety. Walks around with her prayer book clasped to her breast and her eyes raised to heaven." Alice mimicked a child's voice simpering, " 'I'd be Christ's bride if I could, but God has willed otherwise for me.' " Alice returned to her own voice to say disgustedly, "When she says 'Christ's bride', what she sees is herself sitting in glory on a throne beside him, draped in cloth of gold. She wouldn't last a month in nunnery life. I do not like her, nor do I like Somerset, or his wife, or his miserable sons. He's welcome to her! I just want to be left alone for awhile!"

She made a small, angry, almost flailing movement with both hands, then clamped them together, shoved them down onto her lap, and said, looking straight at Frevisse, "There's something else."

Frevisse's momentary urge to comfort her was instantly quelled. Warily she asked, "What?"

"Remember I told you I was afraid of something else but wouldn't say more?"

"I remember."

"Through the last weeks before Suffolk left, he was in a seethe of anger. He kept saying he'd been betrayed. That he'd been betrayed and someone would pay along with him if things went any worse for him."

"He had to mean the duke of Somerset," Frevisse said.

"How had Somerset betrayed him? Everything in Normandy was going and has gone as they planned."

"So far as we know," Frevisse said quickly. "You and I, we truly know very little." And that little had come only by chance.

"But what if there were others in it with them? We don't know for certain there weren't. And if there were others, what do they know? What if they have proofs they could use against John, to his loss?"

Strongly, to convince herself as well as Alice, Frevisse said, "If there is someone else, they can do nothing without betraying themselves. Alice, Suffolk was likely talking out of his fear and anger, and there's no one."

"Mayhap." Despite her voice stayed steady, Alice's hands had begun to twist together in her lap. "But what if he wasn't? And there's this. Frevisse, he was going into exile in *France*. Knowing all he knew and angry as he was, what if he decided to tell everything to the French? How better to assure his welcome than to tell King Charles everything he knew? About the war, about King Henry, about . . ."

"Alice, he would never have been that great a fool!"

"Oh, yes, he could have been," Alice said with a deeper and darker bitterness than she had yet betrayed. "Believe me. He very well could have been. And whoever else was with him in losing Normandy . . ."

"If there was anyone else in it besides Somerset," Frevisse said.

". . . had to be afraid he might truly do it, meaning I have to fear that someone while having no thought of who they are."

"If there's anyone at all," Frevisse persisted.

"Why is Burgate missing instead of simply dead like Hampden and Squyers? Why did he go missing weeks before anyone moved against them?" Alice was speaking more rapidly, as if having the words out might stop them hurting her. "The thing is, after Suffolk's . . . death, when some of our people came back and Burgate didn't and I asked if anyone knew where he was . . . Remember, I told of that?"

"I remember. You said no one knew where he'd gone."

"They didn't, no. But two of them offered that he'd been much with Suffolk just at the end, the day before they'd sailed. That Suffolk and Burgate had been away in another room, writing things."

"The letter to John."

"He had that nearly done before he left here," Alice said with cold scorn at Suffolk. "He showed it to me."

"You didn't go with him to the coast?"

"We parted here. There was nothing more to be said between us."

Alice's coldness ended any more questions that way, and Frevisse tried, "Other letters then."

"If so, they were never sent. There were no messengers. I asked that."

"What you fear is that Suffolk was writing out—or was saying for Burgate to write out—his accusation against whomever he meant when he said he'd been betrayed. And you're afraid that Burgate has this accusation with him, wherever he is."

"That. Yes," Alice said. "Or maybe nothing was written at all. If I could find him and he would tell me that, it would be something. As it is, the not knowing is torture in its own right."

Slowly, Frevisse went on, seeing it more clearly as she said it and watching Alice while she did. "But anything Suffolk may have written in accusation of someone else would suffice to condemn him, too. Why would he do something so foolish as put in writing what would surely destroy him along with anyone he accused?"

"He surely only meant it to be used if he *was* destroyed."

"Even if it could ruin John along with them?"

"To Suffolk's way of seeing the world, if he was ruined, then all was ruined," Alice said with raw bitterness. "For him, if he was dead, what was left alive that mattered? Now he's dead and Burgate is missing and my fear has to be there is an accusation and it will come to the wrong people. And there are so *many* wrong people," she said, her bitterness laced with despair.

Frevisse tried, "But Suffolk didn't know he was going to be killed. Even if he wanted to have everything written down, why trust any man to know it? Why trust this secretary?"

"Oh, Burgate." Alice flicked one hand, dismissing him. "He's been Suffolk's man since he was a boy. In truth, they were boys together. He was the son of Suffolk's father's head clerk and followed his father's way. He probably knows more of Suffolk's secrets than Suffolk's confessor does." Her voice darkened again. "But if there is something and Burgate has it, where is he? Or where is it? If our enemies have it, why haven't they used it? If he doesn't have it, and they don't, who does?"

"If this Burgate were dead, you'd have heard."

"Would I? He could be dead and no one know except whoever killed him. Or look how I'd not heard Somerset was returned to England. How much else is there I've not heard?" She sounded both grim and desperate now, her hands again clamped together in her lap. "I'm tainted by Suffolk's taint. I'm losing—or have maybe lost—my place at court and near the queen, and without that there'll be no one between me and all the enemies Suffolk made for us." She turned toward Frevisse. Her eyes were huge with staring into her fears, and with barely held desperation she said, "Everything is coming to nothing and I don't know how to stop it!"

"You've not come to 'nothing' yet," Frevisse said sharply, in ruthless comfort. "Your place in the world is maybe lessened, but so far you still have your wealth and your wits. Unless you let your fears tear you apart, you're not helpless. You've still time to work against whatever you're afraid may come."

Alice straightened as if from a slap. Momentarily her face tightened with anger; but then it cleared, and she said almost calmly, "There you're right. I'll be defeated when I'm defeated and not before. So, do I tell this Joliffe of yours about this possible written accusation or not? How far do we trust him? Always remembering that you like him and that may undermine your judgment of him."

"You trusted him yourself three years ago."

"Three years," Alice said, as if it were three lifetimes ago. "I've learned a great deal more about distrust since then, with everything that's gone so far astray from where I thought it would."

"Life has that way of going astray from where we thought it would," Frevisse said dryly.

"Has yours?" Alice asked in sudden sideways thought. "You wanted a nun's life and you have it. Aren't you happy in your nunnery?"

"I'm not in my nunnery," Frevisse snapped, hearing too late the betraying anger in her voice even as Alice said back with matching sharpness, "I'm sorry. I've told you I'm sorry. It was wrong of me to . . ."

"No," Frevisse said with quick contrition. "The wrong is mine, to grudge you my help because I'm . . ." She caught on the word, then brought herself to finish, ". . . because I'm afraid, too. For you and John both."

Unexpected tears came into Alice's eyes and she reached out and grabbed hold on one of Frevisse's hands, saying, "Oh, Frevisse, then you know. I'm so frightened I don't know anymore if what I do and decide is driven by fear or reason. That's why I need your help. We have to decide how much more to trust to this Joliffe, and I don't know, I simply and just don't know . . ."

Chapter 11

he afternoon was clouding over. The parlor had been warm with light a little while ago but was gathering gray shadows now, and Joliffe, standing at the window, said without turning his head, "It's likely coming on to rain."

Vaughn, still seated at the low table behind him, shuffling the cards with which they'd mostly passed their time, made a meaningless sound, and the heavy silence fell again between them.

They had tried through the past hours to find a way around their several days of distrust into a semblance of ease between them. They had tried talk, Joliffe asking if Vaughn had been long in Suffolk's service, to which Vaughn said tersely, "I grew up in her grace's service and have never wanted other."

Joliffe noted he had made plain he had served Lady Alice, not the duke. Was that a new distinction, meant to distance himself from Suffolk, or something he held to out of a long dislike of the man?

"What of you?" Vaughn had returned. "Have you been York's man for long?"

"Only a few years." If he stretched a point.

Vaughn had cocked a curious look at him. "These few years haven't been the best of times to take service with someone like York."

"No," Joliffe had agreed. These past few years were in fact a very foolish time to have taken service with a man so openly fallen from royal favor as York; but he had added nothing to his single word, and their talk had mostly ended there, neither of them ready to give away more or trust each other further.

They had tried chess next, because Vaughn knew where a battered board with plain wooden pieces was kept in an aumbry built into one wall of the room—"Not good enough to pack up and take whenever the household moves on," he said as he brought it out—but they were neither of them much good at the game. After one game, that Vaughn stumbled into winning with neither of them quite sure how, they turned to cards with a battered pack from the same aumbry. They had laid the cards out to be sure none were missing, found they were all there, and settled to the least challenging games they both knew, where the shuffling, sorting, and slapping down of cards occupied the mind without need for much actual thought about it.

Getting drunk would have served the same purpose but taken longer and been less quickly recovered from. Besides, they had only the weak ale that Vaughn had brought from the kitchen when he fetched their midday meal.

The little cautious talk they tried between games had gone nowhere, and now late afternoon was come and the

weather was turning and restlessness was creeping up on Joliffe. He could put up a seeming of patience if he had to but
never fooled himself for very long, and he was relieved to
hear a light footfall in the neighboring room where no one
had been all day. He turned toward the door with what
might have been betraying quickness except Vaughn was
rising from the table just as quickly. But they had done no
more than that when Lady Alice came in without troubling
to knock—she being lady here, and everything hers, she
went where she wanted, when she wanted—and both men
bowed, Vaughn saying, "My lady."

"Nicholas," she answered. And stiffly, "Master Noreys."

Joliffe had already noted how "Master" came and went
with her opinion of him. That he was "Master Noreys" again
was probably a sign to the good.

It was surely to the good, too, that Dame Frevisse was
with her, closing the door behind them. With her plain
black Benedictine habit and quiet manner she was like a
shadow to her cousin's more richly garbed widowhood and
bold readiness to make use of her own high place in the
world. But Joliffe knew better than to take those outward
seemings at their outward value. Just as Dame Frevisse
knew him better than he wished she did, he knew that behind
her downcast eyes a sharp mind kept busy. That sometimes
had been to his good, sometimes to his discomfort but never
to his ill, he reminded himself.

As for Lady Alice . . . With the quickness that had served
him well when he was altogether a player and had helped to
keep him alive a few other times, he took in what Lady Alice's
face and body told him about her. She was frightened, and
meant to hide it behind her graceful bearing but her voice
was taut behind her words as she said to him and Vaughn together, "There's another matter I've decided you should know.
I've come to the end of what I can do about it and hope maybe
one or the other of you has some useful thought."

"If we may, my lady," Vaughn said with a bow that Joliffe slightly echoed.

Crisp with an anger she did not trouble to hide, maybe hoping it would serve to hide her fear, she told how and why she thought her husband, at the end, had written out an accusation in damnable detail against those who had agreed together to lose Normandy.

Joliffe's first thought, as he grasped what she was telling him, was disbelief that any man could be so great a fool. Had Suffolk ever seen further than the reach of his own narrow feelings, to want that kind of revenge on his fellows at the cost of what it would bring down upon his son and wife? Plainly his wife believed him capable of such a fool's play, and that well-accounted for her fear.

For Richard of York, though, this thing would be a godsend. It could be the weapon he needed against whatever men around the king were trying to bring him down; and as Lady Alice finished, he asked, to be sure, "You think, then, there were more men agreed to the business than Suffolk and Somerset?"

"Yes." She said the word as if she hated it. Or merely her husband? "Almost surely."

"But you don't know where this accusation is, or even if it was ever written."

"Nothing like it has shown up among any of my lord husband's things that were returned to me. But neither has his secretary returned either, and he's the man most likely to know whether or not this thing ever was."

"You're certain he's someone his grace of Suffolk would have trusted that far?" Joliffe asked.

"Yes."

"Even with something like that?" he persisted.

Curtly Lady Alice said again, "Yes. One has to trust someone, sometimes. My lord husband trusted Edward Burgate."

And presently she hated having to trust Joliffe and he

was scarcely happier trusting her, but he hid that and said, "As it stands, then, there may or may not be an accusation that this secretary may or may not have either written or at least known about, and presently you know neither where this secretary is or if he's alive or dead."

"I pray to God he still lives," Lady Alice said curtly.

"What you want, then, my lady, is to find this secretary and to learn what he knows. Want *us* to find him," he corrected, including Vaughn.

"Yes.

"Because if there is an accusation all written out and signed and sealed by your late husband," said Joliffe—and did not add aloud, God rot him, "then it would serve both you and my lord of York to have it. Because whoever was in this business with Suffolk—Somerset for certain and whoever else there might have been—they're surely among my lord of York's enemies around the king and are someone, or someones, likely to prove equally your foe if they're free to lay all the blame for Normandy on Suffolk, should things come to that."

"Yes."

"What crosses my mind is what guarantee have I that, should your man and I find this secretary, I won't end up dead and my lord of York out of luck in the matter? Since you've assuredly considered that he could use this accusation against your interests as well as against whoever else was part of it."

"A point well put," Lady Alice granted crisply, "and one you'd do well to keep in mind if you were dealing with my late husband in anything. But he was a treacherous cur and I pray to all the saints that I am not."

Her blunt bitterness startled Joliffe and, by their faces, Dame Frevisse and Vaughn, as well; but Lady Alice went on, to only him and still bitterly, "Listen, Master Noreys. There are too many people glad to have Suffolk out of their way. If Somerset doesn't grab his place next to the king, others will be trying to. My son is too young for anything but to be shoved aside, and in myself I have very little power. The most I really hope for is to be given control of his wardship and marriage, but I've no guarantee of those. They could as easily be given to someone else and my son taken completely away from me. Your duke of York is neither my rival nor my enemy. I'd keep him that way. Even more, I think he and I would be best served, the both of us, in making common cause together, and this—through you—looks my best way to that."

"How do you know my lord of York won't betray you, use whatever this is to bring on Suffolk's attainder and ruin your son anyway?"

That was possibly a fool's challenge to make, but better to have it in the open than lurking, since it had to be something she had already thought of; and she asked straight back at him, "Do you think York is that sort of man? To ruin a child for revenge on its father?"

"No." Joliffe's answer came on the instant and without need for thought. "I think my lord of York has more honor in his little finger than Somerset in his whole body."

Bitter humour flickered up in Lady Alice's eyes. "I think that, too. That's York's weakness in dealing with those around the king." She paused, perhaps bracing herself for the next before she went on, "You spoke about the use of a marriage alliance. If this matter ends well, I will indeed be more than willing to a marriage between one of his daughters and John."

Since they seemed to be dealing so openly, Joliffe asked, "What if my lord of York uses this supposed accusation to bring down Somerset, and Suffolk's part in it becomes known?"

"We can hope it will not come to that. I doubt it would serve the government well to have everything made known.

Let York show it to the king and to the chancellor. That should be enough to shift Somerset, and whoever else was part of it, out of royal favor and keep them there."

It should be, yes, Joliffe inwardly granted. It should likewise put paid to whoever around the king was trying to build a case of treason against York, which was an even more immediate need; and he said, "Well enough. Do you have any thought how I should go about searching for this Burgate? Or learning what's happened to him?"

"Master Vaughn can tell you what he's learned thus far toward finding him," Lady Alice said, with a look at Vaughn that gave him leave to speak.

He promptly did, saying, "Unhappily, it's mostly what has not been learned. He was set ashore at Dover with the rest of my lord of Suffolk's household. That's the last we know of him."

"Nothing else?" Joliffe asked. Somehow he had not expected them to know less than he did.

"Everything was in disorder. Some of the men were keeping watch over my lord of Suffolk's body on the beach, waiting for the crowner and sheriff to come. Some left to take word to my lady and elsewhere. Some just left, wanting to get away from the business altogether. Burgate did neither of the first two things, and I've failed to find that he did the last."

"No," said Joliffe. "But there's report he was taken into custody at Dover, maybe by a royal officer, maybe not."

"Arrested you mean?" Lady Alice said, as Vaughn demanded, "How do you know that?"

Joliffe answered Vaughn first, with a smile that probably made Vaughn like him none the better. "Because we have someone there better at learning things than you have?" Before Vaughn could make answer to that, he turned to Lady Alice and went on, "No, not outright arrested, it seems, or there would be some record of it. It's more as if he was taken in hand and hasn't been seen since. He seems gone from Dover, though."

"So it's not that he's willfully disappeared," Lady Alice said.

"Why would he want to disappear anyway?" Dame Frevisse asked. "Presumably taking this supposed accusation with him."

"To make the accusation disappear with him?" Joliffe suggested.

"If there's such a thing exists at all," Dame Frevisse reminded them.

"Can you think of another reason why he should disappear—by choice or otherwise—other than that he knows or has, or had, something worth disappearing for?" Joliffe asked.

"No, that wouldn't be Burgate's way," Lady Alice said unhappily. " Someone has to have . . . disposed of him."

"Or the man that reported him being taken was wrong," said Vaughn with a hard look at Joliffe. "It seems an uncertain enough report at best."

"What have your questions turned up about him?" Joliffe returned, not in challenge but simply to know.

"That no man of his description hired a horse in Dover," Vaughn answered stiffly. "On the chance he had walked away, I had questions asked after him at ports along the coast in both directions and at the nearby inland towns. There's no word that he hired passage overseas or bought or hired a horse or stopped at any inn or tavern or was seen by anyone at all."

"So however he left Dover, it wasn't by any reasonable means," Joliffe said. "We want unreasonable, then."

"Secretly carried off and held somewhere," Vaughn said. "As your report suggests."

"Or simply killed," said Dame Frevisse, "and his body unfound."

"And all hope gone of learning what he knew, one way or

the other," Lady Alice said, "until I learn the hard way, when someone uses the accusation against me." Her words hardened. "I need to know for certain whether this thing is or is not, and if it is, whether it's safe or in someone else's hands."

"You're presuming Burgate wouldn't make use of it for his own gain," Joliffe said. "Sell it to the highest bidder for money or favor."

"He wouldn't," Lady Alice said with flat refusal of the thought.

Quickly, as if to cut off any protest Joliffe might make to that, Vaughn said, "I judge the only place we have much hope of finding out anything is among people near the king, since questions elsewhere have gone nowhere."

"What of family or friends he might have?" Joliffe asked.

"None," Vaughn answered; then added, "None I know of."

"Nor I," Lady Alice said. "It's why he was free to go abroad with my lord husband."

The man might have been specially made to disappear without track or trace, Joliffe thought disgustedly; but aloud he agreed with Vaughn, saying, "Then people around the king it will have to be. That's where we're most likely to find anyone who could be threatened by whatever Suffolk knew." He looked to Lady Alice. "You've surely a spy or two in your service in the royal household keeping an ear out for any talk that way."

"My 'privy friends' in the king's household," she said, using the more courteous term but with a mocking edge, "have reported nothing. They've heard nothing that might be about him or in particular against me. Or at least not at last report from them."

"What about the queen's household?" Dame Frevisse said.

"The queen's household?" Lady Alice was surprised. "She'd have no part in Burgate having vanished. She's not even with King Henry now. The last I heard the king was at Westminster with I don't know which lords, while she's still at Kenilworth, safely away from the worst that's been going in the south and around London."

"She doesn't have to have anything to do with Burgate vanishing," Dame Frevisse said. "Her household is simply one more place someone of your spies might have heard something."

No courteous "privy friends" for her, Joliffe noted.

"Yes," Lady Alice granted slowly. "Among her women, maybe. Women talk."

"And women have lovers who talk," said Joliffe. "Maybe about Burgate."

"Word could pass that way from the king's household to hers, yes," Lady Alice said.

"Could you go there, to the queen?" Dame Frevisse asked her. "You're fairly much her friend, and you'd be best placed to ask questions about your own man."

Lady Alice shook her head. "That would be the simplest way, but I've been given widow's leave from court, to gather up my life and spend my grieving. It would look very odd for me to suddenly return. I'd be very wondered about and there would be too much heed taken of any questions I asked."

"Send Dame Frevisse, then," said Joliffe.

Dame Frevisse said harshly, "No," as Lady Alice said, "That's possible. Yes."

"No," Dame Frevisse repeated with an angry look at Joliffe. "It wouldn't. I've no reason to be there."

"To take my greetings to her grace and give her my hope that she's doing well," Lady Alice said. "You can say you came to tell her that I'm well enough and that I'm praying for her and King Henry in all these troubles. I'll write her a letter for you to put into her hand. That will serve to get you into the heart of the household, and once you're there . . ."

"Alice," Dame Frevisse said, warning in her voice.

". . . you can ask questions without making much of them. And besides and more than anything, you see things differently than others do. You hear more than people say and see things others of us don't."

"And you're a nun," Vaughn said. "Who will suspect a nun?"

Joliffe held back from saying he would, if it was *this* nun; instead he said as if it were settled, "I'll be part of her escort to Kenilworth. I can ask questions of my own there."

"Better you keep your distance from my lady's business," Vaughn said. "There's too much chance someone will know you for York's man."

"A point well taken," Joliffe granted with a slight, agreeing bow.

"Nicholas will go," Lady Alice said. "He's known as mine. He'll be able to ask questions and make talk among the lesser people around the queen with no one likely to think twice about it."

"And afterwards," Dame Frevisse said stiffly, "he'll see Sister Margrett and me back to St. Frideswide's, because by then we'll have been long enough away."

Before Lady Alice could answer that one way or another, Joliffe put in, "And I'll meet them either on their way there or at the priory, to find out what they've learned."

Lady Alice's sharp look back and forth between them told she understood what they both were saying behind their outward words—that Dame Frevisse would do this much for her but then was done, and that he expected to be set free now. Their demands did not please her, but she said crisply, "Well enough," accepting them.

"With Joliffe to be let free to go about his own business in the meanwhile," Dame Frevisse said, to be sure that was clear.

For which he must remember to thank her, Joliffe thought, as Lady Alice said almost angrily, "Yes."

"And he might as well go now," Dame Frevisse said. "To have him out of the way."

And out of Lady Alice's temptation to keep him after all?

Joliffe wondered. Had Dame Frevisse lost that much confidence in her cousin? But careful to show none of that thought, he bowed to Lady Alice and said, all pleasantly, "I'll go at once, then, by your leave. If I may have my horse and gear again?"

Making a small movement of one hand at Vaughn, Lady Alice said, "See to it."

Vaughn bowed and left the room. Straightening from his own bow, Joliffe met Dame Frevisse's look for one long, unsmiling moment between them before he left, too, wondering as he went what that look had meant.

Chapter 12

Frevisse saw Joliffe from the room with relief. She doubted he would have been content to stay quietly a prisoner if Alice had decided to keep him; but with both men gone she was left alone with Alice, who looked at her from a distance greater than the few feet between them and said, "Satisfied?" Then added, more than halfway to accusation, "You'll be as glad as he is to be gone. And the more glad not to come back."

Under the bitterness there was hurt that Frevisse would have eased if she could, but denial would be a lie. All she could offer was, "Alice, this isn't where I belong."

"It isn't," Alice agreed sharply and moved away to the table where cards still lay where the men had dropped them. Beginning to gathering the cards together, she said, "Sister

Margrett has at least enjoyed John's company, I think. You've enjoyed nothing and can barely wait to be away."

Because neither a lie nor the truth were any good to Alice just now, Frevisse held silent.

Finished with gathering and tidying the cards into her hands, Alice dropped them into a scatter on the tabletop and turned around to Frevisse again. "It frightens me I didn't think sooner that the queen's household was somewhere else to ask questions. I simply set her aside from everything that's happening."

"It's because she's been set aside in Kenilworth safely away from everything," Frevisse said. "Of course you'd look to around the king, where everything is happening."

"But I know better than that. She's not a nothing. There's constant come and go between the households. It frightens me whenever I find my mind has failed me that badly."

Glad for the chance to be kind as well as truthful, Frevisse offered, "You've had too much of too many things in your mind of late. Mind and heart are both tired."

"My heart." Alice dismissed that with a quick, sideways jerk of one hand. "I gave up living by my heart years ago. It's too treacherous a thing to trust."

There was more bitterness than truth in that, but Frevisse did not challenge her. Sometimes bitterness was the only shelter left. Just so long as it did not become a permanent dwelling.

"But, Frevisse, if my wits have started to fail me," Alice said with raw despair, "I'm finished. They're all I have. What else besides the queen haven't I thought of, that I should have?"

"You can go mad wondering that," Frevisse said. "Better that you simply hope that if you haven't thought of it, it's because there's no reason or need to think of it yet."

"Frevisse, I'm so tired." Alice paced away from her toward the window, rubbing her fingertips into her forehead where it showed in the tight circle of her wimple. "I'm just so tired."

"With all you've done and had done to you," Frevisse said gently, "tired is the least of what you are. Presently, while there's chance, with nothing more you can do for now, why not rest? Play with John, or read, or walk in the gardens. Sleep," she added as afterthought. The gray under Alice's eyes betrayed how much she needed that.

As if rest were another thought that had not come to her until now, Alice said with surprise, "I should. Especially the sleep. Even if I have to give myself a sleeping draught to do it." They were both looking out the window, not at each other; and still looking out, Alice went on, "If by some wonder you should find Burgate and he's unable—or unwilling—to return to me, at least ask if he knows where the account roll for the manor of Cockayne might be."

Left behind by Alice's sideways shift of thought—the more so because "Cockayne" was only an imagined place used in stories—Frevisse said blankly, "What?"

"The account roll for Cockayne. That way he'll know you're truly from me. It was something between Suffolk and I, to be sure a message was truly by one of us. Where the account roll 'might be'. Those words."

"Where the account roll for the manor of Cockayne might be," Frevisse repeated. "I'll remember." Trying to sound as if she believed he *would* be found and she was not on a fool's errand to Kenilworth.

The next morning was sweet with a soft rain under gently gray clouds. "Not the best of traveling weather but not the worst, either," Sister Margrett said while she and Frevisse waited in the shelter of the great hall's porch for the horses to be brought. Their farewells to Lady Alice were made, but while Frevisse's thoughts still lingered on regret that their parting had been stiff with damaged trust, Sister Margrett was already looking eagerly ahead.

"John will miss you," Frevisse had said when telling her they would be leaving.

"And I shall miss him." Sister Margrett had suddenly smiled. "But to see Kenilworth and the queen! *That* will be something to tell at St. Frideswide's!"

Frevisse would gladly leave all the telling of it to her if only, please God, they could be back in St. Frideswide's soon.

Sister Margrett's other thought had been that they might well reach Northampton, where her family lived, by their second night. "We'll have to stay at St. Bartholomew's of course." Their priory's parent-abbey, not far from Northampton. "But my folk could come see me there before we ride on. Or we could maybe visit them?"

"We'll visit them, surely," Frevisse promised, willing to make someone happy about something. "But we're not to stay a night at Northampton. The second night we're to be somewhat this side of it, at a place called Rushden. Lady Alice has us taking a gift of pheasants to the Treshams there." And two brace of rabbits to Kenilworth. It seemed Queen Margaret was uncommonly fond of rabbit in a sweet sauce of wine and spices.

"The Treshams?" Sister Margrett had asked. "William Tresham that's been Speaker in Parliament all those times?"

"Several times, I gather, yes."

"But . . ." Sister Margrett had paused with a puzzled frown of thought and a quick glance as if to be sure they were alone, though they had been in their bedchamber at the time. ". . . my mother said at her Easter visit this year that he was Speaker this past winter when Parliament brought down the duke of Suffolk. Why would Lady Alice . . ."

What Alice had said, when Frevisse had asked her much the same, was, "Master Tresham did what his duty required of him. He dealt honestly in the matter, and I don't choose to

belittle either him or myself by holding that against him."
She had lifted her chin and added somewhat defiantly, "Besides, his wife is my friend and I don't choose to forget it."

Frevisse gave only the latter part of that answer to Sister
Margrett. "His wife is a friend of Lady Alice's." Then had
added, as Alice had, "There's this, though. Master Tresham
is not in favor with people around the king and queen for
what he did. At Kenilworth, it may be best if we say nothing about having stayed there."

Sister Margrett had understood that with blessed quickness and said only, "Oh. Yes."

Now, as Sister Margrett was saying she thought the rain
was slackening, Vaughn came to tell them the men were
ready and the horses being brought. Only Vaughn and three
other men were to accompany them, the hope being that
with so few riders—and if the weather went no worse and all
else went well—they would make good time, and they did,
Vaughn keeping them to a mile-passing pattern of walk to
trot to walk again, with occasional brief gallops on better
stretches of road and the weather clearing by early afternoon.

Because both Frevisse and Sister Margrett had been to
Bury St. Edmunds, had already seen the saint's gold and be-
jeweled shrine in the great abbey church there, neither felt
need to stop for it and willingly rode straight through the
town's wend of streets and market crowds, satisfied with
sight of the abbey's sky-scraping spire before their road bent
away, leaving it behind them; and in late afternoon they
came down from the gentle roll of hills into the marshy lev-
els toward Cambridge and not much before twilight stopped
for the night at a small Benedictine nunnery in time to join
the nuns for Vespers in the church. That while of prayer and
praise—the familiar words said and sung in the enwrapping
certainty of a church among other women living their lives
to the same pattern as her own mostly was—was like balm
laid over the raw edges of Frevisse's worry and thoughts. She

let herself sink deep into the peace as the women chanted, trading verse for verse back and forth across the choir—*Domine, salvum fac regem. Et exaudi nos in die, qua invocaverimus te. . . . Fiat Pax in virtute tua. Et abundantia in turribus tuis. . . . Retribuere dignare, Domine, omnibus, nobis bona facientibus propter nomen tuum, vitam aeternam. . . .* Lord, make safe the king. And hear us in the day that we call to you. . . . Create peace in your strength. And abundance in your towers. . . . Deign to repay, Lord, to all of us doing good in your name, eternal life. . . .

For the sake of avoiding questions, she and Sister Margrett did not join the nuns for their evening hour of recreation but pleaded weariness and a need to rest, only rejoining them for Compline before going to their beds in the nunnery's guesthall. They awoke there in the middle of the night when the cloister bell rang its simple summons and returned to the church for Matins and Lauds, with Frevisse praying from the heart, *"Dignare, Domine, die isto sine peccato nos custodire. Miserere nostri, Domine, miserere nostri. Fiat misericordia tua, Domine, super nos, quemadmodum speravimus in te. In te, Domine, speravi: non confundar in aeternam."* Deign, Lord, for this day to keep us without sin. Pity us, Lord, pity us. Have your mercy, Lord, on us, as we have hoped in you. In you, Lord, I have hoped: let me not be confounded forever.

With every Office, with every prayer and psalm of pleading and praise, the tight binding of worry Frevisse had carried with her these past days loosened a little more. What she could do, she would do. Beyond that, all was in God's hands, and—returned to bed after Lauds—she fell to sleep more easily than she had been able to for some few past nights.

Vaughn showed he was not best pleased that in the morning she and Sister Margrett said Prime with the nuns before riding on, but to his good he did not try to make up the time by pushing their pace any harder than he had yesterday. They kept to the same rhythm of walk and trot and gallop, and the miles went by. Cambridge's crowded streets slowed them somewhat, but beyond there the level roads through open countryside of wide pasturelands made for unhindered riding. At St. Neot's they crossed a river by way of a timber bridge—always to be preferred to a ferry or fording—but farther on the land began to rise into hills more definite than the ones they had ridden out of yesterday. That slowed their going, but there was still goodly daylight left when they reached the stone-built market town of Higham Ferrers and Vaughn turned them south toward the Treshams' manor at Rushden. He knew the way, so no time was wasted in asking it, and very soon they turned down from the highway and rode through a small parkland and an open gateway into the foreyard of a manor house with its surround of stables and other buildings.

All was far less fine than Wingfield—its hall smaller and older, the spread of buildings less—but the gates stood open in welcome, and because Vaughn had sent one of the men ahead to warn of their coming, someone had been watching for them, and Master and Mistress Tresham came from the enclosed stone foreporch to greet them as they drew rein. A servant came from the stable, too, to lead their men and horses away while the Treshams greeted Frevisse, Sister Margrett, and Vaughn with the hope their ride had been easy and questions of how Lady Alice was when they left her, and saw them into the house. Because Vaughn was there in Lady Alice's name, he was being given something of the courtesy that would have been hers and went with them, through the great hall to the solar where wine and small, freshly made, berry cakes were waiting.

The Treshams were much as Frevisse remembered them from the few times she had met them in Alice's company: Master Tresham a well-mannered man in his fine later middle years, aware of his own wits and worth without need to wear them heavily for the world to see; Mistress Tresham graciously well-matched to her husband in years and wits and worth and manners. While her husband asked Vaughn questions about their journey and for what news he might have, Mistress Tresham soon asked Frevisse and Sister Margrett if they should care to ready for supper, and having drawn promise from Master Tresham that, yes, he would see Vaughn to his room in just a few minutes, she led Frevisse and Sister Margrett upstairs to a pleasant chamber from which someone looked to have been hurriedly removed.

When Frevisse said as much, Mistress Tresham admitted with a smile, "Our son. Thomas. He has his own home now, at another of our manors, Sywell, not far away. His wife died last year and his little boy is staying with us. We're dealing for another marriage for him, but meanwhile he comes to see Jack, which means we get to see more of him. The only trouble," she warned, half-laughing, "is that he and his father go on at each other at length over where the rights and wrongs of the world lie. They're not of one mind about it, and best I warn you, because you'll probably have to listen to them at supper. I'll send someone for you when it's time to go down, and leave you in peace until then."

She withdrew, and Frevisse and Sister Margrett used the respite to wash their faces and hands and say a hurried Vespers before a serving woman came to lead them downstairs, back to the solar again. The Treshams dined in the newer fashion—apart from their household, the great hall left to their servants while they were private in the solar. Like all else at Rushden, the meal was done with quiet grace, served with no great show but with no lessening of courtesy. There was an ease to it all that told here were a man and wife who had made choices about their life and were well-pleased with it.

Rushden might be less fine than Wingfield, but there was the quiet sense of family and a well-loved home that told that here "less" was no loss. Certainly neither Master nor Mistress Tresham showed any sign of thwarted ambitions, only the grace of people pleased with their lives.

Their son Thomas was something of another matter, Frevisse covertly noted. Much about Vaughn's age, he had all the bearing of a young man ready to be ambitious in the world. His manners were faultless but he joined in his father's and Vaughn's talk with a restless eagerness. When Mistress Tresham had again asked after Lady Alice, this time in caring detail, and Frevisse had told what she could, Sister Margrett asked about Mistress Tresham's grandson, and while they shared stories of him and Alice's young John, Frevisse listened to the men's talk. Master Tresham and Vaughn were past sharing reports of how things were elsewhere to sharing their thoughts on matters, with Thomas joining in strongly, until Master Tresham said somewhat sharply at him, "That's a fairly simple view of matters."

"Simple?" Thomas protested. "Do you truly think the Commons have boiled up over half of England all of their own? That there's no one was behind it?"

"What's behind it are a few years too many of wrongs gone on so long and deep that men were finally goaded into rebellion to make someone listen to them," Master Tresham returned. "No one has to be 'behind it'. However ill-guidedly, most of these rebels are no more than trying to better things."

"They may honestly think that's what they're doing, the most of them," Thomas said. He reached out and tapped a firm forefinger against the table top. "But I tell you they're being used. Behind everything, it's York has stirred them up."

"York," Master Tresham scoffed. "Name me one thing—*one thing*—York has ever done that shows he's treacherous."

"He wants the crown. That's a certainty."

"Certain for whom? He's never made a single move that

way. You can't name one thing he's done that says he's out to have it. Unless you've learned to read his unsaid thoughts and found it there, you're . . ."

"You don't have to read unsaid thoughts to know what's in them. What about . . ." Thomas had taken up a spoon to add ginger sauce over the portion of roast chicken in front of him but forgot himself and was waggling it at his father instead. His mother cleared her throat delicately, without directly looking at him. Thomas paused, said, "Pardon," laid down the spoon, and went on but no less intensely, "What about last April? That shipman, in Stony Stratford when King Henry was passing through on his way to Leicester. That fellow who beat the ground with a flail and yelled that York would do the same to traitors when he came back from Ireland. What of that?"

"You can't condemn York because a half-mad fellow—and how much in the way of wits can a shipman in Leicester, days away from any coast, have about him?—rants his name in the public street. 'There's many talk of Robin Hood who never drew a bow.' These claims that York's behind these risings is as much a fable as 'Robin Hood' is. Just because there's talk doesn't make a thing true."

"Then why is he named time and again?" Thomas demanded. "In this Jack Cade's demands, for one?"

"If you'd read those demands instead of only listening to your friends around the king mouth about them, you'd know the demand was for York to be acknowledged King Henry's heir. Which he *is* and that can't be changed until King Henry has a son, may God and the Blessed Virgin bless him that way soon."

"Ah!" Thomas exclaimed, triumphant. "Arrow to the target's heart! Let York be declared the king's heir and the next thing you know he'll have King Henry dead."

"That's like saying a son, because it's known he'll inherit

when his father dies, is beyond doubt planning his father's murder," Master Tresham said scornfully. "No." He raised a hand, forestalling his son's answer to that. "There's no ground to hold York guilty of anything except being born with royal blood, which is hardly his fault. You show me one thing you can prove he's done . . ."

"These rebellions aren't just happening," Thomas insisted. "Someone is behind them. Someone is the head of it all. Like with the body, take care of the head . . ." He made a slicing motion with the side of his hand across his throat. ". . . and the rest will settle quickly enough. I say it's York needs to be . . ." He made the slicing gesture again.

"And I say," Master Tresham returned as strongly, "that York is the one lord I've seen who's done his every duty honorably these past years and at cost to himself, not gain. Chopping York won't cure the wrongs that have been done or solve people's angers. What's needed is for the king to face up to all the wrongs there've been, satisfy the Commons of their just complaints, and give justice where justice is due and punishment where it's been earned. And it hasn't been *York* who's done aught that needs punishing."

Thomas opened his mouth toward answering that, but his mother said with the calm of a woman used to an ongoing debate, "And now we'll find something else to talk about over our meal's end and this very good wine from Normandy. Our steward was fortunate with it. It's from a cask from one of the last shipments out of Caen."

Her firm turn of their talk took them to easier matters and by unspoken agreement they all kept the rest of their talk that evening no further afield than the likelihood the weather would hold for the next few days; some mild questions about St. Frideswide's and interest in the priory's scrivening business; advice from Mistress Tresham on which of the queen's ladies would most want to hear truly how

Lady Alice was for friendship's sake; the discovery that the Treshams knew Sister Margrett's father, a draper in Northampton—had bought the new hangings around their bed from him two years ago. The great troubles of the world were left to fend for themselves, even by Thomas. Only as Mistress Tresham was leading Frevisse and Sister Margrett to their bedchamber by candlelight did she comment on her son, saying not so much in apology as rueful explanation, "We maybe set him into the king's household too young. Or maybe he simply read too many stories of chivalry while he was growing up." She laughed a little. "He's determined he's one of the queen's true knights, ready to stand in her cause against the world."

"Is so much of the world against her?" Frevisse asked, matching Mistress Tresham's lightness.

"Not that I've heard. But what's the use of being the queen's true knight if you can't protect her against something?"

Still smiling, she left them to their good night's sleep and in the morning, after a plain breaking of their night's fast and thanks given all around—by Frevisse and Sister Margrett for the Treshams' courtesy in receiving them so well and by the Treshams for the nuns' courtesy in stopping there—they rode on their way.

Vaughn again sent one of their men ahead, this time to let Sister Margrett's family know she would soon be there, and despite they made good time, the road easily following a river valley between pasture and open fields, by the time they reached Northampton on its strong rise of ground and rode along and around and into a street near the marketplace, not only Sister Margrett's parents were waiting to greet her at their door, but her brothers and sister, their spouses and children, and a solid score of various other kin whom Frevisse did not try to sort out in the two hours spent with them and with much talk and food and drink, until Sister Margrett said they must ride on.

That saved Frevisse or Vaughn being the villain in breaking up the happy family gathering, for which Frevisse thanked Sister Margrett as they rode away by the Warwick road.

Sister Margrett gave a forceful sigh. "I love them dearly but, dear goodness, there's a great many of them. It will be so good to be back in St. Frideswide's. Mind you, memories of the fine foods at your cousin's may trouble my mealtimes for a while, and St. Frideswide's is going to seem so small and quiet, but still, it will be good to be back. Enough is enough, after all. Except . . ." She turned her head to give Frevisse a shrewd look past the edge of her veil. ". . . I don't know what's troubling you and only hope it doesn't come back into St. Frideswide's with us."

That startled Frevisse, before she realized she had small reason to be startled. She knew she had not been hiding her worries very well; knew, too, that Sister Margrett was no fool: she had to have been seeing more than she had chosen to say. And Sister Margrett went lightly on, freeing Frevisse from need to answer, saying, "At least the weather has been good for most of our journeying."

They lost that good weather by mid-afternoon. The air turning sullen and heavy under thickening clouds, and a little beyond Daventry the rain began, sullen and heavy like the air, bringing no cooling with it, making worse that they had to put on their cloaks with the hoods up. The almost treeless fields to either side of the road blurred behind the screen of rain, the road turned slick under their horses' hoofs, and Vaughn brought his horse alongside of Frevisse to tell both her and Sister Margrett, "I'd hoped to reach Warwick for the night, because Kenilworth is an easy ride from there, but I'm thinking now we'd best stop at Southam. There's a good inn there."

Sister Margrett nodded strong agreement to that, and Frevisse said, "Yes. Very good," the more readily because she was in no great hurry to reach Kenilworth. Later tomorrow would serve as well as sooner for such a useless errand as this one.

Chapter 13

Two main roads crossed in Southam, with Northampton and Warwick opposite ways on one of them, Coventry and Oxford their two directions on the other. The inn was of a size and comfort in keeping with that, and after an ample supper followed by a good night's sleep, Frevisse was in better humour to face the next day than she had thought to be. The rain was done, the clouds were thinning toward a fair day as the sun rose, and as they mounted their horses in the innyard Frevisse could not help thinking that Banbury town was merely ten miles to the south of here and St. Frideswide's not far beyond it. If they turned that way, they could be there before . . .

"Twelve miles or so to go, my ladies," Vaughn said, gath-

ering up his reins. "With luck you'll be there not much after midday."

Frevisse took up her own reins and turned her horse to
follow him out of the innyard.

The day had cleared to open sunlight and few high-
drifting clouds by the time they approached Kenilworth's
rose-gray walls and towers. From atop the square bulk of the
Norman keep inside the walls, the queen's banner with her
heraldic arms of Anjou impaled with her husband's lifted
and fell in a small wind, showing crimson, blue, silver, gold.

"So she's still here," Vaughn said as they approached the
outer gateway with its double stone towers.

In surprise, Sister Margrett said, "They told us in Warwick that she was."

"They can say that in Warwick without knowing that she's
moved on without telling them first," Vaughn answered easily. "As it is, she's been here long enough she'll likely welcome what small change of talk you'll bring her."

He said that just as he turned his heed to the gate-
guards, leaving Sister Margrett and Frevisse looking at each
other, both unsettled at thought they might be supposed to
divert the queen, however slightly. They neither of them
said so, though, even to each other, while Vaughn explained
their business to the guard and showed his warrant as the
duchess of Suffolk's man. Given leave to pass, they rode on,
through the cool shadows of the long stone gateway arch
into the quarter-moon curve of the walled and garrisoned
yard that protected the next towered gateway.

There they had to wait while the guards jested with the
driver of a horse-pulled cart piled with hay before they let
him through, plainly someone they knew and about his expected business. They gave Vaughn hardly more trouble,
glanced at his warrant and waved him on. This time,
though, as they rode out the far end of the gateway arch both
Sister Margrett and Frevisse exclaimed and without thinking

drew rein to stare to either side of them, because rather than riding into another wall-circled yard, they were on a wide causeway raised on an earthen bank across a broad, shining-blue lake that spread away on both sides, curving around the rose-stoned castle walls where ahead of them another stone-towered gateway waited.

Vaughn, stopping his own horse, turned in his saddle and said, grinning, "It's something, isn't it?"

"It *is*," Sister Margrett answered almost breathlessly, while Frevisse nodded agreement. Most often, a castle's best outer defense was a steep-sided, grass-grown ditch, wide at the top, narrow at the bottom, meant to make assault by men and siege weapons difficult or, at best, impossible. This lake would serve the same purpose very well; and meanwhile served for pleasure: several shallow-bottomed boats were afloat on it, one with a man fishing, two others with several people in each, shaded under gaudy-painted canvas tilts, too far away on the bright lake to be certain what they did but looking as if merely easily drifting.

"Would the queen be out there?" Sister Margrett asked, wide-eyed.

"I'd say there'd be far more out there if she were," Vaughn said, and they rode on again.

Beyond the third gateway and its guards the castle's great yard opened in front of them, with all the many buildings needed to serve the castle's many needs—stables, storerooms, workshops, lodgings for lesser servants and workmen—and the great come-and-go of the many people to meet those needs. Ahead, the stone tower of the keep bulked high above it all beyond yet another wall that Frevisse supposed closed off an inner yard and royal chambers. As they neared the plain, untowered gateway through that wall, their man that Vaughn had sent ahead came forward to meet them from where he had been waiting on a bench in a stretch of shade along one building, and to Vaughn's, "All's well?" he answered, "No trouble. I've told the chamberlain you'd be here. He says the queen will likely see them sometime this afternoon."

"Good. We'll leave the horses to you and Symond, then. When they're stabled, you can bring our bags. My ladies."

The gateguard here nodded them through without a question, into a courtyard surrounded on three sides by long buildings of the same red stone as the rest of the castle. The solid square of the keep with its narrow windows bulked against the sky to their right, but the other buildings were lower, graceful with tall, stone-traceried windows and steep blue-slate roofs. Ahead was the great hall, its wide doorway framed in deeply carved stone at the head of a wide stone stairway. At one end a tall oriel window curved outward into the yard, while beyond it the other buildings curved around the yard. Vaughn's question to a passing servant in a livery doublet of green and white turned him and the nuns toward the keep and up an outer wooden stairway to go through a doorway set deep in the eight-foot thickness of the wall to a long room with tables and an array of men busy at writing on scrolls and papers or carrying other scrolls and papers from one place to another. This, Frevisse could see, was where the business of running the queen's household was done—the records kept and decisions made that let the queen and her people live in comfort and ease.

Vaughn clearly knew his way here. He and the man to whom he gave them over greeted each other by name before Vaughn left and Master Faber began to apologize there was nowhere near the queen's own chambers in the royal wing where they could be accommodated as they should in honor be, since that they came from the duchess of Suffolk. Still, there was a very good chamber here in the Strong Tower. If they would be pleased to come this way . . .

A stairway in the thickness of the wall took them another story higher in the keep to where several chambers were wood-partitioned out of what had been a single large space in the keep's younger days. "These are where the queen's gentlewomen stay," the man murmured. And the serving-women who wait on the gentlewomen, Frevisse thought. No, they were not being accommodated as they might have been, coming from the duchess of Suffolk; and although the plain, small chamber into which she and Sister Margrett were shown suited her own needs very well, she had to wonder how much it reflected a lessening of Alice's place at court that those who came in her name weren't given better than this. Was it truly that they "couldn't be"? Or was it something else?

Master Faber pointed out that the beds were freshly made for them and there was water for washing in the pitcher there and a clean towel apiece. He said he would have their bags brought up as soon as they came and there were women in and out all day if they had questions or needed help with anything.

"You'll be summoned when her grace is ready to see you and taken there when the time comes," he finished and bowed and left them.

Sister Margrett, looking somewhat overwhelmed, sat down on one of the two beds and said, "Oh, my." With which Frevisse, sitting down on the other bed, could only agree.

As it was, they had barely time to brush their habits clean, wash their faces and hands, and—after their saddle-bags were brought—put on fresh wimples before a woman came to fetch them. They were as ready as they could be and followed the woman from the keep and across the courtyard to one of the other, newer buildings. Up a wide stairway, they came into an upper chamber, where the woman turned rightward through a doorway framed in ornately carved stone, opening into a broad chamber that was clearly a great lord's—or lady's—reception room. Richly dressed men and women were crowded around it in talking clusters. On both sides rows of ceiling-tall windows rose stone-traceried into arches set with heraldicly painted glass in strong colors above, fully glazed with clear glass below to let in a plenitude of light and give view, on one side, into the courtyard, and over the surrounding lake and countryside on the other. Between the windows, the walls were a deep green painted over with patterns of yellow vines and bright-feathered birds, except at the chamber's far end where, ceiling to floor, hung a wide tapestry showing the royal arms of England— gold lions and lilies quartered on crimson and blue— against a sky of paler blue above white castle towers and green trees across the tapestry's lower half.

Centered below the tapestry was a wide and high-backed chair, painted and gilded and raised on the several steps of a square dais. It had all the seeming of a throne, and there could be no doubt that the young woman sitting upon it was surely the queen.

Margaret of Anjou had been sixteen years old when she came to England as King Henry's queen without either of them having ever seen the other. She was twenty-one now, and all the reasons for which the marriage had been made were failed. The truce with France that had come with her marriage was not only broken but the war it had stopped was lost, and doubt was growing by the month that she would ever produce the needed heir to the throne.

Frevisse could only hope there was a deep affection between her and her husband, to make the marriage worth the otherwise wasted cost of it.

And despite everything and worried though Queen Margaret surely was at the troubles presently tearing England, she sat with outward calm enough, her head bent slightly to one side as she listened to two lords in earnest talk with each other beside her. Because she was a queen, her fair hair, instead of caught up and covered out of sight like all other married women, was uncovered, swept back in smooth wings from her face and spread smooth and gleaming behind her shoulders, bound only by the thin circlet of a simple crown. She was dressed simply, too, in a green, open-sided surcoat over a fitted gown of soft rose . . . silk, Frevisse thought as the light slid sleekly along the cloth as Queen Margaret lifted an arm to draw the lords' heed to her. Both men turned to hear what she had to say, and the woman leading Frevisse and Sister Margrett stopped and said quietly, "She's with the duke of Buckingham and Sir Thomas Stanley just now. We'll have to wait."

She adroitly balanced her pronouncement of the noble and knightly names between a lightness that showed she was familiar with saying them and weight enough to impress these nuns with their good luck in seeing such men. Frevisse, having seen greater, was unimpressed, nor did Sister Margrett look to be over-set with awe. The daughter of a wealthy town merchant might well have had occasion to see and even meet lords before this, and certainly knights. And who was Sir Thomas Stanley, anyway? Because she truly did not know, Frevisse asked their guide who looked startled at her ignorance, then said in a quick, low voice and maybe with pity, "Oh, but of course you wouldn't know. He's an officer in the king's household and chamberlain of North Wales, too. And the duke of Buckingham. He's very close to the king, and wealthy. A very great lord."

In the same low voice, Sister Margrett asked, "Does it fret them that they're here instead with the king, seeing to rebels?"

"It's really my lord of Buckingham who has her grace in keeping. He's mindful of the honor," the woman said, much like a teacher delivering a lesson to a pupil. "There's no saying there won't be trouble hereabouts, you know. He has patrols out every day, keeping an eye on the countryside."

Queen Margaret laughed at something one of the men had said. Sir Thomas was laughing with her, but Buckingham was somewhat frowning, looking as if he had been left behind by their laughter.

"Sir Thomas Stanley isn't usually here, then?" Frevisse murmured.

"He's only just come. He's been with the king at Westminster and is on his way back to be sure of things in Wales."

"There's not report of rebellion there, too?" Frevisse asked. To have that at the king's back while he was facing down rebels in the south would not be good.

But the woman said easily, "Oh, there's nothing stirring there beyond the usual brawling among the Welsh. Not that I've heard anyway. Sir Thomas says the Welsh haven't the wits for more than that and sheep-thievery."

Then Sir Thomas Stanley was a fool, Frevisse thought. It wasn't that long since Owen Glendower's great rebellion had nearly thrown the English for well and good out of all their Welsh fortresses and lands in a rebellion that had taken a king, a royal prince, several thousands of men, and too many years to put down.

The two men moved to in front of the queen and bowed to her.

"They're done," the woman said as, smiling, Queen Margaret held out her hand to Sir Thomas, who bowed again to kiss it. Then they backed three steps away from her, slightly bowed again, turned, and started toward the doorway where Frevisse, Sister Margrett, and the woman stood. The woman quickly shooed Frevisse and Sister Margrett aside, but Frevisse took the chance to have close look at both men as they came. The duke of Buckingham was the older of the two, with a long, heavily boned face and every seeming of someone who would go solidly forward with his duty but hardly be a lighthearted companion to a queen young enough to be his daughter.

If so, that was to the good, because with the power that might be in her hands, a queen—and especially a young one—needed advice and guidance more than she needed merry companions.

Of course, for the health of mind and spirit, diversion in right measure and of right kind was likewise needed, and for that Sir Thomas looked a more likely source. Like Buckingham, he was some years older than the queen but there was a soft-fleshed ease to him that promised readier merriment than looked likely from the duke. He might do his duty as it came, but Frevisse suspected he would have more high-hearted sport about it while he did.

Or low-hearted, if he were a baser sort of man.

She found she suddenly felt old and very possibly dull under the burden of such heavy thoughts. She was in danger of becoming nothing but tedious, she thought.

The two men passed, in talk to each other and through the doorway without giving any heed to the women's curtsies, and their guide said as they straightened from them, "We can go forward now. She's beckoning."

Approaching the dais, Frevisse expected to see sign of the summer's worries on Queen Margaret when they were nearer, but her youth served her well. Her fair-and-rose face was unmarred by frown or worry, and when Frevisse and Sister Margrett and their guide had risen from deep curtsies in front of her, she waved the woman aside and leaned forward with a welcoming smile, saying eagerly, "You're from my very dear Lady Alice? Her cousin, yes?"

She looked rapidly back and forth between them, and Sister Margrett faded back half a step as Frevisse moved forward and said, with another deep, acknowledging curtsy, "I am, your grace."

"We have met . . ." Queen Margaret lightly frowned, then said, delighted probably more at her remembrance than over the meeting itself. "Bury St. Edmunds. Yes."

"Indeed, your grace," Frevisse agreed. There had been another time, too, but it had been very brief and full of blood and deaths, and if Queen Margaret had never heard her named as part of it, Frevisse was more than content to keep it that way.

"How is it with my Lady Alice?" Queen Margaret asked with true concern. "She grieves, I know."

"She does, but sends her most good wishes for your health and happiness, your grace, and bade me say she greatly misses your company."

"As I miss hers. And that of my lord of Suffolk. He was a good man. Her grief is ours. She has not been troubled by these *jacques*? These peasants?"

"There's been no rising where she is. But good watch is being kept."

The queen nodded firmly to that. "So must it be. These little troubles must not be let to grow to big ones. Peasants." She put scorn into the word. "This happens in France and they are put down. So." She made a wiping away gesture with one hand. "It is well and makes small difference, so long as it is not the lords who do it. There was our fall in France. Not the fools of peasants but when the lords turned on each other and fought. You see?"

"I do, your grace."

Frevisse had the feeling the queen had said this often of late—a lesson she wanted to be sure the English did not learn the hard way that France had. The quarreling and warfare among the lords of France was what had given the English their chance there. But who were the greater fools, Frevisse wondered—the peasants who made demands for justice they were unlikely to get or the lords who tore their country apart for the sake of their hatreds and ambitions?

That was not a question to say aloud here, and fortunately Queen Margaret, having given her speech, was asking again, "My Lady Alice, she does well? She is not broken with her grief? She will come back to me?"

"She surely will," Frevisse said. "She is grieved but not

broken." A possibility suddenly opened. Trying not to let her voice quicken, she went on, "There's so much to be done, with all her household upset and disordered by it all. The worst now may be . . ." Lightly, making almost a jest of it, ". . . that her husband's secretary is vanished. Besides the worry of where he's gone to, he would be useful to her, knowing so much of the duke's business and all."

Immediate distress crossed Queen Margaret's face. "Oh. I had not thought of that. But of course. She needs him and I am sorry." Unexpectedly, she laughed. "All this while he's here. I did not know she did not know. I shall send someone to tell her."

Trying to have the words out calmly, Frevisse said quickly, "After seeing us on to our nunnery, the men who accompanied us here will be going back to her. They'll gladly take word to her. But may I see him? I know what particular things Lady Alice was worried about. He might be able to tell me and her men could take her that word, too. If I see him, I can likewise hope to reassure her grace of Suffolk that he's well."

"But of course," Queen Margaret granted lightly. "Would you like to see him now?"

Her readiness to send Frevisse on her way probably meant she had decided Frevisse was unlikely to divert her more; nor had she troubled herself with Sister Margrett at all. Frevisse was too off balance at how quickly and easily it was gone, too busy hiding her surprise, to say more than, "I would, if it's possible and you please, your grace."

"Certainly." She waved one of the waiting yeomen-of-the-royal-chamber standing along the wall in green and white livery to come to her.

Only barely Frevisse remembered to say, "Lady Alice sent several brace of Suffolk rabbits to your pleasure, my lady. They've likely been given over to your cook by now."

Queen Margaret brightened with pleasure. "Ah. Please,

I will see her men take something from me to her in return. Powle," she said to the liveried man now bowing to her and briefly, briskly gave him orders that Frevisse mostly did not hear, only, "Tell the captain so," at the end, before making a graceful gesture that gave leave for him to go, and the nuns with him.

He made his bow, they their curtsies, and he led them out of the chamber, down the stairs to the courtyard, across it, and through a passageway beside the keep to a graveled path along a head-high hedge beyond which was a garden that looked to be—by the glimpses Frevisse had through gateways and along crossing paths—as gracious as Alice's at Wingfield but far larger, with the sound of a fountain playing somewhere. Rather than into it, they went around and then along other buildings built just inside the castle's surrounding outer wall along the lake. Servants and other folk they passed on their way gave them mildly curious looks but that was all until they came to a tower at the far corner of the wall. Even there, when they had gone up a half-flight of stairs and into a room just inside the doorway, the two men seated at a table playing at dice and the man sitting idly sharpening a dagger on a stone window edge with blue sight of the lake outside it showed no particular interest in them. By the men's matching good leather jerkins over dark green doublets, and the weapons-racks of spears and halberds around the room, and the dozen or so helmets sitting aligned on shelves beside the door, Frevisse guessed this was a guards' tower and that these were men at ease, not on duty. Why would a secretary be here?

The yeoman Powle said, "These ladies are come to see the man Burgate."

One of the men at the table asked, "Whose order?"

"The queen."

The man made a grunt that could have meant anything and rose from the table. There were several doors from the

room. Going to a narrow one hung with a heavy lock, he
took a broad key from a peg in the wooden frame around it
and unlocked the lock, saying as he re-hung the key, "This
way, my ladies."

Frevisse and Sister Margrett had already traded startled
looks. Staying where she was, Frevisse now asked, "He's a
prisoner?" Nothing Queen Margaret had said suggested it,
so easy she had been at mention of him.

The man in his turn looked surprised. "Aye. Didn't you
know that?"

"No. Why is he a prisoner?"

The man shrugged, unconcerned. "The duke of Buckingham ordered he was to be kept. So he's kept. That's all we
know." And plainly he did not care. "Sometimes somebody
comes to question him. We feed him. That's it." He opened
the door. There were shoulder-narrow, steep, stone stairs going down into shadows. Leading the way, the man said,
"Mind your skirts, my ladies. It's wet at the bottom."

It was that. And dark. And the stink of damp and mold
and a slop bucket not emptied lately came to meet Frevisse
and Sister Margrett as they followed him. Frevisse heard Sister Margrett slightly gag and said over her shoulder, "Cover
your mouth and nose with your veil. Breathe through it,"
doing the same herself.

The room below was the sort often used for storage—
thick-walled and stone-vaulted to bear the weight of the
tower above and stand against assault. Here, with the moat
coming almost to the wall, the seeping damp made that use
unsuitable: wood, cloth, and food, kept here, would rot.

So they were keeping a man instead.

What light there was came slanted and narrow through
three slits hardly wider than a man's hand and maybe a fore-
arm long, set somewhat above man-height. Pierced through
the walls' thickness, they gave hardly even sight of the sky,
certainly no warmth of sun or light enough to more than

grope by. It was the rattle of a chain that told her where to look, just able in the gloom to make out a man slowly standing up from something along the far curve of the wall; but her eyes were growing used to the gloom and her nose to the smell. The chained man was trying to bow, and Frevisse felt sudden anger on his behalf. That he should still try for such courtesy after probably months in this death-hole said better of him than of his jailers, and she said sharply to the guard, "His slop bucket should be emptied. See to it."

"There's someone does it when——" the man started.

"Not often enough," Frevisse snapped. As a nun she had held too many offices in the nunnery, been in charge of too many duties and servants to hesitate at all over giving orders where orders were needed to those beneath her; and anyone who would leave a man living with his own filth when there was no need was very much beneath her. "Take the bucket. Empty it. Scrub it clean before you bring it back." Her eyes were more used to the gloom by the moment. "With a lid, like it's supposed to have. And take that water bucket, too, and do the same and bring it back with clean water in it."

She felt the man hesitate. She sent him a look that, even in the shadows, decided him to do what he was told; but when he had picked up the two buckets and was heading for the stairs again, it was Sister Margrett who said to him quietly, "God's blessing on you for your mercy, sir," earning a respectful, quick duck of his head to her as he passed.

A little shamed at her own curtness but with no help for it now, Frevisse moved more toward the chained man and asked, "Edward Burgate?"

Chapter 14

The thin, bent-backed man shuffled a little forward. Frevisse could see now that he was shackled around one ankle by a fetter attached to a chain fastened to the heavy wooden frame of a bed, the cell's only place to sit. "Yes, my lady," he said, making another bow. He was roughly bearded, his thinning hair uncut, his clothing fit only for throwing out, but he was clinging to what courtesy he could despite his voice croaked as if not much used. "Edward Burgate, if it please you, my ladies. Are you . . . are you from my lady of Suffolk?"

"We are," Frevisse said to him quickly.

"She knows I'm here?" His voice broke and trembled.

"She will, now that I know," Frevisse assured him. "She's

been searching to know where you were but we've only just now found you out."

"Is she here?"

"She isn't. She's at Wingfield, but I've a man will take her word immediately."

Burgate shuffled a little backward and sank down on the edge of the bed as if unable to stand up any longer. His head hung low, his hands dangled between his knees, and Frevisse heard him say on nearly a sob, "Not here."

She looked around at Sister Margrett. "I need to talk to him alone."

"I'll stay here by the stairs," Sister Margrett said. She probably wanted no more than Frevisse did to cross that wet dirt floor embedded with smells and filth both old and new; but where she had choice, Frevisse did not and went forward, careful footed. The place was large enough that, if she and Burgate kept their voices down, their talk would be private and it was on him and what he might tell her that she had to fix her mind, not the stink and filth.

Burgate, despite she gestured for him to stay seated, forced himself respectfully to his feet again as she approached. Seen nearer, he looked to be one of those men who hovered between old and young for a great many years, weakly neither one nor the other; but all else aside, he was plainly near the end of his strength.

"A week," she said. "Lady Alice's man, riding fast, can be to her and back again in a week and have you out of here."

If it were possible to have him out of here. There was something very wrong about him being here at all, and like this. Wrong enough that after his brief flare of hope, Burgate was apparently gone untrusting, because he said now, peering at her, "Are you truly from her? This isn't another trap of theirs, to make me tell . . ." He faltered. ". . . tell what I don't know," he finished, almost believably.

"Lady Alice told me that if you doubted, I should ask you

where the account rolls for the manor of Cockayne might be. That if I said that, you'd know you could tell me whatever you needed to."

On what might have been a smothered sob, Burgate said, "Thanks be to whatever blessed saint has heard my prayers."

"Then there *is* something you need to tell her, something she needs to know."

He gulped on what sounded like a need to cry and said with plainly forced steadiness, "There is. I was my lord of Suffolk's secretary. You know that?"

"Yes."

"Yes. Of course you do." Burgate ran unsteady hands through his hair. "Yes. I wrote his letters. I wrote . . . whatever he needed written. I wrote . . . those last days in Ipswich . . . I made copies of his letter to Master John and . . . It's a very fine letter. Have you read it?"

"It's a very fine letter," Frevisse agreed because Burgate thought so and Alice's feeling about it had no place here.

"He was a noble man, my lord of Suffolk. A very noble man." The relief of being able to talk was overcoming Burgate's restraint but not enough to let him come straight at whatever he had not been saying these months since Suffolk's death. "I made copies of that letter and wrote his last words to my lady, his wife . . ."

He faltered again and stopped. Frevisse could guess he both wanted desperately to be rid of his secret and was desperately afraid to give it up after clutching it to him all these months, and carefully she said, "Your pardon, but I don't think that ever came to her."

"It wasn't . . ." Burgate fumbled and stopped again, staring at her with a frightened man's great need for something to steady him. A frightened but brave man, Frevisse told herself. Even in his need and fear, he did not reach out for the hold on someone that he looked to desperately need; so, little though she wanted to touch him, sure he was vermined as well as dirty, she put out a hand to him and said with forced gentleness, "Sir, I'm here for her."

With a gasp, he grabbed hold on her hand with both of his, clinging but steadying—like a man adrift and drowning given something certain to hold to for a while. At a whisper that Frevisse even at two arms' length could hardly hear, Burgate said, "It was something he hoped would never have to come to her. It was . . . it tells how he and the duke of Somerset and . . . others dealt together to lose . . ." The final word he mouthed more than whispered. ". . . Normandy."

That finally said, he swallowed, then went on in a stronger, faster whisper. "My lord said that if they played him false—his grace the duke of Somerset and the . . . and the others—if they played him false, then my lady would know how to make the best use of what he was telling her. Against them."

"But she never got it," Frevisse said.

"No. Because after they played him false, they took me and I . . ."

Surprised and alarmed, Frevisse said with forced care, "Suffolk wasn't played false, was he? It was pirates in the Channel took his ship. Men angry at him for . . ." She broke off as Burgate shook and shook his head, refusing her words. "It wasn't?" she asked softly.

"They weren't pirates. And our captain knew they were coming. He wasn't surprised. You could see that. What he did and what they did, it was under orders, and the man there giving the orders he wasn't a pirate or anything like. He was . . ." Burgate stopped, swallowed convulsively, and let her go. Stepping back from her a half pace with a rattle of chain, he straightened a little and said, "No, that's not for you to hear. Nor you wouldn't believe me anyway, maybe. No. It's the letter." He edged forward the little he had retreated, his voice fallen back to a low whisper. "The letter. My lord told me in Ipswich, when he'd finished it, he told me to keep it somewhere safe. Not among his other papers. Safe. And that no one was to know of it but me. Unless he died. Then Lady Alice was to have it. But after they . . . after they . . . killed him, other men seized me. At Dover. Someone must have told them there was something Suffolk had written, but they didn't find it and they're not sure of it and they want me to admit there's something and tell them where it is."

"But you haven't. Haven't given them the letter or admitted it exists," Frevisse said. Because if he had, he would not still be here. He might not even be alive.

Burgate had had time enough and more to think on possibilities she was just guessing at, and with a hunted look around his cell he said, "If I'd told them, they'd have killed me by now so there'd be no one else would know what it said. But I haven't even told them it exists, no. So it's safe. It's safe."

"Where?" Frevisse asked.

Wrapped in his months-long nightmare, Burgate jerked back from her, wild-eyed with distrust, before he remembered she had the right to ask. He was trembling, though, and grabbed his face between his hands as if forcibly to hold himself together, saying hoarsely between his fingers, "They're going to torture me. I know it. They only haven't because he's . . . he's ordered otherwise. But if he . . . he . . ."

"Who?" Frevisse asked before she could stop herself.

Burgate began to shake his head strongly. "No. That's something I won't say. Won't ever say. No."

"The duke of Somerset," Frevisse said. "The duke of Buckingham?"

She was more thinking aloud than asking, but Burgate answered hurriedly, "No, not him, no. The . . ." Again he fumbled at words. "The others. Them. Yes." He seemed to become more certain. "Them."

That was as much as she wanted to know. Come to it, she

did not want to know even that much, and she said in an even, steady voice, "What did you do with this letter my lord of Suffolk meant Lady Alice to have?"

Slowly, as if counting each word as he said it, Burgate half-whispered, "When it was done and closed and sealed and he gave it to me, I wrapped it in oil-cloth and sealed it with my own seal. Then I wrapped it into a package of two new-made shirts and a pair of hose and tied it so it was just a bundle. There was a boy at the inn there in Ipswich. He'd been saying he wanted to go to London. To find his fortune and all that nonsense." Burgate momentarily showed the pride of a man who had "found his fortune" in a far more sensible way, forgetting it had brought him to here. "I gave him money to help him on his way in return for him delivering the bundle to my cousin John Smythe in Sible Hedingham. Sire John. He's priest there, very safely out of the way of everything. I told the boy Sire John would pay him for the bundle and gave him a letter asking John to do so. In the bundle I enclosed another letter telling John that the sealed packet had to be safely and secretly kept. Not what it was. I never told him that. Only that he had to keep it for me until I came for it or . . . or he heard I was dead. Then he should take it himself to her grace, my lady of Suffolk. It was the best I could think of," he apologized. "There wasn't much time to think of anything. We were to sail in the morning and I didn't want the letter on me. It was the best I could do. The thing was . . . the letter was . . . it's . . ." He sank suddenly onto the edge of the bed again and hid his face in his hands. "Blessed St. Peter ad Vincula, I'm going to die here. I'm going to die here. Because of that . . . that . . ."

Frevisse moved quickly forward, laid hand on his shoulder, said strongly, "It's no longer your burden. You're rid of it. Someone besides you knows of it now. It's not yours to bear anymore. All you need do is hold silent and wait for Lady Alice to have you out of here."

Burgate uncovered his face, grabbed her by her hands. "A week," he pleaded. "A week, you said."

"A week," she repeated, with silent prayer that Alice would move that quickly and he would last that long.

She made to step back from him and he loosed her, let her go, wrung his hands together in his lap and began to rock slowly back and forth where he sat. "A week," he said.

"A week," Frevisse said again, in retreat now, back across the noisome floor to the stairs where Sister Margrett still waited, her veil still held over her mouth and nose.

The guard was just coming down the stairs, carrying the two buckets, one with a wooden lid, just as she had ordered him. He would have gone past her without any look, but because her sharpness to him might all too likely be passed on to Burgate, she said quietly, "My pardon, sir, for speaking so harshly before. Thank you for your goodness. If you could give him such kindness after this, too, you'll have my prayers and blessing."

With a look both disconcerted and embarrassed, the man said, "Aye, my lady. I'll do what I can."

"The blessed saints have you in their keeping," Frevisse murmured, mild as honey and milk, ignoring Sister Margrett's surprise-widened eyes.

Having done what she could to appease the guard, she went at haste up the stairs and through the guardroom, escaping the tower at just short of unseemly haste. Only when she and Sister Margrett were outside and away from it, in clear sunlight and clean air under open sky, did she slow her pace and say with sharp need at Sister Margrett, "I want to be away from here. Soon. And far." Meaning not only Kenilworth but whatever darkness moved here under all the outward grace and beauty of the queen's royal court.

Chapter 15

he yeoman who had brought them to the tower was gone about his other business, leaving Sister Margrett free to ask as they went back together toward the heart of the castle, "I shouldn't want to know more than I do about any of this, should I?"

"No," Frevisse answered quietly; then, after a moment, added, "Nor ever speak of it at all to anyone, if you can help it."

Sister Margrett was silent then with what Frevisse hoped was acceptance, until just short of the passageway back to the courtyard, she asked, "Will Lady Alice be able to have him out of there? Before he dies?"

"I pray so."

"So shall I," said Sister Margrett and then nothing more,

to Frevisse's relief. She did not want to outright lie, but neither was she going to share any of the truth with Sister Margrett. For her patience through all of this—and more especially for holding back from questions she surely had— Sister Margrett deserved better than a burden Frevisse would not wish on her for any reason.

In the courtyard below the keep they found a servant to send in search of Vaughn, followed the man as far as the gateway to the outer yard, then waited there while he disappeared into the busyness of men beyond it. He must have known where to go, because he came back soon with Vaughn, who tossed him a coin. The man bowed in thanks and returned through the gateway and Vaughn said, "My ladies?"

Not needing to be told, Sister Margrett drifted aside, out of hearing, and Frevisse told Vaughn of Burgate. Vaughn went grim while she did and at the end said, "I'll send Ned off with word to Lady Alice within the hour. Did he tell you anything of why he's there. Or the other business?"

"What he told me I think would be best saved to tell to you and Master Noreys together."

Vaughn eyed her for a moment in a shrewd way that reminded her of Joliffe. She had thought he might protest that and she was ready not to argue with him, simply tell him that was how it would be—the fair sharing Lady Alice and Joliffe had agreed on in the business. But Vaughn only said, "My lady does well to trust you. You found Burgate when no one else has."

"It was only by chance that I did and so readily," she said.

"Some are more favored by chance than others are."

"I'll count myself well-favored if we can leave here tomorrow." Because talk of chance had made her suddenly wonder, belatedly, whether finding Burgate had been only chance. Had she been deliberately used to get from him what no one else had been able to pry from him? If so, she was now in the same danger he was. But no. No one here had known she was coming or could have known she would ask after the duchess of Suffolk's secretary. Or that the queen would think it of so little matter as to simply tell her. It had all been only chance. It had to have been.

But then, when whoever kept Burgate here—those others he was too frightened to name—found out he had talked with her and that Alice knew where he was . . .

The sooner she was away from here, the better she would feel. Vaughn was saying, "We can leave in the morning directly after you've broken your fast, if you will," and she agreed, "That would do very well. Thank you."

He bowed and went away the way he had come, and Sister Margrett, returning to Frevisse's side, asked, "Done?"

"As done as can be," Frevisse answered and wished she felt the lighter for it.

They dined in Kenilworth's great hall at supper. Seated at one of the tables stretching the hall's length, they were a long way from the dais at the hall's upper end where the queen sat behind the high table that was covered by a shiningly white cloth down to the floor and set with gold and silver dishes that caught and glowed with the evening light through the hall's tall, glassed windows. Queen Margaret was differently gowned from this afternoon, in summer-blue velvet edged with dark fur around the low curve of the neck that showed a gold-brocaded undergown. A close-fitted necklace of gold and pearls circled her throat, and there were pearls and blue jewels in her crown, too—a different crown from the plain one of this afternoon.

She shared the high table with the duke of Buckingham on her one side and a churchman on the other, then two other women and finally at one end of the table Sir Thomas Stanley and at the other another churchman, all of them as finely arrayed as the queen and looking to be in high good humour among themselves, giving as much heed to their own talk as to the several singers, jugglers, and tumblers that performed at intervals in the center of the hall during the meal.

Was their high-heartedness real, Frevisse wondered? Did they really feel so little the harsh certainty of the lost French war and the revolts and rebellions tearing at England? All of that was out of their sight, certainly, but was it likewise out of mind? Or were they feigning, for the sake of those who watched them?

It was not a life she had ever wanted—to be the center of other people's need, having to match her outward seeming, despite whatever she inwardly felt or thought, to what her place demanded of her. Even when something other than a nun's life had been within her reach, she had known it was not what she wanted—to be divided between outward seeming and inward heart for duty's sake to others. In that way, her choice to be a nun had been utterly for herself, she supposed. She had once said as much to Domina Edith, her prioress at St. Frideswide's through her early years there; and Domina Edith, old and grown wise with time, had smiled on her and said, "At the best, yes, your choice was utterly for yourself."

She had left Frevisse standing startled for a moment before she went gently on, "Most people lack the good sense to do something so utterly for themselves. They accept being broken into pieces by life's and other people's needs. By becoming a nun, you are hoping for a wholeness of mind and body and spirit that will let you grow outside the bonds of body, the bonds of even this time and this place." Domina Edith's smile had deepened. "You are unlikely to attain that prize in full, unless you achieve sainthood, but it is surely a prize worth the striving for. Surely better than the death-limited, world-battered prizes for which most people settle, usually without much thought about their choice. It may be said, yes, you were self-willed, choosing yourself over others, but should you begin to feel that as too great a burden on your soul, you need only consider what your self-will has gained you—utter obedience, by oath, to the Rule and whatever orders your superiors may give you under it. You may have come by stubborn self-will to be a nun, but one of the great goals of your nunhood is to learn to *give up* that self that willed you here. Remember that and you'll have no worry about the self-will that brought you here." And when next Frevisse had had to work in patient silence under Dame Alys' ill-humoured, angry orders in the nunnery kitchen, that lesson had come all too heavily home.

It was toward the middle of the last remove that the expected way of the meal was broken when Frevisse happened to see a servant lean over at Sir Thomas Stanley's shoulder and say something in his ear. Even from as far down the hall as she was, Frevisse saw Sir Thomas jerk and stiffen. He rose, moved along the table to put his head between the queen and Buckingham, said something, and apparently received her leave to go, because he bowed and went away, out by way of a door at one end of the dais. A ripple of head-turning along the hall followed him but that was all.

He had not returned when the meal ended and the lords and ladies withdrew the same way he had gone, leaving the hall to whatever pastimes the lesser folk might find for the evening. Rather than linger there, Frevisse and Sister Margrett sought out the castle's chapel for evening prayers and went from there to bed, and only in the morning, as they readied to leave, learned what news had taken Sir Thomas from the table.

"Likely spoiled his digestion, too," said Vaughn as he made a final tightening of saddle girths in the outer yard. "What I've heard is one of Stanley's men rode in from Chester with word the duke of York has had warning there's plotting against him around the king and he's set on coming back from

Ireland. Nobody around the king wants that. Sir Thomas sent a messenger on his way last night to the king and rode out himself with his men at first light this morning."

Since the first full rays of sun had yet to strike over the castle walls, "first light" must have been when the dark had thinned enough to see the road.

"He's going to the king, too?" Frevisse asked. Vaughn was standing aside from her horse now, holding the reins so she could mount.

"No. Toward Wales, I gather."

Frevisse swung up to the saddle. While settling her skirts, she looked down at him, somewhat frowning, and asked, "Why to Wales?"

"He's chamberlain there and York's coming seemingly means he's needed there."

"Why?"

Vaughn shrugged. Beyond them, his man was helping Sister Margrett onto her horse.

"Why?" Frevisse asked again, reading more into his shrug than maybe Vaughn had meant to tell.

But he only asked as he handed the reins to her, "Sir Thomas maybe expects the king will take exception to York's return?" before he turned away to his own horse and mounted, giving her no chance to ask more.

They made a very long day's ride of it, coming in sight of St. Frideswide's when the evening light was lying long across the golden stubble of the harvested fields beyond its walls. Vespers was done, but the priory's outer gates still stood open and they rode straight in. The inner gates, to the guesthall courtyard outside the cloister door, were shut but would have been opened readily enough at any traveler's need because the Benedictine Rule required it, but the guesthall servingman who came at the ringing of the bell opened the more quickly when he saw them. Because both Frevisse and Sister Margrett had sometimes been the priory's hosteler, overseeing the guesthall, he knew them and said, openly pleased as he pulled the gates wide, "You're late-come, my ladies, but right welcome. There's been wondering how you were and where."

"We're here now, St. Frideswide be thanked," Frevisse said. "And well enough, Tom." Supposing she was not too stiff to swing down from the saddle. "Has all been well?"

"Well as might be. No great troubles," Tom said, walking beside her horse as they rode into the yard. "There was some yelling when someone lost a pottery bowl down the kitchen-yard well a few days gone. That's been the most lately."

Frevisse nearly gave a laugh of relief. To have a broken pottery bowl the worst thing to be upset over seemed wonderful. But her laugh faded unmade as she saw Joliffe standing up from where he had been sitting on the guesthall steps.

Partly, she was relieved to see him. She had been refusing to be worried for him, but had been anyway because men had been murdered in this matter and there was no reason he could not be, too. Now, seeing him safely here, she simply, suddenly, gave herself up to her deep weariness. All was as well as it might be, and all that was left to do was give over to both him and Vaughn what she had learned from Burgate and be done with it.

She had had all day to think of how she would discretely do that, and as Tom held her horse for her to dismount, she turned to Sister Margrett and said in a somewhat fainting voice, "I don't feel well."

Vaughn, already dismounted and taking Sister Margrett's horse by the bridle, gave her a sharp look. So did Sister Margrett, and Frevisse had the feeling that whoever else believed her, neither of them did, so she made a clumsy effort of climbing down from her saddle and stood holding to it as if too weak or unwell to dare letting go. Aware of Sister

Margrett's and Vaughn's questioning frowns and Tom's worried look, she faltered, "I wonder if, visiting that prisoner, I may have caught a fever?"

"Oh, my lady!" Tom said, alarmed.

"I pray not," Sister Margrett said with matching worry.

"Should I . . . would it be better," Frevisse said as if uncertain, "if we spent the night in the guesthall, rather than . . ."

Sister Margrett quickly took up her faltering words. "Rather than take infection into the cloister, you mean. Yes. Surely." Dismounted now, she hurried to Frevisse's side and put an arm around her waist to help her toward the guesthall steps. "Tom, fetch Dame Claire. Maybe there's some supper left, some broth maybe, Tom? Master Vaughn, your man can see the horses to the stable, can't he? And if you'd bring our saddlebags . . ."

Kindly, capably, Sister Margrett set everyone around them to doing one thing or another, and in the general shifting of horses and men and helping Frevisse up the steps she took the chance to whisper worriedly in Frevisse's ear, "You're not really ill, are you?"

"No," Frevisse whispered back. "But I have to talk to . . ."

". . . the man who was waiting here," Sister Margrett finished for her, and said loudly, for others to hear, "There now, lean on me, dame. Just a little farther." And to Joliffe, now holding open the guesthall door for them, "Thank you, sir."

It ended with Frevisse put to bed in the chamber saved for the nunnery's better guests and feeling very foolish at the bustle Sister Margrett made of it. Dame Claire, the priory's infirmarian, soon came from the cloister, but she and Frevisse had known each other for all the years Frevisse had been in the nunnery, and Frevisse knew there was small likelihood of deceiving her. So she whispered as Dame Claire bent over her, feeling her forehead and for her pulse, "I need to stay the night here."

Dame Claire gave her a sharp look, continued to examine

her, and finally turned away to tell Sister Margrett clearly enough for the servants hovering outside the chamber door to hear, "I find nothing greatly wrong with her. It may be only she's over-wearied, not being so young as she once was."

Frevisse's glare was wasted at her back, and she went on, "But best we be safe about it. You'll both stay here tonight. See she drinks the potion I'll leave for her, and we'll see how all does in the morning." She turned back to Frevisse in the bed and said, "Mind you behave," with a look that said she was agreeing to help but did not like it.

Her disapproval was evidenced more plainly by the potion. Made of sharp herbs, it did no favors to the ale into which it was mixed. As a kind of penance for her lies, Frevisse drank it all and then pretended she wanted only a little of the supper brought to her, hungry though she was. Beyond that, she decided she must leave Joliffe and Vaughn to find a way to talk with her that would raise no suspicions or curiosity among the guesthall servants. Happily, there were no other guests tonight to make that more difficult, and soon after her tray of barely eaten supper had been taken away, Vaughn scratched at the room's doorframe. Sister Margrett went, and just loudly enough to be overheard by anyone in the hall behind him, he asked, "How does she? Happens the fellow here is a minstrel. Might she care for some quiet lute-playing?"

"That might be good," said Sister Margrett with the same carrying quiet. "She's querulous and a little restless. The music might soothe her."

Frevisse had to feel advantage was being taken of her in her "illness". First, it had been "not so young" from Dame Claire. Now it was "querulous" from Sister Margrett. But she remained leaning back against the pillows, trying to look wan. Which well she might, after Dame Claire's potion, she thought, the after-taste of it still unpleasantly with her.

Sister Margrett had helped her off with her outer gown

and veil before she took to bed, but for seemliness' sake she
had kept on her heavy undergown and her wimple was still
around her face and over her throat, pinned to the close-
fitted cap that covered what there was of her short-cropped
hair, so that she was decent enough to be seen by Vaughn
and Joliffe. She nonetheless felt the lack of her habit's familiar safety—somewhat how a fighter must feel without his
shield, she imagined. Nor did Joliffe help. He came into the
room carrying a lute in one hand and a joint stool from
the hall in the other, bowed to her, then set the stool not far
aside from the foot of her bed and said with respectful concern, "If I sit here, my lady, you need not tire yourself with
speaking but can sign to me with a small movement of one
hand if I play too loudly, too softly, or too badly. Will that
do? You need only nod," he added, the laughter in his eyes
belying his "kindness." He was enjoying himself.

Frevisse narrowed her eyes at him to show what she
thought of his "kindness," while accepting it with a small
nod. When he was seated, though, and began to finger a
quiet melody from the lute, she had to grant he had skill at
the playing—and was displeased at herself to find she a little grudged him that, as if in return for making such a jest
of things, he should at least play badly.

Vaughn had followed Joliffe into the room, had kept back
from the bed what seemed a respectful distance while posi-
tioning himself to block Frevisse from anyone's view beyond
the doorway. With Sister Margrett withdrawn to the chamber's far end to sit with her breviary in apparent prayer, this
was as private as they could, within reason, be, and Frevisse
asked, low-voiced, of Joliffe, "What's Vaughn told you?"

"That you found this secretary," Joliffe sang in a soft
murmur matched to the tune he was playing, watching his
fingers rather than her. "That's all. There have been people
around."

"Not about the duke of York?"

Joliffe's fingers did not fumble the strings but his gaze flashed up to her face, demanding to be told more; and he went on watching her while she said, "Word came to Kenilworth at suppertime yesterday. He's said to be coming back from Ireland. The news took Sir Thomas Stanley right away from the high table."

"Ah." Joliffe dropped his gaze. "The good Sir Thomas."

Behind him, Vaughn said, "He's gone to Wales. He rode out with his men this morning."

"Wales," Joliffe said. A Welsh melody ran from under his fingers.

With a small backward glance to be sure no one was near behind him in the hall, Vaughn said, "If York *is* coming back from Ireland and without royal leave, they'll catch him on that hook if none other."

"My lord of York . . ." Joliffe slid the hint of a marching song into his playing. ". . . had it put in his indenture with the king, before ever he went, that he has the right to come back to England whenever he wants, without need of royal leave."

"Well fore-thought," Vaughn said.

"But Sir Thomas has hied himself away to Wales. I wonder why," Joliffe said, more as if thinking aloud than expecting any answer, and neither Vaughn nor Frevisse gave him one. Joliffe slipped into a lullaby of many rippling notes and said as gently as his playing, "This secretary, my lady. What did you learn from him once you found him?"

Behind him, Vaughn took a half-step forward, this being what he wanted to hear, too, and they all three of them glanced toward Sister Margrett across the chamber, sitting with her head bowed over her breviary open on her lap, reading from it in a low murmur that likely masked from her whatever they were saying. Glad to be done with and rid of Burgate's secret, Frevisse told all that he had told her. Though Joliffe continued to play quietly, she watched his face and

Vaughn's go grim while she did; and when she finished, Joliffe turned his head enough to say over his right shoulder at Vaughn, "You've sent word to her grace he's there?"

"Yesterday. As soon as I knew."

Joliffe made a small nod, as if satisfied by that, and said, now looking down at his fingers drifting at the lute strings, "You're probably going to sleep now, my lady. We'll leave you to it and be about our business, by your leave."

That "by your leave" was pointless courtesy. She had given them what they wanted and they were done with her and her "leave" had nothing to do with what they would do now. But despite she had wanted to be done with it all, she suddenly wanted to know what they intended to do next, and was angry at herself for wanting that and closed her eyes and evened her breathing, willing herself to lie as if gone to sleep while Joliffe lessened his playing away to silence. With her eyes kept firmly shut, she listened to him rise and pick up the stool, and only at the very edge of hearing heard him say then, for no one else to hear, "Well done, my lady."

Chapter 16

There being too much chance of being overheard in the guesthall's main room among the servants bringing out the night's bedding, Joliffe and Vaughn strolled in seeming idleness outside to the cobbled yard between the hall and the cloister and church. The warm last of daylight was just gilding the cross atop the point of roof above the church's west front. All else was in soft-shadowed twilight. They had the yard to themselves and went to sit on the step around the well there, to look at ease in their talk, should someone take especial note of them.

There was need both to talk over what Dame Frevisse had said and what they would do now, but while Joliffe turned over his thoughts, considering where to start, Vaughn said,

"I heard someone besides the duke of York being talked of among Sir Thomas' men in the hurry at Kenilworth. Sir William Oldhall."

Joliffe was aware of Vaughn watching him while he said that and chose to look interested rather than blank. Blank too easily gave away you were trying to show nothing. With outward easiness he asked, "What about him?"

"It was being said among Sir Thomas' men that he's the one took whatever word it was that's set York to coming back on the sudden."

"Damnable spies," Joliffe said lightly.

"What are we, then, if not 'damnable spies'?" Vaughn asked.

"Oh, we're spies, surely. Just not damnable."

"You hope."

"And we're not Sir Thomas Stanley."

"He's no spy," Vaughn scoffed.

"No. He's a cur-dog who thinks he's a wolf, but that won't make his bite much the less if he takes a snap at someone."

"Oldhall," said Vaughn. "Do you have any thought on what he would have told York to set him on coming back to England?"

"Probably what I told Lady Alice at Wingfield. That men on at least one of those commissions of oyer and terminer against rebels have been told to find York was behind at least Cade's uprising."

"Was it someone on one of the commissions?" Vaughn asked, watching him, probably as interested in judging whether Joliffe was going to tell him the truth as Joliffe was interested in seeing how far they could go before they began lying to each other.

For now, rather than lying, Joliffe settled for looking at him wordlessly, admitting nothing.

"Someone in the royal household?" Vaughn tried. Joliffe still said nothing, and Vaughn shrugged and said, "Well enough. Let it be your secret. Just swear to me there's nothing to Lady Alice's harm in what you're not telling me."

"Nothing that I know of," Joliffe said readily. "I swear it on my hope of heaven." And tucked away the thought that yet again Nicholas Vaughn gave every sign of being, first of everything, the duchess of Suffolk's man. There was always the chance he was playing some double game of his own, in someone else's service more deeply than he was in Lady Alice's, but without some sign that he was, Joliffe would take him as he seemed—and tell him no more than need be. Just as Vaughn was likely doing with him.

"It's pity, though, your nun didn't win her way closer to the queen," Vaughn said.

Forebearing to say Dame Frevisse was not "his nun," Joliffe simply asked, "Why?"

"From what I heard, for what it's worth, it seems that the queen, in her own rooms after supper, when she heard what Sir Thomas had to tell her, went into a . . ." Vaughn gave half a smile. ". . . royal rage."

"When he told her that York was coming back from Ireland?"

"At that, yes. One of Sir Thomas' men who was there was laughing at it this morning, saying she had Sir Thomas backed against a wall and was yelling in his face that York had to be stopped, that Sir Thomas had to see he was stopped."

Leaving aside pleasure at thought of Sir Thomas Stanley backed against a wall with a woman yelling at him, Joliffe asked, "Did he have any answer to that besides, 'Yes, your grace'?"

"He did. He said he had orders that way already. That she needn't worry. That it would be seen to. He had his orders."

"He kept saying he had his orders?"

"The fellow telling it in the stableyard this morning fancies himself a player, I think. He was miming Sir Thomas against a wall and blustering. How much he was over-playing

I don't know, but he had Sir Thomas saying he 'had his orders' more than once."

"Already had orders to stop York if he came back from Ireland. You're right, it *was* pity Dame Frevisse wasn't there." It would have been interesting to know what she made of it all.

Still watching him, Vaughn went on, "The queen seems also to have said she wants 'this traitor Oldhall dead'." Vaughn mimiced a French, shrill woman's voice. "'I want him dead. See him dead and do the same for York if he gives you chance.'"

"She said that?" Joliffe demanded. "She told him to kill the both of them?"

"So this fellow was saying. Nor does it sound like something anyone like him would make up from whole cloth and stale wit."

Joliffe shook his head. "No, it doesn't." And it made a believable parcel with what else was going on against York. For one moment his anger flared past his carefulness. "Damn them! York hasn't *done* anything. Nothing that deserves death. Even coming back from Ireland is within his rights."

"He's too royal-blooded."

"And those who have found how fat they can live with a weak king don't like the chance there might be a strong one, yes," Joliffe agreed, impatient with what was all too plain. "But King Henry looks to be a long way from dead . . ."

"Unless there's something about his health we don't know."

Joliffe stopped short over that thought, then shook his head. "No. He's spent a fairly vigorous few months of late, what with riding against the rebels and all."

"What with riding toward them, then riding away from them even faster," Vaughn said, rightly enough.

"And now he's riding against them again," Joliffe said mockingly. "Now that Cade is dead and the rebels scattered.

But be all that as it may, King Henry has been too much seen of late to think his health is poorly."

"It's the rebels' demands that York be finally, openly, fully named King Henry's heir that's done it. That's frighted those who want him nowhere near the king or in the government at all."

"Which doesn't change the fact that, by right of blood, he *is* King Henry's heir."

"And that if someone wanted to," Vaughn said very quietly, "they could say York is *more* than only 'heir'."

The last golden light had gone from the cross, and the twilight in the yard was deepening toward darkness, but it was for more than the creep of the evening chill that Joliffe shivered before—as quietly as Vaughn—he said, "They could say it. But better they don't say it aloud. York has never pushed any claim that way at all, ever, that I've heard. All he's ever done or asked for is what any prince of the royal blood could rightly expect. And far less than some have demanded."

"He's surely thought about it, though," Vaughn said, making it sound half-way to an accusation.

"He'd better," Joliffe returned tartly, "since men are willing to kill him because of it."

"True," Vaughn granted. "My guess, for what it's worth, is that Sir Thomas Stanley and whoever else is in this against York are judging him by how they would be if they were him."

That was a thought Joliffe had had before now. He had had other thoughts, too, and asked, "Was that how it was with the duke of Suffolk?"

"Suffolk?" Vaughn put neither liking nor respect into the name. "Suffolk loved himself too much to think much about anyone else. No. His distrust of York came, I think, from knowing, somewhere in himself where he likely never looked straight at it, that York was by far the better at governing the French war than Suffolk had been when he'd had the chance, and that York would surely have done better at governing England, too. Better than Suffolk ever did or ever wanted to. And remember," he added as if Joliffe had accused him of something, "it's the Lady Alice I serve, have always served. Never Suffolk."

That must have sometimes been a narrow distinction and maybe hard to keep when Suffolk was alive to give orders; but Joliffe understood too well how narrow the distinction could sometimes be between respect of self and humiliation, and he chose not to argue Vaughn's, just as he would have wanted no one to argue his.

"About yesterday," Vaughn said. "There's this you'd best know, too, about what was being said. According to this fellow doing all the talking, when Queen Margaret said she wanted York dead, Sir Thomas answered that once he'd been seized . . ."

"Seized?" Joliffe interrupted with disbelief. "For what?"

"I thought it would be for leaving Ireland without the king's leave but if what you say about his indenture is true . . ."

"It is."

"Then I don't know."

Moving his mind backward through what else Vaughn had told him, Joliffe asked, "He never said who had given that order?"

"The fellow in the stableyard? No. And since he seemed to be saying everything else Sir Thomas said, he would probably have said that, too, if Sir Thomas had."

"But Sir Thomas didn't. Even faced with the queen's rage, he didn't say it. So I wonder who . . ." He let the question trail off. He was back again to asking who—with Suffolk dead—now had that kind of power? "The king?" he said doubtfully.

But at the undeniable root of all the realm's present troubles was King Henry's willingness to leave every choice and decision in his government to someone else. To the duke of Suffolk for most the past ten years. But with Suffolk dead . . .

"Somerset," said Vaughn. "Our fine Edmund Beaufort, duke of Somerset. Back from France with his royal blood and seemingly into King Henry's favor in spite of all."

"He's royal-blooded through a bastard line," Joliffe pointed out. "And from a younger line than York's." Then added, "Which are two good reasons to want York dead, I suppose."

There was still light enough to show Vaughn frowning as he said doubtfully, "It would make Somerset an over-busy man at present. It would have him losing Normandy, returning to England, re-establishing his place with the king, taking Suffolk's place at court, and setting up to destroy York, all in one grand rush."

"He's already done the first three. Why not go for the fourth? Though the timing seems not so good as . . ."

"He ought to be under arrest for treason, not into favor with the king!" Vaughn burst out.

"He ought to be," Joliffe agreed. "But it doesn't look like happening. Which leaves only York for him to worry on. Hence the forethought to give orders against his coming back from Ireland."

Slowly, unwillingly, Vaughn granted, "It all holds together."

It did, but he didn't sound easy about it. Nor was Joliffe. Despite it held together, something about it sat uneasily in his mind. Uneasily but not quite in reach, and he knew better than to nag after it, whatever it was. He could only trust it would come to him if he left it alone and so he said, "It would help to know how old this order against York is. Was it given before Somerset came back from Normandy, for instance. But all we can presently do is decide what to do next with what we know."

"Lay hands on this letter that Master Burgate has hidden

with his cousin in Sible Hedingham. Judging by what he said and wouldn't say about it, it's black-dangerous."

"It's surely that, and we should go together to get it, for safety's sake all around." And to make sure the game was played fair, he didn't say. "The trouble is that I need to see word gets to my lord of York in Ireland of the welcome-home planned for him."

"There's this, too," Vaughn said. "We were followed from Kenilworth."

Joliffe paused, then asked, "Why do you think that?"

"Because I'm no more trusting than you are. I had Symond, the man with me, fall back five times during our ride, starting not long after we left Kenilworth, to see what other riders were on the road behind us."

"It's a well-used high-road south from Kenilworth."

"It is that, so it wasn't easy to sort out and be sure of any of them. But there were two that were still behind us after we left Warwick, all the way to Banbury. They never got nearer. They never fell farther behind. Any of the times Symond rode aside to look back along the road, there they were. When we stopped at an inn at midday and afterward went on, they were behind us again, a little nearer but keeping the same distance all the afternoon. When we briefly stopped at an inn in Banbury in the af-ternoon, the nuns talked openly about being to St. Frideswide's by nightfall. Symond saw one of the men watching us from down the street and saw them both be-hind us just after we left Banbury. Not again, though, but they wouldn't have needed to follow us closely then, if they'd found out at the inn where we were going." Vaughn tipped his head toward the gateway. "I'd take money in wager they're somewhere close out there, waiting to see where I go next."

Joliffe made a disgusted sound. "If they're so far gone at

court they don't even trust a nun, the duchess of Suffolk's cousin . . ."

"I'm not mistaken about we were followed," Vaughn said stiffly.

"No," Joliffe quickly assured him. "They don't seem to have been much good at it, but I'd wager that's what they were at." And even if they weren't, someone else, better skilled, might have been. It was not a risk he cared to ignore. "What I'm saying is that someone at court seems to be more suspicious than I wish he was."

Or more than one someone. Under King Henry's weakness the court had become a nest of greed and wrongs. Lords and men bold in a lord's favor did not even need to be overly well-witted at what they did or how much they grabbed for themselves. It was all become grab as grab can, leave lesser folk to the devil, and be damned to the law. But such men never saw their own foulness of heart. They turned it outward into distrust of others, and hence Dame Frevisse had brought a spy in her wake. Damn it.

"Do you think Dame Frevisse was let in to see Burgate in deliberate hope he'd tell her what he hasn't told them?" he asked.

"I've wondered that," Vaughn said broodingly. "But it was too much a thing of the moment, her asking and the queen sending her off to see him. I'd guess the queen was innocent in it, didn't know it mattered."

"But when someone found out what she'd done, they decided to do what they could to recover her error," Joliffe said.

"And had us followed," Vaughn agreed. "They probably feared he'd told this nun what they want to know and that she'd go back to Lady Alice with it."

"They might take that she didn't go back to Lady Alice as proof he told her nothing," Joliffe said for the sake of argument, though he already knew the answer to that.

Vaughn promptly gave it. "She doesn't have to go back to Lady Alice, and likely she's safe enough if she keeps in her cloister. It's me they'll be watching now. As soon as I leave here . . ." He made a sharp, angry gesture.

"You'll likely be no more than followed," Joliffe said. "In hope you'll lead them to this letter. Or, at worst, you'll end up like Burgate."

"Or dead. That would be their surest way of being sure I pass on nothing I might have learned. I'm only hoping the man I sent off from Kenilworth back to Wingfield keeps ahead of whatever trouble they might send after him. But I gave him his orders while there were half a dozen men standing around, and he set off within the hour, and they could report, if anyone asked, that I neither told nor gave him anything beyond the message that Burgate was there."

"And he was likely well away before whoever has Burgate in keeping knew anything about it."

"Or never knew I sent Ned away at all."

"Also possible." The trouble was that there were too many possibles, too many ways to guess at things in all of this. "The one certain thing seems to be that you were followed. Or Dame Frevisse was, which came to the same thing today, but tomorrow when you ride out and she of course doesn't, it will be you they follow. They're not likely to kill you, though. They want this letter. They have to hope you'll lead them to it and they'll want you unharmed until you do. I suppose you could always lie in wait and kill them," he added helpfully.

"Thereby showing whoever has set them on that, one, I'm suspicious enough to note that I was followed, and two, that I must have something to hide."

"Not if the bodies are never found."

"They only have to disappear for my innocence to come under question."

True enough; but it was good to know Vaughn did not see

murder as his quickest way to solving problems, Joliffe thought; and said, "Where is this Sible Hedingham anyway?"

"A northern part of Essex. There's two Hedinghams, close together and both not far from your duke of York's castle at Clare."

"Back eastward from here," Joliffe said. Somewhere beyond Hunsdon.

"East and somewhat south, yes."

"You could go back to Lady Alice at Wingfield first, rather than straight there."

"I may have to, but the longer this thing is in this priest's keeping, the better is the chance we'll lose it. All it will take is someone asking enough questions at Ipswich to find out Burgate entrusted a package to some fellow there, then find the fellow and ask him questions he won't see any reason not to answer."

"It might not be that easy. Haven't you already asked questions in Ipswich and heard nothing about this package?"

"It was Burgate we wanted. We thought we'd have all our answers once we found him. I didn't ask the right questions," Vaughn said bitterly.

"You asked the right questions. Just not enough of them. I know well enough how that goes." Knew it too well and that there was small help for it when it happened. You didn't look for the key to a lock on a door when you didn't know the door was there. "But our package-carrier might not be all that easily found, even with the right questions. London is large. Or then again . . ." Joliffe liked to see as many sides as possible, as much for the sake of making trouble as to solve it. ". . . maybe he's already tired of London and gone home and is even now sitting in an Ipswich tavern complaining of the package he delivered for the duke of Suffolk's man to some priest in . . ."

Vaughn stood up. "I have trouble liking you sometimes."

"Most of the time, I thought," Joliffe said, standing up, too.

Vaughn let that go. Night was enough come that they had to go inside or else be wondered at, supposing they weren't wondered at already; but when Vaughn took a step that way, Joliffe stayed where he was and said, "We have to settle what we're going to do. I could go to this Hedingham instead of you. I doubt I'm known as part of this at all and wouldn't be followed. But before anything I need to set word on its way to York in Ireland of what's being planned against him here. The sooner he knows that the better. Unfortunately, the nearest man I know for it is west of here." In the Welsh marches, opposite the way to Essex, and damn Sir William for not having a tighter net where help could be asked for when needed. "So why don't you come with me tomorrow?"

Vaughn was openly caught flat by that. "Come with you? To Wales?"

Hiding pleasure at having out-flanked him, Joliffe answered evenly, "Your followers will be waiting to see where you go in the morning. So they'll follow us and we'll be obviously friends and that will make me as suspect as you are."

"West from here?"

"The better to mislead them. You need only keep with me for a day or so. Then we'll split up, and they'll have to split up to follow us. You can head north, then curve away east, losing your man on the way. I'll head south and lose my man before going on west. That should confuse matters."

"Then I head for Sible Hedingham, get this letter, and return to Lady Alice at Wingfield. Yes." Vaughn liked the thought. "But will you trust me—trust her—to play fair with York if she gets it?"

Steadily, Joliffe said, "I do. I'll set the warning on its way to my lord of York, then head back to meet you at Wingfield. Or better I go to Hedingham, too?"

"On the chance I miscarry along the way?" Vaughn was practical rather than grim about it. "Assuredly. However it goes, let's plan we each go to Wingfield after we've been to Hedingham. Will that satisfy?"

Since they were trusting each other—forced to it but nonetheless having to play it out as if the trust were true-rooted—Joliffe said, "Wingfield. Yes."

"Good. Settled then," said Vaughn.

As they started toward the guesthall, though, Joliffe noted that neither of them offered a hand to the other to seal the agreement, as either one of them would likely have done with a friend—or with someone they at least truly trusted.

Chapter 17

Frevisse made sure of not seeing either Joliffe or Vaughn before they were away in the morning, to seem to have no especial interest in them; but she did send Sister Margrett with her thanks to both of them—to Vaughn for accompanying them and to the minstrel for his kindness—and assurance that she was much better. She did not add that an evening spent pretending to be sleeping and ill until, finally, she had truly fallen asleep had done nothing for her ease of mind. Only when she was into the cloister again, safely back into her familiar life, would she be able to count herself done, finished, and free of all the business. She knew she did not hide well her urge to demand her release when Dame Claire finally came later in the morning, because Dame Claire's eyes lighted on her for a moment and brightened with mild laughter before sliding to Sister Margrett standing on the far side of the bed. Despite that, she was serious enough of voice as she asked, "How does our patient? She looks better this morning, I think," while lifting Frevisse's wrist to take her pulse. "Are you better, Dame?"

Resisting the urge to snatch her wrist away, Frevisse snapped, "Yes. I'm well. Whatever it was, it's passed now."

Dame Claire regarded her with that lurking inward laughter and said, "Still, a goodly dose of spurge might not come amiss."

Knowing the purgative properties of spurge and most certainly not wanting a dose of it, Frevisse said firmly, "I think not. I feel entirely well."

Dame Claire's laughter lingered but under it she seriously asked, too low to be heard beyond the bed, "It's done, then? Whatever it was, it's done?"

As quietly, Frevisse said, "It's done. Yes." At least for her.

"Well then." Dame Claire lifted her voice to where it had been. "This time I shall suppose the patient knows best how she does. Pray, return into the cloister and be welcome, Dame. You nursed her well, Sister Margrett."

Through that day and the next Frevisse readily and gratefully settled back into the even ways of the nunnery's life—its carefully balanced times for prayer and work and rest. She let the deep comfort of the Offices, the pleasure of her copying work at her desk in the cloister walk, even the small scrapes of familiar aggravation among the nuns, wrap around her as cushion and curtain against what she wanted neither to think nor worry on, because neither thought nor worry were any use. Her prayers had to be enough, and she found most of them were for Burgate, because Alice stood best chance of coming least scathed from everything, and whatever present perils Joliffe and Vaughn were in, they were come to them by choices made out of fair knowledge of what they hazarded. She doubted the same was true of the secretary. He had likely never thought his service to Suffolk would bring him where it had. Like her, he had been brought into this spreading trouble through no wish or knowing choice of his own, and she was safely back where she belonged, while someone meant for Burgate to die.

That thought came to her during Sext in the morning of her third day back at St. Frideswide's, in the choir as the nuns were chanting, their voices twining around each other. *"Ad te, Domine, confugio . . . In justitia tua libera me . . . Educes me e reti quod absconderunt, quia tu es refugium meum . . ."* To you, Lord, I flee for refuge . . . In your justice free me . . . You will bring me away from the snare they have set, because you are my refuge . . .

Someone meant for Burgate to die.

As quickly as the thought came, she denied it. Whoever held Burgate prisoner wanted him alive, able to tell his secret. If ever he told, then yes, he might well be killed to be sure he told no one else. That was the straight-forward way to see it. But the sudden thought come to her was that he could have been kept prisoner otherwise than as he was. He could, God forbid it, have long since been tortured to have out of him what was wanted. Torture was against the law, but so was his imprisonment, uncharged of any crime as it seemed he was. Why had whoever held him held back from torture?

And who had the power to have him held prisoner in a royal castle at all?

In their pressing need to lay hands on whatever Suffolk had confessed into writing at the last, neither she, Joliffe, nor Vaughn had spent time over that question. It was not even that Burgate's imprisonment was a great secret. Queen Margaret had known of it, had lightly sent Frevisse off to see him.

Or had that been done not lightly at all? Vaughn had sent a man ahead with word they were coming. Had it been planned for her to see Burgate on the hope he would tell his secret to her and she had made it easy for them?

And then she had been followed from Kenilworth.

She had seen Vaughn knew it, but since he had kept silent about it, so had she, with the thought that once she was back in the nunnery, the problem would be all his and he could handle it as he thought best. But that did not stop her wondering who had given the order for it. Queen Margaret? That was possible but was it likely? Young as she was and foreign, could she have that kind of power *and* know how to use it among the lords elbowing for their own places and power around the king? Far more likely was that one of those lords, ambitious and already beginning to be successful in replacing the duke of Suffolk, had dared Burgate's imprisonment and ordered her to be followed. The duke of Buckingham was there at Kenilworth, well able to set someone on to follow her and Vaughn in hopes of making use of whatever damage had been done by their discovery.

Or could it be someone among the household officers, acting on some lord's behalf. Somerset's? Or Sir Thomas Stanley, apparently far more powerful than he seemed behind his seemingly plain knighthood? Or could Stanley be working for and with Somerset? Or . . .

Did it matter who it was, now the thing was done and she was out of it? Not to her. But Burgate's imprisonment joined with the murders of Suffolk's steward and priest made it easy for her to believe someone among the lords around the king was intent on taking Suffolk's place in power with no scruple over men's deaths.

And yet that someone had scrupled against using torture on Burgate. Why?

All three men had taken messages from the duke of Suffolk to Somerset in Normandy. That was certain. And Burgate, as well as that, had written out—not so much Suffolk's confession of guilt; nothing so humble as that—but his accusation of those guilty with him, and that was why Burgate was still alive—because someone wanted what he had written. But except by the vileness of his prison he had not been tortured to have what he knew. *Why?* Kept as he was, his death by neglect or disease was almost assured. It was almost as if it was what was hoped for.

But surely they didn't want him dead before he told where the accusation was hidden, because surely whoever held him had considered that Burgate must have made provision for what would happen to the accusation should he die or even be missing long enough to be supposed dead.

The pieces did not fit together with any way that made ready sense. It was as if whoever held Burgate was of two minds how they wanted this to play out. It was almost as if they were leaving whether Burgate would live or die, with whatever would come of it either way, to God's choice.

That was maybe only her own piety speaking—to see it that way and think someone else might, too. It was maybe simply what it most seemed to be—a brutal foolishness not clearly thought through by someone valuing power over all else.

But then why no torture?

She was suddenly aware that the voices around her were fading toward silence on, " . . . *misericordiam Dei requiescant in pace.*" . . . by the mercy of God rest in peace, and that her voice was not with them. She did not know when she had fallen silent with her thoughts, and rather more hurriedly than reverently, she joined in the *Amen* that ended the Office, while a quick, guilty look sideways toward Domina Elisabeth found her frowning from the prioress' higher place at the end of the choir stalls.

Her failure had been noted.

As with other such failures of duty, nothing would be said about it now, unsettling the day. Both confession and rebuke would come tomorrow in the morning's chapter meeting, a practice meant to keep the hour by hour life of a nunnery undisturbed and give the erring nun time to consider her fault and reach a humility that let her freely admit her wrong and accept her punishment when the time came. That the practice did not always reach perfection did not lessen the value of the intent. Frevisse's own good intention to keep her mind to her tasks and away from where it did not need to go was helped by her afternoon work being presently the copying out of prayers to the Virgin from the breviary, as a gift from the nunnery to a butcher's wife in Banbury who had promised her younger daughter as a novice there when the girl was old enough. Frevisse always silently added to that "and if the girl be willing", but just now there was soothe in laying the letters evenly in firm black ink across the paper, filling what had been emptiness with the beauty both of the letters themselves and the wonder held in the words.

Only in the hour's recreation after supper, before the day's final prayers at Compline and then bed, did her guard against her thoughts fall as she walked in the evening light beside Dame Claire in the nunnery's walled garden along the graveled path between the carefully kept beds of herbs and flowers.

She and Dame Claire often walked together in that hour because they were usually content to keep silent in their own thoughts, not needing to talk for the pointless sake of talking; but in that ease this evening Frevisse's thoughts went back to where they had been. Who had ordered those murders, and was someone purposefully waiting for Burgate either to live and break and tell his secret or else to die with his secret kept, whichever God willed?

The latter question she could least answer. As for the outright murders, the duke of Somerset still seemed most likely. He must surely be hoping to move into Suffolk's place near the king and counting on King Henry's slack sense of justice to protect him against the accusations and outcries already being made against him. But even King Henry would not be able to hold ignorant against Suffolk's open charges in this hidden letter.

The trouble remained that when Suffolk was murdered and Burgate arrested, Somerset had been still in Normandy, waiting to be besieged in Caen. He might of course have men in his service who dealt for him, but could they have acted so swiftly—with no time for orders back and forth across the Channel—against Burgate? Could they have had the secretary not only seized but away into a royal prison before word of Suffolk's death was hardly known? Possibly. But could they be the "others" that Burgate had been too afraid even to name?

She doubted it. Those "others" had sounded more like men equal or nearly equal in power to Suffolk and Somerset themselves—and that would be how they had dealt so well at ordering the murders and Burgate's seizure.

And then the matter of Suffolk's own murder. Burgate had denied the given story that he had been taken in the Channel and killed by no more than angry shipmen taking their chance against him. Burgate had claimed it was all planned. But again Burgate had shied from giving any name.

She was hopelessly hindered by not knowing enough about the lords close around the king to make a strong guess about any of them and their ambitions. The duke of Buckingham, of course, because he was presently charged with the queen's safekeeping at Kenilworth and therefore with the keeping of the castle, which could be explanation for Burgate's imprisonment there. Where had Buckingham been in early May, when Suffolk was murdered and Burgate seized? Frevisse thought she remembered the king had been at the Parliament in Leicester all that month. His great lords had been with him there, including Buckingham. But maybe not. Maybe . . .

She found she had come to a stop, was turned on the path and staring down into the dark heart of a red flower whose name she did not know, without knowing how long she had been there. Dame Claire had walked on; Dame Juliana and Dame Amicia were coming her way along the path in murmurous talk together; but for the moment she was alone save for a bee bumbling among the blossoms and she wondered why mankind couldn't live in simplicity with itself instead of with ambition-driven greeds for wealth and power and the lusts of the body. But there was no simplicity anywhere in life, she thought. There was nothing simple about the flower in front of her, with its deep colors and delicate, many petals and finely detailed veins and stem and leaves, each part of it as different from its other parts as all plants differed from one another. And likewise with the simple, bumbling bee that had nothing simple about it, if she paused to think on it. Even the gravel beneath her feet was not simple. Every rock of it was different from all the others. So why uselessly wish that mankind might be simple among itself? "Simple" was not the way the world was made.

"Gone away again, Dame? In mind if not in body this time?" Dame Amicia asked—somewhat tartly, Frevisse thought; and wondered if there was jealousy about her time spent away from St. Frideswide's.

But of course she had known there likely was, with no one to know how less than happy she had been in it or the burden she had brought back with her; and quietly, with no urge to answer tartly back, she turned and said, "No. Merely giving thanks I'm here again," before walking away, head down and hands tucked into her opposite sleeves, wishing she matched inwardly that outward quiet.

She was ready, next morning in the chapter meeting, to confess on her knees before Domina Elisabeth her distraction of mind at Sext yesterday. Because praying was the center and reason of nuns' lives, failure at it was a grave fault, and her penance was grave to match it: to spend the hour before that same Office on her knees at the altar today, tomorrow, and the day after, and to have only bread and weak ale for her midday meal those same three days.

With deeply bowed head, Frevisse thanked Domina Elisabeth and returned to her low joint stool among the other nuns, both accepting her guilt and soothed at listening to ordinary matters being settled in ordinary ways through the rest of the chapter meeting. Her coming penance did not weigh on her. She had prayed too little while she was gone. This would be chance to recover some of that lost time. And fasting was no longer the great trouble it had been when she was young, now that she understood how acceptance was the greater part of bearing it and knew how to accept.

If only she could as well accept everything she did *not* know—would probably never know—about Suffolk's death and all the ills that were come from it.

The chapter meeting ended with Domina Elisabeth's blessing on them. The nuns rose to go about their various morning work, but Domina Elisabeth beckoned for Frevisse to come to her as the others left and said as Frevisse curtsied to her, "Master Naylor has asked leave to talk with you, Dame. I've told him you'd see him in the guesthall courtyard after chapter. You have my leave to go. Afterward, I'd see you in my parlor."

Frevisse curtsied again, waited for Domina Elisabeth to leave first, then went out and around the square cloister walk to the passage to the outer door. During the day the door was kept neither locked nor barred nor guarded. She let herself out and Master Naylor, the nunnery's steward, came toward her from where he had been waiting in the middle of the yard. She likewise went toward him, to be sure they met well away from anywhere they could be overheard. That she did so without fore-thinking it distressed her. Was she grown so distrustful of everything, even here in the nunnery?

As St. Frideswide's steward, Master Naylor had in hand all the nunnery's properties and oversaw its business interests under the prioress' direction. His long, well-worn face rarely had a smile and had none now as he bowed to Frevisse and said, "Good morning, my lady."

She wished him the same, adding, "You asked to see me?"

"I've a question for you, if you will, my lady."

"Of course, Master Naylor."

"Have you brought trouble back with you from where you've been?"

The question froze her into too long a silence before she answered with a feigned calm she did not feel, "I pray not. Why do you ask?"

"There's been a fellow skulking around the edges here since you came back. Some of the village folk have seen him along the woodshore and on the rise toward the mill, like he was watching things here, but he never lets anyone come up to him. Everyone is too busy with the harvest to make trouble over him if he makes none, and he hasn't, so there he is. They say he was here first, that he stayed at the guesthall one night."

She was not surprised that what went on in the nunnery was known outside its walls. Servants mingled and servants talked and there were times like this when that was helpful.

"Which night?" she asked.

With the grim satisfaction of having foreseen that question, Master Naylor answered, "The night after the one you spent there. You and those two men. Seems one of them left him a message."

"Which one?"

"Old Ela says it was the dark-haired one."

Nicholas Vaughn.

"A written message, I suppose," Frevisse said, keeping her voice even.

"Written and sealed, yes."

So Vaughn had expected the man. Was he one of the men who had followed them from Kenilworth? Was that why Vaughn had seen fit not to say anything about them? Or was he maybe sent from Alice, meant to meet Vaughn here?

If so, why had Vaughn said nothing about him?

But then, why should he? His duty was to Alice, not to Frevisse and certainly not to Joliffe.

Or maybe he had said something to Joliffe. It wouldn't have been easy to write and seal a message privately in the general sleeping and eating together in the guesthall.

"So *is* it trouble you've brought back with you?" Master Naylor asked. "Should we do something about this fellow and keep a watch?"

Slowly Frevisse said, "I don't know. I thought I'd left trouble behind me."

"It seems more as if it was waiting for you here, with that minstrel. He's part of it all, isn't he?"

"Is he?" Frevisse said, trying to sound blank about it and suspecting she failed.

Master Naylor's shrewd look never left her face. "Seems so, the way he and the other fellow rode off together in the morning looking friendly together."

"Rode off together?" They must have determined to go with each other to get the letter.

"Headed westward together like they were old friends," Master Naylor said.

"Westward?" She had only an uncertain thought of where Sible Hedingham was but knew it had to be east. Why would Joliffe and Vaughn have ridden westward? "The man who rode in with us, did he go with them?"

"He did."

Not back to Alice. All of them westward. What had they been playing at with that? Was it meant to be a misdirecting of the men who had followed her and Vaughn from Kenilworth? That was possible. But what of this man now keeping watch on St. Frideswide's?

Slowly, with too many thoughts coursing at once, like a tumbled pack of hounds confusing a trail, she said, "If anyone can lay hands on this fellow watching us, I'd like to talk with him."

"Of course, my lady. There's nothing else you can tell me?"

Fully meaning it, she said, "I'm sorry, no. I don't know what's toward at all."

She thought Master Naylor accepted her answer less from belief than because respect demanded it. He had to settle for bowing and saying, "Very well, my lady." But he paused on the edge of going, seemed to consider, then said, "Whatever is afoot, it's not good, is it?"

Matching his quiet, she said, "No. It's not good." And even more quietly, "I'm sorry."

Master Naylor accepted that with a quick nod, bowed again, and left her. She watched him walking away, across the courtyard and through the gateway to the outer yard. An honest, upright man who wanted only to do his work well and keep himself and his family provided for and safe. Those were the things most men wanted, Frevisse thought. And most women. Why did there have to be men so bound up in their ambition to have more and ever more that they endangered and destroyed the little that others had, the little that others wanted?

With a prayer that she had not brought deep trouble with her into St. Frideswide's after all, she went not back into the cloister but across the yard to the guesthall. As she went up the steps, old Ela came out. She had been "old Ela" and a servant in the guesthall for most of the years that Frevisse had been in the nunnery, but of late years she was grown very old, her body sunk in and bent forward on itself, her lifelong limp become a shuffle. Most work was now beyond her, but there was never thought of turning her out. There had been no need to discuss that Ela would have a corner of the guesthall's hall for her own and be fed and clothed and cared for the rest of her life, however long it might be.

What had not been known was what good value the nunnery would have for that kindness. Her body might be worn out but her eyes and wits had not lessened. From her corner or, on cold days, from beside the hearthfire, she kept a sharp watch on everything and everyone, and no one, including whichever nun might presently be hosteler and in charge of guests, was ever misled when asking what she thought about what was wrong, right, or could be bettered around the guesthall and among its servants.

Now, giving Frevisse a stiff-jointed little curtsy—the best her knees would let her—she said, "I've come out to sit in the sun while it lasts."

It was Ela to whom Frevisse wanted to talk, and from Ela's knowing look at her, Frevisse judged Ela's purpose was the same, so she gestured to a square stool set beside the door, saying, "Sit, please, Ela. I've come to ask you something."

"About what you and Master Naylor were looking so sour-faced at, yes?"

"About the dark-haired man who left a message here before he left with the minstrel. Did the minstrel know he wrote and left that message?"

Done with lowering herself with painful care to the stool, Ela gave a sniff. "That he didn't. The minstrel, I mean t'other took care he shouldn't, seemed to me."

"Oh?" Frevisse encouraged.

"In the morning, when his man and the minstrel went out to see that the horses were fit and ready for the day, he stayed behind, wrote out his letter quick-like, sealed it, and handed it off to Ralph, saying he should give it if anyone came asking for 'the dog's letter'."

The dog's letter? Did Vaughn see himself, then, as Alice's faithful dog? More to the point, he had expected someone to come for that letter, and aloud Frevisse wondered, "Did he have all the means to hand to write this letter, then? That he was able to do it so quickly?"

"Had it all in a pouch he carried," Ela said. "Paper, ink, pen, sealing wax, and a seal."

All planned out ahead.

"Did you happen to have chance to see what device was on the wax seal after he'd gone?"

Ela gave a wide smile that deepened the deep wrinkles of her old face. "Happen I asked young Ralph to let me look at it. Old women have fancies like that and it's easier to give me my way than make trouble over it."

Frevisse smiled back at her. "And you thought someone else might be interested in knowing, too."

"That thought was in my mind by then, yes," Ela granted. "So, for anyone who might want to know, I can say it was a cat's face with a circle around it. That's what the seal was. That means something to you?"

There being no point in denying it, Frevisse said, "Yes." That "cat's face" was likely a leopard's forward-facing head. Three of them were on the duke of Suffolk's heraldic arms. Vaughn must carry such a seal for when he needed to send something to Alice. That he had had everything necessary there to hand told he must do it often enough to make carrying it all worth the while.

But that didn't mean this letter had been to Alice.

There was no reason except unbased suspicion to think it had not been. But if it hadn't been . . .

He and Joliffe could have gone westward to throw off the men who had followed from Kenilworth. He and Alice might well have provided beforehand that someone of hers would meet him here, and he might well want to send her word of what was happening. But why keep the letter secret from Joliffe? For plain reasons of secrecy, of course. There could be very little deep trust between them. But there could be other reasons, too—ones not so plain and maybe nothing to do with Alice. Or did it tell her where to find Suffolk's long-sought final letter, and Joliffe was betrayed? Or did it tell someone else, and both Joliffe and Alice were betrayed? And in any case, why was the man still here, keeping watch on the nunnery?

Unless there had been more than one of them, and while one came into the nunnery, the other had lain low and was now gone back to Alice with Vaughn's message.

Or whomever else Vaughn might be serving.

Because Vaughn might be playing a double game. And he and his man were ridden away with Joliffe. Who was alone.

Her mind hurt with all the possibilities for treachery there might be and with knowing there was nothing she could do except pray, when this was one of the times when prayer seemed a very thin comfort against all her fears.

All Domina Elisabeth wanted from her was whether she had been able to help Master Naylor; and just as she had asked no more at Frevisse's return than if she had been of comfort to her cousin and been satisfied when Frevisse answered that she had been of some, so now she accepted Frevisse saying she had been of no help to Master Naylor and let it go at that, to Frevisse's relief.

* * *

She spent the hour on her knees at the altar praying for the burden of her fears and worries to be lifted from her mind and soul, but nothing had lifted by the time the heavy-noted cloister bell began to clang to Sext. Her soft groan as she climbed stiff-kneed to her feet was less for her knees than for her sense of helplessness under the burden of all she knew and how little she could do about any of it. Then someone's hand under her elbow steadied her as she a little swayed, and she looked around to find Dame Thomasine there.

Dame Thomasine was a much younger nun, though not so young anymore, whose early years in St. Frideswide's had been fraught with almost frantic piety and a much-cherished hope among some of the nuns that she might be a burgeoning saint. That hope had dimmed over the years, and likewise, Dame Thomasine's desperate piety had changed, not lessened but deepened and grown quiet in its strength. She seldom raised her eyes higher than her prayer-folded hands, and Frevisse was somewhat startled to find the younger woman was looking at her now, and was more startled when Dame Thomasine, who rarely spoke except in the Offices, said softly, still gazing at her, "It will help to remember that all things under the sun have their time. The time of keeping and the time of casting away. The time for things to come and the time for things to pass. Whatever our own wishes and hopes may be."

Frevisse opened her mouth, as if there were some answer she could make to that, but found she had none. Besides, Dame Thomasine had already lowered her gaze again and was going toward her seat in the choir. The other nuns were coming, too, and Frevisse went to her own place, taking with her a moment of resenting Dame Thomasine. For someone so quiet, she could be very disquieting. But there was both truth and comfort in those quiet words from Ecclesiastes, and as Frevisse knelt and bowed her head, she set to giving herself up to them, because—as Ecclesiastes likewise said—come what may and despite when men mïght wish or hope, it was God who brought all things to their end, and therefore all ends must be good.

Chapter 18

Having once determined that the two men from Kenilworth were indeed following them, Joliffe and Vaughn kept together for a day and a half, riding vaguely southwestward, meaning to draw them well away from whoever had given them their orders. The longer before the men reported back, the longer before some other move could be made some other direction.

"If nothing else, we may buy time enough for Lady Alice to have Burgate freed," Vaughn said. "Then he can tell her everything, and while we play 'hunt the hare' . . ."

"We being the hares," Joliffe said.

". . . she can send someone else for this unblessed letter."

"We having served our purpose by keeping the hounds headed this way."

There was the worry that when they did go their separate ways, their 'hounds' might guess their quarry had spotted them. "But if we show no especial alarm," said Vaughn, "they may think we're simply parting company to be careful and split themselves to follow each of us. Either way," he added with a frown, "you'll be at the greater hazard, riding alone. I'll still have Symond."

"It's a pity killing doesn't come easy to us," Joliffe said. "That would be the straightest way to be rid of them."

"It would, but we're not going to," snapped Vaughn.

He rode in stiff silence for an hour afterward, but Joliffe did not regret having tried him. As Vaughn had pointed out, he was one to Vaughn's and Symond's two. It helped to know Vaughn did not favor murder as a short way to an end. But neither did Joliffe regret when they went their separate ways the second day, Vaughn swinging away northward, intending to lose his follower and curve back to the east in a day or so, Joliffe carrying on the way they had been going. As hoped, their two followers split to follow them, and Joliffe spent part of another day losing his man in a market-day crowd in Gloucester, doing his best to make the loss seem by chance rather than purpose so that maybe the man would go on looking for him there; and because a very likely reason to come to Gloucester was to take the bridge over the wide Severn River, Joliffe let himself be last seen heading that way, before turning Rowan away and heading north, to cross the river by the ferry at Tewkesbury.

A day after that he was well westward into the Welsh hills, free and clear of any sign that he was followed; and he turned north again, meaning to make as straight as the roads would allow for Ludlow, the duke of York's town and great castle where he would surely find someone to carry word to Ireland. But the weather turned when he did, and a lashing rain too bad for riding held him two days at an inn. He had to fight the urge to pace the hours away, but Rowan did well out of it, taking her ease in the inn stable and, "Eating your head off," Joliffe pointed out to her when he went in the evening to see how she did.

She flicked an ear at him and did not raise her head from the shallow pan of oats he was holding for her. The stable was a clean-kept place. The smells of hay and warm horses prevailed over any other, and the rain on the roof's thatch and Rowan's crunching of oats were the loudest sounds, far from the inn's loud main room crowded with other stranded travelers and villagers short of work in this weather. Sitting on the edge of the manger, his back safely to a wall and no one else there, Joliffe felt a better measure of quiet than he had had in days. Just now, just here, for this little while, there was nothing he could do toward what needed to be done. For this little while the weight of necessity was off him and it was pleasant to be doing nothing in particular except contenting Rowan.

In his youth and young manhood he had enjoyed the contentment that could come from doing nothing in particular. He had even worked to better his skill at it. Only over time he had let himself be drawn into other men's matters and matters of his own and somehow had lost the skill, so subtly that he had not seen it go, only known when it was gone. Sometimes he was not sure why. Had it been ambition? Or blindness, so he failed to see what was happening? Or simply stupidity? There were times when he favored the latter reason. If what he truly wished was to be sitting beside his own hearthfire in his own home, why wasn't he there, instead of here?

Rowan shoved her head at him to let him know the oats were gone. He shoved her back, saying, "Greedy. That's all you get. You don't want to turn into an oats-fattened slug, do you?"

She shoved at him again to let him know that, yes, she did, and he laughed and slid off the manger's edge and set to

combing her mane, not because she needed it just then—
the inn's stableman had done a good job of it—but simply
for their mutual contentment: hers at being brushed, his at
the plain work.

Besides, he knew why he was here instead of simply at
home. One way and another through the years he had
learned too much about the men who had gathered to the
duke of Suffolk and into power around the king. Even if he
was near to nothing himself in the wide weave of power in
the realm, still, whatever he could do, however slight,
against such men was worth the doing. He only wished, at
present, that he knew better what men he was working
against, because surely Somerset was not alone in all of it.

The third morning came with a clearing sky and he rode on
with hope of being a good many miles nearer to Ludlow by
day's end, until Rowan threw a shoe and promptly wedged a
stone into her hoof. Prying out the stone took little time, but
unsure how bruised her foot was, Joliffe chose to lead her
rather than ride and maybe make it worse; and because in
Wales the middle of nowhere was miles from any blacksmith,
they were a long time coming to help. The blacksmith they
found proved to be good, told Joliffe he had done right not
to ride but that once she was new-shod, all would be well
and didn't he want to put all new shoes on her now and save
trouble later? Seeing the sense of that, Joliffe had him do it,
and it was only at evening the next day that he finally rode
up Ludlow's steep Broad Street into the marketplace. The
hour was too late for him to present himself at the castle with
request to see whoever was highest among the duke's officers
presently there—too late to do it without drawing unwanted
attention to himself, anyway—so he paid himself and Rowan
into an inn and waited for morning.

Even then things did not go at the speed he wanted. Seemingly everyone in castle as well as town was more occupied with market day than with any other business that might present itself. He only finally was able to see the castle's chamberlain, present the token that affirmed he was from Sir William Oldhall, and give his warning.

The chamberlain grew grim at hearing how Sir Thomas Stanley was gone hot-saddled to Wales at word of York's planned return.

"Under orders for something," the chamberlain said darkly. "That's what you thought and that's what I think."

"If I had to put money to it," Joliffe said carefully, "I'd lay wager he had orders to stop my lord of York, either from landing or else from reaching England."

"Stop his grace? Sir damned Thomas Stanley is supposed to stop my lord of York? How? Arrest him?" the chamberlain scorned.

Grimly Joliffe said, "I've heard from Sir William Oldhall himself that there are men around the king who want his grace accused of treason, that there's secret order for at least one of the oyer and terminer commissions to claim they've found he's behind these uprisings this year."

The chamberlain swore in Welsh. It was a good language to swear in, ripe with ways of damning to hell, both specific and general and especially for Englishmen. Then he said, "There's no telling, then, what Sir Thomas has been ordered to do against York. Sir Thomas is just the mean-minded wretch to do the worst he can. Not that my lord of York will let him do much of anything, I'll warrant. Right. In any case, you'll be wanting to get on to Ireland to warn his grace. I can give you . . ."

"I fear someone else will have to go," Joliffe interrupted. "I've business in the other direction and it's waited too long as it is."

The chamberlain looked ready to protest that but held back long enough to take good look at him and instead asked, "My lord of York's business, is it?"

"My lord of York's business, and as weighty, maybe, as getting warning to him."

"Then someone else can go to Ireland. I can see to that. For you, do you need any help I can give?"

"Some money wouldn't come amiss, and a day's rest and keep for my horse and me."

"You can have all that and a fresh horse, too, if you want."

"Better the devil I know," Joliffe said lightly. Or, rather, a horse he knew was sound, good for the miles he was going to ask of her. "But my thanks for the offer anyway. Just some money, food, and rest, and I'll be away sometime tomorrow."

"You'll have all that. In the meantime I'll have a messenger away to Ireland."

"Better secretly than not," Joliffe suggested.

"It would seem so, wouldn't it? My wife has been at me to send someone to Shrewsbury with a list of things she wants. I'll start him out as if for that and he can cut away toward the coast when he's well away from Ludlow. There should be no trouble about it."

"Except from your wife," Joliffe said.

The chamberlain grunted agreement.

Joliffe made the most of that evening's supper, a full night's safe sleep, and the next day's midday dinner, before he rode out of Ludlow by the road toward Shrewsbury. He made no haste about it, so that when nightfall came he did not have so far to ride back on his tracks to be sure he had not been followed away from Ludlow before circling the town to take the road to Worcester, the opposite way from Shrewsbury. Favored by both the weather and moonlight, he covered a good many miles before, toward dawn, he gave himself and Rowan a rest along a particularly lonely stretch of road, unsaddling her and leaving her to crop the long, dewed grass of the wayside, her lead-rope in his hand while he slept dry under a hedge, pillowed on his saddle.

As he intended, he awoke to the dawn twittering of birds in the first light of the coming day. With sighing memory of the bed he'd had in Ludlow, he crawled stiffly to his feet, ate some bread and cheese with one hand while wiping Rowan's back carefully dry with a cloth in the other before saddling her. When she swung her head around to make a snap at him in token of her displeasure as he tightened the girth, he told her, "I couldn't agree with you more, good lady. But needs must when the devil drives."

She snorted her opinion of that but took the bit and her bridle with only one try at pushing him off his feet with a hard shove of her head.

He had prayed for dry, clear days for this part of his ride, and his prayer was half-way answered. That day and the others after it either started clear and ended with rain or else started with rain and ended clear. He did not find one was better than the other. Either way, he was rained on every day and twice had to stay the night at inns and once spent a whole midday in a village tavern while a pounding rain-storm wore itself out. He was only glad he need not press onward so hard as he might have. By now Vaughn would have Burgate's letter from the priest in Sible Hedingham. He would come there only to find that Vaughn had been and gone and then have to go on to Wingfield, in hope that Vaughn had played as straight as he was playing it and that Lady Alice was ready to carry through their bargain.

He little doubted that she would. She was frightened and in need of an ally and was not fool enough to think she could find a safe one among the greed-drooling pack around King Henry. He would have liked to think she would not want to lose her cousin Dame Frevisse's regard, either, by betraying their agreement, but he was not sure how much weight that might have in the balance. No, what he most counted on were Lady Alice's fear and her need of Richard, duke of York.

His last miles of riding to Sible Hedingham were by green-hedged lanes through the easy roll of Essex countryside. He was back not so very far from where he had started when he left Hunsdon on his way to Alderton. He had made a ragged figure-eight across England and back, and now to end it all he was going to be rained on some more, he thought, eyeing the roil of clouds mounting the eastward sky ahead of him. He was becoming very tired of weather.

In truth, he was simply becoming tired, he admitted as he rode into Sible Hedingham. The village stretched along the road, with a slope down to pastures in a shallow valley on one side, on the other a rise of land to the village fields. As he had neared it, he had seen across the valley, above another village's roofs, the tall, stone square of an old castle's keep. Over there, he guessed would be the local market, because here all he came on was a slight widening of the street before it somewhat jogged and sloped into another stream valley, leaving the village. This wide place in the road was the village's center, he judged by a green-leaved branch thrust out above a door of one of the houses, telling there was new ale to be had there, with two trestle tables with benches set outside the door to invite folk to sit and drink.

But rather than the few lazing scruff that almost every alehouse seemed to have and the only folk likely to be there this time of day, what looked to be half the village men were there and not idle but crowded up to the tavern's open door and window, with a grumbling throb of voices from inside that told more men were there and, by a shriller note mixed among them, some women, too. Nor were they drinking. Joliffe saw one man raise a fist and shake it over his head, and inside someone roared a "*No*" that was answered with cheers.

As a traveling player Joliffe had learned to "read" any place he came to very quickly, judging whether its folk were likely to welcome a play or prefer the sport of throwing garbage or stones—or simply go on sullenly about their business, not interested if poor players starved for lack of work. As he drew rein in the other side of the road from the alehouse, he thought that if he was come here as a player, he would have moved on without unpacking the cart. Something was getting ready to happen, and the sooner he learned for certain that Vaughn had been and gone so he could go, too, the better. Wherever he'd be when the storm came down on him, it would likely be better than here.

A little farther along the street three boys were kicking a stone back and forth across the dust to each other. Joliffe guided Rowan toward them and asked where the priest lived. They answered by pointing at a narrow lane running up-slope beyond the alehouse. "Just up there," one of the boys said. "Across from the church. You'll know it."

"Is he home?" Joliffe asked.

"Him? Yes," another boy said with unboyish bitterness. "Counting his coins and planning how to get more, likely."

"Yah," the first boy said. "That's your father talking."

"Your father, too!" the other boy defended, while the third boy nodded vigorously.

Joliffe thanked them and dropped a silver half-penny to each of them, bringing wide smiles to their faces and an offer from the second boy to tell him anything else he might want to know.

Joliffe smiled back at him, said, "Later, maybe," and reined Rowan toward the lane. It proved to be brief, steeply sloped with the church set on his right on the point of the slope where the lane ended against another road running both ways from it, making another widened triangle of road. There were more houses here, along the lane and the road it met, but as the boy had said, Joliffe knew without having to ask again which was the priest's house. Like its neighbors, it sat flat-faced to the street, so there was probably a large garden behind it, and probably a byre and barn beyond that for the priest's livestock and the tithes-in-kind from his parishioners' fields, unless—as it seemed from the boys' talk—he had brought his folk to paying their tithes in coin instead of with dried beans and peas and grain. Then only what came from his own fields would be in the barn.

Most priests of villages and even small towns lived the double life of priest and landlord of whatever local land had been given to the parish church. The more fortunate priests could make a very comfortable life of it. The less fortunate did well to scrape by from one year to the next. John Smyth did not look to be among the latter. Not only was his house larger than any of his neighbors, it was newly thatched and all its front freshly plastered, with both windows of the out-thrust upper story glassed and the broad front door painted a warm red as yet unmarred by any winter. It was a rich man's house in a place that looked unlikely to have many rich men, and Joliffe tied Rowan to the iron ring hung from a wooden post set in the street beside the door and knocked with confidence at the door. When dealing with the rich it was usually better to seem confident rather than craving.

He expected a servant would answer—this looked too fine a place for the priest to do his own door-answering—and indeed a thin older man with a chicken-scrawny neck and servant's plain tunic did finally open the door, to give Joliffe a narrow-eyed stare that lacked the warmth of Christian welcome before he demanded, "What?"

Here was a servant looking to be offended at anyone who dared to darken his master's doorstep, so in return Joliffe looked down his nose at him and said, "I need to speak to Father John."

"Sire John," the man snapped. "He's Sire John."

"A learned as well as holy man," Joliffe said, smooth as oiled ice. "I'll be most pleased, in my need, to meet him."

The man's glare said he wanted to find fault with that, but

unable to, he finally grunted, said, "You stay here until I've seen if he'll see you," and disappeared from the doorway, leaving the door barely open. Hardly a moment later he was back and made an ungracious gesture for Joliffe to come in. Joliffe went past him without thanks, into a pleasantly large room with a scrubbed board floor, stairs to the upper floor against one wall, a door to the probable kitchen at the back, and a wide, wooden-mullioned window facing the street. The walls were painted saffron-yellow, the roof beams a deep red that matched the outer door. On one long wall hung a painted hanging of St. John the Evangelist with his goblet and serpent, St. John the Baptist with his lamb, and St. John of Beverley with his shrine and cross-staff. Sire John must take his own name seriously, Joliffe thought. The end of the room away from the stairs was taken up with a beam-high aumbry of closed doors below and open shelves above. Because there was a slant-topped writing table near them, the open shelves might have held a scholar's books but instead served to display an array of polished pewter plates, platters, goblets, and cups.

Beside the writing desk, there was a long-legged stool on which Joliffe doubted Sire John perched very often: the priest looked far too settled where he sat on a long, high-backed, well-cushioned bench near the middle of the room, holding in one hand a small plate with a thin-sliced apple, in the other hand an apple slice on its way to his mouth. Like the bench, he was well-cushioned—ample, one might say—and his priestly gown was austere only in being black, with nothing humble about its fine-woven wool.

No, he was not one of those priests who gave all to his people; and he might be plump where his servant was lean, but Joliffe, straightening from a respectful bow and meeting the priest's eyes for the first time, suspected master and servant were of a kind—men unwelcoming to anyone who might want something of theirs, even if only time.

Since Joliffe wanted no more time in Sire John's company

than need be, that was well enough. Let Sire John tell him Vaughn had the packet and he would be out of here and away before the priest could finish bidding god-be-with-him. And he said with his best outward courtesy—the one that went somewhat less than skin deep, "Good sir, I've come for the packet your cousin Edward Burgate sent to you."

Hand with apple slice still poised, Sire John said, "Have you?" He inserted the apple neatly into his mouth, chewed, and swallowed. "Well, you can't have it."

He delivered that with a flat certainty that suggested the Lord God himself would be as readily refused if he presumed to appear and ask for it—and that Sire John would take equal pleasure in the refusal.

"It's gone?" Joliffe asked, still courteously.

"It's not. It's here." Sire John was heavily self-satisfied about that. "It's Edward's. And there's an end of it."

Joliffe went to wary calculation. Vaughn had had time enough to reach here. If he had not, then something had gone wrong somewhere. But even as he thought that, Sire John went on with a smirk of pleasure, "I didn't give it to that fellow two days ago and I'm not giving it to you. So go away."

Joliffe took a quick breath, shifted his thoughts, and said, "Other fellow?"

"Other fellow. Two days ago. Here, like you are. Standing there asking for it." Sire John held out the emptied plate. His man came, took it, and left the room while the priest went on. "Just as well I didn't give it over to him. He was killed and robbed hardly a mile outside of town. He's lying in the charnel house right now while we wait for the crowner to come view him and for someone to pay for burying him. We've sent to . . ."

"Your cousin is in dire trouble and that packet can save him," Joliffe snapped, done with courtesy, "What will serve to convince you of it?"

Sire John eyed him narrowly, then shook his head. "There's

nothing. If you've report and proof that Edward is dead, that's one thing, but to just demand the packet, no. There's something more about all this."

"It's because of that something more that your cousin went to this trouble," Joliffe said. "It's because of that something more that he's in trouble that we're trying to get him out of. I'll swear on a Bible that I'm here for his good and to finish what he started. I'll twice swear it, if that will help."

Sire John made a sound of rumbling displeasure in his throat and his eyes narrowed. "The other fellow offered me money for it."

"I've offered to swear," Joliffe said stiffly. "That should be enough." Would have to be since Vaughn's offer of money hadn't been enough.

"That's not what Edward wanted. He said I was to keep it until he came, or I had proof he was dead, and even then it goes to . . . someone, and it isn't you."

"The duchess of Suffolk," Joliffe said. "His late master's widow. You're to see it gets to her."

"Very good," Sire John said mockingly. "The other fellow knew that, too." He sniffed. "Didn't do him any good, either."

And a plague on Edward Burgate for not having some word that would pry the letter loose from his cousin, Joliffe thought; and had another thought and said, "Then do you go yourself to my lady. Take the packet and whatever guard you want from among your people here and go to her at Wingfield. She'll pay your costs and a reward besides."

Sire John at least paused before answering, still staring at him narrow-eyed but considering before finally saying, "That I have to think on. Come back tomorrow when I've thought on it."

"The packet . . ."

"Has been safe in my keeping and will go on being safe there. I told you, I'll think on it." He jerked a hand toward the door. "Now go."

Neither sense nor greed nor anything short of violence looked likely to shift the man. That was the "benefit" of narrow-minded certainty that one was beyond chance of ever being wrong, Joliffe thought. Sire John would "think on it" and think well of himself for having thought. What Joliffe bitterly doubted was how *well* the man would think: the difference between "think" and "think well" escaped a great many people.

But seeing no way to shift the man, he jerked a short bow and was only barely careful not to slam the door behind him as he went out, certain that when he came back tomorrow, he'd find Sire John had not shifted an inch from what he "thought" now. Vaughn had come for the packet and Vaughn was dead. Sire John's first thought should be that the thing was likely dangerous and be grateful for the chance to be rid of it, even if it meant going—with his own chosen guard, mind—to Lady Alice. If the man had been *thinking*, that's what he should have thought.

But even while Joliffe jerked Rowan's reins free and swung into his saddle, he knew his deeper anger was not at the fool of a priest but at Vaughn for being dead. He'd had no business getting himself killed.

And mixed with that anger was a spine-tightening certainty that more than plain robbery was behind Vaughn's death. For Vaughn to come here, ask for the packet, be refused, and be immediately murdered afterward . . . to accept his death was chance was a stretch Joliffe was unwilling to make, especially since making it and thereby lowering his guard could get him equally dead very soon.

As he turned Rowan away from the priest's house, there was a growling shout from the alehouse, confirming for him how little he wanted to stay the night in this place. There had been past-counting outbreaks of anger and rebellion all this year and they were likely to go on, because after all there was so far no reason for them to stop. All the grounds for men's angers were still there, unchanged—the greed of the lords around the king, the breakdown of justice anywhere the duke of Suffolk's men had held power, the lost French war. If there was yet another uprising in the making here, it was only another reason to be away from here as soon as might be.

But Vaughn was dead, and Joliffe wanted to know more about how he had died than "killed and robbed." Besides, he owed Vaughn at least one prayer over his body, if only because Vaughn had not killed him when he had the chance.

The church's charnel house was easily found, a stone-built shed with reed-thatched roof and wooden door standing in a rear corner of the churchyard. Joliffe tied Rowan's reins to the low withy fence that marked the churchyard bounds without making a barrier, so that he did not bother with going to the narrow twist of stile into the yard but merely took a small leap over the fence. Crossing the humped and grassy ground toward the charnel house, he found that his bitterness at Sire John was growing, the more time he had for it. A more generous priest might have allowed a murdered man's body to lie in the church for better blessing, instead of shoved into the charnel house before its time. The charnel house was where the bones of the faithful departed were kept after being unearthed from their graves when new graves were being made for the more newly dead, since consecrated ground was limited but deaths were not. What Joliffe sometimes wondered on was how that would be at Judgment Day when all the dead were to rise, their bodies restored. The pictures painted and carved on church walls showed a rising up of whole men and women from graves and coffins, never the jumbled sorting out there would have to be of bones piled at random in charnel houses. Presently, though, he was merely glad the bones were clean ones, the rot of flesh long-gone from them, the smell as he opened the door into the shed's shadows only of small decay and the damp earthen floor.

Except for the door, the only light came from two small, high up windows, one in each side wall, above the bones in their sorted piles—large long bones here, lesser long bones there, jaw bones jumbled in a heap, skulls stacked like rounded rocks one on another against a wall, their blank, black eyeholes staring. Vaughn's body lay wrapped in a length of canvas on the bare floor in the middle of the shed, not given even the slight kindness of a candle left burning beside it, to guess from the lack of any puddled wax. Had Sire John bothered himself with a single prayer for Vaughn's soul? Joliffe wondered as he went down on one knee beside the featureless bundle and folded back the outermost flap of canvas to uncover Vaughn's face.

Except—he saw as he turned the canvas back—it was not Vaughn's.

Chapter 19

oliffe stared, blank-witted.

Not Vaughn.

Someone who had come asking for the packet but not been Vaughn.

He threw the fold of canvas over the dead man's face again and stood up, staring down at it, his mind flung back to everything Sire John had said but finding no help in it. The priest had named the duchess of Suffolk but that meant little. Burgate might have finally broken. Or been broken. Had someone decided torture was needed to have what they wanted from him, after the queen's error in betraying he was there?

If that had been error and not something fore-thought.

Or was it, more simply, that Vaughn had after all returned

to Lady Alice first, had been for some reason unable to come onward, and this man had been sent in his stead?

Joliffe lifted the canvas from the dead man's face again, this time meaning to see more than simply that he was not Vaughn.

Several days dead, his skin was gray and sunken over the skull, and because no one had bothered with binding his jaw decently shut, his mouth hung gaping open. A several-days-dead man was not good to look on but Joliffe did and after a few moments knew that he did know the man. Not by name, no, but knew him. He had been one of the men with Vaughn in Alderton.

That he was here had to mean Vaughn *had* gone to Wingfield instead of straightly here. Why? Had he been hurt? Fallen ill? Whatever the reason, he must have gone to Lady Alice because he could not come here, and so she had sent this man in his place. And now this man was dead.

Joliffe suddenly felt the open door of the charnel house at his unguarded back and took a long step aside and turned enough to let him see it as well as the corpse.

He had too many questions now and too many possible answers to them, and much though he wanted to be out of here, he also wanted to see how the man had died, and leaned over and folded back the canvas from the rest of the body. Because the crowner had yet to view it, the body was still fully clothed. In the shadows of the charnel house Joliffe at first saw only the dark, spread stain of dried blood on the man's doublet-front but when he leaned nearer, holding his breath against the smell of beginning decay, he could make out the black slit where a blade had gone through the doublet into flesh under the left ribs. A well-placed blow that would have reached the heart for a quick kill, leaving a man no time to argue about his fate.

That might have been the murderer's good luck, but Joliffe doubted it. He suspected there had been both skill and purpose to that stroke, that it had been made by someone who knew how to kill.

He sat down on his heels and felt in the leather purse still hanging from the dead man's belt. It was empty not only of any coins but of even the lesser things everyone gathered in a jackdaw-way—slight things that mattered to no one but the gatherer and of no worth to anyone else. Whoever had emptied this man's purse had been thorough. Not that that told much. It might have been done either by whoever killed him, the better to make it seem a robbery, or else by those who dealt with his body afterward, taking anything they could get and afterward throwing away whatever they decided was worthless.

Thankful he could see no reason to go through the man's clothing in search of anything else because whoever had so completely emptied his purse would have been thorough there, too, Joliffe stood up and away from the body. Plain robbery with murder might be the way of it, but he could not bring himself to accept that, because even though the duke of Suffolk was four months dead, the circles of trouble he had caused were still spreading outward, with this accumulation of deaths around his household only part of it and no reason to think they were the end. Men who had known too much about Suffolk's part in losing the French war were being killed, and Sire John was a great fool not to be rid of that packet at the first chance given to him. Even knowing nothing else about it, his cousin's desperation in sending it to him should have been warning enough the thing was dangerous. Nor did Joliffe see he was to be honored for refusing to give it up. His grip on it looked less to be keeping faith with his cousin than pleasure at his power to thwart and anger anyone who wanted it.

So what to do next?

Face down Sire John and have the packet from him one way or another, or else set him on his way to Lady Alice. Either would do, and Joliffe found himself favoring the latter, not wanting to have the thing himself unless he could acquire a full suit of armor to wear while he had it and someone to guard his back for good measure.

He re-covered the body, wished the man's soul well with a brief prayer, and went out of the charnel house, closing the door behind him. The setting sun was large and orange above the spread of trees that edged the western sky here, but the storm clouds that had been climbing black out of the east were now sweeping overhead and would likely overtake it before it set. One more trouble and one more bar to him being away from here as soon as he would have liked. To add to his unease, no one had come to ask what he was doing in the churchyard or charnel house. A village usually knew everything that went on within it, with someone always ready to ask questions of any stranger. That no one had come to question him was warning of how awry things were here.

As he untied his reins, Rowan raised her head from grazing what grass there was along the fence and looked at him with what seemed a suggestion that a dry stable and oats would be well bethought.

"Maybe," he told her, swinging into the saddle. "Maybe not. This isn't going as easily as we could hope."

With a great-heaved horse-sigh, she gave way to his tug on her reins and headed down the road toward the priest's house. As they crossed the lane by which he had come from the alehouse he saw at its far end what looked to be the men from the alehouse clotted in a tight bunch, crowding into the lane and shouting at each other with the rabble-growl of men gone past thinking into blind, ugly doing. Yet they didn't look to be quarreling and readying to fight each other. Whatever they were angry at, they were at one about it and it was for someone else.

A few women were standing in their own doorways along the lane, some with tightly crossed arms, others with a huddled look, many with a hand out to keep a peering child or children behind them, but all of them staring toward their angry men. Joliffe stopped Rowan near one of them with a baby on one arm, a toddler by the hand beside her, and a frightened look on her face. With a nod toward the men, he asked, "What is it?"

"The priest," the woman answered, fear in her voice, too. "They're all stirred up against him."

"For what?"

"For everything." For a moment anger joined her fear. "He's not a good man. He won't leave off about 'his rights', wants his full tithes and heriot no matter how hard things have maybe gone with someone. He . . ." Several of the men at the lane's end made a sudden start away from the others, yelling and gesturing for the rest to follow them along the lane.

"Oh, blessed Saint Edmund," the woman gasped. "They're going to do it."

Joliffe swung Rowan away from her. Sire John's house stood blank-faced, with no one heading that way with any warning, and Joliffe did not mean to be seen doing what none of the priest's own people would do. He cared too much for his own neck, but he set Rowan into a trot along the cross-street, toward where he thought—hoped—there would be a gate into whatever rearyard the priest's house had.

There was, and it was standing partly open. Dismounting, he drew Rowan's reins hurriedly through the gate's round handle and went into the small yard. There were a barn and sheds on one side, a small garden of herbs and vegetables and a grassy square with a bench to the other, with a path through the garden to the house's back door. Joliffe went for the door at a run and on the threshold came almost into collision with the priest's lean servant going out.

"The village is up!" Joliffe said at him. "They're after Sire John. He has to get out of here!"

"That's what I've been telling him," the man snarled. He

had a bundle clutched to his chest with both arms and shoved Joliffe out of his way with an elbow. "He won't go. But I am."

And he did, breaking into a shamble-legged run for the rear gate.

Joliffe opened his mouth to call after him, gave it up as useless, and went into a kitchen that showed Sire John's devotion to his comfort and belly. Pots, frypans, sieves, ladles, and other kitchen gear hung about the broad cooking hearth, a heavy, wooden-topped work table sat in the room's middle, and a closed chest with a large lock against one wall probably held such costly things as spices. The villagers would make short work of the lock, Joliffe thought as he crossed the room. As for Sire John . . .

The priest was standing at the streetward window of his parlor, had opened one shutter and was looking out and along the street with no sign of alarm or fear about him, only—as he looked around at Joliffe—dawning anger. "You," he said. "Why are you . . ."

Joliffe pointed toward the rabble-sound of men coming along the street. "They're coming for you. Against you. You have to get out of here. Quickly. Before someone among them thinks to block the back way."

Sire John drew himself up straight, his thick neck holding his thick head high. "Let them come. I'm their priest. They'll not dare raise one hand against me."

"They mean to raise more than one hand against you," Joliffe snapped, shoved him aside, slammed shut the shutter, and dropped the bar across the window. At least the servant had bothered to bar the front door before he fled. "Have you ever seen what happens when men give up being men and turn into one great, vicious beast? That's what's coming up the street for you!"

Sire John disdained that with, "They're my people. I'm their priest. They'll not dare to . . ."

"Have you ever given them one single cause to love you? Even one?" Joliffe snarled. "Whatever else they do, they're going to burn down your house and everything in it, and it will be over your dead body they do it if you don't get out of here!"

That got him what he wanted more than Sire John's escape. He had already given up hope he could shift the priest fast enough to save him, too fool-pleased with himself as he was to believe he could ever come to harm. Joliffe, on the other hand, had a strongly set sense of his own mortality and wanted out of here. But he also wanted what he had come for, and at his deliberately said threat of burning, Sire John's gaze snapped sidewise toward the closed doors of the aumbry against the end wall, telling Joliffe what he wanted to know. On the instant he let the priest go and went to snatch open both the aumbry's doors, ignored Sire John's outraged cry, and knelt and began roughly pulling out the piled scrolls that mostly filled it. Not pious books but records of property and income. Sire John advanced on him with thunderous anger and intent to hurt, but a sudden smashing at both the shuttered window and barred door stopped him and turned him half around with—finally—alarm.

That was no idle pounding and demands, Joliffe thought. Those were axes being wielded against the wood, and he had reached the back of the cabinet without finding any packet. The shutter started to splinter. Sire John was caught in the middle of the room, unsure against which outrage to move first. Joliffe drew his dagger and dug the point under the bottom board of the cabinet, prying upward, certain that somewhere here there was a hidden place but without time to find the catch to open it. The door, hacked off its hinges, was giving way and hands were through the broken shutters, shoving aside the bar there. The board gave to Joliffe's dagger and he flung it up to show the expected hollow underneath, with a velvet pouch, a wooden box with painted lid, and an oil cloth–wrapped packet that had to be Burgate's.

And too bad if it wasn't, Joliffe thought, snatching it up.

Men were climbing over the windowsill, shoving at each other to be first. Sire John was going toward them, crying out in outraged protest. Joliffe thrust the packet down the front of his doublet. For good measure, since it was there, he grabbed up the velvet pouch, too, feeling the shape and weight of coins through the thick cloth, and thrust it after the packet, trusting to his belt at his waist to keep both pouch and packet with him, leaving his hands free for his dagger as he sprang to his feet.

At the broken front door men were elbowing and pushing at each other, crowding to be in. Sire John, too late frightened, was backing away with nowhere to go because men were coming in from the kitchen, too. From there came the first crash of something being thrown down, and Sire John half-swung around toward the sound, mouth open in more useless protest unheard in the shouting all around him.

Then the men closed on him from all sides and had him. He was grabbed, shoved, struck with fists. Joliffe, shouting, too, and with a fist raised, to seem as if he belonged there, slid rapidly sideways toward the kitchen door, keeping his back to the wall as much as might be. Intent on the priest, no one heeded him. Sire John was down, men were piling over him, and Joliffe was almost to the kitchen door through the men still crowding in from that way when he saw that he was being stared at by a man along the wall the other side of the kitchen doorway.

Stared at as if the man knew he did not belong there.

But then neither did the man. He was no villager; was rough-clothed but for riding, not work, and his hair was cut to court-style more than country—and most betrayingly, he was no part of the rout happening around him, was coldly watching it all with head high and no yelling.

And having probably made much the same judgment of Joliffe, he was beginning to move Joliffe's way with a set, flat intent in his eyes that made Joliffe think letting him come close would be an ill thing, and with new urgent need Joliffe shoved among the men toward the doorway, as hampered by them as the other man but nearer to it. If he could get into the clear and run for Rowan . . .

The sickening thuds of wooden clubs had been added to the pounding of fists and now suddenly the shouting went to a greater roar and all unexpectedly there was a mighty shoving back of men from the middle of the room, crushing Joliffe to the wall just short of the doorway. His foe, with better luck, kept coming. Above the suddenly cleared space in the room's middle someone swung up an ax. Its blunt back struck one of the beams, making the downward stroke clumsy and shortened but ending in a thick crunch that told it had found bone.

Joliffe saw his foe glance toward the sound with flaring laughter. Other men were laughing, too, and cheering, and someone was holding up the priest's head in two hands, lifting it high, blood pouring from it . . . With a final hearty shove of two men out of his way Joliffe broke clear and into the kitchen, moving fast for the rear door but feeling, rather than hearing over the cheers and yelling, the other man come in behind him, and because behind him was not some place he wanted the man to be, he spun around, drawing his dagger as he did, to find the other man already had his own dagger in hand and was closing on him as if he wanted blood more than he wanted answers.

For choice, Joliffe preferred to give him neither.

The kitchen was not wide or high enough for good swordwork, but wanting more than only his dagger between him and the other man, Joliffe shied sideways to the firewood stacked beside the hearth and grabbed up a long and narrow piece. With that and his dagger at the ready, he backed toward the outer door while the other man circled the work table, intent on cutting him off from that escape. But a jostle of village men broke suddenly from the parlor into the kitchen, maybe belatedly having found they did not want to be part of what was happening in there. They caught both Joliffe and the other man in their rush toward the rear door, giving no heed to either them or their drawn daggers. Then one of the men swerved to grab a broad frypan from the wall, and the other men realized what they were missing and instead of flight they were suddenly grabbing what they could, and in their shove and shift, while Joliffe, off-balance, tried to fend his way out the door, the other man reached him. Unable to swing around enough to bring his dagger between them, his other arm hampered by too many men around him, Joliffe wrenched sideways, and broke clear but too late, felt a blow low on his left side in the same moment that he was finally able to bring his rough piece of wood around hard at the man's head. It struck solidly, with all the weight Joliffe could put behind it.

The man dropped, and dropping the piece of wood, Joliffe shoved away from him and out the door into the yard, a hand pressed to his side. He was hurt, he knew, but had no time to find out how badly. Hampered as he'd been, he doubted he'd hit the man hard enough to keep him down for long and wanted very much to be away before the fellow was up again. At more a stumble than run he made for the back gate, to find on its far side that Rowan was gone.

His heart lurched downward before he saw her, hardly ten yards off, head down, pulling at grass growing along a back wall, unconcerned with the world's travails, her reins trailing beside her.

Under his hand his side had begun to be warm and sticky with his blood, nor were his legs so steady as he would have liked them to be as he went toward her, careful not to startle her. She went on tearing at the grass while he leaned over

and took up the reins. She didn't argue about his slow climb
into the saddle either, blundering though he was as pain began to awaken in his side. She only tore quicker grassy
mouthfuls before he pulled up her head and swung her away
from the wall.

Joliffe was thankful both for her forbearance and that the
sun was gone, blotted out by the sweeping storm clouds
bringing an early twilight that would go quickly into darkness. That would help to hide his flight if his foe followed,
and he did not doubt the man would. Maybe not until he
had made certain the packet was no longer in the priest's
house but after that . . .

They had said not one word between them but Joliffe
was certain past doubt the man had been there for the
packet now being blood-soaked against Joliffe's side. The
man had killed Lady Alice's man to have it, and having not
found it on him, had been making use of the villagers' riot
to try for it himself.

Making use of the riot? Or was he the cause of the riot? It
had been by angry villagers and beheading that Suffolk's
priest had died in Alderton.

That was wondering that could wait for later. More immediately, Joliffe knew—pursued or not—he had to do
something about the bleeding.

He had without thinking set Rowan away along the road
they were already on. It had climbed them out of the narrow
valley onto higher ground where there was forest beyond
the village fields, and he'd reached the forest now, the rising
wind under the clouds beginning to whip the trees as he
guided Rowan among them and stopped her out of sight of
the road. She was not pleased, stood shifting from leg to leg
and sometimes sidling, while he reached inside his doublet,
shifted the packet and the priest's pouch to his other side,
then twisted around enough, despite the pain, to pull his
spare shirt out of his saddlebag. Folding it into a thick pad,

he slipped it inside his doublet and pressed it over the wound without trying to learn how bad the hurt was, because there was no point in finding out, there being nothing he could do for it just now except stop the bleeding. If he could.

Chapter 20

easons came more subtly within the cloister than in the outer world. The Offices wove their changing garland of prayers through the days and months but otherwise the shifting of the year into autumn was mostly told by the cloister garth's and garden's fading to the duller greens of summer's end and the longer, lower slant of each day's sunlight into the cloister walk. Beyond the walls was all the autumn haste of harvest, the gathering in of the year's yield, and the nuns took their small part in that—besides their prayers for good weather and a bountiful year—with gathering the apples in their own orchard, enclosed by a grass-grown earthen bank and ditch beside the cloister.

With baskets and ladders among the trees and much

climbing up and down and laughter and eating of apples, they every year made a holiday of the work, and this bright, warm, dry September day as much as any other, with the sunlight green and gold among the trees, and the red bounty of apples filling basket after basket. Even Dame Emma's tumble from a ladder harmed nothing more than her dignity, and there would be fresh apple tarts with raisins and cinnamon and nutmeg for supper tonight and apple cakes drizzled with honey tomorrow.

All the same, for Frevisse at least there was awareness that under the long grass among the trees were all the nuns who had ever died in St. Frideswide's. They were all here, as—God willing—she someday would be, her grave as unmarked, as grass-grown, and as forgotten as all of theirs. She could not even say now, for certain, where Domina Edith, the prioress who had seen her with wisdom and kindness through her early years of nunhood, was buried among the others, and though that was as it should be—the earthly body something to be as free of as possible during life and willingly returned to earth at life's end—still, Frevisse was aware of an autumnal sadness that so much could pass and be forgotten. There were already very few left in St. Frideswide's who remembered Domina Edith. When they were gone, when there was no one anymore who remembered her, that would be the earthly end of all her goodness and wisdom; and when in their own turn they died and some day no one was left who remembered them . . .

"That basket is done!" Sister Johane said merrily, leaning from the ladder to put a last two apples in the willow-woven basket Frevisse was holding up to her. "Best fetch another one."

And there were worse things than being forgotten after death, Frevisse thought as she carried the basket away to set beside the orchard gate. Better a quiet and forgotten grave than a long-lived fame for ill and evil deeds. And weren't the apples piled in their baskets a beautiful sight, she thought, firmly turning her mind to somewhere pleasant to be. With all the beauty and bounty there were in the world, to dwell on only sadnesses was surely some manner of sin— of ingratitude, if nothing else.

She was straightening from setting down the basket beside the others and already reaching for one of the stacked empty ones when Luce, the youngest of the guesthall servant women, looked hesitantly around the half-open gate, exclaimed, "Oh, good!" at seeing Frevisse, made a quick curtsy and said hurriedly, "Old Ela says you should come to the guesthall right away, you're needed."

Old Ela must be growing forgetful, Frevisse thought and went on picking up the basket while answering, "Dame Juliana is hosteler. It's her you want, not me."

"No," Luce said with undiminished earnestness. "There's a man hurt. Ela says he's someone you know and you should come."

Frevisse dropped the basket back into the pile, said, "You'd best tell Dame Juliana, too. And Dame Claire. They're over there," and pushed past her through the gateway, gathering her skirts clear of her feet so she could hurry and then—out of anyone's sight in the cloister walk—run, returning to a swift walk as she went out the cloister door into the guesthall yard, so that she had her breath as she came into the guesthall's large hall where some men and a few women were clumped around someone lying on the floor on his back.

Frevisse thrust in among them before they knew she was there and gasped at the sight of the filthy, bloodied man sprawled there on an outspread cloak, even before she knew him for Joliffe and demanded of the people drawing back, "Is he alive?"

"He's that," a man kneeling beside him answered. "But badly fevered, seems."

She saw Joliffe's chest lift then in a ragged breath and she demanded, "Why is he here on the floor and not put into a bed? There." She pointed at one of the small side rooms meant for such guests as did not share the general sleeping in the hall for one reason or another but did not warrant the large bedchamber.

"The blood," one of the women protested. "On the bed?"

"Which counts more? A clean sheet or a man's life?" Frevisse snapped at her. "See the bed is ready." And to the men, less curtly, "Be careful how you move him. The hurt is in his side?" That being where his clothing was most blackened with blood, presumably his. It looked to be long-dried. How long ago had he taken this hurt? If he did not live, they would likely never know that, or from whom he had had it, but just now those were lesser matters against having him alive and keeping him that way.

While she was giving orders for someone to find and bring Father Henry, the nunnery's priest, and for someone else to tell Dame Claire on her way it was a wounded man with whom she must deal, Dame Juliana hurried in. Presently hosteler, she took over ordering the guesthall servants, demanding hot water and clean rags. Dame Claire came in soon after with her box of medicines and Sister Johane to help her. By then Joliffe was on a bed in one of the small rooms, still raggedly breathing, still senseless. Father Henry came close behind Dame Claire, and since there was neither need nor room for Frevisse in the small chamber, nor strictly any reason she should be there, she withdrew, taking a last look at Joliffe past Dame Claire's shoulder as she went.

He had more than a few days' rough growth of beard. Did that tell how long since he had been hurt? When she had first met him, years ago, his beard had been so fair as nearly not to show. He had been young then—very young, to her mind as she saw the world now—and it came hard to think that he must be older now than she had been when they first met; and harder still to think he was maybe going to be no older if he was as badly hurt as he looked to be.

She made no effort to deny how much that thought hurt, and despite she should return to the orchard and her right work, she stopped in the guesthall to question the men who had brought him in. They were from the priory's village and more than ready to tell her all about it. "Found him about a mile off, by the gate into Westmede field," one of them said. "Was on his horse but all slumped over the saddlebow and the horse was cropping grass on the wayside. Not going anywhere fast, he wasn't."

"Still had some of his wits about him, though," the other said. "When we prodded him and asked what he was doing there, he stirred enough to name St. Frideswide's."

"But that's all he did."

"Except start to slide sidewise out of his saddle. He was gone then. Not another word out of him."

"So Peter propped him up in the saddle and I led the horse and we came on to here."

"God's blessing on you for bringing him," Frevisse said. "He likely owes you his life."

The man Peter looked toward the room where Joliffe now lay and said, "If he doesn't die anyway."

"He looked fair bad," the other agreed, then added with a shrug, "Still, better he be dead here than where he was, making trouble for the village."

"There's that," Frevisse dryly agreed. If Joliffe had died by the road, he would have been the village's problem. If he died here, he was the nunnery's. "And his horse is in our stable?" she asked in parting, to be sure that was where the horse *would* be and not somehow gone with them as no longer needed by the hurt man.

One of the men said, "Oh," and the other, "Aye," with a quick, regretful look between them, and then, "We'll be back to work then."

As they bowed to her, she somewhat assuaged their loss by saying, "See what they can give you to eat in the guesthall kitchen before you leave."

That cheered them, and while they went toward the kitchen, she went to Ela sitting in her corner and asked, "Why did you send to me about him?"

With her head bent sideways from her bowed shoulders to look up at Frevisse, Ela said shrewdly enough, "He's the minstrel was here when you came back ill. Here he is again, all hurt. Seemed a thing you'd want to know. Then, too, if he's going to die, there's none here likely to know his right name except maybe you."

Frevisse held silent for a long moment before saying, "Yes. Thank you." Except she did not know Joliffe's right name, only the several by which he had been called the several times she had encountered him. Still, one of them should suffice if Sir William Oldhall had to be told of his death, Oldhall being presently the only person in his life of whom she knew, and someone Alice would be able to find.

Dame Juliana was now sending the servants out of their clustered talk and back to their afternoon's work. With another thought, Frevisse went to her and apologized for being there at all when the business was Dame Juliana's. Dame Juliana shook her head. "The more help the better in something like this. I've never dealt with such."

That made it easier for Frevisse to say, "You might want to give order that no one not of the nunnery come near him."

Dame Juliana slightly frowned with puzzlement, then gaped as she grasped what Frevisse meant, before saying, "You fear that someone tried to kill him and will try again."

"There's little likelihood they will," Frevisse said quickly. "Whatever happened to him, it happened a few days ago and probably a good many miles away but . . ."

"But better present care than afterward regret," Dame Juliana said. "Yes. I'll see the servants all understand."

Frevisse returned then to the orchard, gave what answers she could to Domina Elisabeth's questions, and went on with carrying baskets for the apple-pickers, silently praying for Joliffe's body and soul while she did. Dame Juliana returned, too, in a while but with nothing to add except that the hurt man still lived. Neither Dame Claire nor Sister Johane were seen in the cloister again until Compline, after which there was only silent going to bed; nor was there chance to talk at the Offices of Matins and Lauds in the middle of the night or at Prime at dawn; and after that, while the other nuns went to break their fast, Dame Claire and Sister Johane went instead to the guesthall and did not return to the cloister until time for Mass. Only finally at the chapter meeting afterward was everyone's curiosity a little eased, if not altogether satisfied, when Domina Elisabeth asked how the hurt man did and Dame Claire answered, "It's not so bad with him as it first looked."

Dame Emma and Dame Amicia, restless on their low joint stools, were openly in hope of excitement and dire peril, but Dame Claire, standing with her hands folded into her sleeves and her voice quiet, only said steadily, "The wound is not deep, only a shallow scrape across his ribs. He lost more blood from it than was good for him. I gather from the little he's said . . ."

"He's come awake then?" Domina Elisabeth asked.

"Twice or thrice. Never for long."

"Has he said who he is or what happened to him?"

"Not who he is but that he was attacked by someone, he did not know the man, miles from here, no use to send word to the sheriff."

Frevisse wondered if anyone else noted that was a great deal for a man to say and still not give his name.

Dame Claire went on, "He seems at some point to have poured wine into the wound. That's likely saved him from worse infection than there is, but it will take time for him to heal. The worse trouble is likely to be that he made himself sick riding when he should not have been. He seems to have gone unfed for several days, leaving him perilously weak, but . . ."

"Days?" Domina Elisabeth interrupted. "Has it been days since he was hurt?"

"Several days at least. I don't know that he's sure how many. Because of the fever."

"How very strange," Domina Elisabeth said. "Why didn't he seek help?"

"He's not said that either. I think, though, that Dame Frevisse knows him."

She looked at Frevisse as she said that. So did everyone else, and Domina Elisabeth asked, "Do you, Dame?"

Frevisse had been awaiting that question, had her words already chosen, and answered carefully, "I've known him as Master Noreys and that one time and another he's been in favor with the duchess of Suffolk." All true, so far as it went. "In matters of some confidence, I've gathered," she added. Also true.

It also did what she had hoped. Domina Elisabeth closed careful silence over her curiosity and said in a more straightened voice, "Then we should let her grace the duchess know that he's here and safe."

"If he's still in her service," Frevisse said. "We don't know that he is. We should perhaps . . ."

". . . find that out from him before we do more that way, yes," Domina Elisabeth said. She looked to Dame Claire. "Will he be fit to talk this morning again?"

"If he's not sleeping, yes."

Domina Elisabeth looked back at Frevisse. "Then after Chapter do you see him and learn what you can from him, Dame, since you somewhat know him."

Frevisse bent her head in acceptance of that and set herself to outward quietness through the few confessions of faults since yesterday and Domina Elisabeth's giving out of penances, followed by the obedientiaries' reports of their offices, until Domina Elisabeth at last dismissed them with her blessing to the morning's duties.

Even then Frevisse made no show of haste, going even-paced with Dame Claire and Sister Johane along the cloister walk toward the passage to the outer door, taking the chance to ask more carefully how Joliffe did, but Dame Claire had nothing more to tell.

"We're going to the infirmary now to make a betony and yarrow poultice that should help to draw any illness there may still be in the wound and keep it cool," she said. "We'll brew something for his fever, too."

"You said the wound hadn't sickened," Frevisse said quickly.

"I said he'd saved himself from worse infection than there is, but there's some. With that and the hunger, he's not well, and what I fear is the fever will give us more trouble because he's too weak from hunger to fight it well. I've given word he's to be fed as much as might be, before he grows too ill to eat at all. If you can get more food into him while you talk with him, that will be to the good. Or if it's a choice of food or talk, then choose food," Dame Claire said and went on her way with Sister Johane, leaving Frevisse far less reassured than she wanted to be.

Chapter 21

For Joliffe the days between taking the wound and reaching St. Frideswide's had flowed into an increasingly uncertain nightmare. He had known he no longer had sure hold on his wits and toward the end had been able to do nothing but hold to the one thought that he had to reach safety. He remembered knowing he had failed at that, before he found himself lying on a bed and nuns tending to him. The older one had told him he was in St. Frideswide's and after that he had been willing to lie quietly, his eyes closed, while she saw to his hurt—had answered her questions as briefly as he could and been grateful when she had gone.

He did not try to see the wound for himself. He had seen it more than enough when cleaning it as best he could beside a stream at dawn the first day after his escape. The storm had been hours over by then. Chilled and shivering, he had wanted warmth and a hot meal and bed and did not dare go in search of them, not knowing how wide a net of searchers his would-be killer could throw out after him. He had only stopped at all because both he and Rowan needed rest. She had grazed while he stripped to his waist and did what he could to clean the hurt with cold stream water until he could judge how bad it was. With his teeth set against his stomach's heave, he had washed away enough of his blood to see the four inches of shallow scrape along a rib, his sliced flesh gaping white and red at him.

It would have been worse if Sire John's coins in their velvet pouch hadn't turned the man's dagger, but it was ugly enough, and with no way to close it, he had had to settle for pouring wine from the leather bottle in his saddlebag into the wound. He had then torn strips from what had been his shirt and was now bandages, tied them together and used them to bind the rest of his former shirt over the wound before struggling back into his bloodied shirt and doublet and belting on his sword and dagger again. He had then gathered up and put into his belt pouch such of Sire John's coins as hadn't been lost from the ripped velvet pouch when he had dropped it to the grass, and put on his cloak that would hide the bloodied side of his doublet. And all the while he had been planning what he must needs do next. To be sure of the letter, he had thrust the packet well down inside his tall left riding boot before he dragged himself back into his saddle, his breath coming short against the pain that cost him.

He did not dare return to Hunsdon. Without Sir William there, he could not count on being well enough protected should there be a "privy friend" to send word where he was to the very people who must not find him. Whoever they were.

Nor was he going to dare Wingfield. Whoever had known to come seeking the priest could well expect him to head for

Lady Alice, or at the least have watch kept there for other reasons. As he had said to Vaughn—damn spies.

He needed somewhere not likely and not watched but where someone would know what to do with the letter if he . . . could do nothing himself.

So to St. Frideswide's.

He remembered little after the first day beyond the fixed need to keep moving, helped at that by seeing, whenever he closed his eyes, his would-be murderer's face as the man had thrust for the kill—the man's gloating pleasure as he had lunged with a twist to his arm that betrayed he was going not for clean kill but a gut-thrust that would have left him time to ask questions while Joliffe died.

Or had the man simply wanted the pleasure of watching him die slowly?

The question had been sufficient to keep Joliffe on Rowan's back and riding even as he worsened. If he was going to die, he would rather die alone than gloated over by some murderous cur; and he had been grateful beyond words for Dame Claire's drug-brought sleep last night and grateful again when he awoke this morning and could remember no dreams.

He was fevered, though, and once awake, could not stop his mind's hot, restless roaming to places he would rather not have gone. Back to the moment of his would-be murderer's lunge at him and the dagger ripping open his side. Forward to what he still needed to do and could not, help-less here as he was. Back to the dead man lying in the char-nel house in the churchyard, except sometimes in his hot wandering mind the body had his own face and then again had Vaughn's. Why had it been someone else of Lady Alice's and not Vaughn dead there? Where *was* Vaughn?

Then, without warning, his mind would twist another way, out of that run of thoughts into a half-wild homesick wishing for where he couldn't be, where he wanted to be, where he had to be, where he couldn't be . . . And he would shift on the bed, deliberately rousing the pain in his side to jerk his thoughts back to here and now.

Until here and now and all that went with it were finished, there could be no going *there*, and until he could go there, it was better not to think of it at all.

When Dame Claire and the younger nun came to change his bandage, he asked about the coins there had been in his belt pouch.

"They're still there. They're bloody," Dame Claire said, sounding disapproving of him for his carelessness in getting them that way.

"Please," he said, "give some to the men who brought me in. The rest are for the priory as my gift. My thank-offering. For keeping me alive."

She thanked him kindly and promised she would see to it.

He was presuming, of course, that he would stay alive, but if he died, he wouldn't care who had the money and either way he did not want it for himself. Greed was one of the seven deadly sins—and deadly in more than the spiritual sense for Sire John. He must have been something less than a loving shepherd of his flock, else his flock would not have turned into wolves against him.

Joliffe had sometime wondered what sort of view of heaven someone like Sire John had. Did they expect to set up in heaven with all their goods around them and live out eternity among their worldly comforts?

He could not even claim Sire John had courage at the end. The priest had not so much shown courage as a fool's complete disbelief that he could be in danger. That was a belief that had brought more than one man to grief.

Not, Joliffe thought, that his own very complete belief in his own mortality had done himself much good this time.

When the nuns left him, a servant came in with a bowl of thin soup for him but the effort was too much. He slept instead, a hot, shallow, restless sleep from which he awoke to find Dame Frevisse standing beside his bed. There had been dreams in that sleep that he would rather forget, and he managed a smile at her, surprised at the effort of it.

"You're not well," she said, as disapproving of that as Dame Claire had been at the bloodied coins.

"I apologize most humbly." He saw she was holding a wooden bowl and added, "I'm not hungry."

"But you will eat." She sat down on the bed's edge, careful not to jar him. "It's plain applemose, newly made, strained, and then cooled in the well. Dame Claire wants it in you to keep up your strength and help against the fever."

She lifted a spoonful. Joliffe moved his head back and forth against the pillow, refusing it.

"In you," Dame Frevisse said. She raised the spoon higher. "Or on you."

Joliffe made a small sound toward laughter and opened his mouth, letting her feed him several spoonfuls before the effort to swallow too tired him and he moved his head again, asking her to stop. She did and he gathered strength that was frighteningly hard to find and said, "The letter." He shifted his head a little on the pillow, showing where his riding boots and saddlebag were thrust together out of the way in a corner of the room. The rest of his belongings were gone, either to be cleaned or burned, he supposed. "It should be in the bottom of one of my boots." He had felt it work down while he was riding until it had been under his foot. Leaving it there had seemed best.

"The letter?" Dame Frevisse's eyes widened. "You have Suffolk's letter?" She set the bowl aside and stood up, then stopped to say at him sharply, "Was that where you took your hurt? In Sible Hedingham?"

"The letter," Joliffe said.

She understood necessity, left her questions where they were, and went to feel inside one boot, then the other, and from that one brought out the packet. Joliffe let his breath out with relief. "Best you have it now," he said. "Take it into your keeping and into the cloister."

She returned to the bed, sat down with the packet hidden under the spread of her skirts, took up the applesauce, and fed him more. He ate only because he knew he should and because she would not ask him questions while he did; but when he had to rest again, she asked again, "Was it in getting the letter you were hurt?"

He made a small nod in answer.

"You came this far without seeking help?" she said. "Have you no good sense at all?"

Joliffe closed his eyes. "Very possibly. But they wouldn't know to look for me here. And if I reached here and then died, you'd know to tell Sir William Oldhall."

"Eat," Dame Frevisse said.

He did, but after a few mouthfuls could feel himself fading toward sleep again, turned his head away from the next spoonful, and said, "One other thing. If it does come to the worst with me and you have to send Sir William Oldhall word of it, the name he knows me by is Simon Joliffe."

"And that one your own?" she asked sharply.

Joliffe quirked up one corner of his mouth into half a smile. "No."

She held quiet long enough that he hoped she was done with questions, until she asked, very gently, "Do you even remember, for a certainty, what your true name is?"

His eyes were so heavily closed he did not try to open them but met the challenge under her question by saying softly, "Aren't names simply tools? To give us something to call each other? If it's sometimes better to use a knife than a spoon, why not sometimes use one name instead of another, if it better matches a present need?"

"What I wonder," Dame Frevisse said softly back to him, "is whether, behind all the names you've been, you remember who you truly are."

Eyes still shut and sleep rising in a welcome tide, he whispered, "I remember." Low enough that maybe she did not hear him.

Frevisse was not sure he meant her to hear that last but she did and watched him either slip into sleep or make so good a feigning of it that she could not tell the difference. How much of his life *was* feigned, she wondered. Had she ever known him when he was not pretending to be someone he was not? Or was it that he *was* all the men he sometimes and another seemed to be?

Among the reasons she had become a nun had been the hope she could pare away all the different guises that came with living in the world, rid herself of them to find out who she truly was, so that then she could give herself, freed of the world, to God. Time and life had taught her she was unlikely ever to have that pure of a self to give. The taints of the world went deep and the cloister was not so perfect a place to be rid of them as she could wish, but she was grown free, much of the time, of the confusions that came with passions and counter-running desires and needs. She was, blessedly, nearer to a single self than Joliffe was.

Or was she? A crystal threw out rainbows of light and yet was single and whole in itself, made by God to make those rainbows. Was that how it was with Joliffe? Did he throw out all these different seemings of himself while somewhere behind them he was whole, was unbrokenly himself?

She had no way of knowing. She could only pray it was so, because he would surely never tell her.

Joliffe's fever did not worsen but it held him in its burning grip through that day and much of the next. It finally broke late in the afternoon, leaving him far weaker than he wanted to be. Through that night and the next day sleep came with disconcerting ease, and he welcomed it both for its healing and its oblivion. His body's necessities now were sleep and food and time to lie quietly and heal, and he knew that if he did not heed that need, he would likely be dead after all. Knowing that at least made his choice straight-forward, and his weakness made the choice even easier. Simply sitting up long enough to be fed or rising long enough to tend to what could not be done lying down left him wanting nothing so much as to be flat and quiet again.

It was his mind that proved troublesome. In the three-part division of the Self—body, mind, and soul—he had, over the years, done with and for his body as he chose and it needed, and given his soul such tending as he could toward what the Church said it needed for its salvation; but his mind had been his best companion. He had enjoyed letting it go where it would and as it would, had taken pleasure in most of its roamings; but as he lay on the straw-stiff mattress, he found his thoughts running along too many paths at once and none of them pleasant.

At best, there was simply worry about his wound—that it might turn poisonous despite Dame Claire's care and kill him after all. Worry over that was useless, since he could do no more than what he was, and the same was true at worry over whether he had truly shaken pursuit or would be found here after all, because there was nothing he could do about that either. Likewise worry that in his fever he might have said things he never meant to say. If he had, they were said and that was that. But sometimes his thoughts went a-drift without warning into that heart-aching flood of longing for where he could not be, not yet, and against that pain when it came, he grabbed at anything to stuff into the breach— songs, lines from plays, stray bits of poems, anything to turn his mind and take it elsewhere. Even prayer. *Salve nos,*

Domine, vigilantes, custodi nos dormientes . . . Save us, Lord, while we are awake, guard us while we sleep . . .

But more than anything and beyond his wish to stop it, his mind went searching and circling through the past few weeks, trying to pry straight answers out of the tangle of all the questions there were and failing at it so badly he began to think there were no straight answers to be had.

By the second morning after his fever had gone he was very weary of his thoughts and the rafters over his bed and the small room's plastered walls; and while Dame Claire was changing the poultice on his side, he brought himself to look at the ugly red line of the healing wound, to guess how long until he could ride again.

Seeing his grimace, Dame Claire said, "Yes. It's going to a fine new scar to add to your others."

"That's an ambition I've never had—to have scars or add to them," Joliffe said.

"Then you should keep away from other people's swords."

"It was a dagger."

"Then it should have been easier to keep away from. Now lie down. But if Tom here in the guesthall will help you, you should try being up and walking a little, to begin building your strength again. But not alone," she added. "Only with someone to steady you. Understood?"

"Understood." In truth, he would understand anything she asked of him if it meant he could leave this room for a while. But, "Since I'm so thriving, would it be possible Dame Frevisse be allowed to talk with me this morning?"

Dame Claire gave him a sharp, long look that made him wonder what was being said about him among the nuns, before she answered, "She likely could be."

As she began to gather her things back into her box, he asked, "Do you know if I talked much in my fever?"

"You did," Dame Claire answered, not pausing in her work.

"What did I say?" Partly not wanting to know but needing to.

"What I heard mostly made little sense. Mostly things from plays, I think. And a woman's name."

Joliffe forced a half-laugh. "Only one?"

"Only the one." Dame Claire closed her box and looked at him. "A great many times."

"Ah," he said.

"You would not care to send her a message, lest she be worried for you?" Dame Claire said, not unkindly. "Could she maybe come to you?"

Joliffe shut his eyes. "No." He let his head weigh more heavily into the pillow. "No." And listened as Dame Claire asked nothing else and left him.

She was true to her word that he should walk, though. She was not gone long before Tom came cheerily in to see if he was ready to be up and walking for a time. Joliffe was not in the least sure that he was, but Dame Claire was right that he needed to build his strength again and with Tom's help he shuffled the length of his room and back again a few times before Tom said that looked like all he'd better do and saw him back to the bed.

He was gratefully lying there, his right arm crooked over his eyes while he wondered when he'd next be fed, when someone paused in the room's doorway. "I'm awake," he said, taking his arm from his eyes to prove it.

"You are," Dame Frevisse agreed, coming to stand beside his bed, regarding him with no apparent favor. "Dame Claire says you're much bettered."

"I am. Or not dead anyway, and I count that as being to the good."

"One does," she dryly granted.

He eased himself a little up to lean against the wall at the head of the bed, careful of his side. "Also, I can feed myself now, and Dame Claire has let me walk a little."

"So she said."

"And I've been thinking."

"So have I."

"Should we make a wager our thoughts have been running the same way?"

"If you think you could depend upon me not to lie to win the wager."

She said it with so little change of voice and no change of face that Joliffe took a long moment to realize she had made a jest at him. Holding in the laugh that might have painfully jerked his side, he said as solemnly, "No wager then. Will we go unheard if we talk here?"

"I've set old Ela aside from the door and told her to send away anyone who makes to come in while I'm here."

Since they could not close the door, leaving her alone with a man, that would have to do, and he began to gather his mind for what he should and should not tell her; but she asked first, "Was it Vaughn did this to you?"

"Vaughn? No. We parted company two days after we left here. I don't know where he is, except not where I expected him to be. This was done by someone I'd never seen before."

"Can you tell me more about it all?"

"Tell me first where the packet is."

"With Domina Elisabeth. I told her it's something of Lady Alice's that needs to be kept secret and safe. It seemed better to give it to her privately in her room than be seen locking something away in the sacristy. I've likewise led her to think you're in Lady Alice's service."

If he had had more strength he would have mocked Dame Frevisse for that 'led her.' As it was, he let it go, said, because there might be help in her knowing, "This is how it went with me," closed his eyes and slowly—as careful of what he left out as what he said—told what he and Vaughn had decided here at St. Frideswide's, then made a brief tale of what happened after, through his escape from the priest's house.

Dame Frevisse listened in careful silence, making neither exclaim nor protest. Only when he had finished and opened his eyes again, she said, "There's this to add," and told him that Vaughn had written and left a message here that someone had collected after he and Vaughn had gone, and kept watch on the nunnery for nearly a week afterward.

"We never learned who he was or why he was here," she finished. "Everyone was too busy with the harvest to spend time hunting him down. My best hope is that he was someone of Alice's, set as a kind of guard for a while to be sure no trouble had followed me back here."

"There's been no other sign of trouble here since then, or since I've come?"

"None. No travelers not rightly accounted for, no guests asking wrong questions."

Slowly, thinking as he went, Joliffe said, "Vaughn's letter could explain Lady Alice's man dead at Sible Hedingham. Vaughn must have told her what Burgate had done with Suffolk's letter. It also means he knew Lady Alice had sent, or was going to send, someone here."

"Something neither you nor I was told," Dame Frevisse said coldly. "Which makes me wonder what else we weren't told."

It made Joliffe wonder, too, but aloud he said, "If the man held here a week before he took the message that could be why Lady Alice's man reached Sible Hedingham only two days before me. And of course I'm supposing the message *was* to her. But either way, where is Vaughn? He could have been there far sooner than that, whatever happened."

Whatever she might have answered was stopped by the cloister bell beginning to ring for the day's next Office, a summons supposed to enjoin silence on a nun. Dame Frevisse turned her head toward it, then she looked back to him, say-ing nothing, but slipping a small book from her sleeve. She held it out and he took it, saying, "To pass my time with? My thanks, my lady."

She wordlessly nodded and left, and he carefully shifted himself somewhat higher against his pillow, opened the book's plain parchment cover to the book's beginning, and choked back laughter. She had given him a copy of Chaucer's *Boethe— The Consolation of Philosophy.*

Chapter 22

Having had small comfort from None's prayers and psalms and had the midday meal, Frevisse again asked and was given Domina Elisabeth's leave to return to the guesthall. This time she found Joliffe sitting more up, propped on a pillow against the wall at the bed's head, with Luce sitting on the bed's edge beside him, a bowl of thick soup on her lap and just slipping the spoon from Joliffe's mouth, smiling at him with her eyes locked to his as if something far more than only feeding soup were going on between them. Certainly she startled at the sight of Frevisse and only barely saved the bowl from spilling as she stood quickly up to bob a curtsy and say, "My lady."

"Luce," Frevisse returned as evenly as if she had seen nothing in particular. She held out her hand for the bowl.

"I'm here to talk to Master Noreys and can feed him while I do, freeing you to go about your other duties."

Luce gave over the bowl and spoon with a regretful sideways look at Joliffe, who gave her a smile and said, "Not to worry. I promise I'll be here when you come back."

Luce left on a laugh and a lingering backward look. Frevisse, standing beside the bed with soup bowl in hand, said at Joliffe, "You should be too weak for bringing servant girls to calf-eyes. What were you saying to her?"

Joliffe laid his right hand over his heart and said languishingly, "Only that stories say sight of a fair woman can wound a man to the heart with love, but that sight of her had put heart into the healing of my wound." Still languishing, he added, "May I have more of that soup?"

Frevisse thrust the bowl at him. When she first saw him this morning, she had been unsettled by the grayness shadowed under his eyes and the deep-drawn lines of pain on either side of his mouth, but impatient with his foolishness, she said tartly, "Use your strength for other than flattering our servant girls. You told me you could feed yourself."

His grin was unrepentant as he took the bowl. "Kind words make for kind hands," he said.

"Was it an unkind word of yours, then, set someone so unkindly at you?" she asked with a nod at his side.

"You wrong me, my lady," Joliffe said, sounding aggrieved. "There was never a word said between us at all. I'd done *nothing*."

"Except be there, taking the thing he'd probably come for, too," Frevisse said at him. "Eat." While he began to obey her, she went on. "The priest there, killed the way he was. That was the same way Suffolk's priest died. Killed by his own parishioners and his head cut off."

Joliffe swallowed and said, "Noted that, did you?"

"I gather, too, you don't think the man who tried to kill you was simply another villager."

Joliffe's face went bleak with memory. "The villagers were one thing. They were no more than a dog-pack turned savage, the wits gone out of them. This man, he was enjoying himself in a whole other way and apart from them. I'd lay good odds he's the one who stirred them up and set them on. Not that the stirring up may have been that hard. The whole of the south and east have been seething for months now, uprisings coming and going like pots going on and off the boil. Someone who set to it wouldn't have that hard a time roiling up a village that's unhappy at their priest anyway. Not given there are always men ready for trouble for the hell of it anyway, even at the best of times."

"And these are nothing like the best of times. Nor, I gather, either of those priests the best of men."

"No," Joliffe said tersely. "It seems they were not."

"Even then, village displeasure rarely goes so far as to kill," Frevisse said.

"And even more rarely to the cutting off of heads," Joliffe said, his voice flat and dry. They looked at each other for a long moment, and then he said for both of them, "Two priests dead in a somewhat uncommon way and both of them linked to Normandy's loss. However unwittingly on Sire John's part."

"Eat," Frevisse remembered to order, and while he did, she said carefully, "There's Suffolk's steward, in Wales, too."

Joliffe set the spoon back into the bowl. "You see that, too? The thing that's like among all three murders? Routs of parishioners savaging their priests. A sudden tavern scuffle that 'happens' to break into the street as Hampden passes by. Always no one man to blame. And Matthew Gough," Joliffe added grimly. "The men who killed him and Hampden were hired to it, unlike the villagers, but his death and Hampden's were meant to look the same as the priests'— deaths with no one to blame by face or name. That's four men linked, one way or another, to Suffolk and Normandy, and all of them . . ."

". . . murdered by too many men for one man to be singled out as their murderer," Frevisse said, finishing his thought with her own. "Murdered in ways that, for Gough and Hampden seem by chance, and with the priests, no one man's fault."

"Except I saw him," Joliffe said quietly. "The man who didn't belong where he was. The man who wasn't a villager and knew on the instant that I wasn't either."

"You truly think he goaded the villagers to both priest-killings?"

"I think it . . . possible."

"But even if we bring ourselves to suppose that this man deliberately set to causing these four murders . . ." Frevisse paused, frowning. Did she believe that?

"There's enough alike among their deaths," Joliffe said quietly, "to make it more than just the fever burning odd patterns into my mind."

"And I'm without the excuse of a fever for thinking it," Frevisse said. "But why would this man trouble to be so subtle at these murders? I have to doubt he has any other link to these men. Gough I can see would be better not to do alone, but the others . . . He could have killed them and been away, with no one to know who did them."

"You surely have a thought on 'why'," Joliffe said.

"And so do you," she returned.

He nodded but paused for another spoonful of the soup before saying, "My guess is that these killings aren't for his own sake, that someone is setting him on to them."

"Someone who wants to keep secret the true reason for Normandy's loss," Frevisse said. "So the murders all have to look like something other than plain murder, to lessen chance someone will see how they're linked."

"With now the added slight problem," Joliffe said evenly, "that I've probably become someone else this someone will now want dead."

"Yes," Frevisse agreed, her voice as level as his own.

He handed her the emptied bowl and closed his eyes. "I think I'll go to sleep again."

Not that he looked to have choice about it. Given his body's present weakness, sleep probably took him when it would, Frevisse thought, and she stood still, waiting while his face slackened and his breathing evened, until he seemed gone too deeply into sleep for her to disturb him as she quietly left, taking her thoughts with her back into the cloister.

Her duties kept her there through the rest of the day. She did not go back to the guesthall until the next morning, again with Domina Elisabeth's leave but earlier, between Tierce and Sext, and found Joliffe on his feet and out of his room, leaning on Tom's arm and not walking steadily but with more color in his face than yesterday. Luce hovered nearby, more than ready to help if need be, until at Frevisse's sharp look she seemed to decide she was needed elsewhere and went away.

Tom scowled after her, either because she had abandoned him or else unhappy with her heed to Joliffe; and old Ela, sitting a little aside from Joliffe's door instead of in her corner, chuckled and said, "You help get him better so he goes and she'll remember you soon enough, Tom-boy. Better the ass in the barn than the horse gone down the road."

Tom grumbled something under his breath and Joliffe wisely did not laugh but said, "I'm ready to lie down, I think."

Back in his room again, he eased himself onto the bed, thanked Tom, and added, "I suppose I'll have to do it again this afternoon."

"Aye. So Dame Claire says," Tom agreed. Frevisse had followed them into the room. He jerked a bow to her and went out.

Joliffe, settling himself against the pillow against the wall, said, "So. I've thought more, and likely you have, too."

"I have," Frevisse granted. She did not bother to hide she

was not happy with her thoughts. "We're well-agreed, I think, that these murders were done to keep secret that Suffolk and Somerset set out with purpose to lose Normandy, yes?"

"Yes," Joliffe agreed. "From that it comes that whoever ordered the murders has to be someone who knew that Hampden and Suffolk's chaplain took messages to Somerset in France. Burgate, too, of course, and he'd surely be dead along with them if he hadn't written and then hidden that letter for Suffolk. Instead, his cousin died. In his place, as it were. Though for all we know, Burgate is dead, too, since they knew where to go looking for the letter."

"Unless Lady Alice got him out of Kenilworth before it came to that," Frevisse said, "and it was from him, rather than from Vaughn, she learned where the letter was and sent her man to Sible Hedingham."

"And if that was the way of it, we can guess that someone followed Burgate to Wingfield," Joliffe said, "and then followed her man to Sible Hedingham. It would be easy enough for a spy in her household to tell someone there was a link between Burgate talking to Lady Alice and that man being sent, without the spy knew why."

"And when her man came away from the priest's," Frevisse said, "he was killed because whoever followed him thought he must have the letter."

"Except he didn't, and the man I saw had to set about getting it the longer way."

"Why? When he could have simply forced the priest to tell him and then killed him, if he had to have him dead."

"Again, to keep from having questions asked," Joliffe said. "One stranger dead in the road and no way to tell who did it—that happens. A priest murdered soon afterward and nearby, again by someone unknown—not so easily dismissed. But one more hurly of villagers killing a hated priest . . ." He shrugged. "This year, with all else going on, who's to take special note of that or link it to the dead stranger? The law would be satisfied with seeing there's enough justice done to close the matter, and there's an end."

Frevisse regarded him in a steady silence for a long moment, understanding what he was saying even while wishing she could refuse it. There was too much ugliness in the thought of someone who could so coldly carry out such business. But finally she said steadily, "The question then is not so much who was the man who tried to kill you but who is behind him, ordering it all."

"The duke of Somerset being the open choice," said Joliffe. "As always."

"Especially when you add the murder we've missed out."

"Missed?" Joliffe did not straighten from the pillow but his eyes were darkly alert. "What murder have we missed?"

"The duke of Suffolk's. His death was much like these others."

Joliffe stared past her at the far wall as if needing time to take in what she had said.

He took so long to answer that she added, very slowly because of her own uncertainty, "Come to it, we might well add in the bishop of Chichester's murder in January and the bishop of Salisbury's in June."

Joliffe's gaze snapped back to her, harsh and sharp. "Damnation twice over," he swore softly. "There's a distance I was nowhere near to going yet. Both of them almost as high in the government as Suffolk and Somerset, with Chichester killed by soldiers rioting against him, Salisbury by men of his own bishopric. Again, no blame to be laid to one man."

"Or it may be only that their deaths gave someone thought on how to do these others," Frevisse said quietly but with anger taut behind her words.

"Suffolk was murdered after Chichester," Joliffe pointed out, "and before Salisbury. Which isn't to say Chichester's death didn't give someone an idea for all the others. And whether Chichester's and Salisbury's deaths are part of it or not, the 'why' behind the murders stays the same, I think."

"To be rid of proof that Suffolk and Somerset deliberately set about to lose Normandy, yes," Frevisse agreed. "Which leaves us with the duke of Somerset, since Suffolk is dead."

"And Somerset could well want to be as rid of Suffolk as of Suffolk's messengers, making very much one less to know his part in it all."

Frevisse sat down on a joint stool near the foot of the bed. "The one trouble with that is that he was in Normandy until hardly a month ago. As we've thought before, that's somewhat a long reach for him to keep a hand on what he might want done here."

"But not an impossible one."

"No," she granted. "Not an impossible one. But . . ." She paused, staring at the floor, trying to thread her thoughts onto a single string, instead of scattered and swirled. Joliffe waited, but the coming-together did not happen. There were too many pieces all shoving at one another, and finally she said slowly, "There's something not altogether right about how we're seeing this. The pieces we have make sense, and yet . . . I can't let go this worry that there's more to it all. A piece or pieces we're missing that would altogether change what we think we know."

"The piece or pieces we don't have are the ones that would make *certain* Somerset is behind all this," Joliffe said.

"Somerset or someone else," Frevisse said. "Or Somerset *and* someone else. Remember Burgate's 'others'."

Joliffe had never found Dame Frevisse to be a comforting woman. She went at matters with a straight eye and a readiness to say what she thought that probably won her few friends. On his own part, that straight eye and ready tongue were much of what he liked about her; but for just an instant now he thought how well he could have lived without she had said that. Burgate's "others" had slipped from his mind.

He slid slowly down to lie flat on the bed, tucked his right hand behind his head, and said, staring up at the rafters, "There's this that goes that way. Having finished with Suffolk, the common folk have been in full cry against Somerset these past months, raging and demanding answers. You could well think the lords around the king would be doing the same. But they have not."

With the slowness of seeing what she did not want to see, Dame Frevisse started, "Which likely means . . ." She stopped, maybe not liking anymore than he did where that thought led.

There was no turning back from it now, and Joliffe said, "It's been over half a year since Suffolk slid from power and more than four months since he was killed. Somerset has come back from Normandy hardly a month ago. If this is all his doing, I can see he might well have long enough reach to order murders from there, but a reach long enough and strong enough to keep a strangle-hold on all the lords and other men around the king? That's harder to believe, because those are mostly men who live to have power. Somerset out of power would mean more power for them. They should be after him like hounds after a downed deer's throat, but so far as I've heard, no one among them has made any outcry against Somerset at all. No demands that he explain Normandy's loss. No accusations of treason from the men with most to gain by his fall. You see where that goes."

Still slowly, Dame Frevisse said, "It goes toward the likelihood that Burgate's 'others' have to be among them. Among the high lords around the king. Others besides Somerset that we've no guess toward at all." Like someone determined to grasp a nettle tightly enough to stop the sting, she went on more strongly, "Men close to the king and with power enough to keep questions from being asked and accusations being made by any other lords."

"Lords," Joliffe said grimly, "who want to go on as unsuspected as they presently are."

"Or as *he* presently is," Dame Frevisse said slowly. She was staring, frowning, at the wall beyond the bed. "I'm trying to remember Burgate's own words. Sometimes he said 'others', but at least once, when he was talking of his fear he'd be tortured, he said, 'he' had ordered against it. I tried to have him say who, but he wouldn't. He fumbled back to saying 'the others'."

"That maybe means there were more than one lord in this with Suffolk and Somerset, probably all along, but only one of them is protecting himself with murders." Joliffe shut his eyes, suddenly very tired in a way that had nothing to do with his wound. "A hydra of conspirators and one of them more deadly than all the others. If that's the way of it, St. Jude be with.us. My lord of York is up against more than is any way fair."

"It being about power," Dame Frevisse said dryly, "what has fair to do with it?"

Little or nothing, Joliffe thought bitterly, and all the more bitterly because here and now he could see nothing to do about any of it at all. Warn York, yes, but of what? That there were men trying to destroy him? He knew that well enough. Knew it the better if word had reached him in time of what was purposed against him in Wales. Or if that word hadn't reached him in time . . . Very quietly, eyes still closed, he said, "There's been no word, even a rumor, about York the while I've been here, has there?"

"Nothing that's come here," she answered as quietly.

"If any comes and I don't chance to hear it . . ."

"If I hear aught, I'll tell you. Though you're likely to hear it from Luce before you hear it from me. Do you have any thought on who these men or this man could be?"

"No. Or too many thoughts and no proof."

"The proof is in Suffolk's letter."

"Suffolk's accusations are in that letter. That's all we know for certain." But he had to get it to York.

"They'll be somewhere to start," Dame Frevisse said. She stood up as if to go, then paused and asked in the same calm and level voice, "Why, of all the choices you surely had, did you choose this manner of life?"

Joliffe kept his eyes closed, considered pretending he had gone to sleep; but she waited, and from among the various answers he might have made he finally said, "It happened. And I didn't stop it happening."

"Then why the duke of York? Why choose his service out of all the less deadly ones there must be?"

"Because Suffolk was dangerous." He said it flatly, meaning for her to take that as his last answer, then found he could not leave it at that and opened his eyes to look not at her but at the roof beam again while he said, his voice low, "Suffolk corrupted more than the French war. He was destroying the government here in England for years longer than he was losing that war. For him, his own profit was all. He was draining the country dry for his own gain and the gain of the men around him. That's much of what has driven men to all these revolts. Justice was dying, and it will still die and everything go to the worse if Somerset simply takes his place. Somerset and the other lords like him. They're dangerous in their ambitions, in their eagerness to grab more power than they can well wield."

"And York isn't ambitious?" Dame Frevisse asked. "And grabbing for power?"

Joliffe finally brought his gaze down and rolled his head enough aside to look at her. She was someone who did not simply let life happen at her. She wanted to understand the why of things, and he answered her straightly, "York *has* power. He was born to more of it than any other lord in

England. It's his power Suffolk and Somerset and the others have been trying to break."

"Hasn't he tried to break theirs?"

"He's stood out against them, yes, because if he hadn't, they would have destroyed him by now. I think he hoped his accepting of this exile to Ireland would satisfy them that he'd leave them alone if they'd leave him alone. Instead, they've set to work against him while he's too far away to defend himself." Joliffe did not try to stop the anger edging into his voice. He even raised himself a little up from the bed on his elbows, strengthened by his anger. "Then there's what York has done with his power. He's used it for more than his own gain, has done other with it than make himself more wealthy at other men's expense. Have you ever heard that Suffolk, Somerset, and their kind have ever used their power for anything *except* their own gain?" The weakness that had betrayed him into that open anger reclaimed him. He sank back on the pillow and closed his eyes before saying with deliberate lightness, "Besides all else, there's the difference between the kind of men the king has let gather around himself—Suffolk, Somerset, Sir Thomas Stanley—there's a man with just enough wits to be a cur—and the kind of men the duke of York gathers to him."

"Such as?" Dame Frevisse asked evenly.

Joliffe smiled. "Myself, for one."

She held silent so long that he finally opened his eyes to find she was still standing there, looking at him with a look he could not read except to know that whatever she was thinking, it was not good. And very quietly she said, "Then very likely whoever is behind these murders to keep their secret are the same men—or man—who want to falsely accuse your duke of York of treason."

"Yes." Joliffe had settled on that likelihood some time ago.

"They'll also claim that anyone who serves York is a traitor."

"Yes." Another thing Joliffe had already faced.

"Which includes you," she said quietly.

Meeting her gaze, he agreed as quietly, "Yes."

Through a long moment then she only went on looking at him, before saying evenly, "So long as you know it."

Steadily meeting her gaze, he said, "I know it."

Knew it included him in all the disgrace and ugly death that could come with being a traitor. Nor was he a nobleman, to die by the headsman's ax. For him a traitor's death would be by hanging until nearly dead, then having his guts cut and pulled out of his living body so he could see them while he died.

That was what would come to him if York should fall and he fell with him, and he knew it all too well.

Chapter 23

Dame Frevisse did not return that day, nor for several days. Joliffe did not ask after her, not of Dame Claire or Sister Johane as they saw to his wound each morning, certainly not of Dame Juliana who looked in on him rarely and never with any show of pleasure that he was there. He was left to his thoughts that were presently going nowhere except around and around on themselves—like a dog trying for a flea on its rump, he thought: moving much and getting nowhere—and to recovering his strength. That went well, anyway. The wound was healing cleanly and he walked twice and sometimes thrice a day now, and only old Ela reminding him from her corner not to be a fool and do too much kept him from doing more, because she was right. Pushing too hard before his body was ready would only set him back. Still, the morning that he reached the guesthall's outside stairs on his own and sat for a time in the sunlight was a triumph, and the next day when he walked to the far side of the yard and back a greater triumph, and never mind that when he returned to his bed he slept the rest of the day away.

After his next morning's walk, he was lying on his bed, trying to judge how tired it had left him, when old Ela hobbled in.

"Just seeing that you're awake and as decent as may be," she said. "Dame Frevisse is come to see you."

Joliffe sat up and swung his legs over the bed's edge. "If she feels you have to see me first, I must be better than I thought."

"Aye, you're better enough that I'm keeping my eye on that Luce. She's about decided you're well enough to be useful to her."

"Ela," Joliffe protested. "I'm saving myself for you."

Ela laughed at him. "You do that, youngling. You do that."

She hobbled out. Joliffe heard her say, "He's as decent as he's likely to get, but if he tries to stand up, you stop him."

Dame Frevisse entered, and to be perverse as well as courteous, Joliffe made to push himself up from the bed.

"Don't," she said. "As you well heard Ela say." She eyed him. "You're better. But not well."

"I'm well," he corrected. "But not strong."

"You're better," she repeated. "You're not well. Dame Claire says the wound is healing, has closed better than you deserve, but . . ."

"Aren't all men deserving of mercy?"

"Some are more deserving than others." And added before he could make answer to that, "I've thought further on our problem."

"To more purpose than I have, I hope. I need to know

more and can't learn it here. So . . ." He made a gesture as if casting away his frustration.

"Will it help to have three more deaths to consider?"

Joliffe sat straighter despite that pulled his side. "Three more? What have you heard?"

"Nothing new. These were this summer in London when Cade had the city. Lord Saye and Sele, and his son-in-law William Crowmer."

"As fine a pair of extorting bastards as ever disgraced a royal government," Joliffe said. "I heard of what happened, yes." James Fiennes, Lord Saye and Sele, and his son-in-law had been of the court party, close among the men around the king. They had held a large piece of southeastern England in their greedy hands and for years had stripped it of wealth by every legal and illegal means they could. That they had been beheaded in London at the height of the rebellion after mock trials at the hands of rebels had had a certain illegal justice to it. More justice, anyway, than Fiennes and Crowmer had given to any number of other men, Joliffe thought.

"What I've been wondering," Dame Frevisse said carefully, "is how they came to be in reach of the rebels. They were among the men the rebels had already named in their accusations to the king, but the only ones King Henry had had arrested."

"A sop to the rebels," Joliffe said. "A 'Look, we've met one of your demands.'"

"Yes. They were arrested and put in the Tower of London, and then King Henry and his lords fled London."

"Leaving Fiennes and Crowmer behind, and Lord Scales in charge of the Tower," Joliffe said. "So they should have been safe enough, but they ended up dead anyway."

"Do you know how?"

"Beheaded, the both of them."

"No, I mean how they came into the rebels' hands at all?"

"No," Joliffe said. "Too much else was happening, and I had no grief at Fiennes' and Crowmer's deaths. I never gave them thought at all."

"I heard from men who saw it happening. Lord Scales took Fiennes out of the Tower to London's Guildhall for the trial that Jack Cade and the rebels were demanding."

"That I'd heard. Didn't Cade threaten to set fire to London if Fiennes wasn't tried?"

"If he did, it was an empty threat. London was still on his side then. He had to know that if he had even looked like using fire, the whole city would have turned against him."

Joliffe frowned. "But Lord Scales gave way to it."

"Even knowing that once Fiennes was out of the Tower, the several thousand rebels baying for his death would never let him be taken back. However the 'trial' might go, Scales had to know that Fiennes was as good as dead once he was out of the Tower." She was speaking rapidly, a smolder of anger under the words. "And then there's Crowmer. Why was he in the Fleet prison and not in the Tower?"

Joliffe startled. "The Fleet?" The Fleet prison was on the other side of London from the Tower and not defensible. A prison was for keeping prisoners in, not attackers out, and he echoed, "What was he doing in the Fleet? Why was he there instead of the Tower?"

"I never heard anyone say, but that's where the rebels found him. Dragged him out, bothered with even less of a trial than Fiennes had had, and beheaded him, along with some clerk they took from prison with him."

"Who was the clerk?"

"I don't know."

Joliffe struck at the bedding with his fist. "There's too much we don't know. Crowmer, who should have been in the Tower, wasn't. Fiennes *was* in the Tower but was taken out and all but handed over to the rebels, despite Lord Scales had to know that once he was out he was as good as dead." Joliffe paused with a sudden, inward coldness, then said, "Which has to mean he wanted Fiennes dead."

"Or that Lord Scales is a fool who made a bad choice?" Dame Frevisse suggested.

"I'll give you there's nothing brisk about Lord Scales' brain. He takes his orders and does his duty, without troubling to think overmuch about it. The king's man straight and simple."

Looking at him strangely, Dame Frevisse asked, "You know him that well?"

Suddenly careful of his words, Joliffe said, "In the . . . work I do, it's good to know more rather than less about men who may come to matter. It's not that I always know the men myself. It's . . ." He stopped, uncertain how much he should say that she did not need to know.

She finished for him. "It's that someone has troubled to learn about these men, then share what they've learned with you and others who do the same . . . work."

"Yes," Joliffe agreed, and offered no more.

She let him leave it at that, going back to, "Then you'd say that whatever Lord Scales did with Fiennes and Crowmer, he did it by someone's orders."

"Yes."

"And that whoever gave those orders probably gave them because he wanted both men dead."

"That all follows together," Joliffe said. "So does the thought that it had to be someone who could not only give the order, but afterward keep questions from being asked."

"The way questions haven't been asked about Suffolk's murder."

"There were questions asked," Joliffe said; and added slowly, "Some."

"The ship was the *Nicholas of the Tower*. With all the records kept in every port, both the ship and its men should have been easy to find, to indict, to bring to trial. Were they?"

Joliffe slowly turned his head from side to side, his eyes fixed on hers. "Nothing has been done about them. Not that I've heard."

Dame Frevisse looked at him, frowning, for a long, wordless moment before finally saying, still frowning, "Nothing has been done about the murder of the king's greatest lord? The man nearest him for ten years and more? Nothing?"

Joliffe tried, as devil's advocate, "With all the upheave of rebellions and the French war there's hardly been time to bother with Suffolk's murderers."

Dame Frevisse gave that the scorn it deserved. "Since nearly nothing was being done to save the war in France and the revolts here did not break out at their worst until at least a month after Suffolk's death, there was time enough."

"Come to that," Joliffe said quietly, "not much has been done about either the bishop of Chichester's murder or the bishop of Salisbury's. Some things, but not much."

Very slowly Dame Frevisse said, "There's nothing to say they all link, the way these later, lesser murders so surely do, to someone trying to keep hidden his part in Normandy's loss."

"But the thought does come," Joliffe said.

"It does."

"Misfortunately, it sets us no nearer to knowing who, besides the duke of Somerset, is behind them, although Fiennes' and Crowmer's murders make it even more certain there's someone besides him."

"Because he was still in Normandy when Jack Cade's revolt blew up, and everything happened so fast then, he would, at best, barely have heard Cade was in London before it was all over. He'd not have had time to give the orders that got Fiennes and Crowmer dead."

"But someone did," Joliffe said. "My guess would be the same someone who learned Suffolk had been making threats and writing letters before he sailed for France, and gave order for Burgate to be seized and held immediately after Suffolk's death. And if those orders, then the orders for Gough's death and Hampden's, too, and probably both priests', though by then Somerset could have sharing in the business."

"Who around the king has that kind of power?" Dame Frevisse asked quietly.

"I don't know," he said, because he didn't know. Among the lords left around the king there was no one who stood out in power as Suffolk and Somerset had done these past few years.

But a fear was beginning to crawl up the back of his mind with small, sharp claws.

It was something he was not going to share, and he gave way and let his body slump as if suddenly he could not hold straight anymore. "I think I need to sleep again," he said and lay down and closed his eyes.

Dame Frevisse made a small sound. Whether of irk, anger, or worry he couldn't tell, only waited, listening as with a soft whisper of skirts and no other word she left, leaving him wishing he was as suddenly tired as he had seemed, because then he might have gone to sleep. Now he was going to have to lie here with his thoughts when he would rather have not.

Dame Frevisse did not return that day or the next. Joliffe walked around the guesthall yard a little more each day, regaining his strength more quickly than he had dared to hope. In the while he had been too ill to note it, the year had slipped well into early autumn. The mornings had more of a chill to them, but the afternoons could still turn warm, and he took to sitting for a time on the guesthall steps then, to breath open air and see the sky a while longer before he took himself back into the hall.

Because he could take his meals sitting at table now and no travelers were there that evening, he was having his supper in the hall alone, save for Luce hovering in talk with him despite old Ela's glare, when Tom came in excitedly, saying to all of them as he came, "Have you heard? Tad of the stable is back from Banbury. He says word's running the duke of York is come back from Ireland without the king's leave and there's been trouble in Wales about it. A battle even, maybe."

"Why'd he be fighting the Welsh?" Luce asked. She flattened a hand to her flat breast. "Are they rising again? Is that Glendower man come back, the way they've said he would? Is that the way of it?"

"Not the Welsh," Tom said. "That Glendower was in my grandfather's time. He's not coming back. No. It was the *king's* own men York fought! They tried to stop him coming into Wales. Or maybe into England. Anyroad, there was a battle and the king's men lost and he's coming this way, they say. York is. Going to London to challenge the king and . . . and . . ." His words failed. He made a wide gesture with both hands. "And *all*."

Luce's eyes were huge with excitement. "Oh! Do you think he's come back to claim the crown for himself? Is he going to take it away from King Henry the way King Henry's grandfather took it that while ago?" She lowered her voice. "There's some say that wouldn't be a bad thing."

Joliffe's hand was tightly cramped around the spoon he had been holding, but he asked as if the whole business hardly interested him, "What do *you* say?"

Old Ela was shuffling from her corner toward the table to hear better and snapped, "If she's her wits about her, she won't say anything."

"I'm only saying what people have said," Luce said righteously. "It's only fools talk that way."

"They're fools, too, who say York is going to make worse trouble than we've already had all this year," Tom declared. "My thought is he's come back to settle it all before it all gets worse. Someone has to and he's the man to do it."

"Rightly thought," Joliffe agreed with outward lightness.

"He's never showed other than loyal, so why would he turn against King Henry now?"

"Puh!" said Luce scornfully. "King Henry! King Henry has been useless for years and everybody knows it, God keep him." She gasped, crossed herself, and said, "I never said that. I've never said anything against the king."

"You never have," Joliffe agreed.

Old Ela snorted. Luce tossed her head to show she was ignoring Ela and said, chin in air, "And even if he is useless, he's still king and that's that. So I don't believe at all the duke of York is going to claim the crown. If he wants to show a few lords where the line is, that's another matter and he's welcome to it."

But if it had come to battle between York and any of the king's men in Wales, that was another matter, Joliffe thought. That would be taken for open treason by those intent on bringing York down.

He wanted to ask more but Tom wouldn't know more, and even what he had said was probably something like tenth-hand. Maybe there had been no battle. Probably the one certain thing was that York was back from Ireland.

He pushed himself up from the bench by heavy leaning on the table, said something about being ready to lie down again, and left Luce and Tom still talking. Because old Ela was watching him rather than them, he gave her a smile and a nod to show he was as untroubled by the news as she was. She nodded back, but with a shrewdness in her gaze that made him doubt her message was the same as his.

Pleased to find himself neither so weak in the legs nor so tired as he might have been, he was nonetheless grateful to lie down when he reached his bed. He had yet to bother putting his boots on, so he did not have to trouble with taking them off, and if he decided not to get up again, he could sleep well enough in the new shirt and someone's old hosen and tunic he'd been given. What he feared was that he would not sleep at all but lie awake in worried thought. His day's exertions saved him that. He was part way through his prayer for blessing in the night when he fell into heavy sleep.

Mercy ended when he awoke at first light. All the thoughts he had escaped in sleep were waiting for him with no way short of strong drink to be rid of his thinking and no way for him to come by strong drink here.

York was out of Ireland and seemed to have won against whatever the king's men had set against him in Wales. How he had won past them was among the worries. Then there were all the others. How many men did he have with him? Had he had time to gather them from his Welsh estates or had he brought them from Ireland? If from Ireland, he could have left matters dangerously unbalanced there, given how ready the Irish were to revolt against every treaty they made. However it was, he'd had enough men not only to fight—or face down—Sir Thomas Stanley, but was he going now to challenge King Henry? Or was that just rumor running the way rumor did? Come to it, how much of anything Tom had said last night was only rumor that had out-run anything like the truth?

Which left the questions: Where was York? What did he intend? And as importantly, what did King Henry intend?

Or would it be better to say: What was the duke of Somerset intending?

Somerset and whoever was allied with him, Joliffe amended.

He could bring himself to stay here quietly a small while longer, let the wound heal a little more, let his strength come back more. But in a day—two days—he would have to go. He would get Suffolk's letter back from Dame Frevisse and ride Wales-ward, learning what he could as he went.

If he was lucky, the most trouble with that plan would be getting a girth strap around Rowan after this while at pasture with nothing asked of her but eating.

Luce came with his breakfast of bread and ale and he asked her, "Any more word about the duke of York and all?" Trying to make it sound as if it little mattered.

"It would be an early traveler brought it if there was," she laughed and went away, easy in her life, content that other people's troubles were their own and nothing to do with her.

Dame Claire and Sister Johane had taken to seeing him turn and turn about. This morning Dame Claire came in, carrying her box of medicines, and Dame Frevisse followed her but stopped just inside the doorway, saying nothing, not even a morning greeting, only waiting quietly while he lifted up his tunic and shirt for Dame Claire to unfasten the bandage and take off the poultice. To her open satisfaction it came away clean.

"The wound is closed very well," she said. "There's no sign of infection left. I'll bandage you but nothing more today, and in a day or so you'll not need even that. Have you been stretching as I told you?"

"Yes, my lady." He did the gentle stretch and twist of his arms and body she had said would keep the wound from stiffening. "I've walked in the yard, too."

"You seem none the worse for it, but take care. If you reopen the wound, you may not be so fortunate with your healing as you've been this time."

"When will I be able to ride?"

"You mean leave here?" she said sharply. "You're healing, not healed. There's a difference. I would say you're some days yet from riding."

Quietly Dame Frevisse asked, "Is tomorrow too soon?"

Dame Claire swung around on her, looked back at Joliffe sitting suddenly very still, his gaze fixed on Dame Frevisse, and said very sharply, "If he's no good sense, yes, he could ride tomorrow. And likely be someone else's problem the day after that." She picked up her box of medicines, added,

"Just so he isn't mine again," and left, brushing past Dame Frevisse who did not move aside.

Joliffe sat looking at Dame Frevisse looking back at him in silence for a moment, before he said, "She doesn't approve of me."

"Right now she doesn't approve of either of us," Dame Frevisse returned and finally came into the room and a step aside from the doorway.

Behind where she had been stood Nicholas Vaughn.

Chapter 24

Frevisse had not gone again to see Joliffe because she did not know what else there was to be said between them.

There had to be some other answer than the one to which they had come near but left unsaid.

Had left unsaid because the answer that seemed to be uncoiling in front of them had to be wrong.

But if it wasn't wrong . . .

If it was right . . .

She had repeatedly pulled back from that thought, then forced herself to think onward, to face that after all the answer maybe was simple: If she and Joliffe were right, there was *nothing* they could do beyond Joliffe going to Alice and the duke of York with what he had, with what he knew. Then the matter, whether they were right or wrong, would be all York's trouble and no more of theirs.

She had been taking her turn at kitchen duties, chopping vegetables, when Dame Perpetua came to tell her a man had asked to see her and was waiting in the cloister's guest parlor. That was the small room just inside the cloister's outer door kept for nuns to receive family and sometimes friends. A plain room, it was barely furnished with a table, a bench, a few stools. The man was sitting on one of the stools, his elbow resting on the table, his head leaning wearily forward into his hand. He was muddy and unshaven, and only when he rose to his feet as she entered did she know him and exclaim, "Vaughn!"

"My lady." His bow was slight, possibly because he might have fallen over had he made a deeper one. He was more than merely muddy and unshaven and weary. As she neared him, she saw he had the hollow cheeks and the gray smears under the eyes of someone who had eaten poorly and slept too little for far too long.

That did not stop her demanding, "Where have you been all this while? Where've you come from? I pray you, sit down."

He sank onto the stool again, against courtesy, because she was still standing, but asked even while he did, "Is Noreys here? Did he get the letter?"

"He got it, yes. He was wounded getting it. The priest . . ."

"He's dead. I know. I've been there. Do you know where Noreys is?"

There was desperate need rather than anger in Vaughn's asking, and Frevisse answered, "He's here. We've been tending him. He was hurt. I told you."

"Does he still have the letter?"

"It's here and safe. What of you? Where have you been this while?"

But Vaughn was laboring to his feet again. "Where is he? I have to see him."

It would be simplest if he collapsed in the guesthall instead of here, so Frevisse said, "I'll take you to him."

As it happened, they were only a little behind Dame Claire going there, and Frevisse told Vaughn they would wait until the infirmarian had done with Joliffe.

"How badly is he hurt? Why is he here?" Vaughn asked.

"He's well-mended now," Frevisse said. "He's here because he didn't know where else was safe and where there was someone he could trust the letter to."

"You," said Vaughn.

"Yes."

"So you have it."

"No."

Dame Claire had looked around at them following her but asked nothing. Frevisse pointed Vaughn where to wait while she went into Joliffe's room behind Dame Claire to see for herself how he did, glad to find he was far better, both of his wound and in strength, and he exclaimed in both surprise and relief at sight of Vaughn, "Where in twenty devils' names have you been!" He stood up from the bed and held out his hand. As Vaughn came forward to take it, Frevisse shifted back to the doorway, both to signal to Ela that food and drink were wanted and to keep watch against anyone coming near. Joliffe, seeing Vaughn more clearly, made him sit down on the end of the bed, demanding while he did, "Why was it someone else at Sible Hedingham instead of you?"

Vaughn took off his hat, ran a hand into his matted hair. "That was Gyllam." Strength seemed draining out of him now he had seen Joliffe; he sounded as tired as he looked. "If I'd reached Hedingham as I should have, he wouldn't be dead at all."

"Where were you?"

"On my way to Denmark," Vaughn said on a bitten laugh. "I couldn't shake that mis-bred cur that was following me. He was like one of those damned stray dogs that won't give up but won't come near enough to be brained with a stone. He even picked up two more of his kind along the way somehow, so then there were three of them against Symond and me, and I didn't dare chance openly facing them. Trying to lose them while *not* going to Hedingham or Wingfield, I ended up at Bishop's Lynn of all places and took passage on a ship just ready to pull away from the dock. *That* lost them, and it was bound for Ipswich and that couldn't have been better. From there it's easy ride to Sible Hedingham. Except the wind turned against us and into a storm. We were driven northward, almost to Denmark, before we could come around and beat back. I didn't land at Ipswich until a hell-damned week ago."

Joliffe sat down where he had been on the bed. "But then how did Gyllam come to be at Hedingham?"

"The man I sent back to Lady Alice from Kenilworth reached her, told her Burgate was there. She swept off to Kenilworth herself to have him freed or know the reason why not. She succeeded. He's at Wingfield now, in no good shape but alive and maybe he'll better. He told her what he'd told Dame Frevisse. With no knowing where I was—or you—she sent Gyllam for the letter. That's how he came to be there and killed."

Frevisse asked, "How do you know all this?"

"Because at Hedingham when I came there the crowner and sheriff were tearing the place to pieces with questions. I named Gyllam for them and saw to him being buried and learned that someone who could have been Noreys had been there, too. All I could hope was that Noreys had the letter and was gone to Wingfield. So I went there."

Frevisse looked at Joliffe. "We seem to have suspicioned rightly."

Joliffe nodded. "Someone set Burgate to be followed, and then Gyllam was followed from him."

"That's how I've read it, too," Vaughn said. "It was all a trap and Gyllam died in it."

"And when you didn't find me at Wingfield?" Joliffe asked.

"I sent word to Lady Alice that . . ."

"Sent her word?" Frevisse asked quickly. "She wasn't at Wingfield?"

"She was still at Kenilworth. The queen didn't want to part with her."

He started to say more but Frevisse, seeing Tom coming with a tray with bread and cheese and three cups, warned, "Wait," and Vaughn fell silent. She took the tray from Tom, thanked and dismissed him, set the tray on the bed between the two men, took one of the cups of dark ale, and stepped back to the doorway. Both men took bread and cheese and ate, Joliffe no less readily than Vaughn, but after several mouthfuls and a long draught of the ale, Joliffe said, "You can't have waited for Lady Alice's reply if you were at Ipswich a week ago and here today."

Vaughn shook his head while swallowing bread. "I didn't wait, no. I came the only other place I had hope someone might know where you might be. And here you are. Dame Frevisse says you have the letter. How?"

"Are you going to suspect me of killing Gyllam to have it?" Joliffe asked.

"I'd have come with more than Ned for company if I thought that," Vaughn replied flatly. "But I'm ready to hear what happened there."

Vaughn went on eating while Joliffe told him all that he'd told Frevisse, and looked the better for food, but before Joliffe had finished, grimness had joined the weariness in Vaughn's face. With bread, cheese, and ale gone by then, he sat staring into his empty cup for a long moment, then looked up to say, "It's like it was with Hampden and Squyers. A setting on of other men to do someone's killing for him."

Frevisse and Joliffe traded sharp looks with one another before Joliffe said, "Except this fellow who set the villagers on is ready to do his own killing if need be."

Vaughn took a deep breath, let it out heavily, lifted his gaze from the cup to Joliffe, and asked, "Have you heard the news out of Wales?"

"Some word of doubtful worth came yesterday that York is back from Ireland, that there was fighting in Wales because of it. And that he's on his way to London to challenge the king."

Vaughn's brows rose. "That's more than I've heard."

"That's because you didn't hear it from Tad of the stable, back from Banbury," Joliffe said easily.

"Even Tad of the stable didn't say all that," Frevisse said. "By Master Naylor's report to Domina Elisabeth, given us in chapter this morning, what Tad told him was there's word running York is come back from Ireland and there was trouble of some kind with some royal officers in North Wales about it. Nothing was said of any fighting at all."

"What I heard in Towcester as I came through," said Vaughn, "is that royal officers made some kind of challenge against York in Wales, but he faced them down without it came to fighting."

"That's to the good, anyway," Joliffe said. "Was there word of where York is now?"

"If word runs true, he's headed for London."

"Which way?"

"This. Up Watling Street." The road that ran from near the Welsh Marches to London with a straight intent unknown to most English roads. "That's what was being said in Towcester anyway, and that's on Watling so there's chance the report runs true."

"That will take him perilously near Kenilworth and the duke of Buckingham," Joliffe said. "But I don't see Buckingham sallying out to challenge York."

"Maybe not," Vaughn answered grimly. "But there were men wearing Buckingham's badge all over Towcester and supposedly headed for Kenilworth. Nor they weren't the first to go through, if the tavern-keeper knew what he was talking about, and not all of them Buckingham's either."

"York can't afford to let them stop him," Joliffe said as grimly. "He has to get to the king to defend himself before more can be done against him. And to face down Somerset before Somerset has time to take firm hold there. But if Buckingham has orders to challenge him, to bring men against him and make a fight of it after all . . . Or if Somerset is fool enough to try it . . ." He fell silent, frowning at the white-plastered wall beyond the bedfoot, probably seeing too many ill ways the business could go.

Quietly into his thoughts Dame Frevisse said, "Master Naylor has sent a man to Banbury to see if there's more to be learned, to know if we need to worry here." Because it was never good to have a large, armed force of men in your neighborhood, even if only on their way to somewhere else.

"York should come no nearer to here than Stony Stratford," Vaughn said.

"Master Naylor has set a watch anyway. If other lords are gathering men to bring against York, they could come this way."

"Men called to join York could come this way, too," Vaughn granted.

Joliffe came back from wherever he had gone in his thoughts and said, "And if they meet up with some other lord's men, who knows what idiot thing could happen. The whole countryside closer to Watling Street and along it is likely swarming like an overset wasps' nest with lords' men not knowing whether they're supposed to fight each other or not. It's going to make getting to York with Suffolk's letter difficult."

Frevisse and Vaughn both jerked their heads toward him, with Frevisse's protest coming first. "You're not fit to ride yet."

"Dame Claire said I could tomorrow."

"Dame Claire said you could if you had no good sense."

Joliffe made a "there you are then" gesture.

"That aside," Vaughn said fiercely, "you agreed it's to go to Lady Alice first. You swore to that."

"I agreed to it," Joliffe returned evenly. "I didn't swear. And matters have changed since we agreed. Lady Alice is in Kenilworth. Do you truly want to walk into there with this letter in hand?"

That stopped whatever angry thing Vaughn had started to say. Joliffe went on, "We could ride in but I'd not give a throw of the dice for our chances of riding out, and that would be the end of York ever knowing what's in Suffolk's letter or being able to do anything about it." Thoughtfully he added, "It would probably be the end of us, too."

In the drawn-out silence after that, Frevisse could hear a distant squabble of voices in the guesthall kitchen—probably Luce and the cook in one of their usual happy discords, getting on with their lives without much worry over the greater discords of their betters. But how "better", Frevisse wondered, were men who could tear a country's peace to pieces for the sake of their own ambitions?

Slowly Vaughn said, "So we go to the duke of York."

A silence drew out between them as they probably considered the difficulties of that before Frevisse said levelly, "I'll speak to Domina Elisabeth about who should go with us when we go."

"*Us?*" Joliffe and Vaughn started together. "You . . ." Joliffe's protest died but Vaughn said strongly, "Your part in this is done."

"It's not," she said, not arguing, merely setting out a certainty.

Joliffe, probably familiar enough with his own stubbornness to know stubborn when he met it in someone else, tried, somewhat more reasonably than Vaughn's flat refusal. "If you come, another nun will have to come with you. It's far from fair to make her part of what she isn't."

"If all were fair in life," Frevisse returned, "none of this would be happening at all."

Joliffe started to answer that, stopped, then said carefully, "I never knew you could be that ruthless."

Frevisse smiled bleakly and said, lightly mocking, "It's given to no man to know everything."

Joliffe returned, with a slight bow and matching her mockery, "Then I must thank you that my ignorance is now a little less."

"You are most welcome," she mocked back. Then said, the mocking gone, "There's this, too. By going with you, I can be my cousin's voice to the duke of York. I'll be able to speak more strongly on her behalf than you can, Vaughn." She smiled very slightly. "Besides, the letter is presently in my keeping, and if I do not go, neither does it."

Vaughn looked startled.

Joliffe laughed. "I didn't know extortion was counted among a nun's virtues."

Frevisse forbore to point out that there was probably much about nuns he did not know, and Vaughn asked, "Will your prioress be persuaded to this?"

Frevisse looked at him and said, unable to keep dryness from her voice, "When I say the business is all on behalf of the duchess of Suffolk, she'll agree to it. She has great hopes of the duchess' favor in return for favors."

Vaughn stood up. "How soon can we leave?"

"Sit down," said Joliffe. "We've not settled how we're to find York."

Frevisse thought it was less in obedience to Joliffe than the discovery of how tired he was that sat Vaughn down again; but he said strongly enough, "Find him? We take ourselves to Towcester and head north until we meet him."

"Do we know where York is or how fast he's moving south?" Joliffe asked. "And what of all the lord's men swarming between him and us?"

"True." Vaughn rubbed at his face with both hands. "I need sleep."

He needed sleep and a long rest and several full meals and soon, Frevisse thought; but Joliffe was saying, "Besides, if the murderous fellow from Sible Hedingham is still out there and after the letter, it will be near York he's lurking now, having lost me. Not knowing more than we do of where York is, I say we cut well ahead of him and let him come to us."

Vaughn nodded frowningly to that. "Well before London, though. St. Albans?"

"St. Albans," Joliffe agreed.

"You know the way from here?"

"Southeast through Bicester and Aylesbury. Leaving this afternoon, we could be there late tomorrow. Meanwhile there should be a bed here for you to have the sleep you need while Dame Frevisse sees to everything for our going." He turned his warm smile that she least trusted toward her and asked, "You'll do that, my lady?"

With no smile and clipping her words, she said, "I'll see to it."

Domina Elisabeth met her request with a long silence heavy with unasked questions, first looking at Frevisse, then away, out the window beside her writing desk where she had been seated to her copying work when Frevisse came in. While Frevisse spoke, she had wiped the point of her quilled pen dry and then sat twirling it between her fingers, first one way, then the other. Only when Frevisse fell silent did she at last withdraw her gaze from the window but only to watch the quill's feathered end as she turned and turned it, until finally she said, "St. Albans. Not to meet her grace of Suffolk, which might be reasonable, but for a reason you have not said and one that I . . ." She finally looked at Frevisse again. ". . . would be better not to know?"

"Yes, my lady."

"This man who's been in our care is fit to ride?"

"He's able to and will, whether he should or not."

"Would it suffice if I sent one of our men with him? Rather than you and whoever else among us will have to go if you do?"

"I wish that would suffice, my lady." Domina Elisabeth could not know how very much she wished that, how much she wanted to stay here in St. Frideswide's, apart from all the tangle of angers, ugliness, and treachery across England, not ride into maybe the middle of it. "But this matter of Lady Alice's makes it something of my duty, too."

"Your first duty is to St. Frideswide's."

My *first* duty, Frevisse thought, is to God. Besides that, Domina Elisabeth had other times been ready enough to send her from St. Frideswide's at Alice's need, whatever Frevisse had wanted. Feeling herself dangerously near to anger, she lowered her eyes in outward humility and said, "Her grace of Suffolk has entrusted me with this business. Unless you say otherwise, I'd do wrong to fail her in her need."

"How trouble-fraught *is* this business you're on?"

Frevisse bowed her head lower and held silent. If ordered to answer, she would have to; but Domina Elisabeth, maybe aware she was better off without an answer, said suddenly, sharply, "Well enough, then. Just mind that when the time comes, you let her grace of Suffolk know how far I've stretched the Rule and my rule here for her sake."

Frevisse sank in a deep curtsy, saying, "I will, my lady. I promise she'll know and be grateful. Thank you, my lady."

"There's going to be displeasure among the others over this," Domina Elisabeth grumbled. "At me, at you, and at whoever goes with you."

"Could that be Sister Margrett again, please you?" Frevisse said; and added before Domina Elisabeth could ask why, "The fewer who know of the matter the better. She already knows something, and that way no one else need learn it." And Sister Margrett had already shown how well she could hold back from questions best left unasked.

Domina Elisabeth made an impatient sound, granted, "Yes. Very well. Send her to me, I suppose," and with a wordless sign of benediction dismissed Frevisse as if glad to have her gone.

Chapter 25

hey rode out of St. Frideswide's in the early afternoon—Joliffe and Vaughn ahead, then the man Ned, then Frevisse and Sister Margrett together, then two men from the nunnery—leaving a seethe of unsettled nuns, Dame Claire's anger, and Master Naylor's displeased glare behind them.

Sleep and another meal had done Vaughn some good. With that and having taken the chance to wash and shave, he no longer looked either so haggard or unkept, and however he and Joliffe truly felt in themselves, they made good miles. Frevisse thought Joliffe held himself somewhat too carefully in the saddle, but the one chance she had to talk with him, when they paused at a ford to water the horses, she thought better of asking directly how he did and only asked, nodding at his side, "Does it hurt?"

"Not beyond reasonable," he said easily.

Never a weighty man, he was even less fleshed now, and the full light of day did him no favors. He was too hollow below his cheekbones, and the fine bones were ridged too sharply in the back of his hands; but he held his reins easily, not like a man taut in pain, so maybe he was right and his wound was healed enough for riding. Frevisse supposed the question was then how long his strength would hold, and she must have betrayed that in her look, because Joliffe grinned and said, "We'll find out, won't we?"

It held through the afternoon, at least, and so did Vaughn's, and they rode into Bicester before sunset. There was an Augustinian priory in the town, but on Joliffe's recommendation they took rooms at the White Hart Inn. "The easier to leave in the morning," he said.

Frevisse and Sister Margrett took supper alone in the small chamber they were given for the night. It was when they were done and readying to say Compline before going to bed that Sister Margrett for the first time asked anything about what they were doing, and then it was, "Dame Frevisse, will you swear to me on St. Frideswide's name that all this is needful?"

Sunk in her own thoughts and grown used to Sister Margrett's accepting silence, Frevisse was startled by the question and said, her surprise showing, "Yes. I swear it. Willingly." She steadied. "I swear I saw no other way to do this."

Sister Margrett regarded her solemnly, then asked, "You trust both of these men, then?"

Frevisse paused over answering that, before saying, "Lady Alice trusts Nicholas Vaughn. Knowing him as little as I do, I have to trust her judgment of him. As for Master Noreys, I know him somewhat better and, yes, him I do trust."

The ease with which that answer came surprised her. But

she did trust him. Each time they had met over the years she had been forced to trust him further. She could wonder whether trust brought on by necessity counted as strongly as trust by free and unforced choice, but then without necessity how could a trust's worth be proved and known? And in necessity, she reminded herself yet again, Joliffe had never betrayed her trust. Had sometimes pulled it nearly to its breaking point but never betrayed it.

Sister Margrett, apparently satisfied, gave a short nod and took up her breviary.

There were a great many miles between them and St. Albans, more than a good day's ride. "Meaning we'll have to make a bad day's ride of it," Joliffe had said cheerily when they parted last night.

Frevisse had not doubted he meant it, and indeed they set out in the morning when the world was still gray, with only barely light enough to show their way out of Bicester, and they were more than several miles on their way by the time the first sunlight spilled thickly gold over the horizon and into their faces. Joliffe looked none the better for it but not so bad as Frevisse had feared he might. No worse than Vaughn, anyway.

Tierce's familiar words, when she and Sister Margret prayed the Office as best they could between one time of cantering and the next, had a different richness to them, with Frevisse knowing what she knew, fearing what she feared. *Dominus lux mea et salus mea. Quem timebo? Dominus praesidium vitae meae. A quo trepidabo?* The Lord is my light and my safety. Whom shall I fear? The Lord is the guard of my life. By whom shall I be frightened?

The countryside became wider, with more open fields and fewer hedges. The day promised to stay clear, was even warm with remembered summer although the lay of light across the harvested fields was entirely autumn and last night had been chill. As always after harvest-time there were gleaners in the stripped fields, people without land to grow food enough for themselves searching for whatever might have escaped the harvesters. The harvest had been fine this year, though, and if people were good to one another, no one should go hungry this winter. The barns and granaries were full and there were goodly numbers of cattle grazing the stubbled grain fields.

It had all the look of a world at peace, but somewhere in it the duke of York was moving southward with men enough that he had been able to face down and force aside the king's men in Wales; and somewhere maybe the king was moving with more men to meet him, and somewhere other lords and men were beyond doubt on the move, some to join York, some for the king. It was the way—given the foolishness to which men could sink—that battles happened. Some place as presently at peace as these fields could in a day or two or in a week or before the month was done become a place where men were killing one another.

And the letter she was carrying hidden might be the thing that brought them to it.

She wished she were back in St. Frideswide's, unwitting of all of this from beginning to end. She knew that was cowardice and did not care.

They stopped in Aylesbury at an inn, dismounting in the small cobbled yard, leaving Ned, Bartelme, and Perkyn with the horses, the rest of them going inside where a cheerful woman served them ale and slices of a meat pie warm from the morning's baking. Some was sent out to the men in the yard while Joliffe asked the woman if she had heard of troubles anywhere near. "Like there were all summer," he said. "We don't want to ride into anything."

"I've not heard tell of any stirrings lately, no," the woman said comfortably. "Harvest-time settled most folk, I think. Set them tending to business instead of to trouble, and not beforetime, either. Haply it was more talk than doing around here, anyway."

Frevisse said with not much outward show of interest, "We heard at the nunnery that the duke of York has come back from Ireland. Have you heard anything of that?"

"Oh, aye, I've heard that. *That's* making some manner of stir. There was a fret of men through here yesterday on their way to somewhere because of it."

"York's men?" Frevisse asked.

"Not his, no. Most of the ones I saw had the Stafford knot for their badge. The duke of Buckingham's men, see you. But there were some of Lord Warrene's among them, too, like it was an in-gathering. One of them said they were on their way to Towchester. That's a fair ways from here, but that's what he said."

"Why?" Joliffe asked as if in all innocence.

"Ah, who knows? They didn't seem to know, that's sure. Only that Buckingham had summoned them up and away they were going. If it means the duke of York is truly back from Ireland, then it's none too soon and I'm only glad of it, that's all I can say. Say what you will about the duke of Suffolk, we didn't have trouble like Jack Cade when he was seeing to things. We can only hope the duke of York, God keep him, takes his place and sees to things. Since it seems the king won't," she added darkly, then crossed herself and added hastily, "God keep King Henry, and never think I mean otherwise. But York's his cousin after all, and so who better to take place close to him?"

"The duke of Somerset?" Vaughn said. "He's likewise the king's cousin."

The woman made a scornful noise. "Don't talk to me of

Somerset. The way he handed Normandy back to the Dauphin as if it was his to give away and never mind all. I've a cousin buried over there, killed these twenty years ago when that French witch made all that trouble at Orleans and afterwards. Don't talk to me about cousins. There he is, Somerset, settling in with the king as if it never happened, if I've heard rightly, while all those poor people who've lost their homes and everything are still on the roads and miserable. There's a family here. Jack Wryght indentured to go to Normandy when the duke of York was governor there. Did so well that when his indenture was up, he bought a house in Falaise and set up to be a blade-smith, just like he was here, and his wife went out to join him five years ago or so. Took their two boys and all. Has had two little girls since then, so it was all six of them came dragging back here not three weeks ago, all ragged and everything they own piled in a little handcart he was pulling while the rest of them walked, all but the littlest girl, and poor Alison was carrying her and looked fit to drop, so people say who saw them. They've nothing here now, of course, and nothing left in Normandy. They're staying with his brother and trying to put a life together here again out of what's left to them. They're better off than many, but that isn't saying much." She sniffed might-ily. "So why Somerset shouldn't be called to account for what he's done, king's cousin or not, I don't know. He ought to be charged with treason, and I hope the duke of York sees to it."

Joliffe said in strong agreement, "We can only pray," and shortly thereafter gathered them all up and had them out of there, leaving Vaughn to pay their bill, but saying to him when they were all a-horse again and riding out of Ayles-bury, "There was a woman who knew her own mind about matters."

"She did that," Vaughn agreed. "I just wish the king was as firm-set as she is about things."

"We can only pray," said Joliffe.

Not many miles further on they made the steep climb into the wooded Chiltern Hills. The hours grew longer and so did the miles as they rode, and their shadows that had been behind them and then beside were now ahead of them. They rode with purpose and no pleasure, paused for food and drink in Berkhampstead and heard nothing they had not already heard, and rode on and came into St. Albans in early evening, the white tower of the abbey church glowing rose-red in the westering light. The long, wide marketplace outside the abbey gates had only townsfolk going about their business—no armed men in the streets, no signs of alarm. Whatever trouble might be spreading to meet Richard of York, it was not here yet.

St. Alban's abbey was one of the great abbeys of England, its abbot summoned to Parliament as the equal of many a temporal lord. Named for the saint who had been martyred in far off Roman times on the very hillside where the monastery now stood behind its enclosing walls, the church was also his burial place, his tomb a well-accustomed place of pilgrimage. Their little company was received at the abbey's gatehouse without trouble, no one even asking to see what bishop's papers the nuns carried to give them permission to travel.

Beyond the abbey's broad gatehouse the wide guestyard lay four-square, with a long line of stables to the right and the various guesthalls around the other three sides. Above the red-tile rooftops the west front of the church rose massive against the sky. Sister Margrett had looked longingly toward it as they rode toward the gateway, and she looked back now, asking Frevisse, "Will there be time to see the shrine?"

"Tomorrow assuredly," Frevisse said. "We're too late for even Vespers tonight, I fear."

Only from the guesthall master was there trouble and—finally—sure word of York.

"His foreriders came in not two hours ago," the black-robed monk said with unhappy fluster. "He's at Stony Stratford tonight and will be here tomorrow. His grace and I'm not clear how many more. Enough to fill us to overflowing, certes, even without the pilgrims already here. Not that there are so many, nor have been these past weeks. With all the troubles there are, people aren't taking to the roads like they would be otherwise."

Unmoved by the man's troubles, Joliffe said, "Fortunate for us we've come ahead of the duke, then, while you've still beds for us. If you'll show us where to go, we'll gladly leave you to your other duties and wish St. Benedict's blessing on you."

The monk started what might have become a protest to that, but Sister Margrett added very gently, with only the faintest hint that she might be going to slide from her horse in helpless weariness, "We're so tired."

Frevisse suspected that, more than anything, got them their beds. Ned, Bartelme, and Perkyn were shunted toward the stable with the horses and promise of places in the lesser guesthall meant for servants. Joliffe and Vaughn were sent to the men's guesthall. She and Sister Margrett were led away by a guesthall servant to the dorter kept for visiting nuns. The woman advised them that supper was nearly finished in the hall, and after a quick washing of face and hands, they went to eat out of plain need for food, more than any wish to stay upright much longer. They saw Joliffe and Vaughn there, looking as weary as Frevisse felt, but they did not speak together, and afterward Frevisse and Sister Margrett returned to the dorter, murmured something like

Compline, and crept with aching weariness into their bed. There was not a worry or an ache sufficient to keep Frevisse awake. She was asleep from the moment of settling her head on the pillow.

Chapter 26

A night's sleep made more difference to his weariness than Joliffe had dared to hope. He awoke in the morning with his side aching but not so badly he had to give it much heed, and after breaking fast in the abbey's guesthall, he was restless enough that he told Vaughn, "I'm going to see what rumors and news are in town."

"I'll go with you," Vaughn said with an alacrity that showed he was restless, too—or else unwilling to let Joliffe go unwatched.

Joliffe, having nothing more in mind than asking questions and listening, did not mind which way it was, was even somewhat glad of his companionship as they, first, wandered the length of St. Albans' long marketplace, overhearing what talk they could but nothing new to either of them. Along the way, Joliffe bought a good, dark blue doublet from a used clothing shop to replace his own, given back to him at St. Frideswide's mended and enough of the bloodstain cleansed away to make it wearable but not much presentable. He and Vaughn then made use of the town's public bathhouse to wash and shave, and with that and the "new" doublet Joliffe felt far more ready for the rest of the day.

For a while after that, the two of them drifted into and out of the several taverns and inns along the marketplace and nearer streets, listening to the talk around them, sometimes asking questions as if they were pilgrims worried how safe their journey home was going to be, "with all this shifting of lords' men about the countryside," Joliffe said several times to lead men on to more talk, but he learned nothing much new. Even talk with a pedlar lately out from London brought hardly anything. "The king's in Kent with that dog's toss-up Somerset and some others," the man said. "They're beating the whey out of the poor bastards as thought they had pardon last summer after Cade's rebellion. Is there more trouble than that? Because I'm heading north and don't want to walk into anything."

"Then I'd head west if I were you," Vaughn answered.

"Or sit it out here," Joliffe offered. "Once the duke of York is gone through, what trouble there is will likely go with him."

The pedlar frowned. "Aye. That business in Wales."

"Word of that has spread, has it?" Vaughn asked.

"It's being talked of in London, aye. People reckon it was Somerset's doing."

"Giving orders to the king's officers in Wales? That's moving fast for someone just come back from France," Joliffe said. "He never seemed that sharp to me. He wasn't when it came to saving Normandy, that's for certain."

"Happen losing Normandy has sharpened his wits, like,"

the pedlar said grimly. He raised his leather jack of ale. "Here's to Richard of York seeing to it Somerset gets what's coming to him."

Joliffe and Vaughn both drank to that with him, Joliffe at least with a whole heart.

To the good was that there was no word of any fighting, giving good hope there had been none because word of even a skirmish between York's men and anyone else's would have come racing up Watling Street like wind-born smoke ahead of a fire.

"Nor it doesn't seem the king or anyone is coming out to meet him on his way," Vaughn said as he and Joliffe sat finally alone at a table in the corner of another tavern, drinking thin wine.

"I wish I thought that was a good thing," Joliffe said.

"You'd rather it came to a fight?"

"Not by half. But for there to be seeming-nothing being done on the king's side is strange. Or seems so to me."

"Um," said Vaughn, which might have meant anything.

Joliffe leaned back against the wall and tried to seem he was not as weary as he was. Far wearier than he should be. He needed more strength than this if he was going to be use to anyone, including himself.

Vaughn ended the silence between them by asking, "Have you read this letter, to know if it's going to make enough of a difference to be worth the trouble we've taken with it?"

Keeping voice and body at ease, Joliffe said, "So far as I know, no one has read it since Suffolk sealed it. As to what it's worth . . ." He shrugged. ". . . *somebody* thinks it's worth the trouble of killing men for it. I'm trusting the letter will tell us who."

Vaughn sat staring into his almost empty bowl a long moment before saying, "I'm going at this as if my lady of Suffolk was already agreed and allied with York. I could be very far in the wrong for it."

"The choice and the burden of it lies on Dame Frevisse, not on you. She's acting in her grace of Suffolk's name."

Still staring into the bowl, Vaughn moved his head slowly side to side, refusing that way out. "I don't know if that's good enough."

Joliffe held back from saying, "It has to be."

Instead, he considered his other answers, then carefully offered, "If Burgate was right and Suffolk's death was purposed and not by merely rogue sailors, then it was ordered, and the order came from someone with the power to stop any questioning about it afterward. Can we agree on that?"

"Yes," Vaughn said stiffly, not looking at him.

"Can we likewise agree that the someone who ordered Suffolk's death is likely the someone behind all these other deaths and likewise keeping any useful questions from being asked?"

Vaughn finally raised his gaze to him, frowning, still wary even while assenting, "Yes. Well enough. It's likely that's the way of it."

"Then if whoever has the power to do all that decides to be afraid that Lady Alice knows too much about the same thing these men are being killed for, what chance will she have against him?"

Vaughn took his time over answering that, not because he did not know the answer, Joliffe thought, but because he hated even to think it. But finally he said, "Now that she's had chance to talk to Burgate and it's known first Gyllam and then you went for the letter, whoever is doing this probably does think she knows too much." He made a frustrated sound and said half-angrily, "Why didn't Buckingham just kill Burgate outright?"

"Because none of this is coming from Buckingham," Joliffe shot back. "The duke of Buckingham never troubled himself with a new thought all his own in his whole life, let alone subtleties like are tangled here. And don't tell me

Somerset, either. Somerset has all the subtlety of a five-year-old who thinks that by hiding his hands with a stolen apple behind his back he can make his mother believe he doesn't have it. Burgate is alive because someone was leaving it to God whether he would live or die, whether they'd have his secret or lose it. That's like tossing dice with God and telling yourself however it comes out, it's God's doing."

"That's mad," Vaughan protested.

"Not so much outright mad as reason working half a step sideways from where you and I do our thinking. Now," he said on anger-shortened breath, leaning toward Vaughn, "can you think of who that might be and with the power to make all of these deaths happen and no one look his way? Because if you can't . . ."

He did not finish. Either Vaughn could see it or he could not. And either way, Joliffe was not going to say the thing aloud.

Vaughn began to open his mouth toward saying something. Then the full weight of Joliffe's words hit. Joliffe saw his eyes widen, and his mouth snapped shut. His hands clamped tightly around the wine bowl and he said back, harsh and low, "You think *that's* what's in the letter?"

Joliffe nodded.

"If you're right, then, no, Lady Alice has no hope against him. There's only York might do it."

"Only York. Yes," Joliffe agreed. "And even then . . ." Joliffe broke off, there being little need to finish. Because even then, how much chance did even York have?

They finished the wine with no more said between them. Joliffe paid and they went out into the late morning's sunshine. The tavern they had happened into was in a short lane off the marketplace and busy with people coming and going. Just now five men were standing a few yards from the door, in close talk with one another and almost blocking the way. As Joliffe and Vaughn shifted to the lane's far side to pass them, the talk turned into shouting, two of the men starting to wave their arms, a third shoved another of his fellows hard and backward, between Joliffe and Vaughn, making them step apart. In that instant what had been talk erupted without warning into a quarrel with daggers and a familiarity that made Joliffe shout in sudden warning at Vaughn, *"Hampden!"* and draw his dagger and go for the two men nearest him, turned from their "quarrel" to go for him, spreading apart and probably meaning to take him from both sides. With a wide swing of body and arm, Joliffe slashed the dagger-arm of the man on his left open from elbow to wrist, completed his spin full around to bring himself in behind the startled other man's guard, stabbing into his side and stepping back as the man staggered, both to free his dagger and give himself room to draw his sword in time to knock aside the dagger of a third man coming for him. He followed through with his own dagger but the man stepped back from it. Joliffe caught movement from the side of his eye and slashed his sword backhanded at his first man, this time slicing him across the thigh, and bringing his sword back around in time to jam its point low into the gut of his third man well before the fellow was in dagger-strike reach. Joliffe was just enough off balance and the man just enough beyond clean reach for the blow to be too shallow for killing, but the man lurched backward, staring down in disbelief at the blood starting through his doublet.

Joliffe could have killed him then, but did not; instead stepped back to put his back to the nearest house-wall for time to see what needed doing next. But the fight was done. Vaughn stood a few feet away from him, sword and dagger drawn, watching the two men he had faced running away for the far end of the lane, hauling Joliffe's first man limping and hopping between them, one of them limping, too, and

Joliffe could not tell if the blood trailed behind them was from one or both. His third man was following, bent over and staggering a little. And beyond them, at the lane's end, watching, was . . .

With a hot rise of the anger there had been no time for in the fight, Joliffe started forward.

"Noreys!" Vaughn said, catching his arm. "Let them go!"

In the moment it took to jerk loose of Vaughn's hold, the man at the lane's end stepped back, was gone around the corner, out of sight.

"There!" Joliffe pointed furiously. "Did you see him? The man in the black cap. Watching it all. That was him. The man at Hedingham!"

"I didn't see him, no. Come on. We have to get away from here."

Vaughn had hold on his arm again, pulling, and Joliffe realized the man he had stabbed in the side lay close by, twisted and unmoving in the runnel down the middle of the street. There would be questions about that and not to his own good, Joliffe knew, and he gave way to Vaughn's pull on his arm, sheathing sword and dagger—they would have to be cleaned later—while following him back into the tavern. The whole business had gone so fast that only now were people starting to come out of other doors along the street, and the few men in the tavern were still getting up from their benches to go see what had happened. Vaughn and Joliffe went past them, into the tavern's rear room, past the two women there, and out the back door into a small rearyard.

"Over the fence, I think," said Vaughn.

"Over the fence," Joliffe agreed. It was head-high and of boards. They scaled it, came down in another yard where, happily, there was no one, but a small alley opened from it into another street. By now there was shouting behind them, but they walked away, into the marketplace and toward the abbey, and no one stopped them. Saying nothing between them, they passed through the abbey gateway into the guesthall yard and to the men's dorter, empty at this hour and the nearest thing they had to a safe-haven just now. By then Joliffe's blood had cooled. His side hurt, telling him he had done it no favors in the fight, but a cautious feel inside his doublet found the bandage dry; he'd not pulled his wound open.

What he had done was kill a man. If not two men, depending on how badly the third fellow was hurt. Or three, if the first man bled too much.

It did not feel good to have brought death. It never felt good.

But it felt better than being dead himself.

He sat down on his side of the bed and took from his saddlebag the cloth he kept for cleaning blades.

Sitting down heavily on the bed's other side, Vaughn demanded, "What in all the teeth of hell was that about?"

"They were set up to kill us the way they killed Hampden."

"Yes, I got that. But how did they know it was us they wanted?"

"The man from Hedingham was there." With his sword unsheathed and laid across his knees, Joliffe began to rub it clean of blood. "At the end of the street. Watching. He must have set them on."

"You yelled about a man in a black cap. That's who you meant?"

"That's who I meant."

"But what's he doing here, and why set them on to kill us?"

"I don't know why he's here, unless it's for York." There was a dark thought. But . . . "If he was, that's likely off, now he knows he's been seen and we'll give warning. It was our vile luck that we crossed with him sometime today and he saw me without me seeing him first. Of course it's his vile luck we're still alive. As for why bothering to have us killed—if we're dead, we can't give that letter to anyone."

"He can't know we still have the letter. It could be long gone to York. Or to anyone."

"I'd say he was hedging his bets. If we still have it and we're dead, we won't be giving it to anyone. If we've already rid ourselves of it, well, what's two more men dead in a good cause?"

"Having me dead is *not* a good cause," Vaughn said with indignation.

Joliffe laughed. "Alas, there are always others who don't see the world as we do." He laid his sword on the floor, pulled out his dagger and set to cleaning it. "Besides, I think he just likes seeing men killed."

When Vaughn said nothing to that, Joliffe looked up from his work to find him staring at the floor as if far off in some thought of his own. Joliffe asked, "Doesn't your sword or dagger need cleaning? One of those men I never fought was limping as they ran."

Vaughn shook his head. "He turned an ankle in that runnel in the lane's middle. His good luck. It threw him off-balance and aside from my sword just as I thrust at him." He looked up from the floor and around at Joliffe. "That's an ugly thought. That he enjoys the killing."

"It is. But I've had a lot of ugly thoughts lately."

"You have that." Vaughn lay down and laid his arm across his eyes. Like Joliffe, he seemed ready to rest whenever the chance came.

Joliffe finished with the dagger and lay down in his turn, closed his eyes and folded one hand peacefully onto his chest. The other he kept along his side, resting on his unsheathed dagger laid beside his leg. He was of two minds about Vaughn having stopped him from following Black-cap. From one way of seeing it, Vaughn had done right to turn him from pursuit to escape. But seen another way—had Vaughn stopped him not for the sake of their own escape but to be sure of Black-cap's?

Another ugly thought to add to all the rest.

Chapter 27

revisse and Sister Margrett began the day with going to Prime in the abbey church. Because they were forbidden the cloister here, they entered the nave by the west door along with the few other pilgrims and such townsfolk as were moved to piety at dawn; and because they had no place in the monks' choir beyond the rood screen, they drew aside into one of the side chapels and shared in the Office from there.

At that hour, save for a few candles burning, the nave was mostly lost in shadows. Even dawn's coming while they prayed little changed that before the Office ended and they went back to the guesthall to break their fast. They saw Joliffe and Vaughn there but did not speak with them, and both men went out of the hall first, apparently with plans of their own for how they were going to spend the time until the duke of York arrived.

Breakfast done, she and Sister Margrett returned to the church, leaving the guesthall yard to cross the abbey's now-busy outer yard to the west door again and into the church's hush, with the sun risen enough now to strike through some of the stained-glass windows, spreading color-patterned light—ruby and saffron and sapphire and emerald—along one long wall of the nave that was lined down either side with stone pillars like giant tree trunks.

In St. Frideswide's church nowhere was distant from any-where else. Here, St. Alban's nave alone looked to be longer than all the nunnery's cloister buildings put together. Its ceiling was so high the paintings there were almost lost to view. The carved stone rood screen at the nave's far end was maybe higher than St. Frideswide's church roof-beams; and beyond the rood screen with its ranks of statued saints painted in greens and golds and reds and blues, the rest of the church, reserved to the monks and St. Alban's shrine, stretched onward.

While Frevisse and Sister Margrett stood still, taking in the awe of it, a monk came at them from beyond one of the pillars. He began a protest that now was not a time the shrine was available to pilgrims, that too much else was happening, that in a day or two perhaps . . .

Frevisse had expected him. She held up a coin from her belt-purse. It was one of Alice's, given back to her by Dom-ina Elisabeth for this journey, and it was gold. The monk changed his discourse in midstream to an interest in show-ing them what he could of the church. Frevisse let him work himself around to an offer of after all showing them to St. Alban's shrine. She graciously accepted that but kept the coin for now, and with a patter of words well-used on other pilgrims, he led them along one of the nave's side aisles. As they neared the rood screen, the transepts opened to either side, giving the church the shape of Christ's cross. One of them would almost have held St. Frideswide's whole church with ease, and still the church stretched onward.

Their way was briefly blocked by a screen of open-worked iron across the foot of a broad rise of stone steps, but their monk opened the gate in it and they passed through and up, and now Frevisse sought to let go other thoughts, to bring her mind to bear on the here, the now. Chances to be in such a place were rare, were to be fully lived in, not thinned to nothing by thoughts of other things. They were coming to St. Alban's shrine, the heart within the body of this place. There, with the saint's earthly remains, the earthly and the divine came visibly together. At a saint's shrine, mankind could come closer to the holy than anywhere in life besides the sacraments. A saint's shrine was something that could be touched, hands laid upon it while prayers were made for the saint to ask God for grace and favor and rescue from earthly trials. Here, St. Alban's shrine was the reason for all else. The building's awe and beauty were nothing when matched to it.

Nor did anything in the church match the splendor of the shrine itself. It stood in the center of its holy place beyond the high altar's screen. Higher than a tall man, it was made of varied-colored, polished stone inlaid to patterns, was gold-gilded and set with jewels that shone with other-worldly richness in the clear, steady light of scores of burning candles set all around on stands among stands of votive offerings given along with past pleas for favor or in thanks for prayers answered.

Frevisse and Sister Margrett both went to their knees beside it. With head bowed and hands clasped, Frevisse lost heed of all else but her prayers. She had never had a particular devotion to St. Alban that would have brought her here otherwise, but now that she was here, with his holiness all around her, prayer to him came readily. Deep prayer that what she was doing would come to the end that God best desired. Prayer that if God's end went against her own desire, she might bear it with quiet acceptance and good trust.

She came back from the far place of her praying to awareness of Sister Margrett rising to her feet and that the monk was restless behind them, probably wanting to get on with his day. Frevisse rose, too, reached out to lay the gold coin on a ledge of the shrine, where the monk would surely collect it later, and was stepping back when she heard the monk saying to Sister Margrett behind her, "This now you'll want to see, too. Duke Humphrey's tomb. The duke of Gloucester who was murdered, you know."

Frevisse turned somewhat too quickly. It was usual for the wealthy and highborn to have tombs made for themselves in churches as near to high altars and saints' shrines as they could, so it was no surprise to see one here, towering with stone-vaulted canopy richly painted in heraldic reds and gold and blues. She had given it no look at all as she passed it, but saw it now, and past and present clamped together in a double fist around her heart.

Humphrey, duke of Gloucester, the king's uncle, had been a man in the way of other men's ambitions. Three years ago he had been suddenly charged with treason and then, before any trial, had been suddenly dead. Of natural causes the men around the king had said. Murdered, said too many other people, and so the monk was saying now to Sister Margrett, making a tale of it, but Frevisse's thoughts were gone beyond his words. She was thinking that if someone as highborn to power as the duke of Gloucester could be called traitor and then be dead, what could happen to people as nothing as she and Joliffe were if what they were attempting went to the wrong?

The rest of the morning and into the afternoon she and Sister Margrett spent going from one to another of the many chapels around the church and in doing the Offices. Sister Margrett seemed happy with all of that. Only as they were returning to the church from the midday meal in the guesthall did she say anything of why they were here, asking very quietly, "Does why we're here have to do with the duke of York?"

Sister Margrett deserved to know that much and Frevisse said, "Yes."

"When it's done, will we go home?"

"Yes."

"Tomorrow?"

"I hope so." But to be fair she had to add, "If it's done that soon."

And that was all.

Their afternoon devotions were cut short by a monk going through the church and shooing people out. "To make way for his grace and his men," he said, herding would-be worshipers toward the outer door with a sheepdog's determination to have them where he wanted them.

"How many is he bringing here?" someone asked.

"We don't know. Most will camp on wasteland north of the town, but how many will come all the way with him we've not been told. You'll want to see his arrival in the yard anyway. Thank you for moving on."

Sister Margrett was holding in unseemly giggles by the time they passed out the west door into the afternoon sunlight and the outer yard. Townspeople and abbey guests were already gathering there and, "There are Noreys and Vaughn," Sister Margrett said, pointing ahead to a man-high stone cross standing atop five stone steps in the middle of the abbey yard, just beyond where abbey servants were urging people back to keep clear the way between the marketplace and the church. Joliffe and Vaughn were on the top step, where they would have good view over other people's heads, and because she and Sister Margrett were nuns people moved aside, making room for them to go up.

They settled into place on the step below Joliffe and Vaughn, with nods among the four of them but not words; but as they stood there among the shift and eager unease of people waiting for something to happen, Frevisse began to see heads turning, one to another, in a different way, with what looked like murmurous dismay from some people and denying shakes of the head from others, until finally the talk rolled to the foot of the cross' steps and up. She caught, ". . . Tresham . . ." and ". . . killed . . ." and ". . . York . . ." and then Joliffe shoved down past her and next to the nearest man talking to ask him, "What's that?"

The man turned, glowingly ready to tell his news. "They're saying some folk have come from Northampton and are saying William Tresham—him that was Speaker in Parliament this year—that he's been killed."

Frevisse gasped. As one she and Sister Margrett crossed themselves, but Joliffe was demanding, "What was that about York?"

"Tresham was on his way to meet him. That's what they're saying. Tresham and his son. They were waylaid somewhere on the way and Tresham was cut down and is dead."

"What of his son?" Frevisse asked, remembering him and his parents that evening at Rushden, and that he had a small son of his own.

"Wounded but not so's he'll die of it," the man said. "So they're saying anyway, yes?" he asked the man beside him who had passed the word on to him.

"So they're saying. But Tresham is dead, that's sure it seems. He was going to meet York and was killed for it, that's what they're saying."

"Who did it?" Joliffe asked.

The men traded asking looks and shrugged. They did not know and neither did anyone around them. "It's what happens these days," someone said. "York should have stayed in Ireland."

"It wasn't because of York he was killed," someone else protested. "Outlaws, likely."

"Ha!" another man said.

Leaving them and their fellows to the heated talk that started then, Joliffe went back up the steps. As he passed her, Frevisse asked, "Is it certain, do you think? That William Tresham is killed?"

"As sure as any such news is. I wouldn't trust anyone's telling how it happened, the word has gone through so many mouths. But that he's dead, yes, that's probably true. And his son wounded. Why? Did you know them?"

"His wife and Lady Alice are friends."

"Widows together then," Joliffe said grimly and on.

"That is too miserably sad," said Sister Margrett beside Frevisse. "They were all so happy together."

Frevisse did not remember it quite that way, could only hope the almost-quarrel between Tresham and his son had not deepened from then, and she said a prayer for both of them—for Tresham cut down in some ugly skirmish of men with no time to make his peace with God; and for his son, that he might recover from his wound. And then for Mistress Tresham's grief, for which there could be little help at all.

Joliffe had just finished sharing the news with Vaughn, and Vaughn had said bitterly, "That's cruel and wrong. It shouldn't have happened," when trumpets sounding from the far end of the long marketplace turned the crowd's excitement that way, all else set aside for present pleasure. More men and women tried to crowd onto the cross' steps, were fended off by those already close-packed there, with the very true claim there was no more room. Some made it anyway and the jostling was still going on when the first riders trotted into the yard with clatter of hoofs and jingling of harness—a half-dozen foreriders liveried in matching blue-dyed doublets, two carrying long trumpets now propped at their sides like staffs, two others carrying long

lances with small pennons parti-colored blue and red-purple
murray fluttering from them, showing York's badge of a
spread-winged falcon inside the curve of a closed fetterlock,
and two others in tabards with his heraldic arms of gold lions and lilies and crimson and azure—royal arms differ-
enced from the king's only by a white bar with red roundels
labeled across the top as was York's right.

Royal-blooded dukes and their knights were always a
good show, and York, riding behind his foreriders, did not
disappoint. Having to know as well as anyone that authority
dwelt in appearance as much as in reputation, he was all and
openly a great lord, wearing a deeply blue surcoat open-
sided over a green, high-collared doublet, with a wide gold
chain set with heraldic white-enameled roses over his shoulders and a long sword in a blue-leather scabbard hung from
his hip, and riding a tall bay palfrey whose green harness was
studded with gold heraldic roses and falcons in fetterlocks.

The score or so men riding behind him were garbed for
show enough though not so boldly and were still a finer
sight than most days gave, but as was right it was York who
drew and held most eyes. Just as it would be York who
would draw the most of any attack, should there be ambush
or meeting with other lords that turned to fighting, Joliffe
thought. That was also part of being a great lord, and Joliffe
did not doubt that under York's doublet and those of his
men were breastplates and other armor, hidden so as to give
no alarm or threat.

While thinking that, Joliffe swept his gaze across the
men behind York, looking for Sir William Oldhall, found
him, and snatched off his hat to wave it in the air just as Sir
William was riding past the crowd nearest the cross. There
were other hats off and being waved, and even scattered
cheers among general shouts of welcome, but Joliffe put a
suddenness into his move and called out, "Sir William!" as
he did, and one or the other caught Sir William's heed. He

turned his head, saw Joliffe, and gave a short, jerked nod at him that Joliffe returned before they looked away from one another. It had been enough. When the time came, Joliffe would have no trouble in coming to York.

That would not be for a while, though. First, there was the abbot's ceremony of welcome to be gone through, and as York and his men came to a halt in front of the church, the wings of the nave's wide west door were pushed open by black-robed monks, to let out a double line of their fellows who spread to both sides of the door, framing it and their abbot as he came forward in abbatial splendor of green damask trimmed with gold-worked embroidery and pearls, his gold-crested crosier in one hand shining in the afternoon light. York dismounted and knelt on one knee to receive a blessing under the abbot's upraised hand. When he stood up, they seemed to exchange a few words before going away together into the church.

Behind them, the procession of monks reversed itself and followed, while York's men dismounted and abbey servants came from where they had been waiting to take their horses, freeing them to follow their lord into the church. The bells in the abbey tower began to ring to Vespers, and a good many of the on-lookers crowded forward for the church, too—more townsfolk than would usually be there for any weekday Vespers, Joliffe thought dryly. But there was no surprise in a royal duke having more power to draw them than did God's worship.

The surprise only somewhat lay in Dame Frevisse and Sister Margrett turning away from the church, back toward the guesthalls. Vaughn followed them, but Joliffe fell into step beside Dame Frevisse and asked, "What? No urge to go in and stare at a duke?"

"None," she returned. Her asperity would have shriveled apples. "And we both think we'll pray better in the dorter than in that crowd."

"As ever," Joliffe said lightly, "wise as well as . . ."

Her look stopped him. But she had looked full into his face for the first time, saw something there he did not mean to show, and demanded, "What is it? Has something more than Tresham's death happened?"

He was caught off guard, not used to being so easily read—although with her he ought to know better by now—and answered, "Something else, yes, but not that matters just now." He shifted to a grin and added easily, "Just don't lose yourselves after supper. I think we'll be wanted then."

She must have seen that was all the answer she was going to get from him, and she answered him with a silent, short nod, he sketched a bow to her and Sister Margrett, and dropped back to join Vaughn, the two of them slowing to let the nuns go well ahead of them. Now there was the waiting until Sir William sent for him. Waiting and more waiting, and no surety that anyone was going to be happy at the end of it.

Chapter 28

Having had little satisfaction from the saying of Vespers and kept away from Joliffe and Vaughn in the guesthall during the supper of vegetable pottage, a large piece of cheese, and a thick slice of buttered bread that Frevisse barely tasted, she and Sister Margrett went to sit on a bench just outside the hall's door. Only then, in that pause, did Sister Margrett ask, at hardly more than a whisper, "Are you to *meet* the duke of York?"

Frevisse answered in kind, despite no one seemed near enough to hear, "I don't know. One of his men more likely. Whoever it is that Master Noreys answers to."

"Oh." Sister Margrett sighed with disappointment. "I should have liked to see the duke nearer than across the yard."

But that was all she said, and Frevisse said nothing else either. Instead, they sat side by side on the bench, their heads bowed, Sister Margrett with her rosary, Frevisse with her hands simply folded together on her lap, unwilling to make pretense of praying when her mind was so completely elsewhere, the packet in her belt-hung purse a far heavier weight on her mind than it was at her waist.

Joliffe and Vaughn had left the hall before they did. She did not know where they had gone, and it was a squire with no lord's badge on his plain doublet who stopped in front of her and Sister Margrett and said, "I beg your pardon, my ladies. The others ask your company, please you."

Sister Margrett stood up immediately, Frevisse more slowly. She had not known she would be so afraid of doing this thing when the time came.

Dusk had gathered in the little while they had waited. The tallest pinnacle of the abbey church still caught the last glow of sunlight, but torches were being lighted beside doorways around the guesthall yard as they crossed toward a lesser gateway than the wide one by which they had first ridden into the yard. A damp night-chill was already beginning to settle, and Frevisse shivered, although not entirely from the outward cold.

Joliffe and Vaughn were waiting in the arch of the gateway. Frevisse wondered if her face was as stiff and carefully blank as theirs. And for no good reason at all, she suddenly wondered if she trusted Vaughn. Joliffe seemed to. Alice assuredly did. But did she?

Come to it, did she trust anyone in this matter beyond what bare necessity had forced on her? She was not sure she did. Not even Joliffe.

But why? Did she sense something she had not yet reasoned out, or was it simply that trust—like so much else—was falling prey to the rot eating through England's heart? A rot of which the treachery and murders there had been so

far were only the outward show, if what she and Joliffe suspicioned was true. And if what they suspicioned was true,
what kind of death was trust going to die? And if trust
died, what was left? The questions and their maybe-answers
frightened her more than anything ever had, and only because now was too late to do more than go on the way she
was, she did not falter but nodded to Joliffe and Vaughn and
walked on, her hands thrust up her opposite sleeves in an
outward seeming of humility that hid how tightly her fists
were clenched, following the squire into another, smaller
yard, cobbled, enclosed on three sides by usual buildings
but on the fourth by the buttressed cliff-rise of the abbey
church itself.

As usual with rich abbeys, the abbot's dwelling was set
apart from the more enclosed and cloistered living of his
monks. This was his own yard, Frevisse guessed, and the
high-roofed hall along one side of the yard, its tall windows
glowing yellow with light, would be where he was presently
dining with the duke of York and his household men in
lordly fashion. Around the yard's other sides would be the
abbot's own rooms and chambers set aside for such guests as
were great enough to receive his hospitality, with several
such surely given over to the duke of York tonight.

Those would be where the squire was going, Frevisse supposed as he led them past the wide doorway to the abbot's
hall and the warm hum of many men's voices inside it to a
lesser door on another side of the yard. A lighted lantern
hung there, but the windows to either side were dark and so
was the short passage inside; but straight ahead stairs went
straight up and another lantern burned at their top, giving
light but likewise making shadows enough that Frevisse and
Sister Margrett, with their skirts to worsen matters, went
only slowly up. The squire waited for them at the top, then
led them aside, through a small, shadowed room into a larger
chamber so quietly lighted by three candles on a stand of

a dozen unlighted ones that Frevisse could tell little about it save there were tapestries on the walls and the windows were shuttered.

There was also a man, standing near enough to the candlelight for her to see she did not know him and that he was not pleased at seeing, first, her, then the others. He dismissed the squire with, "Keep watch on the stairs," then waited until he was gone and the door closed before he said sharply at Joliffe, "I expected you alone."

"Without them, there'd be nothing," Joliffe answered as abruptly. He went forward, into the warm spread of the candlelight. The rest of them, even Vaughn, stayed near the door, in the shadows, leaving this to him. "The man and one of the nuns are here on someone else's behalf. The other nun is here because the first one is. There's no more I'll tell you than that. We have to speak to his grace the duke and no one else. And soon."

Over the years Frevisse had seen Joliffe be—and seem to be—some several things, from a rascal of a traveling player to a careless fool to a spy to almost a friend, with more understood between them than was ever said. As a player, he had any number of voices he could use, could seem to be a great many kinds of men, but until now she had never heard him thus—a man sure of his authority speaking as equal to another man of authority, telling him what they would do. And from the way the man was standing suddenly rigid, staring at him, he had never heard it either, and after that staring moment he demanded back at Joliffe, "Without I know anything more than that?"

"Without you know anything more than that," Joliffe agreed. "Men have died for knowing it, and I will not tell it to you, Sir William."

"But you'll tell it to my lord of York."

That was accusation more than question, and Joliffe answered it as such, not giving up an inch of certainty. "I'll tell my lord of York because likely *his* life depends on he knows it. What he does then will be his choice. Including telling you." Without pause but his voice suddenly lightened, he went on, "By the way, what happened in Wales? Was there truly order for your death?"

It was an unsubtle turning of their talk, and Sir William paused, his gaze still hard and assessing on Joliffe, before he accepted it and said, "There was. And for York to be arrested. Arrested!" Sir William barked a harsh, angry laugh. "It never came to a single blow. He faced down Stanley's officers and there was the end of it. Harry Norris, for one, ended up sitting to wine and dinner and a long talk instead of putting him in shackles and prison!"

Joliffe matched Sir William's laughter and asked on the ebb of it, "Did Harry know who gave the orders? Did York ever find out?"

And Frevisse suddenly understood he was not simply using up time. He was trying to lay hold on another strangling rope of the web there was through all of this, hoping for more answers; but Sir William made a disgusted sound and said, "Everybody had their orders from Stanley and supposed he had them from Somerset. What do you suppose?"

That question came sharp back at Joliffe, who said, "I do think they'd both be hard put to order their dog to sit and be obeyed."

"Hm," Sir William said. Their shallow laughter had fallen away from both of them. For a long moment they only stood, looking at each other, each waiting for the other to speak, and when Joliffe did not, Sir William finally said flatly, "You mean it about telling only York."

Joliffe made a small assenting movement of his head.

Sir William stared at him a dissatisfied moment longer, maybe still uncertain how things had shifted between them from master and man to two masters. Then he shifted his belt with both hands, probably in outward sign of resettling his mind, and said, "No point in our standing about, then. My ladies, pardon for my lack of courtesy. I pray you, sit." And to Joliffe again, "I'll send someone to put a word in his grace's ear, on the chance he can slip free of our good abbot the sooner."

"We can only hope," Joliffe said smoothly, like a gracious guest accepting a host's right attentions.

Frevisse thought he was playing it too far, and maybe Sir William did, too. His look held on Joliffe a moment more before he again chose to let it go, settling for a silent bow of his head to Frevisse and Sister Margrett on his way to the door. They both made curtsies in return but it was to his back as he went out the door, closing it behind him.

"So," said Vaughn.

"So," Joliffe agreed.

There seeming nothing else to say, no one said it, and in their silence, Joliffe went to the candlestand, took one of the lighted candles and lit the rest, the soft light blooming to fill the room.

"Better to wait in light," he said, "than have things come at us out of the dark."

With no knowing how long their wait would be, Frevisse and Sister Margrett went to sit on a short-legged chest against the wall near a window; Vaughn chose a low-backed chair and sat with his head down and hands clasped; Joliffe hitched a hip onto the corner of a table from which he took up a small, plain-bound book and began to turn the pages.

Beside Frevisse, Sister Margrett began to whisper the beginning of Compline, the day's final Office. Without thought, simply from long custom, Frevisse joined her, hardly listening even to herself, until the familiar words and their peace took hold on her and she began to say them with her mind as well as her mouth, and then with her heart.

"Nunc dimittis servum tuum, Domine, secundum verbum tuum in pace . . ." Now dismiss your servant, Lord, according to your word, in peace . . . *"Salva nos, Domine . . . et requiescamus in pace."* Save us, Lord . . . and may we find rest in peace. Taking the comfort there was in knowing that these words, this hope, had outlasted the ambitions and lusts of more hundreds of men than she could count or know.

They had finished and were simply sitting, Vaughn silently watching his thumbs tap together, Joliffe holding the book without ever turning a page, when a footfall on the stairs brought them all to their feet, with Frevisse's momentary peace gone well before the door was opened and Sir William entered and stood aside for the man following him.

Even if Frevisse had not seen Richard, duke of York before this, the broad chain of glinting gold and white-enameled roses worn wide on his shoulders, the rich sheen of his long, deeply blue surcoat, and the way he carried himself, straight-backed and with lifted head, proud with certainty of his place in the world, would have told her here was a high nobleman.

She and Sister Margrett sank in floor-deep curtsies as Joliffe and Vaughn made low bows. By the time she and Sister Margrett had risen and Joliffe and Vaughn straightened, Sir William had closed the door and York had crossed the room to the table and full into the candlelight. "Master Joliffe," he said.

"My lord," Joliffe returned.

"And your companions?"

"Dame Frevisse is cousin to her grace the duchess of Suffolk and here on her behalf."

Frevisse made a curtsy, not quite so low as before, to acknowledge that and, raising her head, met York's gaze, startling in its sharp assessment of her before he slightly bowed his head in return.

"And Sister Margrett, here to companion Dame Frevisse,"

Joliffe went on. Again the curtsy and brief bow of the head. "And Nicholas Vaughn, likewise here for the duchess of Suffolk."

Again the sharp, assessing look and bow of the head to Vaughn's low bow. But with courtesy served, York looked full at Joliffe again and said, "You've been ill, Joliffe?"

Joliffe's surprise showed. "My lord?"

"You look worn by more than merely too much riding. Was it illness? Or were you hurt?"

"Hurt, my lord."

"In this matter that Sir William says you say is urgent?"

"Yes, my lord."

"But you do well enough now?"

"Yes, my lord. Well enough."

Frevisse, watching them, thought that by rights the only thing that might have been alike about the two men was their age—both somewhere around their fortieth year—but there was more than that. Their pride, for one thing: something Frevisse had long known about Joliffe and could easily have guessed about York, he being who he was. Her surprise was at seeing the respect there was between them. She knew well that Joliffe did not readily give respect to anyone, while York could hardly be expected to give it to a hireling spy, which was, when all was said and done, what Joliffe must be. But the respect was there and shared as York said, "So you've come with something to tell me, and they're necessary to the telling."

"To tell you and to give you," Joliffe said. "Save for Sister Margrett, who's the one innocent in this." He turned to her. "If you will go aside and pardon us for it, my lady?"

Sister Margrett, making no objection to being innocent and sent aside, bowed her head and silently withdrew to a corner farthest from them in the room. There, she lowered her head, crossed her hands into her opposite sleeves, and went still, as little there as she could possibly be without leaving the room.

"Dame Frevisse," Joliffe said.

Frevisse went forward to join him in front of York. Time was come to be rid of the letter and unwillingness was on her like a weight of lead, because once it was given, once York had read it, there would be no way to unknow whatever it said. And if it said what she and Joliffe feared it did . . .

She paused, her hand resting on the clasp of her belt-purse. "There's one thing first, my lord. Vaughn."

He came forward to stand beside her, the two of them together in this for Alice's sake; but he left the words to her, and keeping her gaze steady on York, she said, "Without the duchess of Suffolk's aid and willingness, we would not have this thing. She believes it holds truths that could ruin her son. She also believes they are truths that should not stay hidden. What she asks in return for giving it to you is that you will do all that you may to protect her son's rights and title and inheritance if this should prove as . . ." Frevisse sought for the word. ". . . ill a thing as she fears. Will you swear to do that?"

It was no little thing to ask a royal duke for his oath, nor did York immediately give it but regarded her steadily before saying, "Is it as dire as that?"

"We think so, yes," Joliffe said before Frevisse could answer.

York looked at him. "Do you think this is a pledge I should make?"

"Yes, my lord."

York returned his look to Frevisse, signed himself with the cross, and said, "Then I swear to do all I may to protect young John de la Pole's rights and title and inheritance, to save him as much as in my power lies from the consequences of his father's deeds." He signed the cross again and asked of Frevisse and Vaughn together, "Enough?"

She looked at Vaughn, who nodded agreement, and she faced York again to say, "Yes. Enough."

She had done what she could for Alice. Refusing to let her fingers fumble, she brought out the packet and held it out to York, both glad to be rid of it and nakedly afraid. She looked into his face as he took it and found he was looking at her, not the packet, as he took it; and it might have been the candlelight or else her own imagining, but her own feelings looked mirrored in his gaze. He was no fool. He had his fears and suspicions, too, and if the letter said what she thought it did, he was right to be afraid of it.

He turned toward the candles, held the packet the better to see the seal on the cord around it, and asked, "Whose seal?"

"Edward Burgate, the duke of Suffolk's secretary," Joliffe said.

York broke it, unwrapped the cord, set it on the table, began to fold back the oiled-cloth wrapping. Sir William began to move forward to York's side. Joliffe put out a hand toward York, saying, "It might be best if only you read it first, my lord. It may not be for anyone else to know."

Sir William stopped, outrage and uncertainty unsteady across his face. York looked from Joliffe to him and back again.

"Have you read this?" he asked Joliffe.

"No, but I have a strong suspicion what it says, and if I'm right, the fewer who know it for certain the better, my lord."

"Suspicion," York echoed grimly. "After my greeting in Wales, I'm willing to listen to suspicions. Sir William."

With a discontent near to anger and not hiding it very well, Sir William stayed where he was.

They all stayed where they were while York finished unwrapping the packet and laid the cloth on the table. York looked at the imprinted wax holding closed the several-times-folded papers that had been inside the cloth. "Suffolk's," he said, broke it, and unfolded the papers. In the silence of their waiting, he began to read, and while he did, no one shifted or stirred.

For her part, Frevisse tried to hold her gaze to the floor but found herself watching York; and although the candles still burned strongly, keeping the shadows at bay, she saw a darkness grow on him as he read. And when he looked up from the last page there was the bleakness to him, as if he had aged years in the few minutes he had taken to read the thing. For a long moment his gaze did not see any of them. He might have been alone in some far and empty place, and Frevisse had the shivered feeling that alone was what he mostly was, no matter how many others were around him.

Then he came back from whatever far place in his mind he had gone; was folding the papers closed and saying with forced lightness, "Suffolk always did say more than need be. Joliffe, tell me about this. Who else has read this? Where has it been?"

"To the best of our knowledge no one has read it but Suffolk and his secretary who wrote it for him and saw to its safekeeping."

Sir William put in sharply, "Where's this secretary?"

York held up a hand. "Let's have it from something like the beginning. Tell me, among the three of you, how this came into your hands and here."

Most of that telling fell to Vaughn and Joliffe. For her part, Frevisse told why she had been with Lady Alice at all and what had passed at Kenilworth while she was there and, in its turn, of Joliffe coming hurt to St. Frideswide's. "Nor is he altogether healed," she said firmly. "Rest is what will presently serve him best."

"I'll remember," York said with the smallest possibility

of a smile that was more at Joliffe's open discomfiture than at her, Frevisse thought.

There was little left to tell then, except what had happened yesterday, with Frevisse having to hide her alarm at what she had not heard before now. When that was done, York stood silent a time, looking downward, then raised his gaze to them all, his face quiet, his voice merely courteous, as he said, "Vaughn, I'll want to talk with you in the morning concerning Lady Alice. She's more than earned my gratitude and any help that I can give her. Dame Frevisse, I think your part in this is done. I hope you can return to your cloister with clear mind and heart. Joliffe and Sir William, I want you to stay a time longer, but Dame Frevisse, Vaughn . . ." He slightly lifted his voice. ". . . Sister Margrett, I give you all leave to go to your belated beds."

Vaughn made a low bow and Frevisse and Sister Margrett deep curtsies and then they . . . escaped, was the word that came to Frevisse's mind as they went down the stairs and into the abbot's cobbled yard again. The hour was late. Some of the lanterns beside doorways had gone out and there were few men about and no women. If there were stars, Frevisse did not see them, concerned more with her feet and reaching the stairs to the nuns' dorter. There Vaughn left them with a bow and no more than a murmured, "My ladies," before going his own way to the men's dorter, but Frevisse paused Sister Margrett by a brief hold on her sleeve and asked, "How much did you hear?"

"Nearly nothing. You all spoke low, and I hummed psalms to myself to stop my ears."

That was more discretion than Frevisse had hoped for and she said, "Thank you. That was well done."

But curiosity could only be curbed so far, and Sister Margrett asked, "Did it go badly?"

"It went . . . as well as it could. Worse for his grace of York than anyone, I think." Remembering York's stark look when he had finished reading Suffolk's damning letter. Who the letter damned had never been said aloud, and for that she was half-thankful, half-raw with wondering if she and Joliffe had guessed rightly. She might never know. Did not know if she wanted to know. Did not know if she could live unknowing . . .

She wrenched her mind away from that and said, "It's done for us anyway, and that's what must matter. Tomorrow we can start home."

Chapter 29

Frevisse's hope in the morning was that she would chance to talk at least once more with Joliffe, but it was Vaughn who came up to her and Sister Margrett as they left the church after Prime, to ask, "Do you plan to leave today, my ladies?"

"After Tierce. We mean to make an easier journey of it than the one here," Frevisse said. "And you?"

"I've planned much the same."

Frevisse had awoken with a thought that his answer gave her chance to follow, and she asked, "Then may we beg a boon of you? A final favor from my Lady Alice? Given how unsettled all the countryside is, would you and your man join ours and see us safely back to St. Frideswide's? It will hardly be out of your way, if you're going to Lady Alice at Kenilworth."

If he hesitated, it was so briefly she could not be sure of it before he slightly bowed and said, "Gladly. I'll find your men and tell them so."

She thanked him and they parted with courtesy on both sides, Frevisse watching him away toward the abbey's outer gateway until, behind her, making both her and Sister Margrett startle, Joliffe said, "Good morrow, my ladies. I trust you slept well."

"Better than you, by the look of you," Frevisse said, eyeing with disfavor the dark smears of weariness under his eyes.

He was freshly shaven, though, and there was a glint in his eyes that was more mischief than weariness, lessening her worry for him as he ignored her jibe and said, "I've been given permission for us to talk in the abbot's garden this morning after breakfast. I'll send someone to bring you there. By your leave, of course."

"Of course," she said, feeling anything but "of course" about it. "But . . ."

"My thanks," he said, bowed, and slipped away among the people still spreading outward from the abbey doorway, leaving her question unfinished behind him.

Since she wanted to talk with him and they could hardly have talked here, she knew her irk at him was unreasonable but that did not ease it.

Sister Margrett made no murmur over the matter. They broke their fast, then asked the way to the abbot's garden. It lay high-walled behind his house, on the slope toward the river at the valley bottom, and was reached by a narrow passage between buildings. The way in from this wide was by a door in the wall, and a man with York's falcon badge on his doublet was standing there, openly a guard. Without need for them to say anything, he opened the door for them to go in, then shut it behind them, and Frevisse did not doubt he would stay there all the while they did and be there to let them out when they were ready to leave.

The garden was as such gardens were. With walks between beds bright with the last of autumn flowers and flowering herbs; a long arbored walk; a square of lawn with a fountain gently plashing in its middle, it had all the usual graces of a great lord's garden, except for Joliffe standing beside the fountain, watching the water play.

Sister Margrett went to sit on a bench where the morning sun was falling warmly. Frevisse went forward to Joliffe, who turned at her approach but stayed where he was, greeting her with a courteous bow to which she returned a bending of her head before she said, "I hope this isn't to ask anything more of me. Sister Margrett and I are bound for St. Frideswide's this morning, come what may."

"Go freely and with my good wishes," Joliffe said, smiling. "No, I've only asked you here because I thought you might like to have your curiosity satisfied before you leave."

"You know I would," she said. She was afraid to know for certain that what she feared was true, and at the same time knew herself too well to think she would choose ignorance if she were given any choice. "York told you what was in Suffolk's letter, then?"

"He let me read it. Let both Oldhall and me. We feared rightly, you and I."

Frevisse drew a short, uneven breath and had to steady before she could ask, so low the words were almost lost under the soft sound of the fountain, "The king?"

As grim-faced as she had ever seen him, Joliffe said what she did not want to hear. "The king. As Suffolk tells it in that letter, France was lost, Normandy given up to French, the war forfeited not simply by Suffolk's and Somerset's choice and treachery, but with King Henry's willing agreement."

"He . . . couldn't have known what he was doing. He's simple. Men say so. He doesn't know what he does. Everyone . . ."

"There are men say the world is flat, too, when it's been

known for a thousand years and more that it isn't. I think—
though Suffolk doesn't say it—that maybe our King Henry
simply hates being king."

"He . . . That isn't possible."

"Why not?" Joliffe asked with mocking lightness; but this
was a thing he had thought dark and deep about. "He was,
what, nine months old when he became king? He spent all
his childhood being forced and ordered about by lords who
knew what kind of king they wanted him to be, never mind
who he might be in himself. Then he came of age and they
handed his power to him and went on telling him who he was
supposed to be and what he was supposed to do. For him it's
been nearly thirty years of that. His whole life. For myself, I
doubt I'd have much love for anyone—and certainly not for
my much-urged 'duty'—after all of that. Would you?"

But he was the king, Frevisse wanted to protest. The *king*.

And at the same time she could understand what Joliffe
had said and she choked her protest down and said evenly,
"Did Suffolk say all of that?"

"Suffolk did not. I think that much grasp of another person was beyond our shallow duke of Suffolk, wrapped with
love for himself as he was. But I think he had sensed enough
that he'd begun to be afraid of his king, if only at the last.
Hence the letter, written against the bitter possibility he
would be betrayed. Which he was."

"He was murdered on King Henry's order?"

"We can suppose he was, from what we otherwise know."

"And all the murders that followed?"

"There's no proof King Henry ordered them. That's the
trouble with all of this. There's no proof of anything. Only
Suffolk's accusations about Normandy and our own suspicion that somewhere behind all of these deaths there has to
be someone with power enough to order outright murders
and afterward stop any true seeking for the guilty."

"Someone not the duke of Somerset." For reasons on which they had long since agreed.

"Not Somerset. Nor is there any other lord who's shown they have that kind of power. Until we find that one of them secretly does, I think we have to more than suspect the murders were done by King Henry's orders, by men in his service. Or maybe only the one man. The one who nearly did for me in Hedingham. He surely gave every sign of sufficiency that way."

"And there's an on-going trouble," Frevisse said. "Because that man is still somewhere and knows you. Knows you're here, if you're right about seeing him yesterday."

"I'm right."

The fountain played quietly beside them, the garden's only sound for a moment, before she said, "You killed a man yesterday."

"I did."

"You've killed other men."

"I have."

She did not know how to ask her next question; but with his disconcerting way of sometimes seeming to know her too well, he said, "But only when they've intended my death or someone else's." He paused, then added, "And I've prayed for their souls afterward. As I hope someone prays for mine."

"You're prayed for," Frevisse said, and added somewhat more crisply, "Besides, I've done more for you than that. I've asked Vaughn to accompany Sister Margrett and me back to St. Frideswide's, four men being better than only two for guard in these times."

Joliffe smiled widely. "To make sure he doesn't follow me about my business? Don't you trust him, my lady?"

"St. Frideswide's is on his way to Lady Alice at Kenilworth," Frevisse said with feigned austerity. "There need be nothing more to it than that."

"Nonetheless, I thank you for your—shall we call it 'discretion'?"

"Then you don't trust him either?"

"When all is said and done, my lady," Joliffe said lightly, "I find I trust surprisingly few people."

But she was among them and he did not have to say so for her to know it, and before the little silence then could draw out too long between them, she said, back to where they had begun, "So we've found out much, proved too little, and solved nothing. Will his grace of York use Suffolk's accusation against the king?"

"I think not openly. It would be inviting open war. There will be lords who will back the king, no matter what, and those too outraged by the wrong to bear it. What York will do is be far less trusting in his dealings with King Henry, far more willing than he has been to push matters where he thinks he's in the right. And he *will* join in the growing demands that Somerset be brought to trial for his treasonous betrayals in Normandy."

"But if King Henry protects Somerset, which he may well do to protect himself from anything Somerset might say against him . . ."

"Then maybe we'll have war anyway."

And what was there to be said to that? Nothing that Frevisse could think of. Nor Joliffe either, it seemed. All was said and nothing settled, and without more to be said, they left the fountain and its greensward and walked slowly toward the door in the wall. Sister Margrett rose and joined them, but Joliffe stopped, took from inside his doublet a small leather pouch, and held it out to her.

"This is from his grace the duke of York. For St. Frideswide's in thanks for the good help the priory gave in this matter."

Beginning to thank him, Sister Margrett took the pouch but broke off, looking startled.

"Not many coins," Joliffe said. "But gold ones, I think."

Sister Margrett immediately started to hand the pouch away to Frevisse, but Joliffe put out a hand, stopping her, saying, "I think Dame Frevisse has had enough of burden-bearing for a time." He smiled his smile that had surely warmed more than one woman's heart. "I doubt she'll grudge you the pleasure of bearing this one."

Sister Margrett smiled back at him, briefly distracted, while Frevisse assured her, "Bear it and be welcome."

Finishing her thanks, Sister Margrett tucked the pouch away. Joliffe went to open the door ahead of them. Frevisse, thinking he would part from them there, was readying her farewell when, with thanks to the guard, he continued with them, back toward the guestyard. As they reached it, he said, "I'll make my farewell now, my ladies, by your leave." He nodded toward the stables. A stableman was standing, holding Joliffe's red-roan horse. "I'm setting out while the day is young."

The stableman had seen Joliffe, was coming toward them. They stopped where they were, Frevisse gathering her mind back from the dreariment of thoughts she had brought with her from the garden. As suddenly as this it was all going to be done. The man reached them. Joliffe took the reins and gave him a coin and thanks. The man went back toward the stables, Joliffe swung up into his saddle, and she found the farewell words she wanted, saying, "Then now is when I must wish God be with you, Joliffe."

He smiled down at her. "And with you, my lady. May all be well at St. Frideswide's, and no one and nothing come to disturb your peace again."

"Where do you go?" Frevisse could not hold back from asking.

"My lord of York has bid me have that rest you told him I should have." He gathered up his reins. "I'm going home."

"Home?" Frevisse's surprise was naked in her voice. Somehow she had never thought of Joliffe with a home.

Smiling as if he had full well intended that surprise, Joliffe said, "I have a home, yes." He started to swing his horse toward the abbey gateway. "And a wife," he added.

Unable to stop herself, Frevisse started to smile, too, as she called after him, "And children, too, I suppose?"

He looked over his shoulder at her, smiled more widely, which was no clear answer at all, and kept on riding. And watching him go, Frevisse gave way and laughed aloud, because thought of Joliffe with a home and wife to go to was better by far than thought of him riding out alone into a world empty of anyone waiting for him.

Author's Note

The plot of this book is solidly imbedded in actual events of 1450. William de la Pole, duke of Suffolk was indeed killed on his way into exile, and within a few months of his death his steward was murdered at Flint, his household priest beheaded by his parishioners, and his secretary arrested. It was a year of violence all over England, with numerous uprisings and murders, but the cluster of deaths associated with Suffolk caught my interest, and when I found reference to another priest being beheaded by parishioners not very far from the other one and soon afterward, plots and possibilities began to spin in my mind.

I already had questions about events of that year. I've dealt with the possibility that the loss of Normandy was a deliberate act in an earlier book of this series. Again, the duke of Somerset's behavior in the course of the French reconquest of Normandy is strange in the extreme, giving grounds for speculation that easily range beyond assumption of plain incompetence. But the duke of Suffolk's murder raises questions all of its own. No one was ever punished for it, despite the name of the ship that intercepted him was known. Actually, soon after Suffolk's death King Henry wrote to the master of the *Nicholas of the Tower,* saying that since the master had not agreed to Suffolk's death and did not allow it to be done aboard ship, if he would run some information to and from besieged Cherbourg, the king would take him and his fellowship "to our grace." A mild response to a brutal murder. Added to that, on 3 April 1450 Gervase Clyfton of the royal household was ordered, by letters patent, to seize for royal use the ship *Nicholas of the Tower* and the masters and mariners of it, and arm them to resist the king's enemies. That gave me pause, linking as it did the royal household to the ship that, a month later, was used for Suffolk's murder. It might also be of significance that two days before that order the king granted Gervase Clyfton 400 marks as a gift for his past good work at sea. And to his work to come? I wonder.

As for other historical deaths taking place or mentioned in the story, Matthew Gough, a veteran of the Hundred Years War, was actually killed while fighting Jack Cade's rebels in a night battle on London Bridge; William Tresham did die in an ambush on his way to meet the duke of York; the bishops of Chichester and Salisbury were murdered by mobs; and so were Lord Saye and William Crowmer during Cade's hold on London. No reason is known how Crowmer came to be moved out of the Tower of London at such a dangerous time. The fact simply sits there as another curious anomaly, like the *Nicholas of the Tower.*

Sir William Oldhall is among the historical personages

in this book but is not known to have been York's spymaster, even supposing such a personage existed; but given the venom with which the crown pursued him over the following years, he must have done something beyond usual to anger those in power. Why not this?

Richard, duke of York's situation in 1450 was exactly as shown in the story; and when he was warned of an effort to indict him for treason and he returned from Ireland to protest this and defend himself, royal officers of North Wales were actually ordered—it's not known by whom—to imprison York in Conwy Castle, seize and execute Sir William Oldhall, and put under lock and key his councilors Sir Walter Devereux and Sir Edmund Mulso during the king's pleasure. Where Suffolk's murder brought nearly no reaction from the crown, York's justified return from Ireland caused what seems a nearly hysterical response. And whatever the reason for those orders, no following charges were made that explains them.

York's exchange of letters with King Henry through the autumn of 1450, and speculation on them, can be found in *The Politics of Fifteenth-Century England: John Vale's Book,* edited by Margaret L. Kekewich and others. The letters do seem to become progressively more aggressive and demanding and the king's responses were evasive in the extreme. In the months to come, York accepted a place in the government and was among those demanding that the duke of Somerset be brought to trial for treason. Somerset never was. Instead, he took the duke of Suffolk's place in the government and ran things even more bitterly to the wrong.

As you can see, I had an embarrassment of riches in the way of violence, mysterious deaths, and inadequately explained events around which to build my plot. Unfortunately, Suffolk's deadly letter is entirely fictional. Nor is there any documentary support for the conclusions I have drawn about Henry VI, only circumstantial evidence—both that discussed in the story and other events in his life. His reputation remains that of a simplistic, pious, weak-natured man, but there are indications of a possible passive-aggressive side to him that I addressed in the short story "Neither Pity, Love, Nor Fear" in *Royal Whodunits,* edited by Mike Ashley. No historian is guilty of encouraging me in this line of speculation.

This time in English history is of course covered in numerous books—subject headings would be "Henry VI," "Wars of the Roses," "Lancaster and York," and "The Hundred Years War" for those wishing to read further. Of specific and invaluable use to me was *Jack Cade's Rebellion of 1450* by I. M. W. Harvey, covering a far wider range of events than Cade's rebellion alone.

Suffolk's letter to his son can be found most readily in editions of the ubiquitous Paston letters.

At St. Albans, Hertfordshire, the remains of Humphrey, duke of Gloucester's tomb and the saint's shrine are still to be seen in the cathedral, though the monastery is long since gone, of course. Five years after this story the first battle of the Wars of the Roses was fought in the town's marketplace outside the monastery walls, with Richard, duke of York on one side and Edmund Beaufort, duke of Somerset on the other.

NOW AVAILABLE IN HARDCOVER

The Apostate's Tale

A Dame Frevisse Medieval Mystery

By Margaret Frazer

As the nuns of St. Frideswide's priory prepare
for the welcome end of Lent, their peaceful
expectations are overset by the sudden return of
long-vanished Sister Cecely. Nine years ago she
fled from the nunnery with a man. Now, her lover
is dead and she has come back, bringing her
illegitimate son with her.

Sister Cecely may be penitent—however much
Frevisse may doubt it—but fully truthful she
is not, and as the apostate nun's lies begin to
overtake her, dangers of more than one kind—
and maybe murder—become an unwanted
part of life in the priory.

Edgar® Award–Winning Author

MARGARET FRAZER

The Dame Frevisse
Medieval Mysteries

penguin.com